THESE ARE *NOT* SPECIAL EFFECTS

The th[...] [...]e dried fern, watching [...]

The tw[...] [...]d of raptors, except the[...] [...]oved from the edge of the fern trees toward the herd of huge vegetarian reptiles. The cows screeched a warning. Two adult bulls bellowed as the raptors raced past them, hunting the calf farthest from the herd. Their claws, three on each foot and one of them huge, cut through the calf's upper skin layers and gashed the muscle and nerve layers below.

The calf, startled, and bleeding, tried to run.

The raptors pressed the attack.

One moved to the creature's left; the other worked its way to the right. Their claws sliced the prey's flesh, leaving behind long slashes that were inches deep. Over and over, they struck at the beast. Warm, red blood flowed from the gaping wounds. Rod understood the logic of their hunting tactics, although it was not what you'd see from most predators he was familiar with. They weren't going for a neck-crunching death bite. They were deliberately bleeding out their prey.

Rod pulled his cell phone from his pocket.

"What are you doing? Those things don't work," Brian whispered. "There's no satellites, no calling 9-1-1."

"Pictures," Rod hissed back, aiming and clicking his camera phone. "We've got to warn everyone, and I don't even know what to call the damn things."

"I do," Jerry said. "They're Spielberg's monsters. Velociraptors."

The Ring of Fire Series

1632 by Eric Flint
1633 by Eric Flint & David Weber
1634: The Baltic War by Eric Flint & David Weber
Ring of Fire ed. by Eric Flint
1634: The Galileo Affair by Eric Flint & Andrew Dennis
Grantville Gazette ed. by Eric Flint
Grantville Gazette II ed. by Eric Flint
1634: The Ram Rebellion by Eric Flint
with Virginia DeMarce et al.
1634: The Bavarian Crisis by Eric Flint
with Virginia DeMarce
1635: The Cannon Law by Eric Flint
with Andrew Dennis
Grantville Gazette III ed. by Eric Flint
Ring of Fire II ed. by Eric Flint
Grantville Gazette IV ed. by Eric Flint
1635: The Dreeson Incident by Eric Flint
& Virginia DeMarce
Grantville Gazette V ed. by Eric Flint
1635: The Tangled Web by Virginia DeMarce

Time Spike by Eric Flint & Marilyn Kosmatka

**For a complete list of Baen Books by
Eric Flint, please go to www.baen.com.**

TIME SPIKE

ERIC FLINT
AND
MARILYN KOSMATKA

TIME SPIKE

Copyright © 2008 by Eric Flint & Marilyn Kosmatka

A Baen Books Original

Baen Publishing Enterprises
P.O. Box 1403
Riverdale, NY 10471
www.baen.com

ISBN 13: 978-1-4391-3312-5

Cover art by David Mattingly

First Baen paperback printing, January 2010

Distributed by Simon & Schuster
1230 Avenue of the Americas
New York, NY 10020

Library of Congress Cataloging-in-Publication Data:
2008005946

Printed in the United States of America

10 9 8 7 6 5 4 3 2 1

To Ted Kosmatka

CHAPTER

1

"Sorry about the rotation list, Andy." Lieutenant Joseph Schuler shrugged and shot the captain a look halfway between pity and resignation. "We're just too short of people to staff any shift the way we should. As for midnights . . . You know how it is."

Captain Andrew Blacklock knew how it was. The same way it had been since the day he started working at the state of Illinois' maximum-security prison just across the road from the Mississippi River. But tonight's numbers were worse than usual. The coverage was nowhere near adequate. He looked at the men and women ready to punch out and squelched the thought of asking them to work over. They had worked short. They were beat. He knew over half of them had worked a double shift. Probably the third one this week, the sixth this pay-period.

Andy forced a wry grin. *Some things never change. Pay everyone overtime, but keep the other costs low. Don't hire anyone new. The state can't afford the bennies. Health, dental, vision. Nope, overtime's cheaper.*

"We'll make it, Joe," he said. "We always do." Andy looked away from the man he was relieving and toward the metal detectors. Three guards were lined up in front of the machines at the prison entrance waiting to process the oncoming shift. Andy wasn't worried. Just irritated.

He hated taking shortcuts, and that's exactly what had to be done when working a skeleton crew. One set of rounds for every two that should be done. Everyone locked down come morning. Day-shift was going to start out behind, and he knew they could no more afford it than he could afford to send the prisoners to the cafeteria for breakfast. Or to the infirmary for their meds. He stifled a curse. The nurses were always ticked when they had to hand-deliver the morning meds to the cellblocks. They were even more short-staffed than he was.

There was no department within the prison system with enough people. Not even at the top end, the administrative level. It was lean times for the state and cuts had been made. More cuts than could be safely tolerated. The prisons of today were different from those of the past. Prisoners could not be locked down for months at a time. They had to be given exercise periods. They were allowed to talk. Imprisonment was no longer forced labor coupled with solitude. And more had changed than just the rules.

The prisoners of today were as different as the rules that regulated their incarceration. At least at this particular prison. X-house—death row—was filled to capacity. Two thirds of the men awaiting execution were drug addicts who had fried their brains before exiting their teens.

Schizophrenia was rampant; delusions of grandeur were almost the norm. And remorse was something few actually felt. Most could find an excuse for what they did. Those who couldn't, didn't seem to care.

The last man to be given a hot shot—the series of three lethal injections deemed acceptable to the state—was one of those men without a conscience. He had raped, mutilated, and killed little girls. Grade-schoolers, the oldest of whom was nine.

Without a struggle, he had walked out of the small room where he had spent his last day on Earth. Meekly, he had lain on the gurney and allowed the guards to strap him down and roll him to the viewing area. He was sad-eyed, gentle talking, sincere. Claiming to be a born-again Christian. Even at the last minute he was working the system, hoping for a stay of execution. It hadn't come. An I.V. had been inserted, and a saline solution began its journey from the dangling plastic bag to his vein. Then from behind a wall—so none of the witnesses could see who administered the deadly doses—an anesthetic, sodium thiopental, was injected into the tubing by a physician. This was followed by an equally lethal dose of pancuronium bromide, a chemical that paralyzed the diaphragm and lungs. Then came the potassium chloride. It didn't take long for this newest addition to his bloodstream to interrupt the electrical signaling of his heart and cause cardiac arrest. The only tears shed that day had been those of the girls' parents. The monster's mother had been dry-eyed. His father had not come to say good-bye.

Andy suppressed a shudder.

Lieutenant Schuler frowned. "Next week, and the week

after, are going to be rough. The staffing situation is going to get worse before it gets any better. Keith Woeltje is going out on medical. He has to have knee surgery. And Kathleen Hanrahan will be starting her maternity leave."

Andy rolled his eyes, since Joe wasn't looking at him. Schuler was a good manager, but he was close to burning out. He needed to take a little time off. Not that that would happen any time soon, even though the man had the time coming. He hadn't taken a sick day or personal day in years. He hadn't taken a vacation for the last two. They were too short-handed.

Joe was flipping through the stack of papers he carried. He was new to the afternoon shift and was still trying to get a handle on his crew and the new routine. He was also trying to come to grips with a divorce and his children living two hours away. Andy knew all the gossip. Maria Schuler had gotten tired of the long hours her man put in and found herself one who would be home every night by five-thirty. The fact that the guy made two dollars for every one Joe earned hadn't hurt the situation any.

Marriages didn't usually fare well for those who worked the prison.

Andy's own marriage had gone by the wayside three years back. For different reasons, but the end result was the same. His wife had been the personnel director of a good-sized manufacturing firm. The company grew. The promotions and raises came. And she found it harder and harder to introduce her husband to the people she worked with. His job at the prison, fine the day they married, was no longer something she wanted. She reminded him daily of his lack of ambition, of his dead end situation. When the split finally came, he had been relieved. And grateful. Connie hadn't wanted children. Not yet. She felt twenty-eight was too young to be saddled with kids. Deep down, he suspected she would never want any. Kids were too messy, too noisy, and too expensive for her to enjoy.

Andy gave the man next to him a long look. Schuler was a big boy, over six-four, and weighing in at a little over two hundred fifty pounds. All bone and muscle. A member of the E-team, he was on the fast track to making captain.

"Relax, Joe," he said. "Just go home. There's nothing you can do about it. We'll be okay. We always are."

Schuler nodded. "Sometimes, I think that's the problem. We always manage."

He handed Andy the papers he had been going over and took off the radio hanging on his belt. He passed it to his relief with a shrug. "You'll need this before the night's out. There's only about a dozen of them working anywhere close to right. Man, what a mess. Makes me want to play the lottery."

Andy laughed. "Sure. And after you won, what would you do with all that time on your hands? You would miss us. Besides, men like you and me, we're not here for the money. Don't you watch the talk shows? It's the uniform. The ego trip. Get home and catch some shut-eye."

Joe's forehead lost a few of its creases but not all of them.

Always worried. Andy clapped the man on the back. "Joe, don't take this place home with you. If you do, you won't make fifty. Do what you can, then leave it here." He smiled, but this time it didn't touch his eyes. He was thinking of another officer who, the year before, died of a heart attack at the age of thirty-eight. The man hadn't left anyone behind because he gave everything he had to the job. There was nothing left for him to build a life with outside the walls. "Stop off for a beer on your way home. One won't do you any harm, and it could do a lot of good."

Joe shook his head. He didn't drink, except very occasionally. Didn't gamble. Didn't smoke. He ate right. Tried to get at least six hours sleep out of every twenty-four, and when he could he got in eight. He was one of the new breed of guards who took their physical health seriously. It was men like him that changed the title of "Prison Guard" to that of "CO, Correctional Officer." They took their health seriously, and they took their jobs seriously. Sometimes, too much so.

Schuler was checking out the state employees lining up to enter the prison. Andy knew he was counting them. One assistant superintendent, three zone lieutenants, seven zone sergeants, twenty-nine guards and two nurses: that was who he would be running the prison with. A thirty-percent shortage of bodies. They weren't all here yet. Most of them would show up in the last five minutes.

Andy watched Joe watching the midnight shift arrive. *Good man, but he's going to worry himself into an early grave.*

He glanced around the twenty-five by forty-five foot entry area and saw Lieutenant Rodney Hulbert, the afternoon shift's second in command.

Rod seemed as small as Joe did large. Just a hair over five-six and with no extra meat on him anywhere, he looked like a strong breeze could blow him away. Andy knew the appearance of frailty was about as far from the truth as you could get. The man was a survival hobbyist and hard as nails. He was also the best marksman the prison had, by the proverbial country mile. Every year for the past three, he'd been a serious competitor in the National Rifle Matches held at Camp Perry.

"No full moon, but the crazies are wired tonight," Rod said, when he came up. He stuck his hand out and shook Andy's. "I'll be glad to go home."

"That bad, huh?"

"Yeah. Two attempted suicides, a half dozen shoving matches, and I don't know how many solitary temper tantrums. It's been hell. We've had to use the extraction team three times and the first responders were called out on two medicals."

Andy shot Joe a quizzical look and the man shrugged. "I was waiting till the charge nurse called in. It seems quite a few inmates have refused their meds. With most of them it doesn't amount to much. But some of them, well . . . the psych meds . . ." He glanced back toward the bars separating the entrance area from the prison. "Even some of the diabetics and epileptics turned down tonight's med pass."

And he was working short! Andy would swear he could feel his blood pressure climbing, even though he knew that was impossible. Not the climbing—he was damn sure that was happening—but being able to feel it.

"Hey, I told you it was going to be a bad night. But who knows, maybe they'll settle down. It's been crazy for over five hours."

"Yeah, maybe." Andy thought for a moment. "Any chance of getting one of the afternoon nurses to stay over? Or maybe a day nurse to come in early?"

Joe shook his head. "Can't. We worked with only two, and they were both held over from days. I've already told Sterling she has to be here by four in the morning. She said she would. She'll even try to get here a little earlier to help with the set up for the first med pass."

Rod nodded his head in agreement. "They're even shorter than we are. You have to remember, the state doesn't pay squat compared to the private sector. We're lucky we've got any nurses."

Andy almost gritted his teeth. He remembered the last meeting. The nurses and the guards were paid the same. The one took a minimum of two years education plus state licensing; the other was anyone with a GED and up. The workload was the same. The danger was the same. The guards were to *be nice* to the nurses. The state couldn't afford to lose any more.

"Okay, let's get report over with. I have a lot to do." He led them to one of the three six-foot conference tables situated close to the glass double doors separating the entry area and the prison grounds. The wind was blowing in from the northwest, causing the doors to rattle with each new gust. He knew that at forty-three degrees—the temperature the bank's sign flashed as he drove past it a half hour earlier—the wind would feel below freezing. Stacks of insurance forms and in-service announcements lying on the counter that ran the length of the east wall fluttered each time the door opened and a guard entered. Andy hoped like hell the nurses showed.

"Who are my nurses?" he asked, suddenly very worried.

Joe laughed. "Man, listen, I can't do this to you. I'll stay over." He looked at Rod.

"I can't stay. I've hit the maximum hours allowed."

"Who're the nurses?"

"Radford. Jennifer Radford."

"Don't know her."

Joe kept his eyes on the clock. "No one does. She just finished her day-orientation. It's her first night working the floor. And Chris Tompkin—she was supposed to train her on nights—called off."

"Oh, hell." It was a whisper, but it seemed to carry in the otherwise silent room. Andy shook his head. "Okay." He was quiet for a moment, thinking again. If they were going to have an untrained nurse passing morning meds he was going to have to send an extra CO to the infirmary. Things had a way of getting out of hand when untrained personnel dealt with prisoners. The classes helped, but it took time and working in the environment to learn how to stay alive.

Even experienced nurses ran into trouble. It hadn't been two months since the last incident. Stanley Frye had stuck Carper Wayne while on their way to the showers. Then, while the nurse was rolling Carper across the exercise yard to the infirmary, Henry John decided to finish him off. Luckily the nurse had just been in the way, not the target. She'd still gotten a chipped tooth, a black eye and some nasty scrapes when he knocked her to the ground so he could plunge a shank—made from a sharpened pork chop bone—into the downed man's heart.

"How many of my guards are out of the class that just finished?" Andy asked.

"None. That's who I had. They scheduled every damn one of them to start on my shift. Then they didn't give me enough experienced officers to train them. Every member of your crew is experienced."

"Well, thank God for that."

"Andy, there's one last thing. It seems the White Supremacists managed to get hold of that new Mexican kid that came in last week. We sent him to the hospital. Don't know if he'll make it."

"How in the hell did that happen? He was supposed to be in the nursery, segregated. P.C.'d." The nursery was what everyone called P.C., Protected Custody, a small wing dedicated to the care of child molesters, snitches, serial rapists, rape victims and the uncontrollably insane. And lately, it housed more and more children—aged thirteen to eighteen—considered dangerous enough to be tried as adults, but too vulnerable to be put in the general population.

"We have no idea. He came up missing about an hour before supper was served. We went looking and found him inside the garbage dumpster behind the maintenance shed."

Andy shook his head. The brutalized prisoner, Jesse Martinez, wasn't a menace to society. He was just young and unlucky. He was a good student, never in any trouble with the law, a quiet boy. But there had been a wreck, and a woman died; and since he had chosen that night to get drunk, he had to do some hard time.

"Man, things are fucked up," he growled. "A kid like that had no business in a place like this to begin with. Goddam politicians. They always figure hollering about being 'tough on crime' will win them votes—but there's no way they'll raise the taxes to cover the expense of overflowing prisons."

"Yeah." Rod's face was unreadable. "When the bastards finished with him they marked his cheek and forehead with a knife. Their fucking symbol. We tore the place apart looking for the damned thing but came up empty. The prison is on lockdown until that knife is found."

"Is there anything more I need to know?"

Both men shook their head.

"All right, Rod, you go home." Andy already had a headache and knew as the night wore on it would get worse. Lately, they had been on lockdown more often than they weren't.

Hulbert got to his feet. "I would stay if I could, Andy. But the office would shit a brick."

"That's okay." Andy glanced at Joe. "I hate for you to stay . . ."

"I know. But I would expect you to stick around if the situation was reversed. Just let me go to the car and get a fresh pair of socks and a couple bottles of water. What did you bring for supper?"

"Barbeque chicken, salad, and a couple of pears. There's enough for the two of us."

Rod dropped his lunch bucket onto the table and flipped it open. "I didn't get a chance to eat. Two sardine sandwiches, a bag of chips, a packet of cookies and a diet Coke."

"Jeez, Hulbert, no wonder you're so damn scrawny! That stuff will kill you." Joe closed the lid to the bucket and handed it back to the man. "Take it home and feed it to the garbage can."

"Okay, but by about four-thirty, you'll be wishing you had it."

"I don't think so." Joe was laughing now. "Maybe we can feed that shit to the prisoners until someone squeals on who hit the Martinez kid. It shouldn't take more than one meal."

"Sounds like cruel and unusual punishment to me." Andy chuckled, slapping Rod on the back. "Thanks. Go home, we'll be fine."

The door opened and the wind gusted in. Kathleen Hanrahan looked their way, giving them her usual easy smile. Her maternity uniform barely fit. Everyone knew at her age she had no business working this late into the pregnancy. But her husband, a laborer at the coal docks, had gotten laid off six weeks after she discovered her birth control measures hadn't worked. And with three half-grown kids still at home, she was stuck. She either worked until two weeks before the baby was due and came back six weeks after it was born, or she lost her job, her house, her car, and everything else she and her husband had managed to accumulate.

"Good morning," she said, patting her rounded abdomen. "Nine more shifts to go."

"Morning?" Joe shook his head.

"My morning." She looked at the clock. Fifteen minutes until time to punch in. "The roads are so dark. Even the prison lights seem dimmer, like they aren't putting out like they should."

Andy flipped his radio to the maintenance channel. The static on the radio drowned out everything except one word, *Generator power.*

"Just what we need." Andy looked at Joe. "Better check before we let anyone go home."

Joe nodded toward Rod. "Go out to the parking lot and get everyone hanging around out there through the metal detectors. I want them all inside the walls, now. And let the afternoon shift know, no one leaves till I say so."

James Cook sat on the top bunk of his cell, his home for the next many years. He wanted to cry, but didn't dare. If a guard saw any tears, and decided to do his job, that could land him in the psychologist's office and probably chained to a bed in suicide watch. It'd be even worse if one of the prisoners saw him crying.

Suicide. The coward's way out. His mother, her eyes cold and knowing, had stared into his own when she told him that. She wanted him to come home no matter what price he had to pay to do it.

His friends hadn't been so afraid of that. They thought they knew him. He was tough. He could handle himself. He would have to bash a few heads, the red man always had to do that in prison, but he would be okay. But when they said those things, they hadn't looked him in the eye. Instead, they had looked at his wiry frame and suggested he start lifting weights right away. They didn't think he should wait until he was convicted. Just in case.

He had taken their advice. Just in case. But he hadn't bulked up much. He had the wrong body type for that. Still, he was stronger and his endurance was up. He just hoped he didn't need either. He was no fool. He was no match for two or three men looking for a fight and a little fun.

For that matter, unless he had an edge, there was no way he could handle even one of these huge mothers.

The big ones hanging over the rail, whistling and calling out "fresh meat" as the new fish were walked from the processing area to their cells had left his mouth dry and feeling as though it was full of cotton.

He knew he wouldn't commit suicide. But just the same, he wasn't sure he would make it home to his mother. He might—probably would—get killed. He had already made up his mind. He would be no man's cocksucking bitch. He would die fighting if it came to that. If he couldn't die then, he would die later, when he went looking for revenge.

Cook forced himself to take a few deep breaths. So far things had gone better than he had hoped. While being processed, his roommate had been a blond-haired, blue-eyed kid from the streets of Chicago. The boy had spent half his life institutionalized in one form or another. Foster homes, county jails, juvenile detention centers. He'd done them all. This was his first trip to an adult prison, but he was already hooked up and doing a booming business for his *papa.* Since the sharks were being well fed, Cook and the other fish had had a relatively easy job staying out of trouble. As for his new roommate, his permanent roomie, he was a white man in his mid-fifties who made it plain he was doing his own time. He wouldn't be trying to dish anything out, but he also wasn't willing to give a fish any help.

Cook was grateful for that. If the man had offered to help, it wouldn't have been for free. There was no such thing as out of the goodness of your heart in a maximum security prison. He had been warned about the way things worked. Some guy, usually older, definitely stronger and with a track record for busting heads would be friendly enough. Offer a little protection from the others. And then would come the price tag. Loyalty. Sex. And maybe a little hooking to one or two of his friends. But he would keep the others off you. He would make sure you weren't jumped in the shower or shoved into your room when the screws were busy elsewhere. He would remind you it was better to be one man's bitch than prey for an entire cell-block.

Cook shuddered and reminded himself he wasn't effeminate. Young, yes. On the slender side, yes. Girlie, no. Except he didn't have much facial hair, and almost no body hair. He wished he was built more like the man on the bottom bunk; then maybe he too could sleep.

Paul Howard, his roommate, wasn't unusually large. But he was big enough and thick enough and exuded a don't-fuck-with-me attitude without saying one word. He had been asleep for almost an hour, but his light snore wasn't why Cook was still awake. It was the other noises. The ones coming from other cells. Some of those sounds he recognized, and some he didn't. He glanced at the iron bars and was actually glad for them. A two-bunk cell with the right roommate was easier to survive than a bed in an open wing. He knew he had been lucky so far, but he also knew his luck would run out. It always did.

CHAPTER
2

"We've got a big one, guys! Really big!"

Margo Glenn-Lewis leaned over, squinting at the numbers appearing on the monitor screen, a frown gathering on her forehead. "Damn weird one, too."

By then, Richard Morgan-Ash was already leaning over her shoulder. Within three seconds, so were Karen Berg and Malcolm O'Connell. Within ten seconds, Leo Dingley had arrived from the room next door. All five scientists working that night in the laboratory buried half a mile below ground in Minnesota had their attention fixed on the monitor.

"'Weird' is putting it mildly," Leo said, after a while. "If I'm interpreting these numbers correctly, we're talking about incredible energy here."

Berg was already working the figures on her laptop. She carried it everywhere, even to the point of eliciting jokes about whether she took it into the bathroom—jokes which she laughed at but never answered.

"It's as big as the Grantville event," she said, her tone hushed. "According to this."

Morgan-Ash made a face. "Karen, to this day it has never been established what the figures were for the Grantville event." He gestured with his hands at their surroundings. "That was seven years ago. None of this was operating then, you may recall." The same meticulousness made him add: "Well. Not for that purpose, anyway. I admit some stray detections were made, but hardly enough—"

"Oh, cut it out, Dick," said O'Connell. "We've crunched the numbers a thousand times over the years, and we know what it had to have been. A time transposition involving a sphere of space six miles in diameter and including umpteen jillions tons of matter—we've got that number figured somewhere, too, but 'umpteen jillion' does well enough for the moment—requires . . ."

His own tone had grown hushed. His finger pointed at the screen. "*This* sort of numbers."

Morgan-Ash didn't pursue the argument. In truth, he didn't really disagree himself. He just found it necessary, as he had many times since he'd joined the project— The Project, was the only name it had—to restrain his colleagues' enthusiasms. In that, if nothing else, they tended to have the bad habit of conspiratorial rebels since time immemorial to be True Believers.

The reason The Project had no formal name was because it had no formal existence. It was, in point of fact, something of a scientific conspiracy, launched less than a year after the Grantville Disaster by a small group of physicists and mathematicians who'd been completely dissatisfied with the official explanation of the event and just as completely disgusted by the scientific establishment's apparent willingness to go along with that official explanation.

All the more so because, damnation, there was *evidence*. Several of the deep underground experimental facilities located in various places around the world to study such things as neutrinos and nucleon decay and cosmic rays had detected . . .

Something.

But all pleas and requests to pursue the matter had been turned down, by governments and universities alike. And, unfortunately, the kind of equipment and facilities needed to detect the phenomena that they suspected were involved was extremely expensive. Not as expensive as something like CERN or Fermi Lab or the Very Large Array, no. But a lot more expensive than anything that would be financed by any single educational establishment or any single private donor.

Fortunately, the newly elected President of the United States had come to the rescue, in a manner of speaking. Soon enough, his administration had so thoroughly infuriated enough scientists because of its heavy-handed political interference in scientific affairs, that influential figures in academia and even in some upper echelons of various government scientific agencies became more sympathetic to the requests. Not, probably, because they thought they were likely to be successful, but simply because they were antiestablishment. So, eventually, through a complex set of interlocking grant proposals, the conspirators got the funding they needed.

Personally, Richard thought it showed very bad taste for Leo and Margo to refer to their funding as "embezzlement," even if he'd admit that much of the language in the grant proposals had been . . .

Well. He preferred the terms "ingenious" or "creative," himself. "Vague," certainly. In a pinch, in a sanguine mood, he'd even allow "misdirection."

On the bright side, the sort of nosy political overseers who'd have the inclination to ferret out the truth behind what those grants were actually funding were not the sort of people whose idea of a junket would include traveling half a mile down into an old iron mine in the backwoods of northern Minnesota. And even if they did, so what? How many of them would be able to make head or tails out of the use to which the equipment was being put, these days? It was, after all—for the most part, at least— the very same equipment that had been purchased and installed for its original purposes over twenty years earlier. The investigator would have to be a specialist in the fields involved to be able to sort out the truth from the flummery.

It *could* be done. Indeed, that was how Richard himself had stumbled across the truth. He'd gotten puzzled by the reports that were occasionally issued from the Minnesota site and had come to see for himself. But, of course, he was hardly a political overseer in the eyes of anyone except his teenage daughter. Who, fortunately, had taken the transition from southern England to northern Minnesota quite well, even if Richard himself was a bit dubious at times of the results.

"The chronographic configuration looks really weird,

too," said Malcolm. "Nothing at all like the events we've observed before."

"I can tell that much from the numbers," said Dingley, "but you're our chronolotrist, not me."

The term "chronolotry" was what they'd taken to calling O'Connell's esoteric branch of mathematics, much of which he'd developed himself. Richard understood it only vaguely. For that matter, after his third beer, Malcolm himself would admit he understood it only vaguely.

O'Connell was frowning, now. "It's hard to explain. Leaving aside that half of it is guesswork. But the difference—forget the energy involved, for a moment, which is also different—is the trajectory. For lack of a better term."

Margo sighed. "Malcolm, you're speaking English again. Try it in Greek."

He flashed her a grin. "Antique or modern?" He looked around for a moment, as if searching for something. "If I could find a clay tablet and a scribe, I could show you the math. Not that it would make much sense to you."

"And again with the insults."

"Look, I don't ask you how your Gandalf computer programs work. Don't ask me how my Elrond math works, how's that? The gist of it—we've all agreed on this, at least tentatively—is that the Earth has been subjected for years now to a hitherto unknown form of bombardment from a cosmic source of some kind. Obviously, an accidental phenomenon, since the location and angle of the impacts have been what you'd expect from happenstance. But *this*—"

He jabbed a finger at the screen. "This is what you'd expect from a marksman taking deliberate aim. It's dead on. Not a single joule is going to be wasted just moving tons of earth or water at random. I estimate the impact area won't be more than half a mile in diameter. If that."

Karen Berg shook her head. "But, Leo, they've all had a diameter smaller than that. Much smaller, we figure. So I don't see why . . . Oh."

"Yeah. 'Oh.' But none of them had anything like this kind of energy, did they? Not since Grantville." He gave Richard a sidewise glance. "Fine. Not since our *supposition* of the energy levels involved in the Grantville event."

Berg looked back at the screen. "Jeepers. Margo, do you have any idea yet where it's going to hit?"

Hearing no answer, she looked down at Glenn-Lewis. Whose face, pale to begin with, now looked as white as the proverbial ghost.

"Yeah," Glenn-Lewis said. "With this much energy and given the chronoletic readings, the trajectory firmed up much sooner than usual. It's going to hit not far from here. Somewhere around the confluence of the Mississippi and Ohio rivers."

"Holy Moses," hissed Malcolm. "*St. Louis?* That's got a population of . . . jeez, what is it? Two million people?"

Margo shook her head. "It'll miss St. Louis by a comfortable margin. But . . ."

She sprang to her feet. "Who's coming with me?"

The rest of the people in the room stared at her.

"What are you talking about?" asked Karen. "A *field* expedition? You couldn't possibly get there in time!"

Dingley cleared his throat. "And a good thing, too. Margo, this thing is *dangerous,* for God's sake. The last time we got a chronoletic impact this powerful, a whole town got destroyed."

"It might still be dangerous after the fact," added Karen, uncertainly. "The energy involved . . . That *is* the area that has the worst earthquake potential in North America, let's not forget."

Leo looked startled. His eyes got a bit unfocused, as he started calculating.

But this was Richard's area of expertise. "You can at least put that fear to rest. All things are relative. Compared to the energy involved in a major earthquake, this"—he jabbed his own finger at the screen—"is like tossing popcorn."

Dingley's face cleared. "Yeah, Dick's right. And the energy levels aren't directly comparable anyway, since most of the impact happens on the fourth dimension, not the first three." He flashed that same quick grin. "To put it as crudely as I possibly can to you amateurs."

Margo was looking exasperated. "For Pete's sake, don't you understand? They *can't* cover this one up!"

Everybody went back to staring at her.

"Look," she continued, "the only reason they got away with Grantville was because it was a once-only." She waved her hand. "Yeah, sure—*we* know there have been dozens since then. Dozens, at least. But why won't almost anyone listen to us? For the good and simple reason that they've been small events and almost all of them happen where you'd expect random impacts to happen. Somewhere in the ocean. Or, if it was on land, somewhere uninhabited or nearly so."

She shrugged. "So, fine. So some fishermen in the

north Atlantic Ocean swear they saw a sea monster, and a small village in Borneo found some sort of weird carcasses washed ashore. But nobody checked the fishermen's story because fishermen have been telling sea monster stories for centuries and while a biologist did go to that village in Borneo, by the time he got there the remains had rotted and all he could say was that they had definitely been some sort of very large and peculiar marine invertebrate."

Richard started tugging his beard. "Yes, true. And if a small village in the Sudan disappears, there are unfortunately far too many simpler explanations."

"Well, there was . . ." But Karen didn't pursue the matter. She saw the point also.

Margo was heading for the door. "So it won't hit St. Louis. Big deal. That part of the United States *is* populated. And not by illiterate villagers or semiliterate fishermen."

Richard had already made up his mind. "I'll come. I think two of us will be sufficient."

The others looked relieved, although they were trying their best not to let it show. They were quite bold people, actually, in their own way. But theirs was not the sort of temperament you find in tornado-chasers.

Neither was Richard's, for that matter. But he did have military experience—the only one of the group who did—and so he felt a certain odd sort of obligation.

There was the advantage, with Margo driving her beat-up SUV through Minnesota back roads, that Richard figured the most dangerous part of the expedition would be over with by the time they got to the airport. If they got to the airport.

But all he said was: "I believe the fishermen were from Boston."

"Yeah, they were. Like I said. Semiliterates."

Richard was tempted to point out that Boston had probably the highest concentration per capita of universities of any city in North America. But, having once fought his way through a heavy Bostonian accent, shortly after his arrival in the United States, he was not inclined to pursue this argument either.

CHAPTER
3

The prison's generator coughed, sputtered, and fell silent.

The walls shook. The ground heaved upward, toppling chairs and tables and people. Captain Andy Blacklock slid beneath the combination melamine and steel conference table as one of the twelve-foot long light fixtures broke free at one end and then crashed to the floor. From where he lay he could see Kathleen Hanrahan. She was wedged against the glass doors, her eyes wide with fear. He tried to move, go to her, get her away from the glass, but couldn't. He was plastered to the tan colored tiles, unable to lift his head or even his hand.

The dull white walls took on a silver sheen, then dimmed to gray. The metallic blue bars looked almost black. The cream colored, airport style X-ray machine seemed to flatten out, and then regain their shape. His ears popped and the whistling eased, eased a little more, and then was gone. He could breathe again. Could move. The colors returned to normal and the room erupted in shouts as people scrambled to their feet. Few of them were able to take their first few steps without hanging onto walls or tables. They seemed to have lost their equilibrium. Kathleen struggled to her feet and then made her way to one of the white, plastic chairs close to the payroll office. She was flushed red and her breaths came in shallow gasps. Her dark eyes were wide with terror.

Andy's radio came alive with status reports. Maintenance, zones A through D, the infirmary, communications, psych units: within minutes every sector checked in. The guards sounded calm, but Andy knew they weren't. They couldn't be. The prison had a disaster plan for every problem that could be thought up, but it mostly involved just locking down and waiting it out. Staff families were expected to fend for themselves during these emergencies.

The gates were now on manual. The electrical locking system would be nonfunctioning. That was going to slow the guards down. Chits, sign-out sheets and keys. But it didn't matter. All inmates were locked away. When the electrical locking system went out, it went out in the locked mode. That was one of the few things inside the prison that was actually fail-safe.

Captain Greg Lowry hurried toward him, his face pale. For a second Andy was afraid the man might have a stroke. Greg was in his mid-sixties, just months from retirement. He was fifty pounds overweight, and rumor said he had some major health issues.

Andy liked Greg. He was one of those men who kept his head and his temper. He also kept his own council. He didn't join in with the gossip and backbiting common to this type of work.

"If there's ever a disaster, we're going to be in a bind, Andy," Lowry had told him at last week's staff meeting. "The disaster plans are written as though we're fully staffed. When was the last time you worked with a full crew? We need a plan that's for us, not the politicians in Springfield."

Greg came up alongside him and whispered, "We might have gotten lucky. There's a wall integrity breach; it's small and it's outside the confinement area. But we have to find out if we have others—there could be breaches inside the cells."

Andy nodded. He turned the volume down on his radio—loud enough for him to hear the reports coming in fast and furious, but low enough that if something private came through, it would remain so.

"You're right, Greg." With both the afternoon and night crews present, they were still a dozen guards short for what needed to be done. He rubbed his head, trying to think clearly. The dull ache he'd acquired earlier was now a full-blown headache, pounding behind his eyes, across the top of his head, and through every sinus cavity he owned.

"What was that?" Rod Hulbert was on his feet, looking around, trying to get his bearings. "At first I thought it was an earthquake. I figured the New Madrid fault line had let go. Now, I don't know."

The last time the New Madrid fault line had a major slip was back in the early 1800s. But everyone who lived in the area knew that the one hundred fifty mile long fault line was overdue. They also knew that when it went, it would be a national disaster that would make the New Orleans hurricane fiasco look like child's play. Over seventy-five percent of the buildings in the quake zone were older buildings made of unreinforced masonry. Buildings like that wouldn't survive an earthquake measuring a 6.3 on the Richter scale—and the last time that fault line slipped, it was a lot stronger than that.

Nobody knew exactly where the New Madrid earthquake would have registered on the Richter scale, of course, since it had happened almost two centuries earlier. But the three quakes had flattened thousands of acres of forests, changed the course of the Mississippi River, and formed new lakes. Those three quakes—part of a series of two thousand quakes taking place over a two-year period— were the largest earthquakes the continental U.S. had ever experienced in the historical record, and had been felt as far away as Canada. They'd even caused the church bells in Washington D.C. to ring.

Andy looked around the entry area. The personnel closest to the metal detectors were going through the process of entering the prison. They were being patted down by nervous guards. The interiors of their lunch buckets were being visually inspected, since the X-ray machines weren't working. Andy gave a small sigh of relief. The entry routine was helping. No one had panicked, but quite a few were close to it.

"Go inside, Greg," Andy said. "Joe and I will put together a couple of teams to walk the perimeter outside the walls. You get the interior checked." He waved in the direction of the parking lot. "Divvy them up. Send them around to the backside. Make sure everything held."

By the time Andy was done talking, Greg had already

cut through the line and was at the first set of iron gates separating the prison from the main room. The one blindingly good piece of luck involved in the disaster was the timing—thirty minutes later, the afternoon shift would have been gone entirely. Andy would have had to deal with the situation with only forty-two people.

Andy looked at Joe and shrugged. "What a way to start a shift." He looked around at the stunned faces. "Don't let anyone else in. Get them outside, walking the perimeter. That's our first priority. Then radio Lowry. I want No-Man's-Land walked." No-Man's-Land was what they called the killing zone: an eight-foot strip of open ground between two fifty-foot cement walls topped with razor wire that encircled the prison.

A few minutes later the entry area was empty except for Kathleen who was stationed at the gates with orders to let no one enter or leave until Joe or Andy okayed it. The rest of the guards were outside. Their flashlights were on and Joe had passed out one radio to each team of three and sent them to check the walls on the east, north, and south sides of the prison. Hulbert and a half-dozen guards had already gone around to the west end of the facility.

Andy was looking at the administration building. He checked the windows first; none of the glass seemed broken. The bars were all in place. And from where he stood he could see no cracks in the mortar between the brown blocks that made the walls. Everything looked good. There was nothing that indicated structural damage to the three-story, brown limestone building that had been built over a century before.

"It looks solid enough. We might have gotten lucky," he said, knowing that until daylight came and men could walk the building and examine it up close, there was really no way of knowing for sure.

Andy watched part of his crew as they hurried alongside the building's exterior, their flashlights playing against the eighteen-foot, chain-link fence topped with razor wire that enclosed the compound. He turned east and looked at the wall and then toward town. There were no lights anywhere. Even the hospital lights couldn't be seen. The entire area was darker than he thought possible—so dark, he couldn't even make out the shape of the bluff the town sat on.

He felt a tap on his shoulder. He couldn't remember the woman's name, but her face was familiar. She usually worked B-house. "Yeah," he said.

She pointed to the sky.

He looked up and his heart leapt in his chest. The clouds were gone and the sky was filled with more stars than he could remember seeing. Then he realized the temperature had changed. It was warm. Very warm. Almost hot. Hot and moist. And there was a combination sweet and sulfur smell in the air. He looked north, away from the prison, and had to swallow hard. The skyline glowed red.

"Hey, Andy!" Joe motioned toward what should have been the administrative parking lot. "It's gone. So is the gun range and the visitor parking area. Everything's been swallowed up by the quake."

"That was like no quake I ever heard of." Andy looked at where the parking lot had been. The blacktop and the cars were gone. Not destroyed, simply . . . gone. In their place was nothing but bare earth and some sort of odd-looking plants. What sort of earthquake could do that?

"Get inside," he said, "and get on the phone. Call the state police. Find out what's going on. Wake up the warden, and get him down here. Then call in the off-duty first responders and E-team officers."

"Already tried that." Kathleen was coming through the doors. "Greg sent me out here to tell you the phone lines are down, and none of the cell phones are working. He also said the radios are on the fritz. The ones used for communication inside the prison are working better than they've worked in days, but those used for outside . . ." She bit her bottom lip. "They're out. Same for the TVs and the regular radio stations."

James Cook's ears popped. The walls vibrated and hummed. The metal shelf with its two-inch foam mattress the prison staff called his bunk swayed. There was noise everywhere.

Cook wanted to sit up so he could hop down from his bed, but couldn't move. He tried to turn his head, but even that was too difficult to accomplish. His eyes stayed focused on the small, iron-grated ventilation hole on the wall just a few inches below his ceiling. He watched as the six-inch bars vibrated faster and faster. His vision blurred. The bars faded, almost disappearing, then returned. The hum turned into a roar. The roar became a whistle. The bars returned to their original color, and then one of them fell out. It was lying on his bed and he could now move.

He reached out to the black metal bar. It was warm, almost hot.

Cook slid the bar back into the vent grill and then turned to face the door. It was tempting to try to hide it and hope the screws wouldn't notice that one of the bars was missing. That piece of steel could make a big difference if he wound up having to fight one of the slabs of beef he'd seen when he arrived. But being found in possession of it could also add two years to his prison term. The bar was still loose, if he ever needed to pry it back out again.

Paul Howard, his cellmate, was trying to get out of bed, and all hell had broke loose up and down the tiers. Men were screaming to be let out of their cells. They didn't want to be trapped inside during a quake or its after-shocks. Guards added to the bedlam, running up the stairs and down the walkways, slapping the metal bars with metal nightsticks and screaming for silence.

He lay down, forcing himself not to look at the ventilation grill. The wall was probably as strong as ever, and they didn't build flimsy walls in maximum security prisons. Besides, what was the point of thinking about the ventilation opening? Even if he could squeeze himself through—not likely, to say the least—he'd just be looking at a three-story drop to cold, hard cement.

He stared at the blue-gray steel separating his cell from the catwalk, his pulse racing and a thin sheen of sweat glistening above his upper lip. The broken bar would be found the first time the guards dumped the room. And even if it wasn't, it didn't matter. He couldn't escape, and even if he could there was no life on the outside for a man on the run.

James Cook was an excellent poker player. Three minutes later, when the screw played his flashlight around the room, his face was proof of that. He gave the CO a cold look, then closed his eyes.

CHAPTER

4

"Oh, damn," Margo Glenn-Lewis snarled. "Another one!" As she slowed the rental vehicle, seeing the police road-block across the road ahead of them, she slapped the steering wheel in frustration. "I didn't think they'd have this dinky little county road covered also."

Richard Morgan-Ash was surprised himself. It was still the middle of the night, and he wouldn't have thought the local authorities in a rural area would have been able to mobilize such an extensive set of police roadblocks on such short notice. They'd been stopped twice already by roadblocks, on the first two roads they'd taken.

They knew from their contact over his cell phone with their colleagues still in Minnesota that the chronoletic impact had happened right after midnight. The exact time was impossible to pin down because the impact scrambled time around itself. By the clocks in the underground facility, it had happened at exactly 12:11:08. But the time

at the impact site itself might very well have read somewhat differently, to anyone in a position to observe.

Whether anyone *would* be in a position to observe such
an impact, from "inside," so to speak, was a hotly contested
issue among the scientists in The Project. A minority were
inclined to believe that anyone caught by such an impact
would simply be destroyed. But the main school of
thought was that they'd undergo a time transfer but might
come out at the other end alive. By way of evidence,
adherents to the majority view would point out that—
assuming the vague reports were accurate—it seemed
that animals coming the *other* direction—so to speak—
came through it fairly intact.

It would help, of course, if the authorities would allow
anyone except their own scientists to have access to the
remains that had appeared at Grantville. But that whole
area, very soon after the impact, had been declared a
national security zone. The same sort of tight security had
been clamped down around it that you'd expect to find at
weapons test sites and top secret installations.

Richard's opinion was that all the existing hypotheses
were simply rampant speculation. They needed hard
evidence before they could do anything more than suck
theories out of their thumbs.

Margo brought the car to a halt. One of the officers
standing by the police car parked in such a way as to bar
the road started coming their way.

Richard leaned toward Margo and said softly, "Allow
me to do the talking this time, would you?"

Margo scowled. Morgan-Ash decided that amounted to
consent, and got out of the car. He wanted to talk to the

officer himself because Margo's notions of how to conduct a conversation with the police seemed to stem from some sort of deep-rooted adolescent resentment. He'd found that, despite being in her early fifties, Margo had a strong tendency to rebel against authority simply because it was authority.

Richard had no such inclination, himself. Not because he had any greater respect for authority-*qua*-authority than she did. He probably had even less. But if there was one advantage to having been an officer in one of Britain's paratrooper regiments, as a young man, it was that he took authority for granted.

"What seems to be the problem, officer?"

He made no attempt to disguise his pronounced accent. First, because he couldn't anyway. Richard had the sort of upper class English accent that was so deeply ingrained he doubted if he could disguise it to save his life. Having attended Eton himself, he was skeptical that its storied playing fields had much to do with Britain's military prowess. For sure and certain, not one of the very tough paras he'd commanded in the field had ever attended the school or even dreamed of doing so. They came from a completely different class altogether. But the school was superb at drumming in the proper accent.

Besides, it would probably help. Decades of movie-watching, he'd found, had ingrained most Americans with the attitude that a man who spoke English with that sort of accent was a legitimate sort of fellow. They'd suspect he would also prove to be obnoxious and overbearing, true. But Richard could defuse that easily enough. The main thing was not to be dismissed outright.

And, sure enough—where Margo had gotten no explanations at all, just curt commands to turn the car around, this officer was willing to talk.

"I'm sorry, sir, but you can't go any farther." He gestured over his shoulder with a thumb. "There's been some sort of major accident at Alexander, and until we know exactly what the situation is, we're keeping everyone out of the area."

Richard shook his head. "I'm afraid I'm not from this area, officer. Alexander refers to . . . ?"

"Alexander Correctional Center. It's one of Illinois' maximum security prisons." The officer made a face. "It's got over two thousand of the state's most dangerous felons locked up inside. We're not sure, yet, but until we know whether or not any of the inmates have escaped, we've cordoned off the whole area."

Richard abandoned his tentative plan to plead a dying relative. Given the situation described, there was no way the police would let them proceed any farther. And the mystery of how and by what means rural police agencies had been mobilized so quickly was now solved.

He glanced at the logo on the police car, quite visible in the beam of the headlights coming from their rental vehicle. *Illinois State Police.* The cars at the two previous roadblocks had belonged to county or local law enforcement agencies, but obviously the state police were coordinating the effort. And, of course, they'd have contingency plans already in place in the event of inmates escaping from a maximum security prison in the area.

"I see." He gave the officer a very friendly smile. "Well, in that case, I'm afraid our ailing cousin will have to manage on his own for a bit. Do you have any idea how soon the situation will be cleared up?"

"I really couldn't tell you, sir. We still don't know ourselves exactly what's happened. The prison isn't responding to any calls, either by phone or radio."

He was clearly not being reticent for the sake of reticence. The man simply didn't know anything.

Richard got back into the car. "Bad luck, I'm afraid. It seems the impact happened at or near a maximum security prison."

"Oh . . . *hell.*" Glenn-Lewis glared at the cop car, as if it were somehow responsible. "Maybe if we found a really back road . . ."

"Not a chance, Margo. In fact, they're likely to have even heavier coverage of such roads, on the theory that an escaping prisoner is mostly likely to seek them out himself." He shook his head. "No, I'm afraid we're stymied for the moment."

Margo began making a three-point turn. Not, probably, because she was worried about getting a ticket for making a U-turn, but simply because the road was too narrow for one in the first place.

"Now what?" she asked, as they drove away from the roadblock.

Richard had been considering the question himself. Not with any great hope of finding what he needed, he looked in the glove department.

"Alas. No maps, as I feared. Do you know how to get to Collinsville?"

"Never heard of it. And there must be a hundred Collinsvilles in the U.S." A bit defensively, she added:

"Look, I'm from Manhattan. There's New York, there's Jersey, there's California way out there on the other coast, and a bunch of stuff in between."

Richard sighed. "Collinsville, Illinois. It's near Scott Air Force Base."

"There's an air force base in *Illinois*?" She whistled, softly. "Jeez, and here I thought they were all in South Dakota or Nevada or someplace like that."

Richard had noticed before that most American intellectuals were astonishingly ignorant about any and all military affairs. In that respect, quite unlike British intellectuals. Or French, for that matter. He supposed it was a residue from the Vietnam War. American intellectuals tended to see that war as a manifestation of imperialist behavior, which they'd not expected from their country. A betrayal, as it were. They were still quietly seething about it, even these many decades later. Whereas British or French intellectuals simply took it for granted that empires were empires and did what empires did. Whether they liked it or not—and they usually didn't like it any more than their American counterparts did—they weren't shocked by the whole business.

Then again, he reminded himself, that was just a theory of his—which might be as half-baked as the theories of his colleagues that he criticized so regularly. The explanation could simply be that Margo Glenn-Lewis, who'd never traveled more than fifty miles from New York City until she joined The Project, was exactly the geographical ignoramus she claimed to be.

"Yes, there is. It's a very large facility, in fact. Scott is the headquarters for United States Transportation Command."

"You live and learn, as they say." She glanced at him, after negotiating a sharp turn in the road. "And why do you want to know where it is?"

"I have an old friend who works at the base. I haven't seen him in years, but we stay in touch now and then by e-mail. I'm thinking he might be of some assistance to us."

"How?"

"He's been there for many years. It's not that far from here, and I'm hoping he might have some contacts in the various police agencies." Richard gestured at the surrounding countryside, which could barely be seen in the light of a quarter moon. "Look at it this way, Margo. We're not likely to discover anything stumbling around in the dark, now are we? I leave aside the danger of encountering escaped and dangerous felons."

Margo smiled. "Hey, I ain't afraid of no convicts."

She said that with the insouciance of someone who had never actually known any convicted felons. Not the sort who'd wind up in a maximum security prison, at least.

Richard didn't know any, either, so far as he knew. But the paratroopers he'd commanded hadn't been all that different, in some ways. Except they were certainly tougher, if not quite as savage.

"Indulge me, then," he said, smiling also. "I *am* afraid of that lot. They're fearsome folk, by all accounts."

Richard found a map of Illinois in the first petrol station they found that was still open in the middle of night, not far from Carbondale. It took him no more than a minute cross-checking the index with the map to figure out the directions.

He looked around and saw that Margo was already out of the station and climbing into the vehicle outside. He followed, feeling mildly triumphant.

"All right," he said, after he got into the car. "What we need to do—"

"I know, already. We take Route 51 north to I-64, and then take I-64 toward St. Louis. We'll pass the air force base along the way." She grinned at him. "I asked the gas station attendant, what do you think?"

"That's *cheating.*"

She shook her head. "We're in the perimeter of a cosmic catastrophe, desperately searching for assistance to get us past official stonewalling, and the man is obsessed with figuring out how to get somewhere the manly way."

"It's still *cheating.*"

CHAPTER
5

Captain Blacklock took his hat off, ran his fingers through his hair, and then slid the cloth and plastic blue and black cap back on. Three of the four teams sent to walk the prison's outer perimeter had already used their two-ways to call in a report. Lieutenant Rod Hulbert's small band was the only one still not accounted for. That had the captain worried. Even if they hadn't checked everything they wanted to check, Hulbert should have at least checked in.

"Okay," Andy called. "I want everyone without an assignment inside. Get behind the walls and at your duty station. Joe, you drive into town, see what's up." He tossed the lieutenant his radio. "It has a six-mile radius. Broadcast continually; use the maintenance channel. If you wind up having to go to the far side of town and know you're out of range, keep talking anyway. Find out what you can and then get a report to the state boys. Let them know our communications are out. Then get back here."

"Do I take the state truck or my car?"

"Take the state vehicle." Andy looked at the stars, then at the red glow to the north of them, and then toward town. "If you've punched out, punch back in on your way to the garage. If the clock's not working, pencil in the time and initial it. I'll sign your card later, but this way your butt's covered if something goes wrong."

The radio, now clipped to Joe's belt, awoke. The static had disappeared. *"D-David-23—10-3000, 10-2000. Repeat. D-David 23—10-3000, 10-2000."*

A guard was down and a prisoner was out of his cell.

Andy caught Lieutenant Joe Schuler by the sleeve, and shook his head. The man had started toward the administration building and the entrance to the prison as soon as the call was completed. "No way, Joe. I'll take care of this. You get the hell into town! We have to know what's happening." The captain then took off at a dead run. There were three double sets of iron gates, two heavy steel doors and three checkpoints between him and the downed guard.

"How bad?" Andy asked, coming through the door of D-house. It had taken him just under six minutes to arrive.

Greg looked up from the desk he was sitting at, then back down. "We found the knife we've been looking for all day."

"Who caught it?"

"Brown. Elaine Brown. She's one of the new recruits. Black woman. Good-looking as all hell and a sweet kid to boot: just barely twenty-one. They shouldn't hire women like her. She still had her whole life ahead of her. And she shouldn't have to deal with the scum we have in here. She was checking for quake damage and got jumped."

Andy didn't bother to remind Lowry that even good-looking twenty-one-year-olds had to eat. And in this part of southern Illinois that meant a job at the prison, if you were lucky. "Who had the knife?"

"Boyd Chrissman."

Andy looked around. None of the prisoners or guards were to be seen. The extraction team had handled the situation, then left. They were good. Boyd would be in the hole or the infirmary by now, depending on how much resistance he gave. The guards would be back at their regular duty posts. "How bad was she hurt?"

"Brown? Pretty bad. She's in the infirmary. Got her in the gut. Melissa Glasser found her. Luckily they both had enough sense to leave it in place till the nurses got here."

"They taking her out to the hospital?"

Greg shook his head. "We can't move her. We can't raise the hospital, any of the doctors, the police, the National Guard, no one. She stays until we find out what's happening."

"You can't do that, Greg. She could die. We're not equipped for anything major. At this time of the night, all we have are nurses, not doctors. You have to load her up in a state car and just hope the hospital is experiencing nothing more than communication problems." Andy turned toward the door.

"Wait."

"Why?"

"Andy, it's not that simple." Greg stood up. "Lieutenant

Hulbert took six men to do a sweep of the west side of the prison. When they finished, he didn't call in a report, didn't want a panic. But . . . I don't know . . . I seem to think no matter what we do, we'll have a panic. There are just some things you can't keep a secret, at least not for long."

Andy ground his teeth. "What's going on *now*?"

"It seems the river is missing."

"Missing?"

"Yeah. The mighty Mississip is gone. Right along with the coal docks." Greg made a strange sound, a cross between a sob and choking. "The dock, the railroad tracks, and about eight million bucks worth of conveyer equipment is gone, too."

"What are you talking about?" Andy's headache jumped from pure misery to a light-flashing, stomach churning migraine. "Did we get bombed?" He couldn't think straight. Nothing was making any sense.

"A bomb wouldn't dry up the river and leave us untouched." Greg's voice was gruff. Raspy.

"Yeah, you're right."

"And it wouldn't leave two-hundred-year-old trees standing where water used to be. And there wouldn't be waist-high ferns growing in rich, black topsoil where an asphalt road was thirty minutes ago."

Andy looked around the cellblock's entry area. It looked solid enough. Not like a dream. The second hand on the wall clock was circling the numbers at a steady rate of sixty seconds per minute. The lights were dim, on generator power, but no more so than was expected. His flashlight, gripped in his right hand till his knuckles

showed white, was the appropriate weight. This was *not* a
nightmare.

"Where's Hulbert?"

"At the infirmary." Greg Lowry looked every minute of
his sixty-plus years. His eyes seemed glazed, and his hands
shook. "I feel like I'm walking around in the Twilight
Zone. This isn't right."

Andy shook his head. "I prefer romantic comedies and
action flicks."

"I don't think what you like counts for too much, Andy.
At least not right now. We're just going to have to get a
handle on whatever this is, and do it pretty quick, too. See
'em watching us?" He nodded up, toward the tier upon
tier of cells—metal cages stacked five stories high.

Andy turned his head and looked. Here and there prisoners stood at the bars, arms extended through the iron.
Andy saw black skin, brown skin and white. He saw tattoos. He saw fists.

"I think we're in deep shit," Greg said. "And I think it's
going to get deeper." Halfheartedly, he waved a hand at
the prisoners. "As different as those men are, they all have
one thing in common: they're on the *inside* of the cages.
For now." He seemed to shrink a little inside his uniform.
"I just pray like hell no aliens pop out of the walls."

Andy didn't laugh. Greg Lowry was serious. And
scared. "I'm going to check on Brown and talk to Rod
Hulbert. I want you to get someone down here to relieve
you, then meet me in the conference room. I'll join you in
about a half hour. Try to get all the department heads
there. The afternoon and night shift."

Greg nodded but didn't move toward the door. He just

stood behind the metal desk, his face slack. "I think that's probably a good idea. But you better send someone else. I can't go."

The man half-collapsed in the padded swivel chair. He fumbled in his shirt pocket and pulled out a small bottle of pills. "Nitro. I've been using them for a couple of months now. And this has been . . . too much."

Andy took the radio sitting on the desk and fingered the send button.

"Don't," Lowry muttered. "It's not an emergency. At least not right now. I just need to rest a little." He pulled a kerchief from his pocket and mopped at the perspiration on his forehead. "I just need to rest, and get whatever is happening straight in my head. If I could get things straight, I'd feel better. I know I would."

Andy didn't put the two-way back on the desk. Instead, he keyed the send button and radioed for Hulbert to send a relief guard to D-block. He also told him to send a cart for Greg. "You're going, Lowry. I'm not giving you a choice in the matter. A dead man is a useless man, and right now I need you to stay alive. When this is over, if you want to commit suicide by pushing too hard, that's your business. But that's not happening tonight."

Greg Lowry nodded and nodded. He couldn't stop the slow, up and down movement of his head. He knew Andy was right. He had already taken more of the nitro than he was supposed to take. And he was still in pain. He needed to see someone medical, and he needed to do it soon. "Andy, I'm not arguing. I just don't know what to do. I don't know what's going on."

"No one does, Greg." Blacklock kept one hand on Lowry's shoulder and both eyes on the clock hanging on the wall opposite the desk. He watched the second hand crawl around its face. "Just hang in there, friend, and take it easy. There is going to be a logical explanation for all of this; you'll see. Something weird—damn weird—but logical."

Greg closed his eyes and tried to relax. The pain was back. His heart felt like it was caught in a vise and was being squeezed tighter and tighter. His left arm was numb, and his fingers tingled. His neck hurt, and his jaw ached. He tried to breathe slowly and easily, but his chest felt like someone had set a hundred-pound weight dead center on it. He tried to get his mind off the pain. He thought of his dog, alone in his two-bedroom trailer. By this time he knew the food and water bowls would be empty. And he thought of his grandson. He had promised to help the boy with his science project this weekend. They were going to build a two-way radio just like the one Greg had built with his own grandfather a half century before. And he thought of his wife, dead now for almost three years. He had bought a bunch of carnations from the gas station three blocks from the prison. They were for her grave. Pink carnations, because pink had been her favorite color. He was going to stop by the cemetery on his way home from work. He hadn't been out to see her in over a week, and that made him miss her even more than usual. He thought about the half-dozen pink flowers wrapped in green paper, the two spring-topped Eveready, 6-volt, classic lantern batteries he had bought for Richard's project, the phone bill that needed paying and the utility bill on the nightstand next to his bed; and of Barky sitting on the back of the couch looking out the window, waiting for him to come home.

Pain bloomed in his chest like a dark flower, and then he stopped thinking at all.

CHAPTER
6

Andy paced the length of the hall separating the holding area and examination room. He knew exactly what the nurse would say once the door opened and she ushered him in. Greg Lowry was dead. He was dead before Hulbert arrived with his gurney. He died before the nurses, who were now working their third shift in a row, ever saw him.

He stopped pacing and looked down the dimly lit hall that led to the medical records room. He had never been in there. All records were kept under lock and key, and the only ones with access were the nurses, doctors, and psych department employees.

None of this made any sense, he thought, rubbing his pounding head. He wasn't worried about the prisoner who tried to escape. It happened, especially when you were dealing with men who would be in their sixties when they got out of their cage. He wasn't even all that worried about Brown. It happened. Guards got jumped. What he was worried about was the other stuff. That was the part that made no sense.

Andy looked at Rod Hulbert, who was standing next to the outside door. The lieutenant had given him a terse report and then spent his time looking out the window watching the cell houses lining the road inside the prison walls.

Hulbert was tense. Ready for action. A lifetime of weekends and vacations traipsing through the limestone bluffs of southern Illinois with fellow survivalists had prepared him well. He had already skipped over the why, willing to let that wait till later, and was concentrating on the now. Andy watched him, envying the way he had adjusted to the situation.

Be aware of your environment. Know what is going on around you.

These were the words all employees who worked inside the walls lived by. People had a habit of dying when the words were forgotten.

But this wasn't a prisoner uprising. This was something different. Andy couldn't concentrate. He was having trouble even recognizing his surroundings.

Rod Hulbert's voice cut through the silence. "There's movement in the yard, and it isn't ours. All staff is accounted for."

The last count showed everyone locked inside their cell. There had to be a wall breach. Which house had it? Andy gave a silent laugh and glanced at the mirror just inside the door. It didn't matter which house. Inside this facility, unauthorized prisoners wandering the grounds were dangerous no matter where they came from.

The mirror showed a dark yard, but not so dark Andy couldn't see shadows working their way across the open area toward the machine shop.

"Infirmary-11, M control, 10-2000, moving southwest toward machine shop." Rod moved from the door to a window, tracking the prisoners. "Possible C, Charlie-house, not sure."

"How many?" Andy hissed, rushing to the window.

Rod hesitated then shook his head. "Looks to be at least four, maybe more," he said, keying the radio so the control room would know.

Andy stared out the window, trying to count the moving shadows. How many were loose? Who was loose? Were they armed? Could he get help from the outside if things escalated? He shook his head again then waved toward the armory.

Rod nodded, broke regulations by switching his radio to the off position, and then slipped out the door.

Andy rushed to the examining room and pushed open the door. "Glasser, we got 'em AWOL, let's move."

"I heard." Melissa Glasser was removing a blood-soaked paper gown. She had been assisting the nurses. Elaine Brown was on the table, an I.V. of saline solution flowing into her right arm. "Give me a sec." She tossed the soiled gown into a red receptacle marked as biohazard waste, then followed the captain to the door.

"I'm going to the armory. I want you to position yourself so you can see if the prisoners leave the machine shop. If they do, you are not to intercept. Call only, even if it's a single prisoner."

She nodded, checked the battery reading on her radio,

and then took off across the street. She slipped into the dark alley between the buildings.

Once outside the infirmary, it didn't take Andy long to catch up with Hulbert. With their radios silent, and their twelve-inch steel and aluminum flashlights held like clubs, they made their way to the armory, quickly and quietly.

"Who's the E-team leader for tonight?" Andy asked, as they pushed the heavy metal door open. "And who's running K-9?" Report had been interrupted and Andy didn't know who was on the afternoon shift's extraction team, or its dog unit. He wasn't even sure who had made it inside the wall for the midnight shift. "Who's available out of our first responders?"

Hulbert shrugged and said, "Us, I guess." He started pulling vests and face shields from the cabinets.

Andy grabbed the keys from the lockbox and opened the weapons cabinet. This was the part of the job he hated. Unlocking the cabinet, passing out the guns and the ammunition. Watching everyone's eyes. Worried someone would panic and shoot when they shouldn't, or not shoot when they should. He'd seen both happen.

"We just finished the debriefing from the last breakout," Kathleen said, breathing heavily. She had half-jogged, half-walked from south tower to the armory in under three minutes. "Who's making a run for it now?"

"Don't know. It was too dark to make out anything but a few shadows. We think they're from Charlie-house."

"That would make sense. It's the only building we haven't sent inspectors through. Everywhere they've gone they've seen damage, just not enough to be a major problem." Kathleen looked toward what was left of the parking lot.

"We haven't heard from," her eyes dropped to the clipboard she held in her hand, "Mark Suplinskas, in over a half hour." She was answering his unasked question. She then flipped the paper and checked the list on the second page. "All the others have reported in within the last fifteen minutes. Mark's new. He worked three to eleven, graduated from that last class."

Lieutenant Terrance Collins walked into the room. "We found three breaks in the exterior wall facing the river, but only one of them is large enough for a small man to wiggle through. The towers have been notified and I have two armed COs watching it. I've also posted COs at the other two areas. They're not carrying anything more than flashlights and radios."

Facing the river? Andy looked toward Hulbert who gave his head a slight shake. The missing Mississippi River was not common knowledge, at least not yet. Okay, the outer perimeter was as secure as they could make it. Now for the inside of the prison. "Kathleen, see if you can raise Suplinskas, and find out . . ."

Damn. "Have we heard from Joe Schuler?"

"He's been broadcasting almost continuously. But most of what he's saying doesn't make sense. He's on his way back. Should be here within the next ten to twenty minutes." Kathleen picked up the notebook she had been using to record all communications from the three two-ways she had been using more or less continuously for the last hour. "He's the only one outside the walls we've heard from. And we're the only ones he's seen. He says the roads to town are gone. Same for the houses and businesses." She gave a strained laugh. "He says everything, the entire town is gone. There's nothing but trees between us and a volcano about twenty miles out."

Andy wanted to scream. There were no volcanoes in the southern part of Illinois. There were rivers and lakes and hills. No mountains. No volcanoes.

"Okay," he said between clenched teeth, "this is too fucked up for us to deal with in the dark. I want everyone hunkered down for the night. The prisoners on the prowl can't get out, so let's just button everything down. Pair everyone up. One sleeper, one awake. There's no telling how long we're going to be on our own. I want radio contact every five minutes from now till sunrise. Station a couple of shooters outside the machine shop. We'll just isolate the bastards till morning."

"That's only about thirty minutes from now," Terry Collins said. "And when the sun comes up it's going to be in the northwest." He shrugged. "That's not a guess. Before I came in Jeff Edelman had me check it out inside the east tower. The sun is already starting to rise. And another thing, he has one of those watches with a built-in compass. He says the magnetic pole has shifted. It's now somewhere southeast of us."

"Who is Jeff Edelman?" Andy asked. "And how does *he* know all this?"

"New guard. He is—was—a geology graduate student at the university," Collins answered. "He had to break off his studies because his mother got sick and the family needed the money. And according to him, everything is wrong. Even the position of the moon and the stars."

"That's impossible," Kathleen whispered.

"Yeah, but impossible or not," Collins said, "the guy's right. If you don't believe him, just look at the sky. You don't have to know squat about what's supposed to be up there to know it's off."

Andy, putting on his gear, remembered the look of the night sky and felt something inside him shift abruptly.

The headache was gone. So was the indecision. Now all he felt was nervous energy.

He cinched his vest snug and slipped on his leather gloves. "Okay. Kathleen, tell Joe when he gets back from town, stay put. We'll join him after we get things inside the walls under control. Collins, get someone over to Charlie-house. Find out what is going on there. I'm going back to the machine shop. Hulbert, get the E-team, first responders, and K-9 put together, I want them all out on this." He picked up one of the assault rifles and a clip, then pulled his faceplate into position. "I guess we can't wait. Let's gather up our strays before aliens start popping out of the walls."

"What?" Kathleen's face paled to a chalk white.

"That was a joke, Kathleen. Just a joke. Now, get busy. I want everyone in full gear: helmets, goggles, and vests. Then get this prison locked down so tight even the cockroaches can't crawl around without getting an okay from one of us. Radio Glasser, let her know I'm on my way. And Collins, get this Edelman guy off the tower and into the administration building's main room. I'm going to want to talk to him."

Andy Blacklock, Rod Hulbert, Melissa Glasser, and the other members of the first responders team worked their way across the exercise yard toward the machine shop. Andy kept to the shadows as much as possible, but didn't try to kid himself. The prisoners hiding inside the building would know that he was there. They would know all of them were there. His best hope was that they would be unarmed.

Once he was within shouting distance he called to the escapees. "Listen up! You need to come out, and you need to do it now. A showdown does nothing but get people hurt or killed. That's not something you want."

Andy gave Rod a nod and the man took off at a slow jog across the yard, up the side of the building and across the roof. He watched Hulbert long enough to know he had made it across the open areas then held his hand up to stop the others from advancing any farther. He was waiting on a call from Kathleen. Things would go better if he knew who was inside the shop. He also needed to know how many, and that they really were just prisoners. He didn't—deep down—really believe they had been invaded by aliens. But . . . He couldn't think of any other explanation for what was happening.

Once Rod was in position there was no more movement and no more talk from anyone. They waited in the growing light. The sun was rising, and it was rising in the northwest just as Collins said it would.

His men—three of the twelve were women, but somehow he couldn't think of them as anything but men, not if he was going to put them in a position of getting shot at— were in position. He had learned that most team leaders thought like he did. They were women in the lunchroom, the meeting rooms, and on the practice field, but when it came time to go one-on-one with a prisoner, they were men. It was only the younger guys who didn't have to fool themselves on that point.

The guards at the prison were pretty well evenly divided between black and white, and men and women. But the first responders and E-team members were mostly men. Big men, as a rule. Rod Hulbert was the only man on the team under six-foot. And he was the only man on it who weighed less than two hundred pounds. The dozen or so women who were part of it were like Hulbert. Specialists. They weren't going to be sent into a cell to bring a prisoner out. It wouldn't happen.

Prisoners could get huge.

That was the thing that surprised new hire-ins. The sheer size of the prisoners. Natural size, too, not simply the bulk that so many of them added by weight-lifting. It seemed like almost half the men convicted of murder were walking giants. One popular theory among the guards was based on studies they'd heard about, where scientists found that a lot of oversized men had an extra Y-chromosome. That extra Y made them big; whether it made them violent or not was up for debate.

Andy was a bit skeptical, himself. True, he'd read an article once that stated a large number of very successful executives also had that extra Y. According to the author, these men didn't wind up in prison because their parents found constructive ways for their child to burn off the extra energy and aggression. Andy didn't know if that was true or not, but figured it was at least a possibility since some of those high-powered positions took more than a healthy dose of the killer instinct to do well.

Still, he had his doubts that there was any such neat answer to the problem. The still simpler explanation was that most juries and judges were more likely to convict a huge man for murder—just to be on the safe side, so to speak—and throw the book at him.

Whatever the reason, though, the fact remained. A very high percentage of prisoners convicted of murder were just plain big.

He shook his head and forced himself to concentrate on what was happening. He didn't have his usual team. He had only three of his regulars; the rest were from the afternoon crew. He also didn't have a backup of state and county boys waiting to be called in. They were on their own.

Hulbert signaled: he could see three prisoners inside the shop; he could get a bead on two of them.

"You, inside the machine shop! Come out with both hands on your head and hit the dirt as soon as you're through the door." *Kathleen, hurry up. I need to know who's inside that building.* Andy gave Hulbert the wait-at-ready signal.

He checked his radio. It was on.

The sun was coming up fast. The shadows of a half hour ago were gone. The combination sweet and sulfur smell he'd noticed earlier was still in the air. And the sky was the bluest sky he had ever seen, streaked with great swatches of orange, reds, and greens. The clouds were huge, cumulous, and almost fluorescent white. A postcard morning. He wished for a camera and the time to capture what he was seeing, then took a deep breath. It was too pretty a day for someone to die. Unfortunately, that was probably going to happen. The only question was who, and how many.

Andy looked at the building and checked his radio one more time to be sure. Hulbert was on his belly, looking through the scope of his semiautomatic rifle. He was following his target, his finger on the trigger, waiting for the *go.*

"It's Charlie-house," Kathleen called on the radio. *"Mark Suplinskas is dead. They used dental floss."*

He'd been afraid of that. New guards simply didn't realize how many ways convicts could figure out how to kill or injure somebody. In their own way, they could be incredibly ingenious.

"There are six of them," Kathleen continued. *"But it wouldn't have been planned. The back wall opened in the . . . quake . . . and they took advantage of it. Three cells opened, six prisoners out."* She rattled off their names: Cole, Biggs, Porter, Robertson, Walker, Taylor.

"Bless you, girl." Andy gave a small sigh of relief. It was prisoners inside the machine shop—*no aliens, so stop being a jerk*—and they hadn't planned the escape. That meant they wouldn't be heavily armed or supplied for a long siege.

He called out loud enough to be heard by those inside the building, "We've waited long enough! It's time for you to come out."

"Fuck you, badge!" someone yelled from inside the building. "It's time for shit. You want us, get yo' lilly ass in here."

"If that's the way you really want it," Andy called back, "that's the way you'll get it. But think things over. That way someone always gets hurt. And that someone is usually the prisoner." He motioned to his team to be on the ready.

Pop!

It was a zip gun. He could tell by the sound. The small, prisoner-made weapons were usually constructed out of old plumbing pipes, springs and metal scraps. They weren't accurate beyond a short distance, but they carried a hell of a punch, and could easily kill a man. The load sounded like a .45.

He gave Hulbert waiting on the roof of Baker-house the go signal.

Crack!

Crack!

Andy knew two of the six prisoners were now dead or down. Rod never missed.

Frank Nickerson was part of the three-man first responder's setup team. He moved into position and then fired the military issue grenade launcher, sending a canister of C.N. between the bars, through the plate glass window and into the machine shop's one large room. It wouldn't be enough to drive the men out, but it would make them uncomfortable as hell.

Heather Kolb, the second member of the team, moved into position and tossed a canister through a window next to the one Frank's had entered. Jason Lloyd finished the trio, with a canister of his own. His went in the same window Heather's entered.

Smoke billowed out the broken windows. The three of them reloaded and fired again.

Now the men inside the building began screaming.

"Fuckin' pigs! Don't shoot, you cocksucking monkeys! We're comin' out! Fuck! Don't shoot!"

Four black men stumbled through the door, their hands clasped behind their heads. Once through the door they spread out, coughing and hacking and cussing.

"Fuckin' hacks, you had no right. No right. We were comin' out." The prisoner doing the talking slid to his knees, his hands clasped behind his head, coughing louder and longer than the others.

Frank moved toward him. Andy watched, fear rising inside him. The man dressed in prison gray was *acting*. His coughing was too extreme, his breaths too regular for the distress his actions implied. The chemical released by the C.N. canisters, designed to irritate skin, eyes, mucous membranes and lung tissue, did not affect all people the same. Andy took a deep breath to shout a warning.

"No!"

It was too late. The prisoner jerked up, burying a shank made from an old toothbrush into the soft tissue beneath Frank's vest. "Fuckin' wood sucker!" he hissed, glaring at the guard—whose skin was several shades darker than his own. Race didn't really matter much compared to the gap between guards and prisoners. "Fuckin' wood lover!"

Frank gasped, blood running from the wound. The prisoner twisted the toothbrush that had been sharpened to a fine point. He was looking for the artery leading to the leg.

Andy didn't think. He aimed his shotgun, fired, and the prisoner collapsed, knocking Frank over, falling on top of him.

The other three prisoners ran.

Someone yelled, "Halt!"

The men continued running.

Rod fired from the rooftop.

Crack!

Crack!

Crack!

Two of the three prisoners were dead. The third was on the ground and would be gone within minutes. His gurgling, rasping breaths could be heard in the now silent exercise yard. Rod's bullet had ripped through both lungs. With each breath, he sprayed a pink froth across the road.

"Shit, oh shit, oh *shit!*" Heather was close to hysterical. She was a good guard, had worked for the state for over ten years and seen a little of almost everything, but this was too much. First the quake, and now this. She had never watched that many die that way. And Frank was a kid, just twenty-three years old, who looked a lot like her own son. He was bleeding on her lap now. She had sat down and was holding him, trying to help, to comfort him. "Shit, oh shit, oh *shit!*" she repeated, finally getting hold of herself.

Andy was on the radio. He needed medical and he needed them now.

The nurses were coming, but the three to four minutes it would take for them to arrive would be too long if Frank's artery had been nicked. Or his bladder. He remembered Brown. Still in the infirmary, unable to be moved because there was nowhere to move her. He checked the man lying on Heather's lap. Heather was applying pressure, trying to slow the bleeding.

He then took off at a jog to check the two dead prisoners. He recognized their faces, but couldn't recall either of their names or why they were incarcerated. He then knelt next to the third one, the one who was still alive. The man was fighting for each breath. There was nothing Andy could do for him.

The man's eyes went wide and wet. His breaths came quicker. He'd be dead within a minute, with that wound.

Andy heard the nurses coming with their carts. It was still shift change, which meant there were three of them inside the prison. Two afternoon nurses and the one and only night shift nurse. Caldwell, Ray, and the new one, Jennifer Radford. He knew one of the three would stay behind to care for Brown. So that left only two nurses available for cleanup in the yard.

He turned around, planning to ask what he could do to help, but stopped and stared. Nothing came out of his mouth.

Jennifer Radford was all business, taking care of her only patient with a chance at survival. She didn't see him, but he saw her. And was momentarily frozen.

He recognized the sensation, although he'd only had it a few times in his life. Rare as it might be, it was quite unmistakable. And, as before, he was struck by how little the sensation had to do with anything popular culture or certainly the girlie magazines ever talked about. It was never a woman's figure, or really even her face. Just . . .

Something. In this case, perhaps, the calm seriousness in a pair of intent dark eyes. Who the hell knew? Just *something* that told him he really, really, really wanted to get to know this woman better. Really better.

Of all the times!

CHAPTER
7

The summons for medical caught the nurses off guard. They were locked inside the nurse's station, with their guard outside the door, and were completely absorbed in their own problems. The three of them were in the middle of report, trying to take care of Brown, the injured guard, and do the paperwork for Greg Lowry. Two of the nurses were in a hurry, wanting to go home and get some sleep.

"Looks like baptism by fire for you, Jenny," Lylah Caldwell said. The sixty-one-year-old RN smiled half-apologetically. "You're going to have to go. My legs are killing me. They're too old and I've been on them for eighteen hours."

Jennifer Radford nodded and shot Barbara Ray a worried look. Ray was an LPN who looked to be in her early forties.

"Don't panic, I'm coming along." Ray pulled a large red leather bag from the bottom shelf of a metal cabinet. "Grab the portable O$_2$ tank." She nodded toward the back room, then snatched up a radio and grabbed another bag from the cabinet, loading it onto a gurney. "Brown is stable, she should be able to get by with just one of us for awhile."

The woman on the examining table moaned and reached for the I.V. tubing attached to her left arm. The saline solution was infusing at a keep open rate. Nothing more than a drop every three seconds, a precaution. If she started to hemorrhage or go into shock, her veins would close up fast, and then an I.V. could become impossible to insert. None of the three nurses were willing to risk that situation. The I.V. had to stay.

"Oh, God. Please. It hurts. Please." The guard coughed, moaned and then tried to reach the tubing once more. The bandage on her abdomen was fresh, but already streaked with blood.

Lylah Caldwell pulled a couple of sheep skin straps from a drawer and began strapping Elaine Brown's arms down. "There's no sense hanging around. Everyone's short staffed; you won't get an escort. Get going. A guard is down."

Jenny moved toward the back room where the O_2 tanks were stored. Things were moving too fast for her to understand what was happening inside the prison grounds, but ten years of working under pressure—everything from crash sites to emergency rooms—kept her grounded.

She scooped up a small, portable tank and then grabbed a mask and a nasal cannula. There was no way of knowing which would be needed, so it was best to take one of each.

When she entered the examination area, Lylah handed her a Sat. Unit. The small device was designed to slip over a patient's finger and read the amount of oxygen in the person's circulatory system. "Now get moving. And don't worry. The prisoners are on lockdown and the guards have everything under control. The two of you will be safe."

Jenny placed the tank on the gurney next to the bags Barbara had stacked in its center. She then took a clipboard filled with forms and the keys Lylah was holding out to her.

The call for medical had caused her stomach to tie into a knot. The three of them had just finished counting everything in the room. Keys, pills, injectables, bandages, scissors, ink pens. Everything and anything that could be considered contraband inside the walls. Twenty minutes straight. One thing right after another. She had been briefed on the deceased heart attack victim, Greg Lowry, being held down the hall in a small room with bars. Brown's status had been assessed, and they were just beginning to go through the calls for the 3–11 shift when the radio announced a guard was down.

She took a deep breath, forcing herself to relax. Gunshot and knife wounds were not new to her, just something she hated seeing.

So much for moving out of the city and slowing things down.

She could hear Lylah, the RN, talking on the two-way. She was telling someone they were leaving the building. Jenny took another deep breath. This was real. It was what the month-long self-defense classes taught to state employees had been geared toward. She was on her own. And if something went wrong she had just one job. She had to survive long enough for the guards to rescue her.

The average length of time for their arrival—after they knew you were in trouble—was three minutes. That was one hundred and eighty impossibly long seconds. She gave the gurney a shove. The familiar feel of the cart's wheels wanting to turn right while she wanted to go straight helped calm her nerves.

"We better hurry," Barbara whispered.

Jenny sped up.

"The nurses are never hurt," Barbara said, panting a little as she worked at staying up with Jenny. "We're the ones who give them their pills and make their appointments with the doctors. They're nice to us. Afraid to get us mad. Afraid we won't get them what they want."

Jenny looked down the dark side street they were passing. The reassurances that everything was safe scared her. She could tell by the nurse's tone of voice, Barbara's hurry to reach the guards had less to do with the injured man and more to do with her wanting to be surrounded by guards with guns.

Jenny increased her speed. Experience had taught her that anything that has to be said over and over is usually not true.

They rounded the next corner and Jenny came to a complete stop. There were about a dozen COs standing near a man lying on the ground, his head on a woman's lap. The woman was crying. A prisoner, a dead prisoner, lay just a few inches away. There were another three prisoners crumpled on the ground several yards away, obviously dead. A guard was kneeling next to one of them.

She took a breath of the morning air; it was warm, filled with moisture. Then she noticed the sun was rising.

Surprised, she stumbled, caught herself, then kept moving toward the man dressed in blue and black.

Her patient.

The other man, the one checking the prisoners, had held her attention for a little longer than she liked. Even in the dim light she could see his face. It stirred up a set of emotions she still wasn't sure how she felt about.

He was Captain Andy Blacklock. She knew his name even though they'd never spoken. She'd seen him leaving the facility as she was arriving every morning of her orientation.

He was tall and thickly built. His complexion was ruddy and his hair-color a light brown. And even though he looked nothing like her husband Matt, she couldn't deny the attraction. That attraction had bothered her at first. After a couple of mornings, she found herself looking forward to it. Matt had been dead for almost three years. It felt good just knowing she could still feel.

She took a quick glance at her patient, and forgot about the captain. The guard had been stabbed in the groin area, just centimeters from the femoral artery. She knew the artery had been missed because he was still alive. That was the good news.

The bad news was, he had lost a lot of blood.

Jenny patted the woman holding the man on her lap, then gently lifted the young man's head so she could move and the wounded man could be laid flat. She then applied a pressure bandage and motioned for Barbara to apply additional pressure while she checked his vitals. His blood pressure was low, 108/58. That wasn't good, but it wasn't bad enough to cause a stroke or throw him into shock. His pulse was 92, weak, and irregular. But his Sat level was 93 and that meant his blood carried enough oxygen to do its job. He would live.

She set the oxygen level to the 2 lpm mark. It wasn't much, just enough to help him out a little. He looked young and healthy, but you never knew. A conservative approach would be better. She slipped the nasal cannula in place and made a mental note to apply a little K-Y jelly to his nose when they got back to the infirmary.

Using her penlight she checked his eyes. PEARL. The pupils were equal and reactive to light. No brain injury. "What's your name?"

"Frank," the woman answered for him.

"Shh. Let him answer. Frank, what's your last name?"

"Nickerson," he whispered.

Jenny looked at the woman and she nodded.

She stroked the man's forehead. His brown skin looked a little dusky, but it was warm and dry. "Where are you?"

Frank tried to sit up and she gently held him in place. "Can you tell me where you are?"

"Yeah. Alexander Correctional Center. And today is Monday." He waved weakly toward the sky. "Maybe Tuesday. And I don't know who won the ball game, since I didn't get to watch the ending. I can tell you who I rooted for, though." He attempted a smile.

Oriented to person, place and time. Good.

"I guess if you can be all that cocky, you'll live. Let's get you to the infirmary so I can patch you up a little before we ship you." She motioned for the guards to bring the gurney over. "Keep him as flat as you can when you lift him. Barbara and I will keep the leg straight and pressure on the wound."

Four guards lifted the man in one smooth move, placing him dead center of the cart. The move was practiced. She had seen experienced EMTs who couldn't do as well. These guys had had a lot of experience doing this. She steadied her breathing.

"Barbara, take him to the infirmary. I'll check the prisoners."

Barbara nodded and followed the guards with the gurney.

The LPN from the afternoon shift had already checked the inmates lying inside the building and the one next to Frank Nickerson, so Jenny turned to the dead men lying on the street beneath the light. Dressed in prison issue, they were in the exact same position she had seen them when she first arrived. But she had to take their vitals. That was the only way to know for sure.

"There's nothing you can do for them," Captain Blacklock said as she approached. "They're dead."

"I know, but I have to check." She had put the electronic equipment on the gurney and sent it back to the infirmary. It was useless for this job. It would do nothing but beep and flash error over and over, giving her no reading. This had to be done the old fashioned way. So she started with the closest man's pulse. For a full minute she counted. Nothing. Respirations nothing. She then pulled out a manual sphygmomanometer and took his blood pressure. Again nothing. She thought about taking his temperature and decided to wait another fifteen minutes or so. He wasn't exactly warm, but he wasn't cold. Not yet.

She repeated the procedure over and over until all three men had been checked.

"What am I supposed to do with the bodies? The phones are down so I can't call the hospital or morgue to have them picked up."

Blacklock shrugged. "We'll put them in with Lowry for tonight. I'll send a few guards after gurneys for transport and have them load them into body bags for you."

"Thanks."

The captain nodded, the gesture seeming calm and relaxed. That was part of Blacklock's reputation, from what Jenny had heard. One of those people who never lost their composure, no matter what they might be feeling inside. Under the circumstances, that was a quality that would be invaluable to all of them. It also made the man particularly attractive to her—and would have, no matter the circumstances. Despite the lack of physical resemblance, her husband had been the same way under pressure. It had been one of the things about Matt that Jenny had treasured.

Trying to tear her mind away from these completely inappropriate matters, she almost asked how many body bags the prison kept on hand. Fortunately, she kept the inane question unspoken. Instead, she said, "Things don't feel right."

"I know."

"It's the barometric pressure. It feels sky high. And things are damp. Bone-deep damp. You get a combination like that and anyone planning to stroke, will. Same way for having a baby."

"Baby?"

"Yes. If the pressure goes up enough, it can cause a woman close to her due date to go into labor. It can also cause a miscarriage, if she's early on."

"Oh, wonderful." Blacklock turned to Hulbert—the sharpshooter who'd just returned from his perch on the roof of David-house. "Locate Kathleen. I don't want her by herself until the end of shift."

Hulbert nodded. Blacklock turned back to Jenny. "Is there anything we can do to stop the barometric pressure from causing a problem?"

She shook her head. Despite his outward calm, she could sense that the man was upset. The shooting and killing hadn't ruffled him, but mention of a baby being born did.

Well, that was one awkward question she wouldn't have to figure out how to ask somebody. He was married. And his wife's name was Kathleen.

Jenny was met at the infirmary's outer door by Barbara Ray. "Lylah and I cleaned and stitched Nickerson. It was deep, but he's all right." Her voice dropped to almost a whisper and she motioned to Jenny's nametag, which was imprinted with the initials NP. "You're a nurse practitioner?"

Jenny nodded.

"Brown's *not* all right. She's hemorrhaging. We're going to lose her."

Jenny ran down the hall to the examination room the wounded correctional officer was in. Coming through the door to the small cubical, she glanced at the machine giving a continuous reading of several vital signs. Elaine Brown's blood pressure was down; her pulse was up. Her Sat level was an 81. Jenny knew by looking, the woman's skin would be cold and clammy. She was almost the same color as ash and her lips were black and purple.

Years of training and experience made her forget she was the new kid on the block. "Heat me a blanket," she said. She looked around the room. She couldn't remember where everything was stored. The setup was nothing like the hospitals and clinics she was used to. Quick access to supplies and equipment during emergencies where seconds frequently made the difference between life and death was not the guiding principle in the storage and location of supplies and equipment inside the prison's infirmary. Staff safety and prevention of prisoners' access to anything that could be used as a weapon were the only factors. "Do we have anything I can cauterize the wound with?"

Lylah's eyes narrowed. "We're not allowed to do that, the wound is too deep. Best we can do is re-sew her."

"Damn." Jenny slipped on a yellow paper gown and pulled on a pair of rubber gloves. "Get me a suture kit," she said, removing the blood-soaked bandage.

"First things first. Turn around," Lylah said.

Jenny turned and the elderly nurse handed her a pair of latex gloves and then slipped a paper mask over her nose and mouth. "Thanks," she said.

Lylah opened the suture kit.

"Increase the saline to 60 and the oxygen to 6. And turn the lights up."

Barbara came through the door with three warmed blankets. "The guards are making us more, just in case."

Jenny nodded, looking at the jagged tear in the woman's skin. She had been cut from just below the umbilicus to just above the pubis. "I can't see where it's coming from," she said, rinsing the area with saline. "Damn. The stitches are all intact. This is new."

She began the process of applying pressure systematically, looking for the source of the blood flow. She was going to have to open her up.

"I have to take them out, get inside, see what's going on."

Lylah's face was tight. "You're on your own," she said. "I've been awake too many hours. Besides, my eyes aren't any good for that type of work. Never were. And Barbara's an LPN. She's good, but she hasn't been trained for anything invasive." Lylah stepped away from the table and returned with a suture removal set.

"Do we have anything to put her under with?"

"No. Just a local, and that's not very potent. And even if we did, none of us has been trained to administer it."

Jenny suppressed a groan. If the local was what was used earlier, it was almost useless for what she was going to have to do now. "I've served with the military overseas. Plus, I did missionary work in Latin America. I can administer anesthetic. I've also done surgeries under conditions much more primitive than we have here."

"Surgeries?" Lylah Caldwell spread one of the heated blankets over the woman's chest and shoulders. "Maybe you have. But that was then and that was there. Now, here at the prison, you don't have the authority to do anything more than snip those stitches and re-sew her."

Jenny looked up from what she was doing, then back down again. Her voice was firm, clipped. "We are in an emergency situation. This woman will die if we wait until someone with the authority shows up. Are you willing to have her death on your hands?"

"It wouldn't be. But if I let you pretend you're a doctor and she dies, then I would be as responsible as you. Sorry, but I'm not willing to join you in prison just because you say you know how to do something. I know you're a nurse practitioner, but here, with no doctor present, you're a nurse. Nothing more." Lylah stepped back from the table. "You will lose your license and get at least ten years if you do anything more than re-sew her. That is practicing medicine without a license."

Barbara Ray, the LPN, gave Jenny a sad look then turned toward the older RN and said, "Lylah, you're right, practicing medicine without a license is illegal." She draped an arm across the woman's shoulder. Her voice was soft, almost a whisper. "We won't do anything we shouldn't. Relax."

She reached across the table and handed her a set of keys. "Go on break. You need it. You've been here too long. Take a pillow and a blanket, go to the records room and lie down on the desk or the counter and go to sleep. I'll take care of this."

The older woman's eyes lost their cold, angry look and filled with tears. "I can't; I'm exhausted. You understand that, don't you?"

Barbara nodded. "I know that; we both are. And Jenny is no fool. She understands the rules. You go get some sleep, and we'll do what we can here." She motioned toward the CO standing outside the open door. "Glasser, how about helping her with the blankets and pillows."

"Sure. No problem." The guard gave the RN a quick

hug and said, "When you wake up I'll have coffee waiting for you."

With no one in the room but the two nurses, Barbara handed Jenny the tools she needed to cauterize the wound. "We have just about anything you need for emergencies. It's the comfort measure materials we have trouble getting."

Jenny looked at the gleaming metal tip and inwardly winced. This was going to be rough on the woman. The anesthetic was completely inadequate. But she would hemorrhage to death without it.

The procedure took less than five minutes. Twenty-five minutes after they started, Brown's bandages were in place and the woman was asleep.

When Jenny finally sat down at the desk it was Barbara who spoke first. "I have to get some sleep. I've been awake for over thirty hours. I'll be in the break room on a table." She grinned. "That was some mighty nice work you did. Half the doctors we have here are druggies, doing community work to stay out of the slammer. They couldn't have done it."

"Thanks. For the compliment, and the warning about the docs. I didn't know that. I thought they were hired by the state."

"Some are, but some aren't."

Jenny nodded and made a mental note to nose around and learn which was which. "For a woman with no training in invasive procedures, you didn't do so bad either."

Barbara Ray's smile was replaced by a look of worried concentration. "Yeah, well, Lylah was just talking. Working here, as short as we are and as violent as some of our emergencies get, you stay up on your skills. And you wind up stepping out of your area of official expertise fairly often. You just don't talk about it. Not if you're smart."

Jenny picked up on the hint and decided it was time to change the subject. "How many of the psych docs are here as part of a plea bargain?"

"None. They're here because they want to be." Barbara shrugged. "They have to think they're helping. It can't be for the money. The state doesn't pay enough for that."

"How's Brown?" Blacklock asked Jenny as she walked out of the examining room and into the wide hall that doubled as a reception area and rest stop.

"I think she'll be okay. I've started her on I.V. antibiotics. That room is not exactly sterile. If I don't give her something, she'll get a hellish infection."

She sat in a chair next to the door. "How long until the phones are working?"

"I don't know."

"This is the craziest thing I've ever gotten myself into," she said ruefully. "No wonder you guys can't keep nurses."

The captain chuckled. "It's usually not this bad. Honest." He looked at Hulbert. "I've never seen anything like that . . . quake. Have you?"

Hulbert shook his head. "I just hope we don't get hit with an aftershock."

Five minutes passed. "I'm really out of my element and I'm betting you guys are, too." Jenny pulled the rubber band from her hair and started reapplying it. "What's up with the sun? And the barometric pressure. And that quake. And the way the sky looks. I have never seen such a blue sky."

Neither man answered. They were looking at the floor, their brows creased, their elbows on their knees and their hands dangling between their legs, still and calm.

Jenny slumped in her chair. Exhaustion, caused from the tension of the last—she looked at the clock—four hours, washed over her. She had hoped this job would be easier than her last one. That, obviously, was not going to be the case.

She glanced to where Frank Nickerson was lying. In spite of the light and the noise, he was sleeping soundly enough that a soft snore could occasionally be heard. His gurney was parked in the hall, since there was no place else for him. At least no place convenient enough for a staff of one to keep a close eye on him. Jenny didn't think he was in any danger, but medical emergencies had a tendency to occur when you least expected them.

Barbara was in the break room catching a nap. Lylah was asleep in the records room. Glasser had said the RN fell asleep as soon as she lay down. She had also said tonight was the woman's third double in a row, and that she was usually very caring and giving. Very reasonable. Jenny had been assured that when Lylah woke up she would be a totally different human being. She would be glad Brown was fixed, and would go to bat for Barbara and Jenny if she had to. She was loyal to her nurses.

Jenny hoped so, but she wasn't really too worried about what she had done. She hadn't done *much* more than she was licensed in the state of Illinois to do. Plus, she was actually pretty good at the art of C.Y.A., covering your ass.

She could do it without lying or stretching the truth. It was a matter of how and what you charted. She just hated the fact that she had needed help, and that need had put Barbara on the hot spot right along with herself.

Brown's vitals were stable. The knife had, by some miracle, missed the intestines. That gave her a good chance of avoiding peritonitis, and just as good a chance of being back on her feet in a week or two. It would be at least a month before she'd be back to work, though, maybe as much as six weeks. But with a little care, the woman should do all right.

Jenny had to suppress a small smile. Brown was one of those black beauties who made most women jealous, including white women. She had the high cheekbones, huge black eyes, and full lips that were money in the bank for magazine models. Which she probably could have been, except she was too short and curvy. And according to Barbara Ray, the CO was as good as she looked, too. She sang in the church choir, helped with the food pantry, and spent every Thanksgiving cooking for those who would normally not eat that day. Prison guard or not, she was a kind-hearted sweetie.

Jenny sighed. Now that things were beginning to settle down, she found herself wanting to look at Andy Blacklock. She actually had to work at not staring at him. Finally, she caved in and gave him a quick glance—and discovered he was staring at her.

"How's your wife doing?" she asked. It was her way of reminding him not to look too much, and remind herself not to enjoy his looking.

"Wife?"

"The lady having the baby."

"Oh. Kathleen." He seemed flustered by the question. "She's . . . just Kathleen. Not my wife. One of the midnight COs. She's got a husband and three other kids." He shrugged. "She's fine. I offered to let her wait this out here, in the infirmary, but she didn't want to. She said she was too big and clumsy and this place was seeing too much action. She felt safer in the communication center. So I sent Keith Woeltje over. He threw his knee out, so he's not much good right now. He'll call if she runs into trouble."

Jenny nodded, hoping he wouldn't be able to read her feelings. *Not his wife. Not his baby. Just Kathleen.* She straightened in her chair a little, then pushed the feelings that had surfaced back down. This was business. A job. You don't date men you work with. It complicates things.

You dated Matt.

She stood up and stretched. It was time to start pulling the meds for the morning drug pass. It took well over three hours to set the meds up, and another hour to pass them. According to the sun, she was way behind schedule. But the clock told her, if she hurried, she might get it done before day-shift arrived.

If they arrived. She was starting to have her doubts about that.

Less than one hour after Jenny entered the large room with its three, twelve-foot-long combination work table/medicine cabinets, Andy Blacklock slid open the metal door slot and said through the small rectangle, "Unlock the door. I've sent for Barbara. She'll have to finish setting up for the morning med pass. I need all department heads in the administrative building for a meeting, stat. Joe is back."

Jenny turned just in time to see him leave.

Department heads? Joe was back?

Jenny was the new nurse, not the head of the department. True, it was technically the midnight shift, and she was the only midnight nurse on duty, but that was just a technicality.

In charge.

She sighed. She had always been the one in charge. Even as a new grad working an emergency room at a free hospital smack dab in the middle of the inner city.

Years ago, she had given up fighting the situation. Back then she was naïve enough to believe she hated being the one others looked to for orders. She had thought she preferred to follow. But her time in the jungles of South America had changed that. It taught her a lot about who and what she was. She was no follower. She preferred to rely on herself. She had more faith in her judgment and her skills than she did in anyone else's. And time and time again, she had proven herself right.

She put the lid on the bottle she had just taken from a drawer and then locked the cabinet. She didn't know who Joe was or where he had been but she needed a notebook and pen. Meetings meant new information. And new information usually meant new ways of doing things. Taking notes was her way of making sure she didn't forget anything, or remember something wrong.

When she climbed the stairs to the upper level conference room she could feel the tension in the air. The guards rushing up and down were in full gear. More than a few wore bulletproof vests and helmets with faceplates pulled into the up position. Watching them in their black leather gloves, leather pants and knee pads made her feel foolish and frivolous, in her pale blue nurse's uniform. Silently, she cursed the idiot who had picked out the balloon and heart pattern that decorated her top, and wished she had thought to grab a lab coat. The uniform, issued by the prison, was ridiculous in this setting.

The purple stethoscope draped around her neck looked just as silly. She slipped it off, folded its tubing, and shoved it inside her pocket. The guards were wearing guns. Big, black guns. Not candy-colored tools.

She slipped into the conference room intending to grab a seat near the back, but was spotted by Rod Hulbert. He waved for her to join him at the front. He had saved her a seat.

"I know things look pretty bad, and they are," Rod said, "but we have good people."

Jenny nodded. "I hope so. What's going on? Really."

He shrugged. "You're going to know soon enough. Andy's going to have Joe give a detailed description of what he saw when he went to town. And since I've been out there, at least a little ways, I have a feeling it's going to be an eyeball popper."

"Why?"

"Haven't you heard?" He didn't wait for her to answer. "The Mississippi River is gone. And if that mother has dried up and left us with trees the size of two-hundred-year-old oaks, town has got to be even more messed up."

Gone. Two-hundred-year-old oaks. She could feel her stomach turn over and fought the wave of nausea that came with it. She didn't feel the need to argue that those things couldn't happen. Some instinct told her that they could, and had. The same set of instincts was telling her to jump up, run out of the room, find a dark closet and hide. To stay there and never stick her head into the sunlight.

Instead, she opened her notebook and checked to be sure the pen she had pulled from her pocket protector was a good one.

Jeffrey Edelman flicked the lights off, then on. Instantly, the room became silent.

Andy Blacklock was at the front of the room. Standing next to him was a man that made his 6'1" frame look small. "Quiet," he said to the people in the room, who almost instantly obeyed him.

"Joe Schuler has just gotten back from town and is ready to give report. You will be hearing what he has to say at the same time I hear it. I'm willing to do things this way as long as the information given out in these meetings goes no further until I say it does."

"We won't be telling the others?" Terry Collins asked. His face was flushed.

"They'll be told. Everything. Nothing held back." Blacklock looked around the room. "There will be no secrets. None. But there's no sense terrifying them. That situation never helps. We will give ourselves enough time to decide the best approach to dealing with things. Then when we tell them the bad news, the newest problem, we will have some sort of corrective action in mind. That will make it easier for them to accept. And no one goes off half-cocked, crazy with fear." He sat down in a metal folding chair facing the audience.

"Lieutenant Schuler, go ahead."

Joe nodded, then began talking. His voice shook, but Jenny knew it wasn't from stage fright.

"First things first. Don't nobody boo me, and don't nobody call me a liar. I didn't cause the things I'm going to be telling you and I'm not going to be saying anything that isn't the God's own truth. Even though I find it hard to believe it myself."

He ran a hand through his hair. "First, the road to town is gone. It leaves the prison, goes for about a quarter mile, then stops. It looks as though it's been cut at a hundred and twenty degree angle. One side is blacktop; the other is ground cover. I say 'ground cover' instead of grass because whatever the stuff is—I didn't recognize any of the plants—it isn't grass. Some kind of ferns, is what most of it looked like. Waist-high ground cover and trees. The trees are big, too. I didn't recognize them either, except for a number of gingkos. But whatever kind of trees they are, they've obviously been there for decades. At least. And out in the distance, I could see trees that were even bigger. Huge things. Trees that have to be hundreds of years old. Could be thousands of years old, for all I know. I thought they were redwoods at first, but Jeff Edelman says my description doesn't quite match. The one thing for sure is they're conifers. In the distance, that's it. Only conifers.

"It took me over an hour to get to what should have been the city limits. The truck couldn't go but about a mile or so and I had to walk the rest the way. I found this where I guessed the police station should have been."

He held up what looked to be an unadorned, well-worn pocket watch. Instead of a chain, a strip of leather hung from the ring above its winding stem. "The man who used this was leaned against a stump, dead. He was dressed in old-fashioned garb, like for a parade, but different. And from the insect infestation and deterioration of the body, I would say he had been gone for several days." He set the watch back on the table. "That man was all I found. There is no town. No railroad tracks, no cars, buildings, factories, or streetlights. Nothing. No people." He shrugged. "No living people, anyway."

"What happened to them?"

Joe shrugged again. "It wasn't a bomb or anything like that. This is something else. Nothing is destroyed. It's just . . . vanished."

He waved toward the outer wall, to the area beyond. "And I don't think this is just a local situation. If the sun is wrong here, it's wrong all over the world. And, according to Rod Hulbert, the river is gone. It hasn't dried up. *It's gone.* I talked to Jeff Edelman about it. He said moving that much water would have affected other things in other places. It would change things over a wide area. According to him, since the Mississippi is over two thousand miles long, if its bed is gone, things have to be messed up all over the world."

"That's right," Edelman said. "It's as though the planet quivered and everything is now different. The tower guards have been spotting strange animals prowling around the perimeter of the prison, and even stranger looking birds. Woeltje says he saw a creature with a hell of a wingspan flying over the prison just a little after sunup, that wasn't anything like any bird he'd ever seen. And there has been an increase in temperature as crazy as what we're seeing in the plant and animal life. This is November and it's eighty degrees out there. And the sun rose six hours ahead of schedule, in the *northwest*. And last night, the stars were wrong. They were in the wrong place, and there were too many of them."

Jenny swallowed, working at staying calm. She could tell by the reactions of those around her, most of what Edelman was saying was old news. But for her, it was all new. She could feel the sweat on her palms and on her upper lip. She looked at Hulbert and knew even though he had already heard most of it, he was taking the situation no better than she was. He looked calm enough, but his respirations were up to sixteen. That was high for him. He was in such unusually good shape, his resting respirations were usually around twelve to thirteen.

Kathleen, the CO in charge of the communications and control room, stood up. "I have a husband and three children in town." Her voice changed to almost a wail. "Where are they? What does all this mean?" The man sitting in the chair next to hers put his arm around her and drew her back down into her seat. Her quiet sobbing filled the room, driving home what had been said.

Andy stood and Joe returned to his seat. "It means we have to get ready for a long stay."

Hulbert nodded his head and sighed. "Well, I guess now we know."

"Know what?" Jenny whispered.

Hulbert looked at her and gave a thin grin that held no humor. "We know we're fucked."

CHAPTER 8

Geoffrey Watkins sat next to what was left of the small fire used to heat their afternoon meal. He didn't do so for the warmth. That was hardly needed now. It just gave him something to do.

The women and children lay in the shade. The old men sat next to the women, watching the woods. The soldiers had their camp by some trees not far away. A horse whinnied. A bird called.

He listened to the whispering of the trees in the breeze and forced himself to sit straight. He was weary, bone weary. At the age of fifty-four, he felt too old for this trip. Many of those with him were too old. That, or too sick.

The Treaty of New Echota had forced the evacuation of all Cherokees. He, and those with him, had been among the last to leave for the new land across the big river assigned to them by the United States.

They had left Ross' Landing in November of 1838 by wagon—a party of three hundred and seventy Cherokees, escorted by a unit of U.S. soldiers. They had crossed the Tennessee River, the Cumberland River, and then the Ohio River. The trip had been long and hard. It was still months from completion. And now he did not know if it would ever end, or where they would be if it did.

It had been winter and the snow was inches deep. They had been in southern Illinois, near the confluence of the Ohio and Mississippi rivers when their world disappeared and this new world showed up. Everything familiar was lost.

The snow and cold had been two of the things that vanished when their world shook and screamed. Watkins was grateful for that. He was not grateful for the other things that were missing: the food, tools, equipment, and people.

Their wagons and most of the horses were gone. Some of their people and the soldiers, too. Only eight soldiers were caught up in the storm that blew the Cherokees to this land, wherever it was. Eight soldiers and three hundred and twenty-one of his own people.

The soldiers relinquished any authority they might have over the Cherokees to Geoffrey, once they realized they were no longer in southern Illinois. That had been a wise move on their part, as outnumbered as they now were. The Cherokees had been stripped of their land and many of their possessions, true, but they still owned some things. Among them were guns and knives.

Even then, had the soldiers been Georgia militiamen instead of U.S. regulars, they would have been killed. The Georgians had committed many personal atrocities against the Cherokees in the course of the relocation, including murder, rape, robbery and mutilation. But all you could honestly accuse the regulars of doing was following the orders of their government. Their own conduct had been well-disciplined. And many Cherokees knew from Chief John Ross that Major General Winfield Scott, the man in charge of the U.S. troops overseeing the relocation, had tried to get President Van Buren to stop the relocation once he saw the epidemics developing in the camps. But Van Buren had refused.

So, there had been no violence toward the soldiers, even if relations were tense.

His people were tired unto their soul, and they were hungry. And many of them were sick, including his wife of twenty-five years. She had pneumonia. She was burning up with fever. Her labored breathing had kept him awake most of the night. Now, in the light of day, she seemed even worse.

"Chief," Bradley Scott called. "We've got company."

Watkins stood up. Things had changed, but in some ways they were still the same. The Cherokees in his group were traditionalists. Not all of them were full-blood—he wasn't, for instance—but many of them were. So they were not encumbered by the need to watch over black slaves, and they retained many of the skills that most of their people had lost in their attempt to emulate the Americans. There'd been enough men in the group with the needed skills that he'd been able to send out scouting parties almost immediately. Now, another one was returning.

But he had nothing more to report than the others. They'd all encountered strange creatures and strange plants, some of them quite fearsome, but none had found the missing farms or the missing towns.

"Sorry, Geoffrey. I could find nothing. Not even a hunter's lean-to."

Watkins nodded, letting no trace of apprehension show. "McQuade is still out. He was to follow the river three days, and then return. Perhaps he will be more successful."

Stephen McQuade had been his close companion for many years. They had fought together in alliance with the American general Andrew Jackson at the Horseshoe Bend during the Creek war, almost twenty-five years earlier. He was a man Geoffrey had counted on many times.

And he was starting to get desperate. McQuade had to succeed.

They needed food and shelter, of course. But most of all, they needed the tools and instruments by which they could obtain those things. Blankets, pots, knives, and ammunition. Even traditionalists like his people had come to rely on the technology of the white man, to a large extent.

Most of all, though, they needed information. Ignorance was the greatest enemy of all. It had taken more lives than disease, war, and weather combined.

The sun was down and the fires were lit. Watkins looked at the flickering flames, hoping they would be enough to keep the new animals at bay.

"Chief."

Geoffrey didn't turn around to look at Susan Fisher, one of the Cherokee healers. She was good at what she did, but she didn't perform miracles. And without food, water and medicines, a miracle would have been needed. He knew what she had to tell him. He had been listening to the sound of his wife's ragged breathing for hours, holding his breath each time she grew silent. Breathing a sigh of relief when he heard the gurgling sound of air being dragged into lungs laden with water.

The mother of his children—three sons and two daughters—was gone.

He had known the second she passed. The death rattle was something no man could mistake for anything else, once he'd heard it. And he had heard it many times over the years.

"I'm sorry," the small woman whispered.

Chief Geoffrey Watkins nodded. Hard times, bad luck. They seemed to be his fate these days. And the fate of his people.

Hernando de Soto, Pedro Moreno, and Hernando de Silvera spent the morning looking for the missing river. The huge watercourse had disappeared the night the demons broke free of hell and carried them from North America to this accursed land. The fertile soil that had stretched for seventy miles north to south, and ran twelve miles east to west, had also disappeared. In its place was a conifer forest, and soil so thin that it would do poorly for growing the corn and other food the conquistadors and their men needed.

Worst of all, most of the natives who would have provided that food for their new masters had vanished also. Some remained, but not the great numbers they needed.

As the sun rose to its zenith, de Soto's second in command, Luis de Moscoso, was six *legua comuns* south of the main camp. He was dealing with one of the devil-worshippers who had cursed the expedition, thus causing God to abandon them and giving the devil the power to torment the Spaniards in this evil land. He sat on his horse staring at the native. The heathen was one of six such men found over the last few days. The slaves—taken before the spawns of Satan were loosed upon the Spaniards—had not recognized the tribe these men were from.

This newest one was dressed like the others. He wore nothing more than a loincloth. He carried no weapon and had no food on him. He was obviously a fool, or took the Spaniards for such. Each of the interpreters had tried to talk to him. And each time the captive indicated he could not understand what was being said.

Disgusted, Moscoso gave his orders. If the savage continued to pretend not to understand what he heard, chop his ears off and feed them to the pigs. If that didn't make the man talk, cut his tongue out and force it down the fool's own throat.

The Spanish soldiers holding the Indian by his arms shoved him to his knees. In the Year of the Lord 1541, if you were part of Hernando de Soto's expedition to North America, it was unwise to hesitate when a direct order was given.

The Indian, a member of a nascent Mississippian chiefdom from the year 637 A.D., struggled to get away as the men dressed in elaborate body armor advanced with steel knives drawn.

CHAPTER
9

It wasn't until Wednesday that Richard and Margo were able to learn anything. Nicholas Brisebois, Richard's friend at the air force base had been quite friendly and willing to cooperate without pressing for any serious explanations. The problem was simply that he didn't know anything himself.

Neither did anyone, it seemed.

"It's weird," he told them over dinner that night. "Even my buddy in the state police is in the dark. All he knows is that the area surrounding the prison is crawling with people from a branch of FEMA he never heard of."

"Feema?" asked Morgan-Ash.

"You have to make allowances, Nick," Margo explained. "Richard didn't move to the U.S. until six months after Katrina. So the acronym doesn't come tripping off his tongue the way it does for most people."

"Ah. An acronym. God, you Yanks dote on the wretched things. And it stands for . . . ?"

"Federal Emergency Management Agency," Brisebois supplied. "But according to my friend Tim, these aren't regular FEMA types. They're from something called the Special Investigations Bureau. Annoying bastards, from what he says. It didn't take the EMTs on the scene more than an hour to start calling them the 'siblings.' *They* were annoyed because the siblings wouldn't let them through to do their job. Said there were no injuries, as if anybody in their right mind is going to believe that."

Brisebois took another bite of his steak, chewed, swallowed, and then shrugged. "But the truth is that Tim just doesn't know much. He got assigned to help coordinate the search for any missing inmates, and didn't spend much time near the site itself. He says he never even got a glimpse of the prison, so he doesn't know what sort of accident might have happened."

Margo had ordered the only fish course on the diner's menu, for health reasons. Now, she was regretting the decision. Whatever it might do to your arteries, the air transport specialist's steak looked good, damnation. Whereas her so-called perch looked as if it had been dredged from a canal somewhere. Tasted like it, too.

She pushed what was left, which was most of it, off to the side with her fork. She wasn't really that hungry anyway. "'Special Investigations Bureau'? I never heard of it, either. Of course, that's hardly surprising. There must be eight thousand federal agencies I never heard of"—she gave Brisebois a smile—"including yours. When Richard told me you worked at the air force base, I assumed you were in the military."

Nick worked through another large bite of his steak.

"Was," he half-mumbled, before finishing his swallow. He wasn't a sloppy eater, but he didn't waste any time, either.

He wiped his mouth with his napkin. "I was in the Air Force for over twenty years. Trash-hauler. Flew a C-141 cargo plane. Then I wound up in the Pentagon coordinating air transport for the first Gulf war. I guess that got me labeled as an expert, so I wound up finishing my career in the Air Force here at Scott. When I retired four years ago, I pretty much just swapped my uniform for a suit and started doing the same job for the Defense Department working in an office across the hall from the one I used to have."

He was a rather attractive man, she decided, in a stocky sort of way. Not all that much older than she was, either. But he was also quite obviously someone who came from a very different world than her own. Quite well-educated, but somehow very blue-collar. She wondered if that was a common combination among military officers. She'd ask Richard. He'd know, unless British customs were wildly different.

She wasn't sure if she found that attractive or repellent. Both, probably, although she had a dark suspicion the attraction was winning out. How else explain the fact that she'd had to suppress—twice, in fact—the completely inappropriate urge to mention that the "Lewis" part of her last name was of purely historical significance. The only reason she'd kept the name was because, by the time of her divorce, that was the name she was known by professionally.

Not to mention that she'd had to suppress—twice, again—the urge to ask Richard if his friend was single or married. It was all a bit ridiculous, really. She was a scientist here on serious business, not a middle-aged woman on a singles' cruise.

She suddenly realized that Richard was looking a bit grim. "I have heard of the agency, as it happens," he half-muttered. "They're quite secretive, apparently."

Brisebois frowned. "Secretive? What the hell is there to be secretive about, if you're with FEMA? It's not as if natural disasters are exactly covert." His easy grin came again, this time with a slightly sardonic twist. "I grant you, the current administration is obsessed with secrecy. Still, even for them, that seems over the top."

Richard seemed on the verge of saying something, but only shook his head. The gesture was so minimal that Margo barely spotted it at all. But she saw that Brisebois hadn't missed it either.

"What's this all about, Richard?" he asked softly. He pushed aside his plate, having finished the steak and baked potato. "And please spare me the bullshit."

Margo wondered how Richard was going to finesse the question. Then, seeing the expression on his face, she realized he *wasn't* going to finesse it.

She started to place a restraining hand on his sleeve. Then, realizing how pointless that would be, almost snatched the hand back. Then, to her discomfort, saw that Nick Brisebois hadn't missed that either.

"Speaking of secretive," he added.

Morgan-Ash gave him a thin smile. "Would you settle for 'need-to-know'?"

"Not likely, buddy. Seeing as how I could just as easily turn the question around. Why are a mathematician and"—he poked a thumb in Margo's direction—"a specialist in whichever arcane branch of physics she works in, the name of which I don't remember and it didn't mean squat to me anyway, rooting around in southern Illinois and expressing a burning interest in whatever happened to a state prison?"

He leaned back in the booth seat, his hands planted firmly on the table. "No. Please. *Don't* tell me you think this wasn't a natural disaster and the authorities are actually covering up flying saucers."

Morgan-Ash's smile widened. "You mean this *isn't* Roswell? But I would have sworn the sign specified Route 51."

Brisebois chuckled. "It's Area 51, dimwit. And don't tell me a light infantry officer who could make his way through the Falklands doesn't know the difference between Illinois and New Mexico. Area 51's in Nevada, anyway."

Richard was the only one of the three still working at his meal. He ate the same way he did his professional work. Slowly and meticulously.

"Well, no. In fact, both Margo and I are quite sure that a natural disaster is involved. Not a flying saucer anywhere in sight. What we also believe, however, is that the authorities are maintaining a veil over exactly what sort of natural disaster it is."

Brisebois stared at him for a moment. Then he shifted the stare to Margo for a longer moment, before bringing his eyes back to Richard. Suddenly he grinned from ear to ear.

"My God. Richard Morgan-butter-wouldn't-melt-in-his-mouth-Ash. A genu-ine Grantville Freak. Who woulda thunk it?"

He clapped his hands and started rubbing them together. "Join the club, you Johnnie-come-latelies. You should've told me right at the beginning, though. My buddy Tim in the state police is a charter member. That would have *really* gotten his interest sparked."

Richard was almost gaping at him. Margo suddenly realized she *was* gaping at him. Hastily she shut her mouth.

Brisebois flashed her that same, slightly sardonic grin. "What, Ms. Glenn-Lewis? Did you honestly think the two of you were the only skeptics in the country regarding the Of-fi-cial explanation of the Grantville Disaster? For Pete's sake, my garbage collector thinks it's garbage—and he knows garbage when he sees it."

Not knowing quite what to say, she slipped into being defensive. "Well, there are actually more than just the two of us. We . . . Well." Now a little flustered, she asked the first question she could think of. "How did *you* get interested in the matter?"

"My ex-wife. Laura got her Ph.D. in European history not long before we split up. The one more-or-less solid fact that slipped out from under the government's quarantine was that the material transposed with Grantville was of German origin. Probably from the first half of the seventeenth century."

"Yes, that's right."

"But they claim they found no remains, except those of a small number of people. No villages, towns, nothing. Just a few bodies, right?"

Margo and Richard nodded together.

Nick shrugged. "Well, Laura told me that had to be

nonsense. Because, according to her, any time after the middle ages you couldn't have found *any* part of Germany six miles in diameter that didn't have at least one village in it. It wasn't exactly the Wild West."

He looked through the window at the darkness outside. His expression seemed a little sad, although Margo wasn't sure because of the dim lighting in that corner of the diner.

"Laura's got a more . . . Well, let's just say that my view of the world is harsher than hers. She assumed that what was involved was simply error on the part of the investigators. Me, I figured we could just as easily be looking at a cover-up. Because—what if the information is true?"

His eyes came back to them. "Huh? What then?" He jerked his head toward the window. "Who do they have, somewhere out there, in some sort of witness protection program? Or, more likely, locked up somewhere and they're trying to figure out how to lose the key?"

Margo had . . . never thought about it, she realized. So far as she knew, neither had any of the scientists in The Project. Their approach to the mystery of the Grantville Disaster had been entirely driven by interest in the physical phenomena involved, and what they implied about the universe. Their frustration with the authorities and their tendency to be secretive about their work was simply a matter of finagling the needed funds to do the research. It wasn't as if they'd ever *really* thought there was a conspiracy involved on the highest levels. Not, at least, a conspiracy that went beyond the rather humdrum tendency of most establishments to keep a lid on truths simply because they might prove somehow awkward.

More a matter of bureaucratic reflex than conscious thought. Much less . . .

With some annoyance, she realized that a corner of her brain—obviously located somewhere in the primeval stem—was distracting her with its muted chortling.

So. There's one question answered. No, he is not married.

Richard pulled out his BlackBerry and punched in a number. After a pause, he spoke into the receiver.

"Leo? Richard here. I think you'd best come down here yourself. Bring Malcolm also. And Karen, if she can get away. And call my wife and tell her I won't be back for a bit."

There was another pause, as he listened. "No, that won't be necessary. It's not that urgent, and that's an extra expense for no purpose. We have a rental vehicle already. We'll pick you up at the St. Louis airport once you let us know your flight and estimated time of arrival."

He disconnected. "This will all prove quite interesting, I believe."

CHAPTER
⟨⟨⟨⟩⟩ 10 ⟨⟨⟨⟩⟩

Anyone not on duty was crowded into the administrative building's second floor briefing room. Almost two hundred men and women stood shoulder-to-shoulder to hear what had happened to them, and what they could do about it. Forty-two from the night shift, and over a hundred and thirty from afternoons. Forty guards had not been able to make it. They were the temporary crew standing watch so the others could attend the meeting. Kathleen had made arrangements to tape the proceedings, so that once their shift ended they could hear and see what had taken place.

The Quiver—that's what those who had talked to Edelman were calling it—had taken place fifty-eight hours back. Since then a dozen guards had left, looking for home and family members—and all of them had returned within a few hours, some of them downright terrified. They'd returned with stories of strange animals, stranger insects, and no roads and no homes.

The prisoners had also heard the stories. They knew what had happened. But so far their reaction had been subdued. There had been no confrontations. Even the inmate fistfights that normally erupted almost hourly had disappeared. The prisoners seemed to be holding their collective breath, waiting to see what was going to happen next. As one guard put it, they probably felt safer behind their bars than they would outside them.

Most of the guards and all of the department heads knew this situation would change soon. There were over two thousand prisoners inside the walls and just a little over two hundred guards watching them, divided into two twelve hour shifts. That was a very dangerous ratio.

Andy stood to the left of Joe Schuler. Rod Hulbert stood at his right. Joe had just finished giving the guards the same report he had given the department heads the day before. He had left nothing out. Andy had watched Jenny as Joe talked. Her eyes never left the man's face.

Before the meeting she had told him she needed to talk to him in private. Her department's needs had to be addressed quickly. When he'd asked what the needs were, she had only shaken her head and said now was not the time to discuss them.

Other department heads had not been so reticent. The head of the kitchen had told him they were just about out of bottled water, and that they would be out of propane in less than three weeks. Jake Conner, the maintenance supervisor, had caught him in the hall with still worse news. It turned out that the reason many of the toilets weren't working was because all the laterals buried three feet beneath the soil on that side of the one-hundred-year-old

prison were crushed or missing. The same thing went for
the septic tanks.

They could make do for the time being, for a while.
But if the rest of the toilets went . . . Andy suppressed a
shudder. Without plumbing, the prison would quickly
become unbearable.

His eyes went back to the new nurse. She had been
under more pressure than most of the people in the room,
yet managed to look fresh, even crisp. Her face betrayed
none of the stress of the last two days.

Lylah Caldwell, on the other hand, looked exhausted.
Her lined face was now pale and puffy. It was as if she had
aged five years for each of the last two days. Barbara Ray
wasn't here. She was in the infirmary with their two
patients, Elaine Brown and Frank Nickerson.

Andy had left a guard at the infirmary. They couldn't
really afford it, and since there were no prisoners within
the clinic, it was probably foolish. But he couldn't make
himself pull the only protection available to the three
women. They were not trained for this. Not that the
guards were either, really. Everyone inside the prison was
out of their element.

Andy looked at Jenny again. She was listening to the
speaker, ignoring everything else going on around her.

Andy forced himself to look away from her and listen to
Joe's recap of his trip into town.

"So, with what Rod and the rest of the guards saw, it's
obvious that we're on our own. There's no help coming
from the outside. I'm going to let Jeff Edelman explain
the technical side of this."

Andy watched Jeff walk to the front of the room. He was nervous, and Andy knew why. The room was filled with people who had had enough bad news already. They certainly wouldn't want to hear what Edelman was about to tell them. They just wanted someone to reassure them that they would be getting their world back in a few hours, days or weeks. Not the forever stuff he was going to explain. Andy sighed and Jeff began talking.

"I'm sure most of you have heard all the rumors by now. One of them is that we're somehow in a different dimension. Another is that there was a war, and we were hit with a new weapon. Or, we were the only people *not* hit, the sole survivors of the weapon. We're part of a secret government, or alien abduction experiment and we're being tested. Hell, I wouldn't be surprised if, deep down, some of us think this is just a dream and we're going to wake up and be at home in bed."

He took a deep, somewhat shaky breath. "Well, it's not. This is real, people. We just don't know what *it* is. We do know there are no satellites in the sky. I had three staff members watching for one all night. From our location, we should have seen dozens of them in the course of just a few hours. All radio and television signals are gone, and this is also worldwide. There aren't any ham radios in operation. Nothing.

"The parking lot ends, our world disappears, and the dirt and grasses begin. And if you go a little farther, even the grasses end and the ground cover changes completely."

He let that sink in, then continued.

"I don't know what has happened to us. And I'm not sure if it even matters. But since I can't think of anything else that makes any sense, my guess is, we've moved in time. The position of the stars strongly suggests we aren't in our own time line. Exactly when we are, I don't know. But my second guess is—from what we've seen of the landscape—that we went back, not forward."

"Well, whatever's happened, can't it reverse itself?" That came from one of the guards standing toward the back of the room. He needed to half-shout to make himself heard over the little hubbub that had filled the room after Jeff's last pronouncement.

Edelman shook his head. "That's a nice thought, but don't count on it. If we let ourselves think like that we would be committing suicide. We're here. And if we don't accept that fact, we won't survive. We'll run out of food and water."

"If you don't know what it is, then that means it could have been some sort of weapon. You can't say it's not. And if it was a weapon, something else could happen. We could get hit again."

"You're right. We can't say what it is or isn't," Joe answered for Jeff. He shook his head. "It could be any one of the explanations people have come up with. It could also be one of a hundred things no one has thought of. But does it matter? We don't know why things are like they are. But we do know we have to deal with the situation. We take care of business now, and then later, when we can, we try to figure out what and why. As for it happening again, we don't have any control over that, so we have to hope everything's going to be okay from this point forward and work with what we have."

Rod Hulbert cut in. "Joe is right. We have too many

prisoners inside these walls. We can't afford to panic. Besides, as far as we can tell, whatever happened is over. It's like the Quiver caused it, and now we're in a new time for us."

Joe nodded and added, "We need some short-term and long-term plans. And we have to get busy right away. Otherwise we'll get caught."

"*When* are we, then?" Keith Woeltje asked.

Jeff Edelman shrugged. "I'm not sure. To find out exactly, I would need a computer programmed for that purpose. The plant and animal life in the area right outside the prison is not what was there before the Quiver, but they seem modern enough. Yet, when we look at the stars, we know we are definitely not in any modern time frame. We're at least a half million years back. But keep in mind that is a conservative estimate. I could be off by a million years or more." After a slight pause, he added: "A lot more."

A woman in the back of the room called out, "Couldn't the situation be temporary? Couldn't we go back home, someway?"

Jeff Edelman shook his head. "No. We're not in Oz and we don't have a pair of ruby slippers. We're here. And the odds of another Quiver or weapon blast, or whatever, coming along and refilling the river and taking out those mountains and trees and putting our town back . . ." He shrugged. "I believe whatever happened occurs very rarely. I believe we will never experience another one. But I don't know that because I don't know what caused this one."

The room suddenly erupted. It took almost two minutes

of shouting for quiet to finally bring the room to a stunned silence.

The room was dead quiet now, and people were listening. It was time for Andy to talk. He knew Jeff had fudged, right there at the end. When the two of them had talked privately, Jeff had said they were tens of millions of years back in time. He had actually guessed, a minimum of fifty million years. And he also believed it could be as much as a hundred million years.

But Andy didn't see any reason to bring that up here. Fundamentally, it didn't matter anyway. Half a million years back in time or half a billion, they were still the only human beings anywhere in the world. So he would concentrate on what they needed to do.

"With things the way they are," he said loudly, "we're going to have to change a few job descriptions and decide what we should do with the prisoners."

Before he could go any further, Terry Collins marched to the front of the room. He was angry, and it showed. "If all this is true, winter could be on its way. We need to get off our duffs, quit jawing about what has or hasn't happened and get ready for God knows what. Are we headed for a three-month freeze or are we sitting at the beginning of an ice age? We don't know how long we have to get ready, and we don't know how long we have to get ready for. We have to get the prisoners out of their cells and put a shovel in their hands. We've got work to do, and they're the ones who need to be doing it!"

Andy gritted his teeth. Until they knew more and had made plans, the idea of letting two and a half thousand inmates in a maximum security prison out of their cells was insane. Literally, in some cases, since dozens of those inmates were in fact psychotic. And while most of them weren't, they were hardly what you'd call good citizens.

The prisoner-guard ratio was too low, it was as simple as that. They were covering twenty-four hours a day, seven days a week with a staff smaller than what just the day shift normally ran with. He caught a glimpse of Collins' eyes and knew he wanted something that had nothing to do with the possibility of an upcoming winter. He had his own agenda and instinctively Andy knew what it was. This was Collins' first move in a play for power.

He had to stop this, now. Collins was one of those guards that, unfortunately, sometimes worked their way into the ranks and even managed, as he had, to get promoted. Callous, completely self-centered, not much different from the men he was protecting the public from. If the man gained control it would be work crews this week, slaves next week. This week, it would be all guards under his protection, next week it would be just his favorites. The rest of the guards would find themselves needing protection.

"Sit down, Terry." He kept his tone level, but it was very cold. "You and I know it sounds good, but can't be done. We have to get ready for tomorrow, but first we have to figure out what that tomorrow is."

Andy hesitated. What did the people need to hear? Then he knew. The truth. That was what they needed, and what they had the right to. "You've all heard the numbers. We have a two-month supply of food, if we stretch it. Our water is almost gone. Our sanitation system is shaky. And we have no heating or cooling after tomorrow. Medical supplies are limited. Our firepower is limited, because we only have so much ammunition. We don't have enough clothing."

Collins was nodding, as if Andy was agreeing with him.

"We don't know our environment. We don't know what is going on around us. You heard Edelman. You heard Hulbert. You heard Joe. We don't know when we are. We don't know who is outside these walls, if anyone. There could be a friendly, advanced, civilization on the other side of the mountain, or no one but us anywhere on the planet."

The room was completely silent. Collins was actually smirking, now.

It was time to lower the boom. "And before we've had time to figure out how to deal with any of this, Mr. Genius here"—he pointed at Collins—"thinks it's a really bright idea to let over two thousand of the state's most dangerous felons out of their cells. Maybe he thinks some good ideas will emerge from the ensuing debate between Boomer and his boys and the Aryans."

That brought a sudden gust of laughter from most of the guards. Collins seem to wilt a little.

"No, I don't think so," Andy said forcefully. "There will be no get out of jail free cards passed out. Not yet, anyway. Not until we know who and what is outside the prison walls, and until we're sure we have the situation under control."

"If we wait too long," Collins shouted, "it will be too late! We will die!"

"No. If we move too fast in the wrong direction, then we will die. We can't afford to get careless. And I can't think of a better definition of the word 'carelessness' than poorly supervised prisoners."

He looked at Schuler.

"Joe, how many men are on exploration duty?"

"Four teams of three."

Andy looked at the men and women crowded into the room. "These men are out there looking for water, food, and anything else that we might be able to use. They are also looking for signs of civilization, for other people."

He looked at Jenny. "What's medical doing?"

She stood up and faced the crowd. "We are doing very little. We're holding back on everything and anything that doesn't have to be used to keep a person alive today. We're looking for replacement treatments and replacement meds. We're setting up first aid classes to teach people how to deal with medical emergencies common in a more primitive environment. We're also in the process of developing hygiene classes. Careful washing of small cuts has suddenly become very important. The same thing goes for avoiding worms and other parasites. We are all going to have to learn new ways of doing things if we want to stay healthy."

"Baker," Andy called, "what are you doing about our heat source?"

Laughter rolled from the man. "We're trying an experiment. I don't know how well it'll work, but I read once in a magazine where villages in India do it. We're setting up methane toilets. Little outhouses designed to turn fecal waste into a gas that can be burned."

A moan came from the crowd, followed by boos and shouts of, "Oh, how gross!"

Baker shrugged. "Look, folks, it's what we got. The Indians use pig crap, and we don't have any pigs. On the other hand, we've got almost three thousand people in the prison, counting everybody. That's a lot of crap. So much, in fact, that with the sewers down the maintenance guys are wracking their brains just trying to figure out how to get rid of it. We figure we may as well do this while we're at it. If nothing else, it should generate enough methane to keep the kitchens going."

"Okay," Andy said. "You get the idea. We have problems— a lot of problems—but we're working at solving them. We'll use our prisoners' favorite recipe for pruno to make a form of fuel. When it's done we'll be able to mix it with what gas we have. That will allow us to stretch our supply and use some of our older vehicles and generators. During the Second World War, the Germans used alcohol to fuel their war effort. It's not the greatest answer, but it will do the job, at least for a while.

"When we get these things under control we'll get busy solving some of our other problems. Have a little faith. Man has survived a long time with nothing but his brains. I really think we're smart enough to get through this."

He shot Collins a look. For the moment, at least, the bastard seemed cowed by the ridicule he'd gotten. "I've appointed over a dozen project managers. Each of these managers will need volunteers. They will be posting lists sometime within the next few days. Anyone interested in helping out, sign up. If you don't see something that will utilize a skill you have, come talk to me. I'll give your name to someone who can use what you know."

Jeff Edelman spoke up. "I need people with mapping

skills. That means people capable of drawing a straight line, and good at drawing things to a scale. It doesn't mean someone who has actually drawn a map professionally. We need to send someone capable of mapping an area with each exploration party that leaves the prison. It would be nice if that person could also catalogue the different plants and animals being found."

Rice was next. "I'm building a green house. I need laborers able and willing to do some shovel work, and people with green thumbs. I'm also looking for anyone who understands sprouting and herb production."

Collins flared up again. "And when are we suppose to do all this volunteerism? We're working twelve-hour shifts with no days off. We need to put the prisoners to work, I tell you!"

Andy took a deep breath to steady his nerves. He really wanted to take a poke at the jackass standing in the middle of the room. "Collins, you aren't going to force me into making a snap judgment. So, sit down and be quiet, unless you have something constructive to say. Everyone here is aware of our limitations and most of us are aware of our responsibilities."

Kathleen stood up next. Her face was a combination of pale white areas and red blotches caused from crying. "If this is going to last for more than a few days, we need a place to rest. Is there a way we can move prisoners in with each other? We, the guards, we need bedrooms. Someplace to get away that is our own. Someplace quiet. And we need a place to go when we're off duty and want to be around people. Maybe we could keep the cafeteria open."

Andy looked at Hulbert.

"Sure," the man said. "I'll open the cafeteria as soon as we finish here. But I don't want any bloodshed so it's going to take a couple of days to arrange sleeping quarters. We can't just pile the prisoners in together. Imagine sticking Boomer in with one of the skinheads."

The room erupted into laughter. "Boomer" was the nickname for an inmate named Timmy Bolgeo, and it fit the man. He was a three-hundred-pound black weight lifter who was normally easy enough to deal with. But he did have an anger management problem, and when his temper went things got pretty thermonuclear. The skinheads were his favorite method of venting.

Andy grinned and motioned for Woeltje to open the doors. The guards' laughter could be heard all over the building. And laughter was as good a way as any to end the meeting. Actually, it had ended a lot better than he'd thought it would. In retrospect, Collins' opposition had given Andy the handle to settle people down.

With the meeting over he asked Jenny if he could walk her back to the infirmary. Her easy smile and soft voice were two things he had come to lean on, these past two days. They eased his tension and made making bad choices easier.

And all the choices had become bad. Like his decision to cut water rations in half. And food rations by one third. And his decision to not notice that the only diabetic getting an insulin shot was a young guard who stood watch in the east tower. The nurses had agonized over that decision. They could keep all the insulin-dependent diabetics alive for sixteen days, or one diabetic alive for six months. They had chosen the six months. And they had chosen the youngest person in need.

Jenny was the one who finally made the call. She was having to make all the tough calls coming out of the infirmary. The other nurses had basically jumped into the back seat, leaving it to her to drive the bus.

She was making and then living with her bad choices, just like he was.

"Before the meeting you said you had a problem." He walked slowly, enjoying the fresh air and sunshine. He'd spent almost all his time since the Quiver in meetings of one sort or another.

"Yeah," she smiled, but it was thin and didn't hold any humor. "I'm running out of supplies. Seizure medications, antidepressants, blood pressure meds, heart meds, you name it. Unfortunately, we were running low on a lot of medications when this hit. Starting tomorrow, people aren't going to get their regular doses. I juggled the diabetics. Put them on oral meds instead of their injections and changed their diets to buy them a little time. I could do it with the prisoners because I could control their activity level as well as their food intake. A guard was different. If she was going to work she had to have her meds."

They were at the door to the infirmary.

"I'm sorry you were put in the position of choosing, Jenny."

"Sorry or not, I have to do it again. And then again. And again."

He had to restrain a powerful impulse to reach out and stroke her hair. It was hanging loose today; the rubber band she had been using to tie it back was gone. "We're all doing it. We have no choice."

She nodded, then leaned against him. They stood like that a few moments, her head on his chest. He could feel her tears as they soaked through his shirt.

"Jenny!" Barbara called from inside the building.

She straightened and smiled. "Thanks for the shoulder."

He nodded and watched her disappear into the building and mentally kicked himself. Some men would have come up with something to say that would have made her feel better. They wouldn't have stood there like a lump of clay.

CHAPTER 11

Two days later, Andy, Jenny, Rod, and Joe sat inside the cafeteria sipping their one and only cup of coffee for the day. Knowing that coffee would be gone soon made it taste all the better. According to the head cook, the kitchen was stretching what they had as far as they could. But stretching it or not, six days from now the black brew would disappear from the face of the Earth. Never to be seen again, probably, at least not in their lifetime.

"We're getting behind at the infirmary," Jenny said. "We have to have some help with the cleaning. Those floors and cabinets haven't been washed down since the Quiver. And with only four of us, we don't have the time. The guard you've loaned us spends most of her time working as a medical assistant. I can't spare the time for her to do a little cleaning. As for Barbara and Lylah, they're putting in fourteen-hour days just caring for patients. There's no time left for the grunt work. And without it, we're going to start getting epidemics."

Andy nodded. The kitchen had already asked for a few prisoners to help with their workload. So had the project managers. "Okay, I'll start sending a few prisoners to work, but I hate to. I can't spare the COs to make the situation safe."

Jenny chewed her bottom lip for a second then said, "I have the prisoners' charts. Let me go through them and then give you a list. Not everyone here is psychotic, after all. I can give you a list of those who aren't in for violent crimes, or at least the ones I don't think are dangerous."

Andy nodded, although he was skeptical. The guards never saw the charts, but they always knew the reasons for a man's incarceration. And that rumor mill was probably more accurate than the official tags. "Okay, but keep in mind that most of their convictions were after the plea bargaining stage of our justice system. What you see may not be what you get. And try to find some first timers without juvie jackets. They'll be a little easier to deal with. Especially if they haven't been here long." He shrugged. "After what Collins wanted, I hate to pull any of the prisoners out to work the prison, even if it was their job before the Quiver."

"Is Collins going to be a problem forever?" Hulbert asked.

"Probably," Andy answered. "There's always one. And I guess he's ours." He debated gulping the last few ounces of his coffee, while it was still hot, tasting like it should, or sipping it. Making it last as long as possible. In the end he sipped.

"He was transferred here from upstate. A *problem child.* Not enough to get him fired, but close to it."

Terry Collins was almost six and a half feet tall. Thin, athletic, and full of venom. Andy had seen his record. He had been in a half dozen confrontations with prisoners in the six months since he'd come to Alexander. Each time the prisoner had been the one to cross the line first, but experience had taught Andy that six was too many, in that period of time. Way too many. Collins had to be starting it. Or, at least, not defusing the situation.

Defusing was what the guards were *supposed* to do. Men were not locked up in maximum security prisons because they had a lot of self-control. They needed help keeping themselves out of trouble. And rumor had it Collins had trouble with that one, himself. The stories circulating about him and his ex-wife, if true, were evidence of it. The fact that the man was divorced wasn't unusual. But rumor had it when his wife left she skipped state. She took the kids and ran.

"It sounds like this Collins character would be an element in a lawless society. A dangerous element." Jenny looked at Hulbert and Joe sitting across the table from her and Andy. They both nodded.

"We just have to be sure we're not lawless." Andy could feel another day, another headache, coming on.

Hulbert grinned. "Oh, there's no danger of that. We've got a library full of legal books. We have nothing on agriculture, but we have lots of law."

"Yeah, well, I'm not so sure that's the type of law we'll be needing." Joe had tried to make a joke out of it, but the truth in what he said made the comment hang in the air instead of blowing away with a smile or chuckle.

Hulbert stared at his empty cup. "You're right. We're

not ready for slick lawyers and loopholes and technicalities. We need strength. The people are scared. Hell, we're all scared. We either give the guards what they need, or they're going to look for someone who can." He nodded toward a small cluster of men sitting at a table in a corner of the cafeteria. Those were the men who had stood next to Collins at the last meeting. "Each time one of the cooks says we're out of something new, that little group grows. One can of vegetables at a time. And Collins knows it. He's just biding his time. Waiting on our first emergency."

"I read once that no country is more than three missed meals from a revolution." Jenny shrugged. "I guess we're talking truths. And it doesn't hurt to say out loud what everyone else is thinking."

Hulbert reached across the table and patted her hand, then smiled at Andy. "Okay, we won't let them miss any meals."

"How?" all three of them asked at the same time.

"We already have exploratory expeditions going. They're doing the day-trips, gathering everything they find that might or might not be edible. Let me lead a few hunting parties that don't have to be back by nightfall. Give me three men, unlimited access to the armory and make my time my own. I've talked to the scouting parties. There is plenty of wild game out there. In a week's time, two at the most, I should be able to get us enough meat to run a month or so. After that I can keep us stocked through the winter."

"Meat's not enough," Jenny said. "We need grains and vegetables. We've had a few people outside the walls looking, but they aren't bringing in enough. The last trip didn't net a bushel basket full."

"I know, Jenny. I was there when they came in last night." He drummed his fingers on the table, looking at Collins' men. "I've spent two-thirds my adult life playing the weekend survivalist. I guess all those years of learning what's edible and what's not is about to pay off." His face lost all signs of emotion. "Let me get the protein, then I'll take a handful of people on foraging parties. From what little I saw while outside the walls, I think I could teach a small group of a dozen or so people to find tubers and other edible plants. They wouldn't have to go far. It could be done with the same type of day trips we're doing now. I didn't recognize too many of the plants, but I did recognize a few general types. And they were high in carbs, vitamin A and E. I also saw a couple that should give us our calcium and plenty of C."

She nodded. "Okay. That's good. But there is something else, and I hate to say it, but I'm going to. You guys have been great. But . . ."

Jenny wasn't the type to be lost for words. "Just say it," Andy said. "I don't think the four of us can worry about what's politically correct. At least not for right now."

"Actually, that's the problem. We do have to worry about it. And we have to worry about it now. Not later. Rod wants to take three *men* with him. Not three experienced hunters. We can't fall into that trap. When the work gets divided up into men's work and women's work, we lose. We have to keep things focused on experience and who's good at what. Gender and color has to stay out of it. Otherwise we're dead in the water. When the hunters come back, if a woman provided part of the food, women retain their value."

She wasn't pleading, but her voice had an edge. "People respect strength and brains. But if women aren't given a chance to show off the things they know and the strength of character they have, then they lose it. We all lose when women become pets to be cared for. And later, to be kicked."

Hulbert shrugged. "Okay, you're probably right. I know quite a few guys I wouldn't trust not to mistake me for a buck, even if I was wearing hunter orange, which I won't be. But no tokens. That's almost as bad as not allowing a minority to participate. Stories about screw-ups get around even faster than those about successes. And they're never forgotten. If there's a woman on grounds who *wants* to go, and has the experience, real experience, I'll take her."

Jenny grinned. "That's not a problem. Her name is Marie Keehn. She's no token. She's a fisherperson and hunter from way back. Took her first bear up in Canada when she was fifteen. She showed me a picture of it. She also told a story. A little tacky for mixed company, but what the hell."

Jenny dropped her voice and leaned closer to the men. "Marie and her family were up in Canada, hunting. They hadn't been able to find anything their entire trip and it was their last day. She had started her period that morning and her father's rules were, if she was bleeding, she couldn't hunt. The smell, which humans wouldn't even notice, would attract any wild animals in the area. Well, she was young. So, she decided not to tell anyone. She went to her bear stand; her brothers went to theirs. It turned out, her father was apparently right. Her period did seem to attract the local wildlife. She was the only one who took a bear that trip and she's never told any of them about her *secret bait.*"

Hulbert was laughing so hard he spilled the last of his coffee. "My God! I'm in love! I want to meet this woman."

"I'll tell her to come see you."

"You wouldn't happen to know when she's supposed to come around again, would you?"

Jenny stood up to leave. "Ask her yourself."

Andy jogged to catch up with her. "I think you made Hulbert's day."

"I'm glad someone's happy." She slipped her hand into his and gave it a squeeze. "What I'm going to tell you won't be so good, Andy."

"It never is." He rubbed the top of his head, applying as much pressure as he could along the temple areas and across the top.

"Another headache?"

"Yeah."

She handed him a small white envelope filled with aspirins. "I figured you would be running low by now. Some of your headaches are caused from tension. But I'm betting some of them aren't. You're off all sugars now. And your caffeine intake has dropped to one cup of coffee a day. Caffeine and sugar are both addicting. And withdrawals from them include headaches." She gave his hand another small squeeze. "If you feel irritable, exhausted or develop diarrhea, don't be surprised."

"At this point in my life, nothing can surprise me. Now, what's your bad news?"

"We're going to lose about one hundred prisoners within the next month or two."

"*What?*" Andy stopped walking and stared at her. "That can't be right."

"A little over one hundred of our prisoners have health problems that will cause them to die within the next month or two if left untreated. And I don't have the means of treating them. I've run out of their meds." Jenny pulled her hand from his and started walking again. He followed a half step behind her.

"One hundred," he whispered. He had known this was coming, he just hadn't realized how many were going to die.

"Yes. But the numbers are actually worse than that. Over the next year, maybe two, we will lose five hundred. Diabetes, high blood pressure, kidney failure, heart failure, transplant rejection, and liver failure are going to cause us to lose about half of them pretty fast. My guess is at least seventy within the next two weeks. Another thirty the following two weeks. Tuberculosis and hepatitis will kill the others within the next year, maybe two. Then things will slow down a little. But over the next five years, we will lose our inmates with AIDS. The grand total when we're done will actually be close to one thousand."

She slowed her pace, giving them a little more time to talk before reaching the infirmary. "This is not an estimate. I've been going through their medical records. Speaking of which, we should suspend those rules. At least you and Joe and Rod should start looking through the convicts' records. Sooner or later, you're going to need to start paroling some of the prisoners. You'll need to know everything you can about them."

Andy set aside her last suggestion. She was right, but that could wait. It was her medical numbers he needed to digest. One hundred prisoners would be dead within two months, five hundred within two years, and a thousand within five years. That was just under half the inmate population. The horror of that was followed by quiet panic. "What about the guards? How many of them are going to die?"

"Relax. It won't be nearly as many. Most of them are healthy. Healthier, in fact, than the American population as a whole. They're younger, on average, and they have to take a screening physical to get the job. Prisoners, on the other hand, are far unhealthier than most people, especially the kind of prisoners you get in maximum security facilities. There are a lot of reasons for that. Some of it is simply because they generally come from poor backgrounds, and 'poor' and 'unhealthy' are almost synonyms. But some of it is more personal. They run more heavily toward addictions than most people, and addicts are almost always unhealthy. And even if they aren't addicted to anything, as such, they usually come from dysfunctional families and don't have much in the way of self-discipline. Their diet is likely to have been as bad as you could ask for since they were infants."

She shrugged. "But, whatever the reasons for it, the fact remains that the health of many prisoners is really lousy. As for the COs, we have a few on blood pressure meds, a couple on heart meds, one on insulin. They may have other medical problems I don't know about, of course. Unless they come to me asking for help, I have no way of knowing."

He nodded. "What are we going to do with all the bodies? We can't possibly bury them."

"No." Her tone was flat, almost emotionless. "We couldn't. We don't have the manpower. We'll have to burn them. Preferably on raised platforms because of the smoke and the odor." She squeezed her eyes shut for a moment, as if blotting out a memory. "I've seen this before, Andy. If we screw it up, we're going to be in real trouble. We can't afford an epidemic on top of everything else."

Real trouble? Seen it before—epidemic? Andy had wondered more than once about Jenny's past. The nurses at the prison were good at their job. And they had nerves of steel or they didn't stay. But even so, Jenny wasn't a typical prison nurse. She was at least one cut above the average. What she knew, how she carried herself, the way she stayed one step ahead of everything, none of it was typical. And the control she kept on her emotions was unbelievable. He had seen her cry several times over the last few days, but her tears didn't cause her to lose control. She would be crying one minute, giving orders the next. Medical was the best-run department in the prison and she hadn't been there long enough to draw so much as one paycheck. All three nurses plus their guard had sleeping areas. They had work schedules with a priority listing that let them get things done that used to take eight people.

"There are a couple of things you need to know. I took Woeltje off tower duty, permanently. That knee of his is pretty bad. He was wearing a brace when the Quiver hit, so that helps. But he is to do zero stairs from today on. You also have to take into consideration how far he has to walk each time you assign him. And he can't be posted some-place that requires standing for long periods. He has to be able to stand, sit, and even prop that leg up on a regular schedule."

Andy nodded, then braced himself. Jenny might be unusual in a lot of ways, but she was also predictable. She always saved the worst for last. Always.

"We've admitted Kathleen to the infirmary. She's on complete bed rest. I'm going to induce labor if the baby doesn't move in the next twenty-four hours."

"Why?"

"It hasn't moved much since the Quiver came. And it should have. I'm still getting a heartbeat, but it's weak and irregular." She shrugged, and he could tell she was working at keeping her voice steady. "This close to being born, the baby needs to be moving on a regular basis, and it's been twenty-four hours since . . ."

Andy's headache went from a dull throb to a knife cutting, anvil pounder. He had to close his own eyes.

"You need a shoulder?" she asked.

"Yeah. Yeah, I do."

She hugged him and laid her head against his chest for a moment before walking into the infirmary. But this time, instead of tears, he thought he felt a soft kiss.

CHAPTER
12

"Hulbert's hunting party left a little before sunup,"
Lieutenant Joe Schuler said. "The first of the methane
toilets are now online, so we'll find out soon enough if
they work. The construction of the first greenhouse will
be finished sometime today, and we now have a working
well. It's only nineteen feet deep, but it's good water."

Andy nodded. He already knew. He had heard the
shouts the second the work crew hit it. If he hadn't known
what they were digging for, he would have sworn they'd
struck oil. The way they laughed and shouted reminded
him of some of the late night movies he had watched with
his grandfather. He had been ten years old and his grandmother had passed away, and his grandfather—it turned
out to be his last summer—had reluctantly moved into the
spare room in the basement. Every Friday night the two
of them had sat on the lumpy green couch the old man
had insisted on bringing with him, drinking soda, munching
chips and staring at an old black and white television.

Twice that summer the two of them had stayed up past midnight in order to watch *Giant*. He could still close his eyes and see James Dean covered in Texas' black gold, shouting to the heavens.

"We will be finished with the inmate relocations sometime today," Joe continued. "When that is done, we'll start the cleaning. And then we'll be able to start assigning permanent sleeping areas for the staff. And you can tell Jenny I've got the solar showers hung. People can start showering again." Joe stopped his report when he realized Andy wasn't listening. "Is something wrong?"

"I hope not," Andy answered. He looked at the door to medical then asked, "Did you hear about the east wall, and the—God, I can hardly say the word—the dinosaur?"

"It didn't get in, though. All it was doing was scratching itself."

"This time. And I don't care if Jeff says it wasn't a meat-eater. The damn thing was *huge.*"

Joe Schuler nodded. Everyone knew they had been lucky. No one had been outside when the creature showed up, and the wall had held.

Andy's face was grim. "I can't turn them out. If a pterodactyl flies overhead and takes a dump, coating the entire exercise yard, it doesn't matter. And it doesn't matter if a dinosaur scratches his ass on the east wall. But if something else shows up, like a tyrannosaurus . . . I can't turn the prisoners out."

"I know, Andy. Besides that, if we're here, there could be other people. And it would be morally wrong to release some of these guys until we know for sure. You have to wait."

Andy scanned the interior of the prison, then shrugged. "I don't believe ten percent of them would last more than twenty-four hours on the outside, in any event. We have men who've been inside these walls for over forty years. Over fifty years, in a few cases. If they couldn't make it when things were organized and easy, they aren't going to survive when one screw-up means you don't eat, or you get eaten."

"Hey, Andy, I know that. So does everyone else. We're protecting whoever else might be living in this timeline, and we're protecting the prisoners from themselves and . . ." he shrugged. "None of the prisoners or the COs are talking about leaving. They're all scared. No one thinks surviving outside the walls is an option. Not right now, for sure."

"Do you know what killed Greg Lowry?"

"I heard he had a bad heart and it gave out because of the Quiver."

Andy shook his head. "No. Aliens killed him! He died because he was afraid some frigging alien was going to jump out of the wall at us."

Confused, Joe shook his head. "That's crazy."

"Yeah, well, that's what killed him. And if we aren't careful we're all going to die because of aliens or God knows what."

"We'll do okay, at least for a while. Most of what's crawling around out there seems content to leave us alone."

"Joe, I'm not talking about tomorrow. I'm talking about next year, or the year after, or twenty years from now. We have to look ahead to the point when the prisoners are out of their cells and we are living outside these walls. We are going to have to farm and hunt and build factories. And do it in a way some God-awful creature the size of a blue whale doesn't knock it all down. And none of it can be done with over two thousand men in chains.

"And the water, we have a well, but how long till it runs dry? We need something more reliable. We need a river."

"Hey, Cap, maybe you should . . ."

"I'm sorry, Joe." Andy Blacklock clenched and unclenched his hands, stretching his fingers out then curling them tight. "Today isn't a good day." He gave the second lieutenant a phony smile. "Kathleen Hanrahan is in having her baby."

"Oh." Joe gave Andy's shoulder a squeeze, then walked away as fast as he could without actually breaking into a jog. He had heard that the kid was probably dead. Everyone had heard that.

"Kathleen, wait. Don't push, not yet." Jenny wiped the woman's face with a cool cloth.

"I don't understand this. I've had three babies. None of them were this hard to bring. None of them. Each baby is supposed to get easier." The woman's water had broken and she had been in hard labor for over fourteen hours. She was exhausted, close to the breaking point. She was also terrified that the reason she was having such a hard time was because something had gone wrong with the baby.

"You are a lot older than you were back then. Your muscles have been stretched and pulled by those other births. They don't ever go all the way back. Just relax and don't worry. It won't be much longer now. The last time I checked, you were dilated to an eight." She flashed the woman a smile. "When you hit the magic number ten, the baby will be here."

"I know, but I just can't." Another contraction came, arching her back and causing her to moan. "I can't," she sobbed.

"Relax," Jenny said to the woman and moved to the "catcher's position." Barbara replaced her near the woman's head. She took one of Kathleen's hands; Lylah took the other. Jenny made a quick check then smiled. "Magic time, Kathleen. You're ready."

She motioned for Barbara to join her at the foot of the examining table. "Okay, Kathleen, you have to relax and work with the baby. The baby needs you to help it be born. Do you understand?"

Kathleen nodded. The contraction had ended. For the moment she could concentrate.

"I want you to take a few deep breaths. Come on. You need to oxygenate your blood, and the baby's. Come on, breathe."

Kathleen did as she was told. She took deep breath after deep breath. A new contraction was coming.

Jenny could feel the woman begin to tense up. She started rubbing her legs, pressing on the flesh as hard as she could without causing pain. "Kathleen, it's a wave. Feel the wave. Ride it. Up. Up. That's it, ride the wave to the peak." She could feel the contraction through the woman's skin. "That's it, it's peaking. Push. Push. That's it. It's plateauing. Good. Stay with it. Now. Feel it. Stop pushing. Relax. It's coming down. Down. You can take this. Ride the wave down."

Kathleen relaxed. The contraction was still there, but

she was on the back half of it. She could relax. She could do it. "How many more?"

Jenny's eyes had never left the woman's pubis. The baby had crowned. "One, maybe two more. Then you're done with the hard part."

Kathleen nodded, then said, "Another one's coming."

Jenny concentrated on the baby, her heart in her throat. The infant's hair was plastered to its scalp. Black hair streaked with blood. A thin dusting of white. The baby moved forward a centimeter. "Push, Kathleen. Push!" Another centimeter. The contraction peaked. "Push!" The baby's head was free. Quickly she worked her fingers around its neck. *No cord. Thank you, God.* She could see the baby's pulse beating in the top of its head. It was regular and strong. *Maybe we're going to be lucky.* "Kathleen, don't push. Wait for the contraction."

They waited. Twenty seconds, thirty, the contraction began. Another twenty seconds, thirty, and the baby was free.

As the umbilical cord prolapsed, Jenny suctioned the baby's nose and throat with a new ear syringe she had found inside the med room. He was gray and chilling quickly, but his heart beat within his thin little chest. "Please," she whispered. "Please . . . breathe!"

The baby jerked in her hands, gave a small choking sound, took a breath of air and then whimpered. It was such a small sound, but it could be heard by everyone in the room. The three nurses had been holding their breath. Barbara and Lylah's tears were flowing as fast as Kathleen's. Jenny fought to keep from joining them. She lost the battle and gave a soft sob.

"My poor baby." Kathleen reached for the newborn. Jenny wrapped a heated bath towel around the infant, gave the child a quick hug, then handed him to his mother.

"Congratulations, Mom," she said. "You have a beautiful, healthy son. What are you going to name him?"

Kathleen's tears came harder. "I don't know. He was supposed to be called Samuel Ray. He wasn't going to be named for anyone. We had done that with the older boys. It was just a name from a baby book that we liked. It sounded good. But now, I don't know if that's good enough." She gazed at the baby and wiped her eyes. "I think his name is too important to have picked it from a book."

Jenny patted the woman's leg. "You don't have to decide today. You have time."

CHAPTER 13

Stephen McQuade didn't expect the rifle butt slammed into his lower back. He fell to his knees, gasping in pain. He'd been floating in and out of consciousness for hours. Maybe days. It was hard for him to decide. He had been beaten too many times to be sure of anything.

But the beatings were the easy part. The hard part was the fear. The knowing what was next. After each beating he'd been tied to a tree and was able to watch one Indian after another tortured and then killed. He assumed they were Indians, anyway, although he didn't recognize their language or their manner of dress and personal decoration. They certainly weren't Cherokee or any other of the southern tribes he was familiar with.

He did recognize the language spoke by their captors. They were Spaniards. He couldn't speak or understand Spanish, beyond a few words, but he knew the sound of the language. These men could be nothing else.

They were brutal beyond belief. Not even the worst sort of Georgia militiamen would have been this savage.

First they'd torture and eventually murder the children, so their parents could see them die. Then, apparently not getting the information they demanded, they started on the women. That was just as slow and even more degrading. Finally, the men. One at a time. Hour after hour.

Hands pulled him to his feet, then a moment later he was back on the ground gasping, bleeding from a blow to the back of his head. Kicks were coming from all directions; he closed his eyes in an attempt to protect his vision as his head and body were pounded. Someone ground the heel of his boot onto McQuade's left ankle. His hands were tied behind his back, so he couldn't fight back. Stephen curled his legs towards his chest, protecting himself the best he could.

Someone kicked him in the groin. The world faded to gray.

The beating continued. Stopped. Then continued. His nose broke and his sinuses closed. He had to breathe through his mouth: His lips were split and some of his teeth were gone. The pain was too much for him to know how many. Hands grabbed at his hair, dragging him through the dirt and over the bodies of those already dead. The pain was everything. There was nothing else.

A voice came from somewhere. He thought that was the man the others called de Soto. He was demanding something. Stephen tried to answer, but it hurt too much to open his mouth. He wondered if his jaw was broken, then decided it didn't really matter.

Someone grabbed the leather that bound his hands behind his back and jerked him to his feet. His shoulders screamed. One of the soldiers wearing chain mail, leg armor, boots and a steel helmet, stepped in front of him.

The man aimed his ancient-looking gun at McQuade and fired. The flesh of his right side tore and burned, and the impact knocked him down.

He tried to crawl away.

The Spaniard standing to the left of the man with the matchlock reached out with a wood-handled halberd and hooked Stephen's left hip, dragging him back to the center of the small crowd. The one called de Soto placed a booted foot on Stephen's stomach while the Spaniard with the halberd wrenched its metal tip from where it was buried in bone and muscle. That finally brought blessed unconsciousness.

Stephen woke to the sound of silence.

He forced himself to roll to his side; stopped as the nausea washed over him, then slowly turned his head so he could catch a glimpse with his right eye, which was the one not swollen completely shut. There were no Spaniards, and no Indian corpses. There were footprints and animal tracks. Strange tracks from strange creatures.

He tried to think through what he was seeing, but it was too much for now.

He was alive. And the cave he'd passed the night in was not far from where he lay. He forced himself to get up, as difficult as that was. He needed to walk.

He knew he would die. There was no way to survive his injuries, even if his hands weren't tied behind his back. But if he stayed out in the open, the dried blood on him would surely attract one of the strange creatures he had seen. The cave would be a much better place to end his life.

Lieutenant Rod Hulbert's small band of hunters had been out since before daybreak and was starting to tire. They had already taken a buffalo of some kind and what he thought was a ground sloth and were headed back to the prison with more meat than they could comfortably carry. Hunting was going to be even better than he hoped. He nodded to himself and swatted at one of the strange insects flying in circles around his head. On their next foray he would take a larger party with him. That way, carrying their kill wouldn't be quite so hard.

As heavily loaded as they were, he guessed they wouldn't get home until sunset tomorrow. Then he grinned when he realized he already thought of the cement and razor wired structure as home.

He called a halt, and the four of them dropped their bundles and stretched out in the grass. They still had four hours of daylight left. They could afford a short break; two hours more of walking, and then they could make camp for the night. Their prey had been boned-out on site, which made carrying the creatures a lot easier. Marie carried at least sixty pounds of the meat, and each of the men was loaded down with still more. Carrying the meat bundles plus their regular gear was hot, hard work that the insects hadn't made any easier.

"We'll take twenty," he said.

The four of them lay in the grass for almost five minutes without talking. They were tired. It was Jerry Bailey who broke the silence. He sat up and waved toward the small rise to the new north. "You guys go ahead and take a break. I keep hearing something that sounds like water. I wanna take a peek."

"All right," Hulbert said. He had heard the noise and guessed it to be a small creek. "But no more than five minutes out. And keep your whistle in your mouth."

Bailey stood up and stretched. "Be back," he said.

Rod watched him go, suppressing a grin. Bailey was a hell of a hunter. It had surprised him. The soft-spoken guard hadn't struck him as much of an outdoorsman. But he was. As a matter of fact, so was Brian Carmichael. And Marie Keehn turned out to be worth more than both of them combined. The four of them had worked well together. Marie had been the one to actually make the kills, but it had been all of them working together that made it possible in such a short time. That and luck.

"I hope Jerry finds a lake with a few crappies, or maybe a bass or two in it."

Marie laughed. "Brian, if you're going to make a wish like that, wish for a few catfish."

"Nope. Bass or crappies. Maybe a pike." Brian Carmichael sat up. "I grew up down by Kentucky Lake, eating catfish. Every Sunday afternoon we went to Grandma's for fried kitty-fish, cornbread and greens. I haven't found anyone who can make those bottom feeders taste like she did. So, I gave up on them."

"Well, you've never tasted my old man's recipe. You get me the fish and I'll . . ." Marie's grin changed to a frown. "Hulbert," she whispered. "We've got people."

Rod sat up and looked south, the direction Marie was looking. It didn't take him long to see what she'd spotted in the distance. A dead fire, obviously made by people.

When they went over to investigate, all they found was a broken arrow and a bead necklace. There was also a mix of tracks—human and animal—leading off into the woods. Blood. Another set of footprints going the same direction Bailey had gone.

A second later, Jerry was back, waving for them to follow him.

The three of them moved quick and quiet.

"There's a corpse at the edge of the river, and I don't think it's very old," Bailey said, as soon as they were close enough for him to be heard without shouting. "The guy was killed by humans, but his body's been chewed up pretty bad by a scavenger of some sort. And by the looks of the blood trail, there could be others. Human and scavenger."

"Damn," Hulbert hissed. "Okay, we need to be careful, here. If there are people, we need to find them."

When they reached the corpse, he knelt down to inspect it. "This guy was stabbed, with some sort of big knife. It's not a wound caused by any sort of animal, that's obvious. Okay." He straightened up. "I guess it's no longer an 'if.' We are not alone, and someone had to have done this."

He glanced at the two men with him and then at the small brunette. "Remember, we don't know who the bad guy is." He waved at the corpse. "It could be him. He might have been killed by someone trying to defend himself. Or, he could have been a victim. He could have been robbed and then murdered. Hell, he could have been killed for the fun of it. We know that happens way too often. But it doesn't matter. He's dead and someone did it."

Hulbert checked their ammo. They had enough. But

the body armor was back at the prison. You didn't need it when you were after anything but man. He considered going back to the prison for reinforcements and the proper gear but changed his mind. There were more than human prints in the mud and dirt. The animal tracking the people wouldn't wait until he got back.

"Marie, haul the meat this way, then wait here. Stay out of sight, and don't make any noise. We'll check it out."

The raptor—a large female weighing over a thousand pounds—stopped. The male that had joined her several days before also stopped. The two of them were inside the thick brush of tree ferns not far from the herd they had been tracking for the last half hour; their brown-red skin blended in with the brown-red of the dried ferns.

The large female sniffed the air.

The two of them stared at the lone iguanodon. The big plant-eater had been placidly feeding on the tender shoots of seedlings growing close to the rapidly flowing stream. While he grazed, his herd had moved downstream. He was young, not full-grown, and careless.

A female iguanodon bawled to her calf.

The three-year-old bull heard her and lifted his head. He looked around. He rose on his stocky hind legs and took a half dozen steps toward his herd. His nostrils flared. The cows were starting to bunch up, herding the yearling calves into their center.

The three men lay hunkered down in the dried fern, watching and listening, afraid to breathe.

The two predators—they reminded Rod of raptors,

except they were reptiles and not birds—moved from the edge of the fern trees toward the herd of huge vegetarian reptiles. The cows screeched a warning. Two adult bulls bellowed as the raptors raced past them, hunting the calf farthest from the herd. Their claws, three on each foot and one of them huge, cut through the calf's upper skin layers and gashed the muscle and nerve layers below.

The calf, startled and bleeding, tried to run.

The raptors pressed the attack.

One moved to the creature's left; the other worked its way to the right. Their claws sliced the prey's flesh, leaving behind long slashes that were inches deep. Over and over, they struck at the beast. Warm, red blood flowed from the gaping wounds. Rod understood the logic of their hunting tactics, although it was not what you'd see from most predators he was familiar with. They weren't going for a neck-crunching death bite. They were deliberately bleeding out their prey.

The calf lunged awkwardly at the tormentors. They jumped back, and then pressed forward, hissing and screeching.

The attack continued. Back and forth, over and over, the instincts and coordinated moves of the pack-hunter allowed the raptors to keep the adults of the iguanodon herd at bay without slowing the attack on the calf.

They lunged toward their prey—*rip, twist, turn*—and then ran at the herd—*force the creatures back*—and then returned to the attack on the calf.

More and more muscles and nerves were severed. More and more blood flowed. Blow by blow, the two raptors worked together, weakening the beast. It didn't take long for the great creature to fall to the ground, bleeding and dying. After it collapsed, the herd moved away and the raptors began tearing the flesh from the calf, consuming the meat while the pitiful creature was still alive.

Rod pulled his cell phone from his pocket.

"What are you doing? Those things don't work," Brian Carmichael whispered. "There's no satellites, no calling 9-1-1."

"Pictures," Hulbert hissed back, aiming and clicking his camera phone. "We've got to warn everyone, and I don't even know what to call the damn things."

"I do," Jerry Bailey said. "They're Spielberg's monsters. Velociraptors."

Marie Keehn sat impatiently, waiting for Hulbert, Carmichael, and Bailey to return. It had taken her over forty minutes to haul the four bundles of meat to the river's edge, and another ten minutes to scout the area. Now, three hours after sitting down on a fallen log, she was definitely getting spooked. She kept hearing something, over and over. It wasn't loud, and it wasn't continuous. It was just a soft sound that she felt she should recognize, but couldn't.

Then the sound changed. It grew a little louder. It was a moan.

She circled the area. Back and forth, holding her breath, hoping to hear it again.

There it was. Soft. From . . .

She turned around, scanning the area. Yes. Behind the

brush. She approached the area slowly and carefully. Behind the greenery was an opening. A cave. And inside the entrance, a . . . man, yes.

Bloodied. Broken. But alive.

She used her steel, prison-issued whistle to let the others know she had found something, then squatted to get a better look. The man's chest rose and fell. His face was swollen and misshaped. This was not an injury from a fall; his hands were tied behind his back. The man had been beaten. He had also been shot.

She could hear the guys coming and gave the whistle she wore around her neck a small puff, creating just enough sound to allow them to locate her. She didn't want to move the man without help. He didn't appear to be in imminent danger from his surroundings. And his injuries were extensive enough she could complicate them if she tried to move him into the sunlight. She leaned closer, trying to get a better look at him.

The breeze momentarily changed direction. The hair on the back of her neck stood up, and her heart raced. She could smell wet fur.

"Marie!" Bailey yelled. "Don't move!"

She froze, scanning as much of the area as she could without turning her head. Her rifle was on the ground. Her knife was on her belt.

From somewhere to her left she felt, more than saw, movement. Hulbert was now in front of her. He was on one knee, his rifle raised. One second after that her ears rang from a loud boom.

A big catlike thing lay on the ground less than two yards from her. Its head was the size of a bear. The body was stockier than that of any cat species she'd ever seen, but it was definitely some kind of cat. Its canines were enormous.

"Shit." She stood up and looked at the giant "kitty" Hulbert had taken down with one shot. A head shot, right in the left eye. The kind of shot that only an expert marksman could pull off—and probably the only kind of shot that could have saved her.

"Thanks." She blushed and picked up her gun. That was really stupid. She knew better than that. Her father and her brothers had taught her the rules long before the prison preached them to her. You had to know what was going on around you. *Know your environment.* Don't get sidetracked. *Be aware and be alert.*

"I appreciate the help." She gave Hulbert an apologetic grin and then nodded toward the cave's interior. "I guess I was messing with its dinner." She pointed toward the man lying just inside the opening to the small cave.

CHAPTER
14

Jenny Radford sat looking at the charts in front of her. It had been another long day. She should be in bed, but knew she wouldn't sleep if she didn't take care of the charting. Insomnia plagued her anytime she tried to leave something until the following day. She would just lie on the small cot twisting and squirming until she finally got up and did it. And today had been one of those days that left a dozen loose ends waiting to be tied up after everyone else had gone to their rooms for the night.

The routine charting had been done, and now she was doing a journal entry. The journal was something she'd started more or less for herself. It was a recording of what happened in the infirmary, and everywhere else inside the prison. She was keeping track of the steps they were taking in an attempt to solve all their problems. It made it easier for her to stay upbeat if she could see the progress being made. Besides, if it were in writing, even the small successes wouldn't be overlooked. And so far, they were all small successes.

No, not all. They now had water. That was a biggie. It was the biggest biggie, in fact.

The infirmary was in the process of being cleaned. Really cleaned. Andy had sent over three prisoners to help out. It had been wonderful. The prisoners cleaned while Casey Fisher, the infirmary's permanent guard, watched. They worked about four hours. It wasn't a lot of time, but it had helped. They had managed to get the actual work areas cleaned up and all the laundry aired out. Tomorrow she was going to have them start washing linens. They would have to do it by hand, but at least it would get done. Once the laundry was caught up, they could start on the deep cleaning.

She sighed and stretched, trying to focus on the page in front of her. Each day's med pass took less and less time as the pills, elixirs, patches and powders ran out. In less than thirty days, there would be no med pass of any kind. That's when the workload would double.

Andy had stayed out of the infirmary's business, for which she was grateful. Too many chiefs slowed things down. She smiled. Captain Andy Blacklock, with his newly sprouted beard and eyes that missed nothing, was the only bright spot in her life right now. Without him, the place would be unbearable. Their relationship, whatever it was, had been growing one day at a time. Short talks, short walks, and now, tonight, a short kiss. Well, it was more like a peck on the forehead, but it was a step. Even though she was alone, she smiled.

She knew he was divorced. And that he had dated a little afterward, but nothing serious. And that was a good thing. If he was grieving for anyone left behind, it wasn't someone part of his day-to-day life.

There was a lot of he-ing and she-ing going on right now between the guards. And rumor had it, between a few of the guards and the prisoners. She had been told that romantic liaisons between staff and prisoners happened, but it was rare. Sometimes it was a homosexual relationship; sometimes it was heterosexual. Regardless, it was never tolerated and it always ended with the CO or nurse being dismissed. That wouldn't happen this time. No one could get fired, but they could get transferred from one building or department to another.

Jenny knew the reasoning behind those types of decisions, and approved of them. What she disapproved of was how nothing stayed confidential. How everyone knew everyone's business. And how nasty and crude the rumor mill could get.

The need for affection was a normal reaction to stress. When a person came under the guns, he or she would reach out for someone who could make them feel safe.

Does he make me feel safe? Her smile faded a little. No, nothing could do that, under these circumstances. But Andy did make her feel warm, and cared for. And she needed that feeling. But she didn't know if she needed the other feeling. The one of her caring for him. And she was pretty sure that was what was happening. A little more each day, she was falling in love with Andy Blacklock and that scared her.

But it didn't scare her enough to push him away, did it? The smile returned and she picked up her pen. It was time to get back to work.

Twenty minutes later she was reaching for the switch that would turn out the light when she heard a pounding on the glass doors separating the infirmary from the prison-yard. It was midnight. The pounding continued as she made her way down the hall to the entry area. Rod Hulbert, Marie Keehn, and Jerry Bailey were on the other side of the glass.

She unlocked the double set of doors. The three of them carried in a man she didn't recognize. He had been hurt. And by the amount of blood on his clothes and the way his head drooped to the left, he was in bad shape.

"You have a patient," Hulbert said.

She gently turned the man's head so she could see his face. She knew before letting them in, he wasn't the fourth member of the hunting team. She had watched the team leave and knew Brian Carmichael was a black man with a bald head, a round, friendly face, and big brown eyes.

"Where's Carmichael?" she asked. "And who is he? Prisoner or staff?"

"Brian's helping the kitchen staff take care of the meat we brought in. This guy's not either one, prisoner or staff."

Jenny stared at Hulbert for a moment. She then motioned them toward the examining room. The questions would have to wait.

Jenny filled a metal bowl with water and grabbed a washrag and towel. She had to get the grime off his face. She needed to see how extensive his injuries were, and that was the only way she could see. The man flinched, but didn't cry out.

"He's been beaten and shot," Marie said. "I don't think the bullet caught anything vital, but he's hurt pretty bad."

Jenny nodded and set to work—a quick rinsing of

his face and neck, a head-to-toe assessment, an I.V., oxygen—then she had the guards help her remove his outer clothing. Clothes had become too precious to waste by cutting them away. She then used blankets and straps to immobilize him.

He had been shot once in the side. The wound was bad, but wouldn't kill him, unless it was already infected. In the freakish way that sometimes happened with gunshot wounds, the bullet had traveled around the flesh instead of passing through the body. It had come to lodge not far under the surface of the skin near his kidney, where it was easy to remove. There was a lot of tissue damage, but she didn't think any critical organs had been touched.

His nose was broken. His left eye was swollen shut, but the eyeball itself looked to be okay. She would know more once the swelling went down. He was bruised all over, even in the groin area. Some of the bruises were raised and hard. Most of them held a little heat. Neither of those were good signs.

"Are you sure he isn't a prisoner?" she asked. But, deep down, she already knew the answer. Beneath the injuries, the man's physical appearance wasn't any different from that of any number of prisoners—or guards, for that matter. But he was wearing a necklace that no prisoner would have been allowed to keep in his possession. It was a wide, flat band with intricate carvings that wrapped around his neck much like a snake would wrap itself around the arm of its handler. An expensive-looking piece that appeared to be hand-tooled. He also wore the strangest silver earrings she had ever seen. They were attached at the top of his ears, rather than the lobes.

Marie shook her head. "We're sure. And he's not a CO, either. He doesn't belong to us."

Jenny stopped; her scalpel shook, then steadied. "Not one of ours," she whispered, and went back to work.

For the next twenty minutes the room was silent except for an occasional moan from the man on the examination table.

Jenny hoped he would live. His injuries were extensive: broken ribs, probable concussion, multiple contusions and bruising with a lot of soft tissue damage. He was going to have to be luckier than he had been or he would be gone by morning.

Rod Hulbert moved so he could get a look at the spent bullet Jenny dropped into a small metal pan that sat on the portable tray she used to hold her equipment. "We found him about an eight-hour hike from here. He was by himself curled up inside a small cave. The place was filled with primitive tools and weapons, and looked like quite a few people lived in it, but he was the only one around. And he doesn't speak English. All he would say was something that sounded like Ka-nun-da-cla-ga."

Jenny gave a sigh. No English. The word—or words—didn't sound like anything she had dealt with.

"We thought at first he was saying who did this to him, but we're not so sure now. He looks half starved, and like he had been through quite a bit even before he was beaten and shot. He might be part Indian, but we're not even sure of that."

"Could he be from town?" Jenny asked.

"I don't think so. It's a small community, and someone who dressed this outlandishly would be someone you'd notice, and remember. He could be a drifter, or maybe one of the tourists. We get a lot of people through here. They want to walk part of the Trail of Tears. And a lot of them are Indian. Or at least part Indian."

Marie held up one of the man's shoes. "This is the weirdest looking footwear I've ever seen. There's no heel and no instep." She dropped the shoe to the floor and picked up the man's pants. "His pants button; they don't zip. And the material is thick and the weaving looks a little uneven. Look at the seams. These were hand sewn."

Jenny had noticed the buttons when she stripped the man. They were *real* buttons made out of shells, not plastic. She had also noticed the man wore no underwear. That wasn't unheard of. Even in this day and age, some men would go without them. But the buttons, that was a new one for her.

She took off the hospital gown she was using to protect her clothes and tossed the latex gloves into the sink. They would be washed, and then reused. The rules were simple, one pair of gloves per patient. Later, when the gloves ran out, they would have to reexamine how things were done. She didn't look at the patient; instead, she stared at the three members of the staff who had brought him in. "I guess we've done about all we can. Now we just have to wait and see if the antibiotics can turn the corner for him."

Hulbert was shaking his head slowly. He used a pencil to scoot the bullet around and around in the small metal container. "This damn thing is weirder than his pants or his shoes. A lot weirder. Huge caliber, for one thing. How did a bullet this big stay in his body? It should have blown right through him, unless . . ." He shrugged. "Low velocity, I guess."

He sat the pan down and pulled his small camera phone from his shirt pocket. "But that's nothing compared to what else we've seen."

Andy groaned, then glanced at the clock. He hadn't been asleep but two hours. "Yeah, give me a second. I'll be there!" he shouted at whoever was pounding on his door.

He stumbled around the room trying to get dressed in the dim light filtering through the window. He slept with the curtains opened. The sun was his back-up alarm. But it wasn't up yet. All he had for light was the soft glow of the moon and a few thousand stars. "Who is it?"

"Jenny."

He opened the door. The two vertical worry lines situated between his eyebrows had deepened. "What's wrong?"

"I'm sorry," Jenny said. She glanced down the empty hall toward the stairs that led to the prison's entry area. Andy slept in what had been the human resource office. "You have to come see this," she whispered. "You really do have to see this now."

CHAPTER 15

"Okay, Rod." Andy slipped Hulbert's camera phone into his pocket. He would have Edelman take a look at the pictures and then maybe they'd know what they were up against. "We'll deal with Jurassic Park later. For now, let's see if we can figure out what happened to our mystery man. His injuries weren't caused by dinosaurs. Give it to me from the beginning. Don't leave anything out."

"We weren't out more than six hours and had taken down two large animals." Rod looked at Jenny and smiled. "Marie got both of them. One buffalo of some sort, and something that's probably a giant sloth. Marie's amazing. The cooks are going to cuss her trying to figure out how to cook the stuff, but she's the best I've ever been out with. She has a real gift. That woman . . ." He shook his head, never losing his grin.

Andy smiled absently. "Good. Then what happened?"

"We were on our way back and ran across evidence of a battle, or an animal attack. We went to check it out.

While we were gone, Marie found him." He motioned to the wounded man. "He was curled up inside a cave, moaning. Anyway, there he was, too weak to even stand. We got back just in time to stop an attack from some animal related to the cat family. I didn't get any pictures of it before we boned it out. We probably shouldn't have taken the hour a job like that takes, but I couldn't let any of the meat go to waste. Too many of our people could wind up going hungry if we don't have the right priorities.

"Anyway, after we took care of the cat, we scoured the area looking for others, but didn't find anyone. We back-tracked about a mile, following what we believe was this guy's trail. There were plenty of footprints—not his—but definitely human. After wasting what was left of daylight, we bedded down for the night, and then started home first thing this morning. With all the meat we were packing, and with him in such bad shape, the trip back took all day and part of the night.

"You get a short distance from the prison and the world changes, Andy. It is nothing like home. And the plants and animals are nothing like home, although you do occasionally spot something familiar. We've got problems. And I don't mean the routine problems of finding enough to eat and ways to keep warm. That world out there is our biggest problem, and we had better get to know it pretty damn fast. We'll either know it, or it'll bite us in the ass. It'll kill us all."

"Can you find the spot you found him in?" Andy asked.

Hulbert nodded. "I can also show you where those creatures in the pictures were."

"Is there anything else you can tell me?"

Hulbert shrugged. "I don't know. There's probably too much for now. Once you get away from the prison, the forest floor in a lot of places is as clear and clean as a mall floor. When there is ground cover, it's usually ferns of one kind or another. There are animals out there with infants the size of an elephant. There are insects the size of toy airplanes. And man, don't even go near the water. I've seen some birds, a lot of reptiles, and a fair number of mammals. But the plants and animals don't seem to mesh. It's like everything has been tossed into a pot together, and the heat's been turned up. It's just sitting there. Simmering. Waiting."

"Thanks." Andy Blacklock picked up the two-way sitting on the nurse's desk. It was about two in the morning, but this couldn't wait. Jeff Edelman had to be wakened and Lieutenant Joe Schuler needed to be relieved from duty so he could attend the meeting that was going to take place within the next hour. Andy silently cursed their bad luck. Brian Carmichael had been sent to the kitchen as soon as they arrived at the prison. He had shown up with three exotic animals and without a gag order. That meant the rumor mill would be in full swing by sunup. If they wanted to prevent a panic they needed to know what they were facing. They needed to know what Spielberg's monsters were, and they needed to know what and who their houseguest was. As for the other department heads, they would be told about another meeting, one that would take place about nine, right after breakfast.

Andy stood next to the cot and watched the man struggling to get loose from the straps that held him to the table. Things were *completely* screwed up now. He had a prison full of felons he was trying to protect from themselves and from whatever it was outside the walls. He had around two hundred overworked, exhausted COs looking to him for answers. And now he had what? A war going on outside?

Jenny was afraid the patient would try to pull the I.V. out of his arm so they had tied him down. The man's eyes were glazed and feverish. His dark skin managed to look pale and flushed even to Andy's untrained eye. The captain stared at the man's face. Here was someone who could tell them what was happening outside the walls. And the someone was in bad shape and apparently couldn't speak one word of English.

"Is he going to make it?" the captain asked Jenny.

"I don't know."

"Ka-nun-da-cla-ga. Ka-nun-da-cla-ga," the man moaned. His voice was raspy and soft. Almost inaudible.

"Man, I wish I knew what he was saying."

Jenny nodded. "When I moved into my apartment in town, the landlady made a point of telling me the area receives visitors from all over the world. If he is one of the tourists he could be talking just about any language. Whatever it is, it's not Spanish. I'm almost fluent in Portuguese and that's close enough that I'd recognize Spanish if I heard it."

Andy shook his head. "No, you're right. I took four years of Spanish in high school. That's one I would recognize, even if I didn't understand the exact words."

Jenny shrugged. "Well, what he's saying doesn't sound Arabic or Asian, either. That I would know. And I would bet he's not American."

He looked at the man on the cot. "Why are you so sure he isn't American?"

The nurse waved a hand at her patient. "He's somewhere around fifty, maybe older. And he was never given a smallpox vaccine. I checked his hips, arms, and legs. Anyone that old, if they had been born in this country, would have been given the vaccination, unless their religion forbade it. Also, he's had no dental work done. And believe me, he needs it. Those teeth have got to cause a lot of pain now and then. From that and the fact he doesn't seem to speak English, I'd guess he was a new immigrant. And he had to come from a country that didn't have a comprehensive health program. He might even be an illegal alien." She raised a hand to stop Andy's complaints. "I know; that's not an accusation you want to make too readily, but look at him. He's starving. He's been beaten. But he's not an addict. The damage to his nose is from the beating; the interior is not drug damaged. He has no track marks. His liver isn't distended, and neither are his intestines."

"How does being beaten and starved make you an illegal alien?"

"Andy, if someone starved you, beat you within an inch of your life, shot you, then left you for dead, you would go to the hospital. And you would press charges. You wouldn't be hiding in a hole in the ground. The only people who don't go to the police are those who can't. And since most dealers are users, he probably had other reasons to steer clear of the authorities."

Andy looked at the man on the cot. "I guess you're right. I would call the cops. But I don't think this guy had a chance. And I don't think it had anything to do with being afraid of the badge. My guess is, this happened after the Quiver." He handed Hulbert the pan with the spent bullet. "He was shot with a matchlock, you said."

Hulbert nodded. "That's what I figure. I can't think of any other explanation for a bullet that big and that slow-moving. I'd bet he's Indian. Probably pretty close to full blood."

Andy stared at Hulbert. "You're talking Native American, not an India Indian." He was wide-awake now.

"Yeah, I am. And I'm thinking he's *extremely* authentic. And I have a hunch he has enemies just as authentic as he is."

The captain stared at Hulbert, then at the man strapped to the examination table. "We can't jump to any conclusions. That bullet could have come from a replica. Or maybe an antique."

Hulbert was shaking his head. "I thought of that. But not too many reenactors play around with matchlocks. They're usually interested in later historical periods. Then you have the guy's clothes and all the things Jenny mentioned."

Andy pulled the clothes from the biohazard container, careful not to touch the blood. He turned them over and over in his hands, checking the seams and the buttons. "If these are part of a reenactment costume, they cost the guy a pretty penny. They're the most authentic looking things I've ever seen."

"He doesn't look rich enough to be into that type of fun," Jenny said. "He looks like one of the homeless I used to care for when I worked on the coast."

Marie entered the room, carrying a tray of sandwiches.

"And if that's not a reenactment costume, and if he wasn't shot with a replica, where is the guy who did it?" Marie shrugged and then answered her own question. "We don't know."

Now it was Jenny's turn to look surprised. "Oh." She looked at the man on the table and then at Andy. "It doesn't matter if that stuff is real or fake. Does it? We have people out there. Real people. And they're armed and shooting."

Hulbert shrugged. "Like I said, we've got problems. And if the animals are mixed up, jumbled up, the people are likely to be, too."

Marie Keehn moved so she was standing next to Rod Hulbert. Her voice trembled slightly, "More than two thousand prisoners to feed and water, multiton dinosaurs to avoid, and to top it off, out of sync people using other out of sync people for punching bags and target practice. And we don't know why."

Jenny hissed softly. The captain and the lieutenant both nodded, their faces grim.

Jeff Edelman stared at the pictures on the camera phone for a while, and then shut the phone off. "I want the best artist in the prison to copy this onto paper. The same thing for the jewelry our visitor is wearing." He looked at Hulbert. "The camera phone is a great way to record what's going on in the field, at least until the batteries wear out."

"You're right," said Joe Schuler. "We'll go through all the cars on the lot and through the lockers. We'll gather up all the picture phones and have them placed in the armory. That way when we send people out for whatever reason, they can take one of the cameras with them. When they get back we can have the pictures transcribed to paper. If Hulbert had one in his car when the Quiver hit, I'm betting we'll get a couple dozen of the things."

Hulbert nodded. "Andy, we might want to do a technology check. See who has what, and if it could be useful put it under lock and key."

"No, we *don't* want to do that," Andy said. "We don't want to confiscate anything. That includes the picture phones. Ask what's in everyone's lockers and lunch buckets. Ask if people will donate their stuff, or loan it. But I don't want anything commandeered."

"Nothing?" Edelman asked.

"Nothing. Now, what can you tell me about Spielberg's monsters?"

Edelman frowned. "The nickname Jerry Bailey gave these animals is more appropriate than you realize. The two large birdlike creatures doing the attacking are called Utahraptors. They are the jumbo-sized relatives of the velociraptor. While the velociraptor weighs around fifty pounds, their larger cousins will tip the scales at eight hundred to a thousand pounds. An amateur, Bob Gaston, found the first of this species in 1992. This was the same year work was being done on Spielberg's film, *Jurassic Park*. Spielberg hadn't liked the idea of his meanest creature being such a lightweight, so he wanted to cheat and make them larger. The technicians working on the film, of course, did it Spielberg's way. Bigger was better. Anyway, with the discovery of the Utahraptor, you would think the raptors in the movie would get a name change. It didn't happen. They left the name of the beasts velociraptor, but gave them the size of their Utahraptor cousins."

Hulbert shrugged. "Hollywood is not here. The animal killed by those things was not happy and neither were we. That was the scariest thing I ever saw in my life."

"I bet." Jeff suppressed a yawn and then sighed. "Sorry, three hours a night, every night, it's not enough sleep for anyone." He yawned again, but this time didn't try to fight it. "You have to look at the whole picture. That stegosaurus that used the prison wall for a scratching post a couple of nights back was from the Jurassic period. The Utahraptors on that picture phone were from one hundred and twenty million years back. The animal the raptors ate, the iguanodon, was from the early Cretaceous period, which was around one hundred and forty-five million years before the modern era. The T-rex in Spielberg's movie was from the late Cretaceous period, around seventy million years ago."

"I thought you said the tyrannosaurus was from the Jurassic period," Jenny said.

"No, the book and movie was called *Jurassic Park* because it sounded good. Most of the animals it depicted were actually from the Cretaceous period, the same timeframe we seem to be dealing with. Much of the plant life a few miles out from the prison is also from that time period, but not all of it. Too much of it is unfamiliar to me, and a lot of what I recognize, I can't name. I can't remember what it's called."

"I don't care about the name," Joe said. "I just want to know what is happening. Are we going to be dealing with the animals from that movie? Velociraptors and Tyrannosaurus Rex?"

"Well, *Jurassic Park* depicted a theme park populated with dinosaurs built from found DNA left over from the Jurassic and Cretaceous periods. The plants and animals inside the park were basically from the same period, but that doesn't mean they coexisted. Very few species last eighty million years, which is the length of time the Cretaceous period lasted. Or even eight million years, for that matter. The only time we know for sure two species coexisted, is when we find them together. All else is guesses. Good guesses based on a lot of facts, but they are still guesses."

Jeff walked over to the dry erase board and began sketching a time line. "Utahraptor was from approximately one hundred and twenty million years ago. They lasted about a million years, it's estimated. The iguanodon was from about one hundred and forty million years ago. No one knows how long they were around. But if you looked at the picture closely enough, you'd see a couple of other creatures in the background. There was what I think is an ornithocheirus flying above the trees and near the water's edge there was something that looked like a crocodile."

"Crocodiles lived one hundred and twenty million years ago?" Jenny was surprised.

"Yes, they did. They're one of only a handful of creatures with that type of longevity. I didn't see one in the picture, but turtles are another group that has managed to live that long without a lot of changes."

"What's an ornithocheirus?" Hulbert asked.

"That was the creature flying above the trees." He looked at their faces and sighed. "It's a type of pterosaur. Also called pterodactyls."

"So, we're one hundred and twenty million years in the past?" Andy asked.

"That would be my guess." His grin had very little humor in it. "Give or take maybe fifty million years, you understand."

"Are you telling us we're going to have to deal with brontosauruses and tyrannosauruses?" Joe Schuler asked.

Jeff shrugged. "Brontosauruses, as such, no. The brontosaurus was a combination mistake and scam. The man who found it, Othniel Charles Marsh, popped a head of a camarasaurus onto the body of an adult apatosaurus and called it a brontosaurus. The men who proved this, James McIntosh from Wesleyan University and David Berman from the Carnegie Museum, figured the wrong head was done on purpose. But they also figured Marsh didn't know that the body was the adult version of a dinosaur Marsh found earlier. They believed Marsh assumed both skeletons were adults and were of different species. I guess we'll never know for sure. The mistake and scam took place in 1879, and wasn't discovered until 1970."

"Jeff, we don't care what the creature is called, or what type of head it has. We just want to know what we have to deal with," Andy said.

"Yeah. But it's important that you know that what you've been taught, or saw on television, may not be what you get." Edelman frowned, looking worried. "We're used to animals of a certain size, with a certain speed and strength. Predictable abilities. Predictable limitations. The animal we're talking about, whatever you call it, is unpredictable because we've never dealt with it. It wasn't a meat-eater, but who knows how placid or belligerent it was? And if it was—is—belligerent, then you're dealing with a creature the length of a northern blue whale. It doesn't weigh as much. It only weighs thirty tons, where the blue whale weighs about a hundred. But that doesn't make it any less dangerous, if it develops a peeve at us.

"As for a tyrannosaurus, it could be here. I just don't know how likely it is. According to our *limited* fossil records, they didn't show up until the end of the Cretaceous period. They could have coexisted with these other plants and animals, or they could have been separated by about sixty million years."

He grinned again, every bit as humorlessly. "I guess the one bright spot is that we probably aren't near any seacoasts. The top marine predator nowadays is likely to be a mosasaur. That's a giant seagoing lizard that was probably the most dangerous animal that ever swam the seas."

"So, you're telling us Cretaceous Park just became real," Marie Keehn whispered.

No one else said anything.

Jenny had gone back to the infirmary, Marie was asleep in the dorm set up for off-duty COs, and Hulbert had taken Bailey and Carmichael to the armory. He wanted something a little more deadly the next trip out. Joe Schuler, Andy Blacklock, and Jeff Edelman were alone in the conference room.

"Okay, Jeff. Spill it. There was something you weren't saying earlier. Say it now."

Edelman laughed. "You know, you say that like you think I should learn to talk up, but we both know you would rather I gave you bad news in private, or as close to it as I can manage."

The captain smiled. "Maybe. What is it?"

"I've told you my theory; that somehow, we have been dragged back through time. Well, along the way, I think we picked up other times. So far, everything we've seen has been from the same geographical area, just different time frames."

Blacklock closed his eyes and leaned back in his chair. Edelman had explained his theory of time travel to him. And if Edelman was right, then Hulbert was going to be righter than the man could possibly guess. They were going to have problems.

If they had been dragged back in time to the Cretaceous period, and Edelman was right about others being dragged along, that meant any and all creatures that lived from then till the day the prison disappeared could be outside the walls waiting on them. Including people.

"Edelman."

Andy and Jeff turned to look at Joe Schuler. "Yes, Lieutenant?"

"If you're right, we're in even more trouble than that, aren't we? That stegosaurus outside the wall three days ago was from the Jurassic period. That was even earlier than the Utahraptor and the Cretaceous Period."

"Actually," Jeff Edelman said quietly, "I was holding back. I didn't want a panic."

"Holding back?" Captain Andy Blacklock asked.

"Yeah. There was another critter, and since no one asked, I didn't volunteer its origin. It was almost hidden in the trees. It was no more than ten feet long and wouldn't weigh more than fifty pounds. But it had a mouthful of teeth that could do some real damage. The thing might have been a Coelophysis. And if it was, we are looking at a meat-eater from the Triassic period. That means, if my theory on what is happening is correct, we have the possibility of running into any creature that roamed the Earth in the last two hundred and forty-five million years."

Blacklock glanced out the window, then at his watch. He had less than an hour to shower and eat breakfast. Then it would be time for his meeting with the department heads. He gave a low groan. This meeting was not going to be pleasant.

CHAPTER 16

Adrian Luff sat on the floor of his cell next to the bars, a mirror angled so he could see what was happening in the corridor. It wasn't much. The corridor was empty. The only things he could see were the mesh-covered light hanging from the ceiling and the gray metal door at the end of the hall. The door would be locked. He was the only prisoner inside the cell house. The others had been moved.

He listened to the silence and checked his watch once more. *He's late. The sonofabitch is always late.*

Adrian looked like a mild mannered accountant. Which is what he had been, in fact, before the cops dug up his basement and found the bodies encased in cement. His short, sandy hair, pale skin and pale blue eyes were combined with little open features that inspired trust. He was clean-shaven and soft spoken. Things had worked out fine, would have continued to work out fine, except he forgot his manners. One time. One slip. And the old bag he offended had focused her binoculars on his house day and night till she caught him. And turned him in.

For a long time, he hadn't understood what happened. It kept him awake at night. Tossing and turning. Trying to decide what had aroused her suspicions. Then one morning, listening to the prison wake up, he remembered his mother. She was one of those soft-spoken little women who wouldn't say shit if she had a mouth full of the crap. He was in fourth grade and she was at school *again*. He had spouted off to the teacher who had turned him in to the principal—and that's when they found the girlie magazine tucked into his binder. The magazine had been stolen, but no one noticed that. They didn't ask how a kid his age could come up with the thing. They glossed over the smut rag, shrugged it off as pubescent curiosity, and concentrated on his foul language. On his lack of manners.

Yes, he was young. But not too young to learn. And that was the last time his mother ever came to school in disgrace. After that, her son was a pleasure to have in class. *Such a nice boy. A hard worker. So polite and well mannered.*

Two years later, when the school was vandalized, no one looked at him. They tried to pin it on other boys. The loudmouth boys without manners.

And thinking of that day, remembering what he learned, he finally understood what went wrong. The neighbor hadn't gotten suspicious. She was just pissed off at him. That's why she'd spied on him, hoping she would find something she could tell the neighbors about, or better yet, the cops. She was simply *offended*. She didn't care about the old man and old woman buried under his basement. She didn't care about the social security checks direct deposited into an account he accessed each and every month. She was just out to get him.

The only thing that had kept him from getting the death penalty was his insistence they were dead by natural causes. He'd been their landlord and had just taken advantage of their deaths. He'd been careful, so the autopsies couldn't prove any different, and the lawyer had gotten him a plea bargain. He would pull a double dime train—two ten-year sentences served back to back.

That first year behind the bars had been the worst. The innocent looking face that helped him on the outside had almost gotten him killed behind bars. Almost. But not quite. A month after the *unfortunate incident*, just before he was discharged from the infirmary, he had been offered a place in the nursery. He had turned it down. Protective custody was worse than death. It was solitary confinement for the duration of a man's sentence. No. Twenty years of hiding in fear wasn't in him. So, he turned things around. A knifing here, a rumor there, a bribe slipped into an open hand, and when there was nothing else that could be used, blackmail. He learned the system and then worked it. Working other prisoners had been tough at first. But he caught on. The guards hadn't been so tough.

They wanted to believe in people. Oh, some of them were hard-asses, pricks. But that was okay. They were predictable. And that's all you really needed. You just had to know how they would react in any given situation.

You had to know who could be bought and for what price. Sex, drugs, money, power—or maybe it was something on the other side of the coin—the feeling of being useful, of being needed. A savior to some poor man's damned and tormented soul.

He could feel himself calming and concentrated on his breathing. Panic is what landed him in prison. He couldn't afford to do it again. When old Mrs. Haywood asked him what he was going to build with all the cement he bought, he should have been polite. He should have told her it was for a patio. Or a sidewalk. Not, "It's none of your fucking business!"

But he had learned. A man with something to hide can't drink. And that was the second piece to the puzzle. The reason he forgot his manners. A half-pint of Jim Beam.

Now he smiled and waited for the door to open. He waited for the man dressed in a light blue shirt, dark blue pants, and shiny black shoes to step into the corridor. He thought about the guards and what he would do and how he would handle things if he had their job. If he were a guard he would have no pity. No grudges. No bad habits.

Then he thought about the kitty-kitties, the women guards. He liked the sound of that. *Women guards*. He didn't use the term female, not even when talking to himself. And he never called them bitches unless he was talking about them to another prisoner. He wondered what it would be like, being a woman and walking these halls. He knew what it would be like if he was a guard at the women's prison. Those little connets would love him. He gave a soft chuckle, then adjusted his mirror.

"Glad you could make it," Adrian said. "I was getting nervous, afraid something went wrong." He kept his voice light. None of the irritation showed. None of the anger or impatience.

"Yeah, we had another meeting and it ran over." The man stuck his arm through the bars and dropped a small package no bigger than a cigarette lighter into Luff's hand. "I don't know who's the bigger fool, Andy Blacklock or Joe Schuler. But I guess it doesn't matter as long as they stay that way."

Luff pulled himself to his feet using the bars. "What was the meeting about?"

"You haven't heard?"

Luff shook his head. He *had* heard, but he wanted it confirmed. It sounded just too good to be true. Blacklock was letting the prisoners out of their cells once a day. He was going to give them time to dump their chamber pots—fancy ass name for an over-sized tomato soup can—grab a shower, and get a little fresh air and exercise. The nonviolent inmates in good standing were even being allowed to volunteer for work details.

And all the bosses had agreed, no one was going to mess it up. The first man to slime one of the guards, died. Before the Quiver, it was fun to see a guard gunned down with piss or shit saved by a bored con. But not now. Getting out of the cell for a little while was too damn important. Everyone knew it. Those with brains knew they had better watch those without them.

He shook his head again. "You know how it is around here. I've heard a few bits and pieces, but didn't believe none of it. It was way too stupid a move, even for them."

Terry Collins leaned in close even though there was no one to hear what he had to say. "Well, you better believe it. Believe every word. And smile. Smile nice and big. Show your teeth, baby, because we're about to bite 'em in the ass!"

Luff smiled. "When?"

"Soon. If our boys do their job right, we're about to change the way this place is run."

"When?" Luff was having a hard time controlling the anger Collins always stirred up in him. "When do we move? I have to know so I can make sure my people are in place."

"Your people?"

Luff hesitated, trying to decide how to respond. Collins was one of the crazies. Not off enough to be spotted, unless you knew the type really well. Collins was a sadist. A Bible thumping whacko who used scripture to justify whatever it was he was doing or not doing.

The man was nuts. But he was also cunning. An operator. Collins loved twisting the knife on someone weak, but he loved sparring with the strong even more.

So Adrian shrugged. "My people. If you want them, you have to take them."

Collins laughed. "So serious today, baby. *So serious*. You should be happy. It's not everyday a man gets to be a part of history in the making."

"When do we move?"

"Soon, I told you. I have to see how many guards are going to be on and where. There's a lot of planning with something like this. When I get it figured out, I'll let you know. Then you and our boys can get ready."

"What happened at the meeting?" Adrian allowed a little of the agitation to show. Not enough to send the man off in a huff, but enough to get a response.

"Blacklock and Schuler just saved us a hell of a lot of trouble. It's as though they know what is coming down, and are going out of their way to help us out."

"How?" Adrian Luff hated begging for answers. He hated trying to sort through Collins' bullshit to come up with what was happening.

Terry Collins lost his grin for the first time since entering the corridor. "Soon, this empty wing will be full of prisoners. The list I gave Hulbert has been approved. So the men you told me you wanted are in the process of packing up their old cells and getting ready to be marched across the yard to their new home." He looked at his watch. "They should start arriving in about fifteen minutes. Andy Blacklock's own orders, the stupid bastard. And once the move is completed, the sign up sheets for work crews will be passed out. And we're not just talking about the infirmary. The lists are for the whole ball of wax, even the machine shop."

Luff nodded. His sources were dead on the money. That meant they were probably right about the other bits and pieces of gossip flying through the pipeline. "I hear we got company last night."

Collins frowned. "Yeah. They found some shot up piece of shit out in the woods. The fucker can't even talk English."

"Too bad. If he could talk, we might find out where he came from." Luff didn't give a rat's ass about where the fish came from. He came from somewhere. And he had been shot. That meant there were others out there. And for right now, that's all he needed to know. Other people meant other opportunities.

That night, Adrian Luff lay in the dark, listening to the sounds of three hundred men breathing, snoring, coughing, farting, and spitting. Collins still hadn't given him a day or a time. And no details on how the coup was going to take place. Nothing except, "Be ready. I'll unlock the gates. We'll use the guards' own guns to take over the place." Nothing but bull and shit.

But he had filled the tier with the men Luff asked for. Twenty cells, three men to a cell, sixty men in total: his personal crew. Collins was a waterhead. He thought he was going to rule the roost once the lid came off. He thought they would forget he was a badge just because he was the one who opened the gates. But even fools had a use. And sometimes they could give you information that would come in handy.

And sometimes they gave you something to worry about.

"It's as though they know what is coming down, and are going out of their way to help us out."

Why would Collins say that? What would make him think it? Could it be true? Did they know? Were they setting them up? If they were, why?

He considered one possibility. Blacklock and his people wanted them all dead. They *wanted* them to revolt so they could just gun them down. That way they wouldn't have to feed the convicts.

He rolled over on his bunk and looked out between the bars. No. That wasn't the right answer. If they wanted them dead all they would have to do is quit feeding them. There was a war going on. That was obvious. Either the

Muslims, Arabs or Chinese had come up with some new weapon, and the prison had taken a hit. They had been blasted right out of middle-America and into wherever they were. Captain Andy Blacklock had no one to answer to. He could do anything he wanted to do, and no one would care. So why were they still alive? Why hadn't he ordered them shot?

Adrian rubbed his head and tried to think. He needed information. And he couldn't count on Collins to give it to him. Besides, he didn't want the bastard to know what he was thinking. Ducks like him loved to quack; it made them feel important. But they tended to spook easy. He needed someone else to supply him with gossip. Reliable gossip.

Mentally, he went over the list of inmates already on work detail. He figured the infirmary was the best bet for getting reliable information. That posed a problem, since he didn't have anyone working inside it.

There were four prisoners who worked the infirmary. Two were high-ranking rugheads. No way he would get anything from one of them. The third hung out in Boomer's corner. He wasn't the man's galboy; Boomer didn't lay the track with anyone. But he took care of his boys. He was retired—a lifer—so he didn't have anything to lose. Each time he went off, he'd do the hole and the thorazine shuffle for six months, then he'd be back in the general population looking for revenge. No. Adrian didn't want to mess with that. They didn't call Tim Bolgeo "the Boom" for nothing. The little bit of information he was after wasn't worth getting 10-10'd over. The last guy Boomer labeled a poacher got greenlighted. The contract hadn't taken forty-eight hours to be filled. The man was a crazy. But he was a crazy who paid well.

It would have to be the fourth one, the Indian.

He had run the guy's tags as soon as he showed. He had been transferred in just three days before the Quiver. His name was James Cook and he was an unknown. But the word was he was an amateur. This was his first trip and he was an independent, and that meant he hadn't been schooled. He could be used. He was also in the cell house, just one tier up from him and was scheduled to work the infirmary's afternoon shift.

But he'd have to be softened up first, and softened up good. Luff needed full cooperation and he didn't have time to screw around with the usual slow and easy methods.

Luff scribbled a quick note, stuck it in a tin hooked to a thin rope, and whipped it into the next cell. "Work this over to Butch. As soon as the screws open the gates for supper, I've got something I want him to do."

CHAPTER 〜〜17〜〜

"You're sure about this?" Margo asked, peering at the graphics display on Leo Dingley's laptop screen. "I mean . . . it seems . . ."

"Really weird?" Dingley chuckled. "As opposed to everything else about these . . ." He turned his head to half-glare at Richard Morgan-Ash, who was sitting next to Malcolm O'Connell on the couch in the living room of the large suite he'd rented at the hotel in Collinsville. "Whatever we're going to call these things, which we've never been able to decide because Mr. Fussbudget over there shoots down every proposal I make."

Morgan-Ash smiled thinly. "I have probably ruined my reputation as it is, associating with you heretics. I will be damned, however, if I will hammer the nails into my own professional coffin by presenting a paper entitled 'Some Observations on the Mystery Bombs from Outer Space.' Much less 'Some Observations on the Bizarre Bolides from Beyond.'"

"They're good names," insisted Leo. "'Myboos' and 'Bibobs' are right up there with quarks."

"'Myboos' will be turned into 'Mybobbs' within eight seconds of reaching the blogosphere," said Morgan-Ash. "I shudder to think what would happen to 'Bibobs.'"

"Will you two quite clowning around?" Margo said crossly, still peering at the graphics. "Dammit, this new data you brought down here with you just doesn't make *sense*. Why would there be a time dilation? We've never seen it before."

Malcolm O'Connell shook his head. "That doesn't mean anything, Margo. The data that exist on the Grantville event are sketchy, to say the least. None of the equipment that detected anything at the time was designed for the purpose, the way our stuff is now. And all the other events since Grantville have been tiny in comparison. The energy levels either weren't high enough to produce this phenomenon, or—more likely, in my opinion—the phenomenon existed but we simply weren't able to detect it. The fact that you can track a jumbo jet's trajectory from miles away doesn't mean you can track a sparrow's from the same distance."

He heaved himself up from the couch and came over. "And it's weirder than you think." He pointed to a sidebar in one corner of the screen. "See this? If I'm interpreting it correctly, it means the time bolide or whatever the hell we wind up calling it isn't simply speeding up—so to speak—relative to our own timeline. It's . . . I'm not sure what it's doing, exactly. Call it stuttering."

"What do you mean?" asked Nick Brisebois. He was sitting on the other couch in the room next to Timothy Harshbarger, his friend from the state police. Every time Margo looked at the two of them next to each other she had to struggle not to smile. Where the air transport specialist was stocky and on the short side, Harshbarger was at least six feet, four inches tall, and as lean as a rail. The effect was even more striking when they were standing next to each other. Mutt and Jeff, absent the facial hair and the antique costumes.

Neither man had said anything since Richard explained the gist of what The Project had been doing in Minnesota for the past few years. Brisebois seemed interested, at least. Harshbarger's expression had been completely neutral. Margo wondered if the policeman thought they were all half-nuts.

O'Connell looked over at him. "What I mean is that— if I'm interpreting this correctly, mind you—the bolide's timeline isn't speeding up steadily in relation to our own. It's stuttering. Stopping and starting. At various points, it seems to suddenly slow down and match our own. Or slow down even further. It's hard to know, of course. And there seems to be a wobble in the spacial dimension. If I'm right about that, what it means is that the area of impact as the bolide moves back in time isn't holding steady. It's moving around. Not much, but some. And it keeps getting bigger too. Well. I think."

Brisebois looked a little cross-eyed, as if he were trying to visualize the process. Margo had tried that herself and suspected she looked cross-eyed too, when she did.

"In other words," Nick said, "it's like a spike being driven back in time. But the penetration isn't steady. It stops or slows down at points. And the—tip of the spike, I'll call it—is shifting around. And spreading out."

"Hey, that's not bad!" said Malcolm. "What if we call them 'time spikes,' Dick? You can't possibly object to that."

"Oh, I can manage to object to almost anything. To start with, there doesn't seem to have been anything 'spiky-ish' about the Grantville event. That was more like a time scoop." He shook his head. "But forget that, for a moment. Nick's translation—yes, yes, it's a layman's attempt to put mathematical concepts into words, with all the usual imprecisions but it's still damn good—brought something into focus for me. Is there a *correlation* between these stutters, as you call them, and the shifting of the spacial locus?"

"Huh!" O'Connell frowned. "I dunno. Actually, I'm not sure exactly how you'd match the two." He peered at the screen. "I mean, the way these figures are generated . . ."

"Sure we can," said Leo, sounding excited. "Hold on a minute." For just about that period of time, he typed furiously at the keyboard. Not the laptop's own, which Dingley found a nuisance, but a full-sized keyboard he'd brought with him and had connected to one of the computer's USB ports.

He finished whatever he was doing and, quite dramatically, pressed the "Enter" key. A completely new graphic appeared on the screen.

"God damn. Will you look at *this*?" He lifted the laptop a few inches off the table and swiveled it so that everyone could see.

Brisebois laughed. "Oh, swell. Leo, that spiderweb or whatever it is may mean something to you, but it's Greek to me."

The reaction of the scientists in the room, however, was quite different. All of them immediately understood what was being displayed. And all of them—including Margo herself, she was pretty sure—practically had their eyes bulging out of their sockets.

"Jesus," she whispered. "It's a *perfect* correlation."

Morgan-Ash, naturally, interjected a cautionary note. "Nothing in nature is 'perfect,' Margo. Not to mention that this is simply a graphic depiction of some mathematical concepts which may or may not have any correlation to the real world."

O'Connell rolled his eyes. "Oh, great. Just the time and place to have another philosophical debate about whether mathematics inheres in nature or is simply hard-wired in the human brain and our way of interpreting data that has no inherent mathematical nature of its own. God, I swear. If the day ever comes that we master this stuff enough to create our own time machines, I vote that the first expedition goes back and shoots David Hume."

"You'd probably have to shoot Locke and Berkeley too," Brisebois said, smiling. "And just to be on the safe side, jog forward a bit and plug Immanuel Kant. I'm afraid that debate's pretty deeply rooted in the western intellectual tradition. In fact, it wouldn't surprise me at all if, in the end, you wound up putting out a contract on Plato and Aristotle."

Margo stared at him. It would never have occurred to her that a man whose institution of higher learning had been the Air Force Academy would be familiar with the history of philosophy.

He must have spotted her stare, because he shifted the

smile to her and shrugged modestly. "I read Will Durant's *History of Philosophy* when I was a teenager and got interested. I don't have the training to work my way through Whitehead and Russell's *Principia Mathematica*, but I've read most everything else. Even worked my way through Hegel's *Science of Logic* once. The Big Logic, too, not the condensation in his encyclopedia."

His friend Tim spoke, for the first time in over an hour. "Good thing for him he was just a lowly trash-hauler. They make allowances for such. If he'd been a fighter jock, he'd never have lived it down."

Again, Brisebois did that little modest shrug. "What can I say? I simply didn't have the wherewithal to be a fighter pilot. My reflexes might have been good enough, but I lacked the key temperamental ingredient."

"Which is?" Leo asked.

"You've got to be a complete asshole to make a good fighter jock. I'm just not that arrogant. Even my kids admit it."

A little chuckle went through the room. Margo joined in, although she wasn't moved so much by the humor as by a new peak of personal interest. An impulse made her ask: "What did you think of Schopenhauer?"

"You mean, besides being a misogynistic jerk?"

She decided that maintaining one's focus exclusively on professional matters was probably not what it was cracked up to be. She gave Nick a gleaming smile and said: "No, that'll do quite nicely."

Morgan-Ash cleared his throat. "To get back to where we were, I wasn't actually raising an abstract philosophical issue. I was simply pointing out that even Malcolm will admit that half the principles—if I may be allowed the term—of his invented mathematics—"

"Discovered mathematics," O'Connell interjected.

"—are just first approximations." Richard pointed to the display on the screen. "What *that* is, with all its crispness, is simply a display of logic that's at least partly guesswork. It's more like a drawing—or a cartoon—than a photograph."

O'Connell looked on the verge of exploding. Richard held up his hand in a somewhat placating gesture. "I'm not sneering, Malcolm. I'm simply cautioning against trying to draw too many exact conclusions."

Fortunately, Leo came into it—on Richard's side, where he normally tended to align with O'Connell. "Hey, look, Malcolm, he's right. Still and all"—here he shot Morgan-Ash a reproving look—"the fact remains that while Margo was over-shooting to call the correlation 'perfect,' it's awfully damn good. You're the statistician, Richard. You tell *me* what the probability is that a display like that would emerge from random correlations."

Morgan-Ash grinned. "Oh, there's none at all. Not worth talking about. I agree that we're looking at something real. I'd just be a lot happier if we could match the numbers against—dare I say it—some bloody *evidence*. You know, that filthiest of all filthy four-letter Anglo-Saxon words. 'Fact.'"

The state policeman shifted in his seat. "What sort of fact are you talking about?"

Morgan-Ash tugged his neatly trimmed beard. "Lord, I don't know. If we could just get our hands on whatever showed up in Grantville! One thing that seems clear about these time impact events is that, in their own way, they adhere to the principles of thermodynamics. Action, reaction. Nothing is free. If they shift something into the past, something gets shifted forward to the present. If we had enough data to find out, I'd be willing to bet we'd discover the mass involved was identical."

Harshbarger stared at him, for a moment. Then, suddenly, came to his feet. "All right. I've decided you guys are real. Give me a minute. Nick, I'll need a hand."

With no further ado, he left the suite, with Brisebois on his heels. They were back in less than three minutes, carrying something large and heavy into the suite. It was encased in a peculiar sort of wrapping that Margo realized must be one of the storied body-bags she'd heard of, and seen occasionally on television news footage.

"Clear the table, would you?"

Hastily, the scientists moved aside the remains of their lunch. Tim and Nick placed the body bag on the table, and Harshbarger slid open the long zipper.

"Okay. You tell me. Is this the kind of evidence you're looking for?"

After a long silence, Leo said: *"Holy shit."*

Richard's contribution was more sedate. "Unless there's a hitherto unreported species of large reptile in the central United States, I'd say the answer is yes. This is indeed the evidence we're looking for. And the odds of that being true—I speak here as a expert statistician, you understand—I estimate as being indistinguishable from zero. Seeing as how—"

He peered at the carcass on the table. "Did you weigh it?"

"Yup. Eighty-three pounds, four ounces. Measures six feet, three inches, from the snout to the tip of the tail."

"As I said. The chances that a reptile not much smaller than a Komodo Dragon has been wandering around loose along the Mississippi River without ever being noticed is indistinguishable from zero."

Malcolm—unusually, for him—played the devil's advocate. "We shouldn't jump to conclusions. Maybe it got mistaken for an alligator."

"Wouldn't matter," said Tim. The policeman pointed to the patch on his shoulder. "State Police, remember? There have never been any sightings of alligators in Illinois. This isn't Florida or Alabama. I can guarantee you that if anyone spotted what they thought was an alligator in these parts, we'd have heard about it."

He leaned over. "Besides, it doesn't look the least bit like an alligator, other than having a generally reptilian appearance. But I don't think it's even a reptile in the first place. My partner and I got a clear look at it before we shot it. This critter wasn't running on all fours, the way a lizard or alligator will. Hell, look at those forelimbs. Those aren't designed for weight-bearing. It was running on its two hind legs. Like a bird, except the body was level, with the heavy tail counterbalancing the head and chest. Which is to say—"

Margo finished the sentence for him. "Exactly the way paleontologists these days figure dinosaurs moved."

"Yup." Harshbarger poked the reddish skin with a long forefinger. "That's what I think this thing is. A real, no-fooling dinosaur. Got no idea what kind, though. It's not something I ever studied."

So far as Margo knew, none of the scientists in the room had any real knowledge of paleontology either. She certainly didn't.

"Where's your partner?" Nick asked.

Tim grinned. "Knowing Bruce Boyle, he's probably knocking down his fourth boilermaker at Jimmy's, telling himself he was hallucinating. It was all I could do to get him to agree not to turn this over to the siblings, like we're supposed to."

"Excuse me?" asked Morgan-Ash.

The grin stayed on policeman's face, but the humor in it vanished completely. "The siblings. Those clowns from FEMA. They've given orders—just as arrogantly as they do everything, speaking of assholes—that 'anything unusual' is to be turned over to them immediately and not to be discussed. Apparently, deep matters of national security are involved."

"Huh?" asked Leo. He frowned at the carcass. "I mean, sure, it's nasty-looking. But I really can't see where even a thousand of these things running loose would be more than a local problem, for a while. Hell, it's not even the size of a mountain lion, much less a bear."

Tim barked a little laugh. "Oh, you'll get the news tomorrow. It'll be all over the country's news channels. It seems—no, I'm not joking—that the disaster at Alexander wasn't any sort of natural catastrophe. It turns out it was a terrorist attack."

"Huh?" Leo repeated.

Obviously, Nick had already gotten the story from his friend. His own grin was sardonic. "Oh, sure. We knew Al Qaeda was crazy. Now we know it for sure. They strike at the Great Satan by blowing up thousands of our hardened criminals."

"Good God," said Morgan-Ash, his normal imperturbability shaken. "That's . . . that's . . . *preposterous.*"

"Yeah, it is." Tim's grin was finally replaced by the scowl it had so thinly covered. "I really, really hate being played for a damn fool. Even by people who are polite about it, which these shitheads certainly aren't." He poked the carcass again. "That's why I brought this thing here, after Nick told me about you guys. I just held my peace until I was sure you weren't fruitcakes."

Margo smiled. "Don't jump to conclusions. We're Ph.D.'s, don't forget. Probably a bigger concentration of fruitcakes in academia than anywhere else. Not to mention that we've spent most of the past few years living half a mile underground in an old iron mine. That's got to be borderline fruitcakery, at least."

The state police officer smiled back. "Yeah, I guess. But you're pikers in the fruitcake department compared to the of-fi-cial clowns who are telling me that Moslem terrorists blew up a maximum security prison." Again, he poked the carcass. "I wonder how they'd explain Nasty here? Probably claim it was a stem cell experiment gone bad."

He leaned back and shook his head. "No, I think I'll toss in with you folks. Nick and I spent quite a bit of time talking it over. So. Now what?"

The scientists stared at him. The tall, skinny policeman planted his hands on his hips.

"Look, folks, you might as well understand something right from the start. I guess for you this whole thing is just a matter of scientific curiosity. Well, that's fine. But for me—and there'll be more than just me—it's goddamit *personal*. These are small communities down here in southern Illinois. It ain't Chicago. I knew a lot of the people who worked at Alexander. One of the guards was my high school girlfriend. And the lieutenant in charge of afternoon shift, Joe Schuler, was my best friend. I've known him since we were both six years old."

He looked down at the carcass, glaring fiercely. "I want to know what happened to my best friend. I want to know what happened to my high school sweetheart. What *really* happened. Not some lying bullshit fed to me by federal agents covering up God knows what."

He shifted the glare to them. "Do you understand? I'm not interested in spending years under a mountain somewhere studying more data. You're scientists, I'm a cop. I think a crime's being committed and I want to goddam fucking well know the truth. And I don't much care what gets taken apart in the process."

Margo couldn't help it. She burst into giggles.

"What's so funny?" asked Harshbarger.

She shook her head, weakly. "Sorry, Tim. I wasn't laughing at you or your feelings. It's just . . ."

She shook her head again. "I think you've just ended a debate that we've been having amongst ourselves for almost eight years now. Call it the Eggheads vs. the Dudley Do-Rights."

She gave her companions a serene gaze. "I've always been one of the Dudley Do-Rights, myself. And I do believe we just won the debate."

Morgan-Ash smiled, and stroked his beard. "So am I. Oddly enough, since I'm normally the most conservative of this lot of wild-eyed radicals. And, yes, I think we just won the debate."

He gave Malcolm and Leo—who'd been charter members of the Egghead faction from the beginning—a gaze that was just as serene as Margo's. "Wouldn't you agree, gentlemen?"

O'Connell and Dingley were eyeing the state police officer. His hands were the size you'd expect from a man that tall. And they looked quite capable of taking many things apart, if he was in the mood. Which he so obviously was.

"Guess so," said Leo.

CHAPTER
18

"Hey, Injun!"

James Cook took a deep breath and kept walking.

"I'm talking to you, sister!"

The voice was coming from one level up. The line of sixty men he was in was making its way across the metal grating that porched the fourth floor of the five-tiered cell house. The metal stairs leading to the ground floor were packed. He was trapped. He looked around for a screw. There. At the door. A guard. If he could get close enough to be seen, if he got stuck, at least he wouldn't bleed to death before they found him. The line moving from the back of the cell house to the door slowed to a snail's pace.

He knew the score. He had just hoped it would be someplace else, someplace in the open. His uncle had explained it to him as soon as they knew he was going to be doing some serious time. "Boy, how you start is how you go, so be careful. You're looking at half a lifetime behind bars. So, as good lookin' as you are, you have no choice. If you don't want to be turned out and punked out, you're going to have to be one hell of a hog. You can't back down. You gotta beat the shit out of some big motherfucker. Hell, you might have to kill someone as soon as you get the chance. Whichever way you go, make sure the shit-heads know you got heart, that you done it. But try to do it in a way the turnkeys can't pin it on you. There's no sense upping the ante to a lifetime behind bars."

The old man had looked grim. "And never forget one thing, either. There's no men behind them bars. Just animals. Wolves and rabbits. And you'll be one or the other. So make up your mind as to which."

It hadn't taken James more than a couple of days in the fish tank to realize his uncle was wrong. There were quite a few men behind the bars, actually. They were just hiding it from the wolves because they didn't want to become rabbits.

He slowed his pace to match that of the line. Fear was the one thing he wouldn't show.

"Hey, squaw! What's your hurry?"

Cook resisted the urge to drop his hands into his pockets. The voice was closer, but not close enough for him to play his hand. There was still a chance the guy intended to take it to a blind; someplace the guards wouldn't be so likely to see.

He walked with the line, not crowding the man in front of him and forcing himself to keep his breaths steady.

Finally, they were through the door and onto the street. This was better, but not the best. He glanced around and spotted where he wanted the fight to take place. It was a small area of hard concrete and scattered gravel. It was the same area where he had picked up the small stones he now carried inside his pocket. The footing was good, too, which he'd need against a man a lot bigger than he was. He'd finally gotten a glimpse of the guy who was after him. He probably outweighed James by a good fifty pounds, and it didn't look as if much of it was fat.

He hunched his shoulders, jammed one hand into each pocket, and picked up his pace. He wanted the wolf to think he was scared, running.

It worked. The large man with full sleeves—snake tattoos running from shoulder to wrist on both arms— hooted and followed him toward the open area away from the guards. Cook sped up, forcing the man behind him to break into a trot. When he was sure the guy was closing in, he stopped and turned around. He could see other prisoners a dozen yards away. They weren't here to help with the beating; they were just sightseers along for the fun.

One on one, then. He had a chance.

The man coming toward him had a pillowcase in his hand. James knew it would be filled with batteries, scrap metal or something equivalent. That was okay. It wasn't a banger. He had a chance.

He pulled his hands from his pockets, slow and easy. He wanted one fight and one fight only. He wanted the rumors that followed this fight to tell he was bare-fisted. The small pebbles he had tucked into his right hand wouldn't be visible. There were about a dozen of them, none bigger than a BB.

He waited. He would let his assailant throw the first punch. That was for the audience. He knew the way he wanted to do his time. He wanted to be a man others felt safe around. A man who didn't look for a fight. But he would also be a man who wouldn't run. One who could inflict some damage when pushed.

The big man hesitated. He had expected the Indian to turn and run, but he hadn't. Instead, James brought his fists up in an exaggerated fighter's stance. The big man sneered and swung his pillowcase, aiming for the head.

James had counted on that. A man this much bigger than he was would assume that his weight and strength would be enough. And he wasn't likely to know that James had done a lot of amateur boxing.

He dodged the blow easily, then sent a left jab into the man's face, followed by another. Quick-quick. He had good speed and reflexes.

Most important of all, he'd boxed enough to know you had to control the adrenaline. *Watch.* Take that extra split second to see what the opponent was doing before you threw another punch. If you lost that control, the adrenaline took over and you just started swinging madly. Against a man this much bigger, that was hopeless.

His assailant was surprised, then furious. He howled something and drew back the pillowcase for another blow.

His face was wide open. James hurled the pebbles right at his eyes.

The man howled again and clutched his face. James kicked him in the groin. Not the full swinging kick he'd have used on a football. Just a quick snap-kick. Everything had to be quick. It was his only chance.

It wasn't the kind of blow that would collapse a man, but any kind of blow to the testicles hurt like hell. The guy's hand came away from his face and went to his groin.

Again, his face was open, but that wasn't James' target. The man had the sort of square heavy head that would just break knuckles if James tried a full punch.

He gave him two more left jabs. Quick, stinging blows; designed more to confuse the opponent than hurt him.

The man roared with fury and charged.

Now.

James met the charge with his first full punch. A right cross with everything he had and all his weight behind it. But his hand was open, the thumb and fingers forming a vee, and he wasn't aiming for the face. The throat below was completely exposed.

It was a blow that might have killed a smaller man. This one's neck muscles were just too thick for the impact to collapse the throat. But it took him down, it surely did. Down hard, and down final.

James looked down at his assailant for a moment, gauging whether he needed to start kicking him.

No. He was on his side, clutching his throat, gasping for breath. His eyes were bulging.

The fight was over. It hadn't lasted more than a few seconds. That would do more for James' reputation than any amount of pointless stomping. He just turned and walked away.

Carefully, keeping his face calm and expressionless, he headed toward the infirmary. The crowd parted, letting him walk through. Just as he reached the door to the infirmary he heard someone say, "Injun, you in deep shit now. That was the Butch. Luff's favorite boy."

James stopped and turned around, to see who was

talking. Making sure to turn easily—no spinning around, nothing that looked excited or nervous—and keep his face expressionless.

But whoever it had been was not inclined to speak up again.

Good enough. After a second or so, James went into the infirmary.

Later, as he scrubbed the counter with the foul smelling mixture he had been given by Barbara Ray, James wondered what the nasty stuff was. Back home, when he cleaned the equipment at the firehouse, they used a bleach solution. This was not chlorine or alcohol based. The familiar odor of antiseptics was not present anywhere within the infirmary. Barbara, the LPN on duty, had told him they were out of the regular cleaners. They were using stuff from the machine shop and hoping it would do the job without causing too much damage. According to her, they were in the process of producing a little alcohol. So, hopefully, they would have at least one of the old tried and true products within a few days.

The infirmary had changed since he first arrived. Its six beds were now reserved for COs and inmates who were critical. Now, inmates needing nonintensive medical care were housed upstairs in what used to be the psych ward. The psych patients had been returned to the general population or moved to X-row.

The beds situated inside the holding cell just outside the examining room were occupied by two female guards and an infant. The CO with the baby was Kathleen Hanrahan. The other bed was occupied by a young and very pretty black woman who looked to be in rough shape. She had to be Elaine Brown, the one who took it in the gut right after the shit hit the fan.

There was also one patient tied to a gurney inside the examining room he was cleaning. The guy didn't look like a guard or an inmate. And he looked like he'd been busted up pretty good.

After a few minutes, the man gave a small moan and mumbled something Cook couldn't quite make out, so he moved closer, his heart in his throat. It had been a long time since he had heard Cherokee. His great-grandmother was the last one he had heard speak it, and she died when he was fifteen. But even so, he was sure that was the language the man was using. Its familiar rhythm caused his chest to squeeze tight in an ache for home.

It took him a minute to translate what was being said. The man was in pain. He was also thirsty. Cook looked around and found a cup, then filled it from the water pitcher sitting on the medicine cabinet. The old man gulped the warm liquid down in three gulps, then gratefully patted his hand.

"How did you know what he wanted?" asked Jenny Radford, the nurse practitioner who ran medical. She was standing in the doorway. Captain Blacklock and Lieutenant Hulbert were behind her.

"He speaks Cherokee."

"He *is* an Indian, then. I thought he might be." Hulbert was nodding his head. "And you can understand him."

"A little."

Jenny's grin was almost contagious. "Great!"

James shook his head. "Lady, you don't understand. I

was a kid the last time I heard someone speak Cherokee. I haven't spoken it or heard it spoken in years."

"Try," said Captain Blacklock. "Try hard. I want to know who shot him."

Cook shrugged and looked at the man. "Who shot you?" he asked in English. He had no idea how to phrase the question in the old language.

The old man looked at him then tugged at the straps holding him in place. He spat out a string of words and Cook shook his head.

"Go slow. I can't catch what you're saying unless you slow it down."

The old man surprised him; he slowed down and repeated himself. He was now speaking so softly that James had to bend over and put his ear just a few inches away.

James still didn't understand. He shook his head. "Say it again."

The man repeated himself. Then, said it in English. Perfectly understandable, although the accent was odd.

James looked at Hulbert and Blacklock. He didn't think they'd heard anything understandable, that far away.

So, he shook his head. "I don't know what he said."

"Take a guess," Hulbert said.

"I can't."

Radford walked over and touched the old Cherokee's hand. "I was watching you, and I know you understood what he said. So, tell us."

James took a step back. *Damn! What a day!* He wasn't going to tell these people anything. They were stupid—too stupid to realize the old man understood everything being said. Stupid and nuts. And the old Indian was nuttier. He was claiming Spaniards shot him!

Lieutenant Hulbert smiled, but it didn't touch his eyes. "By the looks of you when you came in today, I would say you need a rest. I'll send you back to your cell. You haven't been here long. You haven't had much time to get to know everyone. Or the way things work. Maybe we could let you have the rest of the day off; let you visit a friend. Luff, or one of the other boys in the cell house might invite you over for tea."

The guards were no different from the cons. Everyone knew that. They would use you, then leave you to die. They were worse than wolves; they were vultures. Vultures that picked you down to the bones but kept their hands clean. You would be dead, but they could pretend their souls weren't sullied.

But James didn't let any of his anger show on his face. "You want something from me, I'll give it. But you have to give me something first. I want a roommate transfer. I want . . ."

He thought fast, picking through the information he'd gotten since he arrived. A lot of it was just scraps and rumor, of course.

What James needed right now—needed desperately— was protection. That meant protection from one of the bosses, not the guards. Unless they kept you in solitary, the guards had no way to keep a man safe, and James didn't want to spend the next twenty years in solitary. Even if he got out alive, he'd be a jibbering nutcase by then.

He decided his best bet was Boomer. He was the only

boss who didn't care what race you were, as long as you weren't full white. And he didn't care what got you behind bars as long as you hadn't done some kid. But even so, to be in his cell and not be one of his men, that could get you killed. It was a gamble, but it was his best chance.

"I want Boomer moved into my house, and no one knows why. And it happens today. Now. I don't go back to my cell until he's sitting on that bottom bunk. And you keep me here during the day, every day. You can let it out that I was an EMT in my former life."

"You were?" Jenny sounded pleased.

"I think he's lying." Hulbert shook his head. "And we don't bargain with the inmates."

"Believe what you want. I don't care. But if I tell you anything, especially what this guy just said, my life's worth nothing. We both know that. Rats don't make it. Besides, things are different now. You can strike deals. And if you had any idea as to what was happening behind those bars you would be stalking the walkways for anyone who'd ride your leg."

Captain Blacklock gave a small laugh. "Maybe. But I'm not sure I need to deal with you. The way I heard it, you're life's not worth much one way or the other. We know about the fight with Butch Wesson."

"You knew about it and didn't do a fucking thing to give a fish a hand." He gave the men in blue uniforms a cold stare. "It doesn't matter. When I'm sent back to my cell I'm done. That bastard has friends, and they'll be looking for revenge and to save a little face. So, why not send me back to a new roomie? You do that for me and I'll sing like a bird."

Blacklock returned the gaze calmly, for a few seconds. Then, shrugged. "Okay, you've got it. But you've got to have two roomies. We're tripling everyone up."

"Okay, then. The Boom and Adrian Luff."

Hulbert chuckled. "Well, I guess that'd be one way to solve your Luff problem."

James Cook shook his head. "I want to live. And if you haven't noticed, I'm not some lily-white-ass. I either get the Boom on my side, or I die."

Andy thought about it. Cook was right. The guards couldn't protect him. They hadn't even been able to protect the Martinez kid before the Quiver. Now, after it, no one was safe.

"Okay, kid. You're in with Boomer. And if your records say you once worked as an EMT, you can have a permanent work posting here in the clinic. But I'm not giving you an upper-level Aryan to put between you and the Boom. You'll have to work it out on your own. I'll pull Paul Howard out of your cell for a few days. Six days, counting today. Then he gets popped right back in. The man is white, but he's level headed and doesn't mix with trouble. He and the Boom won't become the best of buds, but they'll be able to coexist."

He then gave Cook a little headshake. "Just for the record, we didn't find out about the fight until it had already started. And by the time we got there, you'd ended it and were already gone. Believe it or not, I actually hope you live till tomorrow. But, just in case, what did this guy say?"

Cook shrugged. "Ask him yourself. He speaks English."

CHAPTER 19

Jeff Edelman shook his head. "History isn't my area. I don't know any more about it than anyone else does."

"We don't need a historian," Joe Schuler hissed between clinched teeth. "We need a scientist. We need someone capable of reasoning this shit out. We have an Indian who swears he's from the mid-eighteen hundreds and was shot by a Spaniard named de Soto, who we know was from the mid-fifteen hundreds. He further swears that he ran across a small village filled with primitive people who can only be the early Mounds people. That culture existed still earlier. They're the ones who built the mounds you see around this part of the country. And to top it all off, everyone is fighting a bunch of animals they've never seen before, but which have to be things that died back in the Crustaceous Period. And, God help me, I believe every word of it."

Jeff nodded, slow and easy. "Okay, but I don't think there is any figuring *this shit* out. I've already told you what I think. I think we've been dumped back in time. Along the way we picked up hitchhikers, or maybe they got here first. I don't know. But Joe, it doesn't matter. We just have to go with it. See what we're dealing with, and do whatever we have to do."

"It does matter." Joe scratched at his newly sprouted beard. "What happens if we do something to screw up the future? What if we do something that will let Adolph Hitler win World War II, or maybe prevent penicillin from being invented?"

"Or kill our own grandfather?" Andy Blacklock stood up and walked to the window. "I don't think that's a problem. I think what we're doing now is actually in the present. We're still moving forward, but in another place."

"Alternate universe?" Joe nodded. "Yeah, I've heard about them. On TV, and in books. It makes sense. In that other universe, or home place, the Cherokees are still traveling the Trail of Tears, de Soto is still butchering his way towards his own un-grieved demise, and the Mounds people are quietly disappearing from the face of the Earth. Yeah. That would be good. Real good."

"This is crazy!" Jenny exclaimed. "You're saying there are two of us now? Well, which one is the real one? Which one has the soul? The one back there or the one that's here?"

Andy shook his head. "I'm not saying that is the way it is. I'm saying an alternate universe makes the most sense."

Jeff Edelman snorted. "Jenny, don't get pissy. If a theory makes any sense at all, we have to at least consider it. And I think Andy and Joe might be right. I think history is continuing. And I don't think we have to walk on eggshells because I don't think we can have an impact on the history of the world we came from. We're on a new time-line. And this change might have left behind a half-dozen or more possible universes. One for each disruption in the original line."

From the window, Andy could see what had once been the parking lot and bluff. In the distance, he could see a volcano. Fortunately, it didn't seem to be active.

"Does it really matter?" he asked. He turned to look at the others. "I don't believe there are now two of us. One at home and one here. I think we're gone. That the people back home are as confused as we are. I also don't believe we can change what happens in our future. I don't think we're in our own timeline or that we're in our own universe. Not that what I think matters. Even if everything we do and say is happening in our own past, we still don't have to worry about doing something that changes man's future."

"Why?" Joe asked.

Andy motioned for them to come to the window. "Look to the east, right above the tree line. See that bird? We're over a mile away. That thing is huge. It's a prehistoric creature. It died out when life on Earth was all but destroyed by a comet strike, or whatever. We had the Permian extinction about two hundred and fifty million years ago, according to Jeff. Then, about sixty-five million years before the Quiver, something—once again—wiped life's slate almost clean.

"We don't know if that is going to happen tomorrow, next week, next month, or twenty million years from now. It doesn't matter. If this is our own past, then the one thing we know is that we didn't make it. Whatever civilization we manage to start will disappear without a trace. So, we don't have to worry about which timeline we're in—ours or a new one. All we have to do is build our present. The one we want to live in and the one we want to leave to our children."

Jenny wiped her eyes on her sleeve. "So, we're the new Adam and Eve."

"What are we going to do?" Hulbert asked.

"Go meet the Cherokees. Our guest says he was traveling with them on the Trail of Tears. By then, the Cherokee weren't even close to what any sane man would call 'wild savages.' They even had their own alphabet. I figure we can get along with them okay."

Joe looked dubious. "Has it occurred to you they might be holding a grudge?"

Andy shrugged. "Against who? Americans almost two hundred years back? A lot's changed since then. I don't see any reason to think they can't figure that out for themselves. I think Stephen McQuade already has. It helps, you know, that he can look around and see for himself that we're now a multiracial society."

He picked up the pad he'd used to take notes while talking to Stephen McQuade, the wounded Cherokee. The Cherokees had been in southern Illinois when the Quiver caught them. So had the prison. "Yeah, it's starting to make sense. Everything we're running across is something that existed somewhere in this area, at one time or another. Not exactly where the prison is, maybe, but pretty close. The Trail of Tears passed through this area. So did de Soto. And I'll bet money the Indians McQuade spent the night with were Mounds people."

He handed the pad to Edelman. "I think your theory about us getting shoved into the past and taking others with us is pretty accurate. Look at this. All of these people were here in Southern Illinois, within a few miles of the prison. They were just here at different times."

Edelman looked at Andy's notes. "If it's the real de Soto, we're in trouble. That bastard was nothing but a butcher. Everywhere he went he stole everything he could get his hands on, and enslaved anyone he could. Of course he only murdered, robbed, tortured and raped in the name of God and gold."

Jenny gave him a strained smile. "Christians didn't exactly corner the market on that type of behavior, you know."

"True enough," Edelman said. "But the conquistadores were right at the top of the class. It wasn't just de Soto. When I was in high school, I did a report on gold mines. During the 1500s, the Franciscan monastery was running the show in Cuba. Those Spanish monks were so ruthless, the Indians they enslaved to work the mines would commit mass suicide. They would get their hands on enough rope to hang themselves, and then during the middle of the night they would say goodbye to each other, wrap those ropes around their own necks, then jump."

Andy suppressed the urge to shudder. He knew the way things used to be done. He had the same history teacher Edelman had. Mr. Carter had refused to sugarcoat anything. He believed the only way to correct things was to make sure kids grew up knowing just how evil people could become if left unchecked. And he didn't restrict that lesson to the Europeans and Adolf Hitler. He had rubbed man's inhumanity to man in their faces using every civilization on the planet. He wanted them to know there was no such thing as the good old days.

"When we get through with the Cherokees, assuming we can," Andy said, "then we'll try to work something out with de Soto. He'll be a lot tougher to deal with, I expect. But he might not be impossible. He was greedy. He wanted to be rich and move up the ranks in power. Once he realizes there is no gold, no Catholic church, no monarchy to give him land that does not belong to them, we should be able to come to some sort of agreement with him and his men. When the only thing of value is your next meal, a man's perspective tends to change. I speak a little Spanish, and some of the COs are fluent in it. We won't have trouble understanding each other."

"I hate this place!" Jenny didn't look at any of the men in the room. She kept her eyes on the floor. "Andy, you're talking about dealing with people who act worse than the ones we have behind bars. If you strike a deal with de Soto, how do you justify keeping our murderers, our rapists, our thieves, behind bars? How do you say, this devil is our friend, but that devil has to stay locked up?"

"Jenny, we have no choice. We can't go back to our world. We have to live in this one. We have to adapt, or we die."

"Adapt, or sell our souls?"

He walked across the room and stood directly in front of her. "I will do whatever I have to do to keep us alive. I'm trying, Jenny. The first thing we have to do is warn the Cherokees. From what McQuade told me about the shape they're in, they won't be able to survive an attack from de

Soto. Then, we'll try to warn the Mounds people. Then, we will try to talk some sense into the conquistadores. When we get back we will start releasing the nonviolent prisoners."

"Release them, or let them out of their cells?" Joe asked.

"That's going to depend on what we find out there. Until I know more, I'm not willing to hand any of them a gun or a knife. Every gun and every box of ammo given away is less we have to defend us from dinosaurs, Spaniards, and I don't know what else. So, how do they take care of themselves? You've seen the things roaming around outside the walls. If I open the gate and send them down the road, unarmed, they're dead. And if I unlock the gates, and then let the prisoners remain inside the prison, every one of us could wind up murdered in our sleep. The decision on what we do with and for the prisoners waits. Now," Andy said, "get the department heads together. We have a trip to plan."

Lieutenant Hulbert stood at the door to the cafeteria waiting for Marie Keehn to finish briefing the kitchen staff on food preparation and storage. He felt foolish, but didn't care. He figured the woman would probably laugh at what he was going to say, think he was paranoid, but he was going to say it anyway. He had to.

She was amazing.

She was also as far from his so-called type as any woman could get. He preferred athletic looking women. Usually light complexioned blondes. Sometimes redheads. But they were always slim and muscular. She was none of these things. Instead, she was dark haired and dark eyed. Tiny but curvy. Almost, but not quite, chubby. Buxom. *Voluptuous in miniature.* He smiled at the thought then frowned. She was damn good with a gun. She worked well under pressure, didn't lose her head. And when instincts counted, hers were right on the money.

And she could smile. And laugh.

That's what it was. The other stuff was just gravy on the potatoes. It was that laugh. She had a dry sense of humor and knew how to take a joke. And she was smart. He hoped she was very smart. She was staying behind with Joe. And Collins.

He didn't like that. He wanted her with them. But Andy had been stubborn about it. He insisted Joe might need her. She was the only sharpshooter besides Hulbert the prison had. And since Hulbert was going, she had to stay.

Andy was probably right, although that hadn't stopped Rod from arguing. Instead of sending half their force, Hulbert wanted only a handful to go. He wanted to just make contact and begin the negotiations for peace.

But Andy had shot that down. No negotiating. There wasn't time. With de Soto roaming around loose out there, not to mention dinosaurs, the Cherokees needed to be behind the walls of the prison. They were already worn out from the trials they'd undergone in the course of the Trail of Tears.

The same went for the Mounds people. Once everyone was inside, then they would figure out what to do about the animals and about the Spaniards.

Rod hadn't bothered to point out that the prison,

with over two thousand prisoners, was not exactly "safe." Everyone knew that. But everyone also knew there were Utahraptors beyond the walls, and Spanish conquistadores, and who knew what else. Hulbert had argued a smaller group could travel faster, which meant safer. He had pointed out that emptying the prison of well over half its guards might be for nothing. They might not be able to find Watkins or the Mounds people. Or, both groups might refuse to join them. Or, once Andy met with them, he might not want them to join the guards inside the walls.

But the bottom line was, there always had to be someone in charge, someone calling the shots, and that someone was Andy. So that meant Hulbert was leaving and Marie was staying behind.

And that also meant Jenny went with them.

Andy hadn't wanted the RN to leave the facility. He believed the prison was the safest place for the women. But Jenny insisted she was the only nurse in good enough physical shape to make the trip. And a nurse had to go. Even though Jenny had explained how risky the trip could be, Stephen McQuade was refusing to give them directions to the Cherokee camp. He was going with them, or they would have to find the camp on their own.

McQuade was still in guarded condition and there was too much that could go wrong. So, a team of six guards had been assigned to carry his stretcher. Three teams of two. And Jenny was going and Marie was staying and Hulbert and Andy both wished like hell it was the other way around.

"What's up?" Marie said, exiting the lunchroom.

"We need to talk. I'm leaving with Andy and you're being left here with Joe."

"Doesn't surprise me." The look she gave him was different from the one Jenny had given Andy when they had argued over who was going and who was staying. Marie wasn't mad. She was disappointed. Disappointed in him.

"I tried to get him to let you come along, but he wants you here. Joe has to have someone with sharpshooter status."

"I see."

He watched as she thought about what he said. He could see the war of emotions going on below the surface, and he could see when that war ended. She accepted the logic in Andy's decision faster and easier than he had.

"Marie," he looked at the wall behind her, not at her face. He couldn't look her in the eye. "I don't want you to turn everything in. Hold back a little something you can carry with you at all times. Even in the showers."

She didn't ask why or what. Instead, she said, "That's against the rules."

"And you've never broken one?"

"Maybe, one."

"Okay, break one more." There was so much he wanted to say, but settled on, "If you get caught, and they dock your pay, I'll make it up to you."

"You bet you will. You'll be out the dough for a steak dinner, drinks and dancing at the swankiest place in town."

"You got it." His voice became gruff. "And anything else you want."

"Hulbert, you have no idea what this is going to cost

you." She smiled that easygoing smile of hers, then grew serious. "You're not asking me to do anything I didn't want to do anyway. Things aren't right. The tension in this place can be cut with a knife. Something happened while we were hunting."

"Yeah, that's why I want you to be real careful. Don't get caught up in anything. If things start to look a little iffy, bail. If you guess wrong and wind up in a tub of hot water, I'll tell Andy I told you to do it."

"When do you leave?" she asked.

"In about an hour."

"Walk me to the armory. I have a rifle to turn in; you can distract Stacy while I get something easier to conceal."

"And get enough ammo to hold off an army."

She looked him in the face and this time he returned the look, letting his eyes meet hers. "Marie, I'm serious, dead serious about this. I have this gut level feeling, and it's a bad one."

"Okay," she said. "I'll do it. But you tell Joe you transferred me to the field, and I'm not assigned to a post. Scratch me off the shift roster altogether. That will give me the ability to be anyplace I feel the need to be. But when you get back you have to tell me why."

"Collins—"

She shook her head. "No. Not Collins. I want to know why you warned me. Why you felt you wanted to protect me."

He touched her hair. "That's an easy one."

"No. Don't tell me now. It'll jinx it." She stood on her toes and gave him a quick peck on the cheek. "Luck, for us," she whispered. She then turned toward the armory, all business.

CHAPTER
20

The men who had been so eager to join Hernando de Soto on his expedition into the interior of the New World were now desperate to go back to Spain. The gold and silver they'd sought were nowhere to be found in this land of demons. The plantations, worked by slaves taken from native villages, were nothing more than a dream either. There weren't enough of them. They'd found hardly any more than the Tula slaves they'd brought with them, before the great river disappeared and the dragon's sulfur breath began rising from cracks and fissures in the ground.

So many Spaniards had died—so many Spaniards, and so many of their horses. Most of the pigs were gone too. Not from dying but from running away.

The only creatures doing well were the dogs. They had not lost one dog.

CHAPTER
21

Stephen McQuade dozed off and on as he was carried along the riverbank. Occasionally he would mumble something and the small team that carried him and his stretcher would assure him they were still following the river. They passed the cave where Marie Keehn found him and started the upward climb leading to the pine forest. It wouldn't be long and they would leave the water's edge. They would be well inside the forest by nightfall.

Jeff Edelman would occasionally wander away from the slow moving group of COs and would return, always carrying something new that he'd show the others. The conifers that Jeff found so fascinating did not register much on Andy. They didn't really seem that much different from the ones he'd known in Illinois. But the six-inch long tooth certainly got his attention. So did the egg the size of an ostrich's.

But no one talked much. It was as if they could barely breathe.

The volcano not too far from the prison had been apparently dormant. But on the second day they came into sight of a volcano in the distance that was sending a thin plume of gray-tinged smoke into the air. That might be a problem some day, but the potential threat was so distant in comparison to the others he faced that Andy decided it wasn't worth worrying about.

Around noon the next day, Andy took his share of the cold rations being passed out and sighed. They couldn't afford the time to build a fire and heat the slabs of meat, so he took a bite of the sandwich and forced himself not to make a face. *Gristle and grease on rye.* He then took a swig of water, immediately regretting it. The liquid, instead of washing the taste from his mouth, caused the grease to solidify, coating his tongue and teeth.

Gunshots sounded. And what he was sure were screams.

Andy dropped his sandwich to the ground and unslung his rifle. The COs all did the same. The gunfire and shrieks were coming from somewhere up ahead.

Rod Hulbert was by his side. "That doesn't sound like people fighting off an animal. It sounds like a war."

Andy nodded. That's exactly what it sounded like. And from the timber of the shrieks, it also sounded like women and children were the ones being attacked.

Andy motioned for Jerry Bailey to stay with Jenny and her patient, Stephen McQuade. He then motioned for the others to follow him.

The prison team worked its way through the woods. It didn't take them long to spot the men doing the killing.

They were dressed in armor and wore helmets. A good number of them were on horseback. Several of them were shooting into the center of a village whose houses were made of downed branches and animal hides.

Eight men of the village came rushing out, naked except for loincloths and wielding nothing more than decorated clubs. They weren't trying to attack the Spaniards, though. They were just trying to rescue two women and five children who'd been caught in the open, unable to get to the safety of their homes or the woods. The women had draped their bodies over their children in a pathetic attempt at protection.

Several Spaniards fired, but none of them hit anything. Given the matchlocks they were using, that wasn't surprising. The Indians were a moving target—moving fast, too—and the range was at least fifty yards. Andy was pretty sure they'd only started shooting to panic their victims. They could have already killed the women and children, if they wanted to, huddled the way they were in the open. If the kids had been on their own, they might very well have been killed by now. But the instinctive protective gesture of the two women had kept them alive. The conquistadores might not want the children, but they'd want the women intact.

One of the Spaniards on a horse, wearing a fancy-looking blue coat, bellowed something and the rest of them lowered their guns. He got off his horse, drew his sword, and the rest started following suit. Two of the Spaniards, it seemed, would be left behind holding the horses while the rest went into the village.

Clearly, the leader intended to save whatever

ammunition they had left. Conquistadores like this, armored and armed with steel swords, would have no trouble butchering natives completely unarmored and with nothing better than clubs. All the more so, since most of the Spaniards would be veterans of Europe's ferocious wars.

Andy did a quick count. Fifteen Spaniards. Seventeen, counting the two holding the horses. They were probably the same detachment from de Soto's forces who'd attacked McQuade and the Indians he had been with.

He made his decision just as quickly. This wasn't a prison uprising. This was war. There would be no negotiating and no prisoners taken. He had too many behind bars to take care of as it was. The bastards died. That simple.

He nodded at Hulbert and made a summoning motion. Rod started heading his way, moving carefully so he wouldn't be spotted. Fortunately, there wasn't much chance of that since the Spaniards' attention was entirely on the village and the prison guards were well off to the side and slightly to their rear.

Brian Carmichael was right next to him. Andy leaned over and said softly: "Take ten men with you into the woods. Circle the village about two-thirds of the way around. Whatever you do, make sure you don't wind up directly across from us, where we might get ourselves in an accidental crossfire. After we start firing, if any of those bastards try to get away, kill 'em. We want just one prisoner, no more." He glanced at the Spaniards approaching the village. "The one with the fancy blue coat. He's the only one we leave standing."

Brian nodded and took off, tapping a guard here and

there as he went. Those he tapped fell in line behind him. Seconds later they were gone from sight.

By then, Hulbert was next to him. "We'll aim for the ones with guns first. Pass it along. I'll give the signal with my first shot. Except for that asshole in the blue coat. I want him for questioning."

He gave Rod just enough time to pass the word down and then lifted his rifle. For a moment, he hesitated, wondering if Carmichael was in position yet.

Andy decided it didn't matter. He couldn't wait. The Spaniards were almost into the village. Within seconds, they'd be starting the slaughter.

He picked out his first target, the Spaniard slightly in the lead. Andy's marksmanship wasn't in the same league as Hulbert's, but it didn't need to be. Leaving aside the training he'd gotten as a prison guard, he'd been hunting deer since he was thirteen. So had probably every man with him. With modern rifles, at a range of not more than seventy yards, this was going to be every bit as much of an overmatch as the Spaniards against the Indians would have been.

Andy pulled the trigger and the man went down. Less than a second later, the rest of the guards did the same. Only two of them missed their target, and one of those managed to send a helmet flying. That was enough to stun the man who'd been wearing it and drive him to his knees.

It took the Spaniards a fatal couple of seconds to realize they were being attacked from the woods. By then, only six of the fifteen were still standing, including the leader. The man whose helmet had been shot off was not one of them. Whoever had sent the helmet flying had sent the owner's brains after it with his second shot.

The two men holding the horses had also been shot, and the horses were scattering. The six that remained didn't even try to get to their mounts. Instead, they bolted for the woods on the other side of the clearing. It did them no good. At Rod's shouted command, the rest of the guards held their fire and let the marksman take them down. One. Two. Three. Four. Just about as quickly as that. Hulbert really was a fantastic shot. He would have taken down the last of his targets before the man reached the shelter of the trees, but a volley from the side swatted him like a bug.

The only one left was the leader. Whatever else the man was, he wasn't a coward. He brandished his sword and rushed directly at the trees from which the volley had come. He was shouting something that might have been "Jesu Maria!"

Belatedly, Andy realized that he hadn't considered the fact that he'd ordered Carmichael to capture a man still intact and armed with a sword—and who was obviously willing and able to use it.

Hulbert solved that problem. One more shot and the blue-coated conquistador was sent sprawling. There was blood spreading across the left leg of his trousers.

Gutsy bastard, though. He started rising again, still holding the sword and snarling. But he was moving slowly now, so Hulbert's marksmanship could really come into play. Another shot knocked the sword out of his hand and left the hand a mangled ruin.

Carmichael came out of the woods. He trotted up and

bashed the Spaniard on the head with his rifle butt. The
man still had his helmet on, but Carmichael was strong as
an ox. Helmet or no helmet, the blow drove the man down
on his belly. Unconscious by now, probably. Close enough,
anyway.

Andy stood up. His eyes searched the village but couldn't
see any signs of the inhabitants. That wasn't surprising, of
course. Given the savage nature of their rescue, you could
hardly blame them for being as afraid of their rescuers as
they'd been of the Spaniards. From their viewpoint, it
must have been like watching a tyrannosaurus devour a
smaller predator who'd been threatening them. Would
you come trotting out of hiding, waving and smiling at the
tyrannosaur?

Jeff Edelman and Rod Hulbert came over. "We have to
go out there and get the guns," Jeff said. "Right away."

"What?" Hulbert blinked.

"We have to get the guns and the ammunition. They
saw what the guns could do, so they'll take them. Some of
them will die, trying to figure out how to use them."

Andy saw his point. "Besides that," he added, "until we
know more about these people, I'd just as soon they didn't
have firearms. Just because they were somebody else's
intended victims doesn't make them sweethearts. If I
remember right, the Mounds people could get pretty
bloody-minded themselves. Some of them might get
killed learning how to use the guns, but they'll learn soon
enough. I remember that much from Mr. Carter's history
classes. If there was one piece of European technology
that everybody who ran across it learned to use right
quick, it was guns. Stone age or not."

Jeff nodded. "Yeah, that's true."

"What about the rest?" Rod asked. "I hate leaving them with nothing. These bastards we shot weren't the only men de Soto has with him."

Andy thought about it for a second or two. "I don't see any reason we can't leave the rest with them. The swords, whatever other weapons there were. They'll strip the clothing, too."

"What about the horses?" asked Jeff. "We could use those ourselves."

Andy looked to see where the horses had gotten to. They'd bolted away just about as rapidly as their masters had. Former masters. He could only still see one of them, and that one was at least fifty yards off.

"Yeah, we could. But how many of us are good enough riders to know how to sweet-talk a scared horse into settling down, in the first place?"

Carmichael had arrived, just in time to hear that.

"I am," he said.

The three white officers stared at him. Carmichael clucked his tongue and grinned. "Stereotypes, stereotypes. Just 'cause I grew up a ghetto boy in East St. Louis doesn't mean I didn't have cowboy daydreams. Except in my case, I kept them long enough to learn how to ride a horse. I'm pretty damn good at it, if I say so myself."

"I'm a good horseman too," said Hulbert. That wasn't surprising. Hulbert was good at anything that involved survival in the wilderness. He probably knew which type of cactus provided water and which snakes and insects you could eat. There were times Andy thought the man was just a little bit nuts.

Edelman weighed in. "We should at least try, Andy. For one thing, if we don't, the horses don't have much chance of survival. That'd be true even if they were wild horses. There's nothing in their evolution that'll have prepared them for being hunted by dinosaurs."

Carmichael scowled a little, at that. Andy knew he belonged to one of the fundamentalist churches that thought evolution was nonsense, at best. But he didn't say anything. The immediate truth of what Jeff was saying about these horses was obvious, regardless of whatever explained it.

Andy hated to take the time to round up the horses. They had other pressing matters to attend to. Still, there was no question that horses would be very useful. In fact, without roads and with a very chancy fuel supply for the motor vehicles, horses could make the difference between survival and failure.

He looked back at the village, wondering if . . .

But he dismissed that idea almost at once. Whoever these Indians were, Mounds people or not, they clearly dated from some time before horses had been brought to America. They wouldn't know how to keep the horses alive. In fact, they'd probably try to hunt them and eat them.

"Okay. Rod, you and Brian—and take whatever men you can find who have the skills—see what you can do with the horses. I'll see if I can get the villagers to talk to us, in the meantime."

"What about him?" asked Carmichael, jerking a thumb at the one still-living Spaniard. The conquistador was still lying on the ground. Two of the guards were watching him, with rifles ready at hand.

"He'll keep. I doubt if he's even conscious yet, as hard as you belted him."

Brian grinned again. "Hey, boss, *you* see what it's like some time, having a wild man charging at you and waving a sword. Damn thing looked ten feet long. I wasn't taking no chances."

"I wasn't criticizing. Just making an observation. And you'd better get going, unless you figure on tracking those horses for a week."

Hulbert and Carmichael left. Andy turned to Edelman.

"I'll go into the village alone. And I'll leave the rifle behind." He patted the pistol holstered to his hip. "I'm thinking they probably won't recognize this as a weapon. Or, if they do, they'll think it's just a tiny little club."

Edelman looked dubious.

"Jeff, they'll be scared to death. And all they've got in the way of weapons are those decorated clubs. Probably ceremonial weapons."

"Like hell they are! Andy, I hate to break the news to you, but those 'decorations' you're talking about are actually inlaid pieces of obsidian or some other sharpened rock. Don't kid yourself. Those are real no-fooling weapons. And your recollections about the Mounds Indians are on the money. 'Bloody-minded,' for sure. They found one mound with over two hundred skeletons in it, a lot of them missing their heads and hands. The Mounds Indians don't seem to have been as purely murderous as the Aztecs, I grant you, but nobody in their right mind is going to confuse them with the mythical Noble Savage."

Andy shrugged. "So our new world is not risk-free. What a shocker. I'm still doing it." He glanced at the village, estimating the distances involved. "Look, we'll compromise. You and the rest can move up within thirty yards, with your rifles ready. If the people in that village were watching the fight at all, they'll know the guns can kill them at that distance if they try anything."

He handed Edelman his rifle and started walking toward the open center of the village. He moved more slowly than he normally walked, to give the villagers time to realize what he was doing.

Once he reached the center, he looked around. Up close, he could see many pairs of eyes staring at him through gaps in the hut walls.

He tried talking for a while, in the hopes that one of them would come out. After a minute or so, realizing that an endless repetition of "I mean you no harm" was pointless as well as boring, he started reciting what he could remember of *The Ballad of Eskimo Nell*. When he ran out of verses he remembered, he went on with a recital of *The Night Before Christmas*. He'd committed that to memory when he was eight years old and, for whatever odd reason, had never forgotten a single line.

". . . *heard him exclaim, ere he drove out of sight,*
"Happy Christmas to all, and to all a good-night!"
Nothing.

So much for slavering Aztec warriors. Andy had heard the theories that the Mounds Indians practiced ritual sacrifice. But, even if the theories were true, that was probably something done by their kings or chiefs or high priests. Whatever they had in the way of rulers. This was just a local village. The inhabitants were no more likely to be prone to ritual bloodshed than the residents of a small town in southern Illinois were likely to stage a New Orleans-style Mardi Gras parade.

"Screw it," he muttered. "Deeds speak louder than words, and all that."

He turned and hollered at Edelman and the others, watching him.

"They won't come out! Gather up all the swords, all the armor, all the helmets—anything loose you can find in the way of weapons or tools or coins—and we'll pile them up here. Then we'll be on our way."

That didn't take but a few minutes. The guards were thorough, too. By the time they were done stripping the corpses, all that was left on them was their clothing. The resulting pile in the center of the village was pretty impressive. All except the two silver coins they found. Andy decided to highlight those by balancing them on top of a helmet at the center of the pile.

"Okay, let's go." He gave the villagers peeking at him one last slow look, turning almost completely around. Then, gave them a snappy salute and led the way out.

"What'll they do, do you think?" asked Jeff.

Andy shrugged. "I have no idea. But I figure the one skill they're bound to have is that they'll be way better trackers than any of us are. If they decide they want to find us, they'll manage it."

"What do you mean these aren't the same guys who attacked you? They have to be!" Jenny, usually so self-controlled, now seemed on the verge of tears. Her voice was shaking a little. She reached out and took Andy's hand.

Stephen McQuade shook his head. "They are the same sort of men. But from what you described, I do not think they are the same men."

He nodded toward the one Spaniard they'd kept alive. Jenny had attended to his wounds, as best she could. The man was conscious now, sitting upright and glaring at them. Andy hadn't seen any need to tie his hands or feet. The gunshot wounds Rod had inflicted on him served that purpose just fine.

"I am certain this one was not among them," McQuade said. "I would not have forgotten his face. Certainly not the blue coat."

Andy wasn't happy at the news, certainly, but he didn't share Jenny's distress, either. In retrospect, it was not surprising that de Soto would have several parties of soldiers foraging the area. The more parties he sent out, the greater the likelihood they'd find something useful. And given the disparity in military power between the conquistadores and the scattered groups of Indians, there wasn't any real danger involved.

Or wouldn't have been, if a twenty-first century prison with guards armed to the teeth hadn't gotten caught in the mix. But there was no way de Soto could have foreseen that.

The questions that were now raised were:

How many men did de Soto have, all told? Where was his main force? How many other parties did he have scouring the area?

Andy was sure they were looking at a war. He'd do his best to negotiate with de Soto, but he didn't have any real hopes anything would come of it. From what he could remember of his history classes and what Jeff said, the conquistadores rarely negotiated—and when they did, they were being duplicitous.

"Okay," Andy said, "so these goons weren't the ones who attacked you. Were the villagers part of the same people who befriended you?"

Stephen shrugged. "The description sounds the same. But I was only with them for less than a day, and never learned more than—I think—four or five words of their language."

His English was perfectly fluent; even idiomatic, all the way down to the swear words. But the accent kept throwing Andy off a little. It was a weird combination of a heavy sorta-hillbilly accent with a cadence and occasional use of terms that reminded Andy, more than anything else, of a couple of Shakespeare plays he'd seen. He remembered reading somewhere that there was a theory that Appalachian dialects were actually the closest to Renaissance English. Apparently, the theory was right.

Edelman hissed. "How many people got caught in that damn Quiver, anyway?"

Andy rubbed his head, then shrugged. "There's no way of knowing that. All we know for sure is the prison, the Cherokee, the Spaniards and the Mounds people are here."

Edelman shook his head. "I don't think these are really Mounds people. In its heyday, the Mounds people were an advanced civilization for their time, and even for villagers these people seem too primitive. I think they're more in the way of precursors. Call them early Mississippian, the culture that eventually produced the Mounds people."

"Okay, what else can you tell me about this area? I don't care when you're talking about. If they were within fifty miles or a hundred miles of the prison, sometime in the past, I need to know about them."

"Not a lot." Edelman looked at the volcano on the skyline. "Most of what I know is from working the local tourist traps as a teenager. Cahokia appeared sometime after 800 A.D., then disappeared around 1200 A.D. No one knows why. At their peak, they had over twenty thousand people.

"After they left, what would one day be called Illinois became part of a huge, empty corridor no one lived in. The area was still empty when de Soto came through three hundred years later."

"Just our luck," Rod muttered.

"Actually, I think we're better off without them." Jeff made a face. "They were farmers, hunters, builders, and artists, yeah, so they'd have had more in the way of resources we could maybe trade for. But they were a people living in harsh times. They were capable of mass violence. They were also like a great many primitive cultures when it came time for a funeral. If an important person died, they would bury quite a few people with the dead. And you can bet your ass the people were not dead before the funeral rites. There has also been some evidence the Cahokia might have practiced a little cannibalism and some form of human sacrifice. That's never been proven, but I wouldn't want to have to find out the hard way."

Later, Andy lay under a wool, state-issued blanket, listening to the sounds of the night and watching the stars.

Exhausted, he'd thought he would fall asleep before his head hit his makeshift pillow. But he hadn't. Instead, he lay there and thought about the last few days. Things, gone crazy the day of the Quiver, seemed to have escalated out of control. There were too many pieces to the puzzle and he had a feeling he still didn't know who all was inside the woods.

He rolled over so he could look at Jenny. She was less than a yard away, wrapped in one of the flannel blankets used inside the infirmary. She was using her medical bag for a pillow. Her back was to him. In the dim light of the moon and stars he could see the rise and fall of her breathing. He could also see the way her shoulders seemed to shake. She wasn't asleep. She was crying.

He slid next to her and dropped his arm around her waist. Now he was close enough he could hear the small sobs. He didn't say anything, and neither did she. Instead, she nestled against him. After a while, they were both asleep.

CHAPTER
22

Geoffrey Watkins studied the giant lizard-birds working their way across the clearing toward the rudimentary village the Cherokees had put together. He estimated they weighed about what a horse did, and they were about the same height. Their bodies were longer, though, with a very heavy and stiff-looking tail. The biggest difference was that, like birds, they moved on two legs instead of four. Their hind legs were hugely muscled, much bigger than the forelimbs, and ended in birdlike feet with three talons. But one of those talons, unlike any bird Watkins had ever seen, was enlarged and cocked back and out of the way while the creature walked.

Their heads swung from side to side and their tongues darted in and out of their mouths, as though they were tasting the air. And even from this distance, he knew their mouths were filled with teeth that made the teeth of two-hundred pound gars seem as nothing. Everything about them shrieked *predator.*

To make things worse, predators that were also like wolves. Pack hunters. The six creatures moved together, obviously hunting as a team.

He watched them, more fascinated than horrified. He'd dealt with dangerous animals since he was a boy. He figured they could deal with these also.

The animals had been spotted ten minutes before. Luckily, Scott's eight-year-old son had been exploring away from the village and had spotted them at a distance. Still more luckily, the beasts hadn't spotted the boy. He'd been able to get back and give the warning in plenty of time.

By now, clearly, the lizard-bird hunters were already honed in on the village. By smell, he assumed. They'd slowed down quite a bit, and were picking their way across the clearing, trying to spot their prey.

Unless they had the eyesight of eagles—which was always possible, of course, but Watkins didn't think that was likely with land animals—they wouldn't be able to see the humans yet. Everyone except the warriors and the soldiers was hiding in the log huts, and the armed men were positioned for ambush. Still, Watkins was wary. He simply wasn't familiar enough with these monsters to know what their capabilities were. He'd have felt a lot better if they were giant bears or wolves or cougars.

"Chief," Bradley Scott whispered. "We're ready. Sergeant Kershner says the soldiers are ready too."

From somewhere south of them an animal bellowed. None of the people inside the camp recognized the beast making the sound. The six lizard-birds hesitated, and then became agitated. They sniffed the air and turned this way and that, using small hopping motions. For a few seconds, Watkins hoped they might get attracted by other prey. But, after a while, they resumed their careful stalking of the village ahead of them.

The Cherokee chief was glad now that he'd instructed his warriors not to try for head shots. The way the creatures' heads bobbed and swayed as they moved would make them very difficult to hit. Ammunition was getting scarce, but time was even scarcer. To fire and miss would mean taking time to reload. Even for a man good with a musket, or a well-trained soldier, that took at least a third of a minute. And while the creatures were moving slowly now, everything about the way their bodies were designed made it obvious that they could run very quickly when they wanted to.

The soldiers, with their better muskets, had agreed to fire first. Watkins and Scott and their fourteen warriors would hold their fire until they saw what effect the soldiers' guns had on the monsters. They'd divided themselves into two groups of eight men each. Scott's men would fire after the soldiers, and Watkins' group would be the final reserve. If these things were like most reptiles, they wouldn't die easily.

The soldiers were either very brave or very well-trained. Maybe both, but Geoffrey suspected it was their training. Sergeant Kershner was a stern disciplinarian, when he felt it necessary. Whatever the reason, they waited until the lizard-birds were thirty yards from where they were hidden before they fired their volley.

Kershner, Geoffrey realized at once, must have come to the same conclusion that Watkins had. They hadn't had enough time to develop any detailed plans beyond the rough division of forces. The U.S. sergeant had obviously ordered his men to aim at only the leading two of the six monsters. Probably worried that if they spread their fire they wouldn't hurt any of them enough to matter.

Those two creatures went down, as if they'd been poleaxed. The soldiers were all armed with muskets made at the Harpers Ferry armory. As big and dangerous-looking as the lizard-birds were, each of them had been struck by at least three .69-caliber bullets.

That still left four, completely unharmed. The beasts had scattered at the loud and unexpected noise, but they were already coming back. And now, unfortunately, they weren't bunched in a group.

"Aim for the one on the far left!" Scott shouted. That was also the nearest one to his group, about fifty yards away. "And don't shoot until—"

But three of the warriors had already fired before he got halfway through the command. Even when the Cherokees fought as allies with the Americans, which they often did, they fought as skirmishers. They weren't trained or accustomed to firing in volleys.

Only one of the bullets hit, so far as Watkins could tell. Not surprising, at that range. The targeted monster screeched and jerked around, slashing with its teeth at nothing.

The bullet had struck the tail, not far behind the hip. Geoffrey realized the creature must have thought it was being attacked from the rear. It suddenly dawned on him that the lizard-birds were under the same handicap he and his people were. They didn't know the capabilities of humans any more than humans knew theirs. This would be the first time they'd ever encountered gunfire—and as nasty as those heads looked, they also didn't look as if there was too much room for brains in them either.

Bradley must had come to the same conclusion. There was no point in waiting until the monsters got closer, because they were now just milling around. Agitated and confused, smelling blood and knowing some of them had been attacked, but not knowing from where or by what.

"All right, shoot at him again!"

The other five muskets went off. At least one of the bullets struck something vital. The monster twisted, screeching, twisted back—lashing out now with that ferocious-looking huge claw, again at nothing—and then staggered and fell. When it hit the ground, it kept writhing and lashing out with the claw.

That was enough. These were predators, not fanatics or soldiers trained to fight to the death. Even the most ferocious predators avoided dangerous prey. They went for the weak or lame or young, and ran if they encountered anything that looked like it might put up enough of a fight to kill or injure them.

The three survivors took off at a run, heading for the other side of the clearing. Their speed was frightening. If they'd known enough to charge the soldiers after they fired, they'd have been upon them long before the soldiers could possibly have reloaded. Watkins would remember that.

Belatedly, he realized he was forgetting something even more important. The best defense humans ever had against predators was the knowledge those predators gained that humans were prey to be avoided. And these monsters *still* had no idea what had happened to them.

Cursing his years and the creakiness of his joints, he lunged into the clearing, waving his arms and shouting as loudly as he could. A few seconds later, Scott and several other Cherokees joined him.

Maybe one of the monsters looked back. He wasn't sure.

"Will you look at those crazy savages?" sneered Private Sam Underwood. He'd broken off from reloading his musket to watch the Cherokees in the clearing, shouting and carrying on like wild men. "I told you they wasn't no different from animals."

Sergeant James Kershner decided he'd had enough of Underwood. The Georgian's prejudices were so deep-rooted the man couldn't even think. And he was a nasty bastard, to boot.

"Shut up," he said. "They're smarter than you are. They're trying to make sure those damn lizards learn to stay away from us."

That didn't even budge the sneer on Underwood's face. "You say."

"One more remark like that, Private, and I'll have you arrested. You're still under army discipline, and I'm still in command."

His anger made Kershner's accent thicker than usual. Although he'd been born in Pennsylvania and his parents had given him what they felt was a proper American first name, he hadn't learned English until he joined the army. His whole town was populated by Swabian immigrants and still spoke their dialect of German.

Underwood was just about as stupid as he was nasty. For a moment, he gaped at the sergeant. Then the sneer came back.

"Arrest me, how? You ain't got a brig, Kershner, in case you ain't noticed."

By then, Corporal John Pitzel had his own musket reloaded. "Good point." He cocked the weapon and shoved the barrel into Underwood's neck, just below the jaw bone. He wasn't gentle about it, either. Although English was his native language, Pitzel came from German stock also. He had less use for the Georgian than Kershner did. The man was even stupid enough to make wisecracks about Germans.

Which, given that four out of the eight men in his unit were either German immigrants or born into German immigrant families, including the sergeant in command, qualified him as Stupid First Class. Especially since two of the other three men were Irish immigrants, and Underwood made just as many wisecracks about the Irish.

"I think an execution in the field is called for, Sergeant," said the corporal thinly. "Insubordination during combat."

It finally registered on the private that he'd crossed a line and was in serious trouble. His eyes widened and the sneer vanished. "Hey! Quit jokin' around!"

Kershner considered Pitzel's proposal—which, he knew perfectly well, wasn't a joke at all.

Normally, of course, he'd have dismissed the idea immediately. But there wasn't anything normal about their situation. And the fact was, they were heavily outnumbered by the Cherokees. Even if Underwood's attitudes and habits didn't get them killed, they were bound to produce an ever-widening schism between the soldiers and the Cherokees. Relations were tense enough, as it was.

But what finally tipped the balance had nothing to do with military issues. James Kershner was twenty-four years old and had all the normal desires that a man that age had. By now, he was certain they were stranded in this new world for the rest of their lives, with only the Cherokees for company. And he was pretty sure one of the Cherokee girls was even showing some interest. One of Chief Watkins' nieces. He thought her name was Ginger Tansey. A pert and lively girl, about nineteen or so, with a nice smile and bright eyes.

"Shoot him," he commanded.

The bullet damn near took off Underwood's head. He was dead before he hit the ground.

The sergeant swiveled to bring the rest of the men in the unit under his gaze. "Any of you have a problem with this?"

David McLean grunted. "Not bloody fucking likely. I plan to end my days surrounded by grandkids, like a proper Irishman should. And if their grandma is an Indian, I can't say I much give a damn."

The only soldier who looked disturbed was one of the Germans. More confused than disturbed, really. The man was a bit slow-witted.

The one and only native-born American soldier of old English stock in the unit looked downright pleased.

"I couldn't stand that son of a bitch," he pronounced. "And I got no problem at all becoming a squaw man. Beats the alternative, hands down."

"I don't think they like being called 'squaws,'" Kershner said mildly.

"Fine. I got no problem at all becoming the swain of an Injun princess. That beats the alternative even better."

"What's that all about?" Bradley Scott asked. The sound of a gunshot had drawn their attention to the woods where the U.S. soldiers had been waiting in ambush.

"I don't know," said Watkins. "I guess we'll know soon enough."

And, in fact, less than a minute later the soldiers emerged from the woods, dragging the corpse of one of their own with them. They laid him down a few feet into the clearing and several of them took out spades from their knapsacks. Obviously, they planned to dig a grave, right here and now, with no further ado.

"At a guess," Watkins said, "Sergeant Kershner decided to lance a festering boil before it got any bigger. That's the one they called Underwood. I had a feeling he'd be a problem, just from the few times I had to deal with him. He must have finally crossed a line."

Scott rubbed his chin. "It occurs to me, Geoffrey, that we all crossed a line today. Or if we haven't, we should."

Watkins thought about it. Once he'd gotten used to Kershner's accent, he'd come to realize that the young sergeant was very shrewd. Quick-thinking, too. And, it was now obvious, prepared to be decisive and ruthless when he needed to be. All the things a smart old chief looked for in a successor.

And why not? Cherokees had been intermarrying with whites for generations. So had all the southern tribes.

Watkins himself was at least a quarter white, in his ancestry. The top chief of the Cherokees, John Ross, was seven-eighths Scottish, if you calculated things the way white people did, by race instead of clan.

They had a lot of years ahead of them. Very dangerous years. But, maybe, their children and their children and their children would have forever. If they started the right way.

"Yes, I think you're right."

That evening, before the soldiers started their usual separate campfire, Watkins went over to Sergeant Kershner.

"Why don't you and your men start eating with us from now on?" he suggested. "We cook better than you do, anyway."

He gave their tents a glance. "And starting tomorrow, we should build you a real cabin. Who knows? Winter might be coming."

Kershner's smile was a lot more serene than you'd expect from such a young man. "Good idea. I was just thinking the same thing myself."

CHAPTER
23

After they were ushered into the room—chamber, it might be better to say—that served The Project as its operations center, Nick Brisebois and Timothy Harshbarger spent a minute or so looking around with interest. Their companion, Harshbarger's police partner Bruce Boyle, even lost the apprehensive expression that had been on his face since he arrived at the site in northern Minnesota.

Eventually, Boyle whistled softly. "This looks like something right out of a sci-fi movie." He gave the big table at the center of the chamber that the scientists used as a conference table a somewhat reproachful look. "Except you oughta have a captain's chair and a pilot's chair."

Richard Morgan-Ash chuckled. "And how, exactly, would you fly an iron mine?"

Boyle shrugged. "Don't ask me. But it wouldn't seem any stranger to me than the rest of this does."

"Why'd you put it down here in the first place?" asked Harshbarger.

"We didn't, actually. This facility was originally built back in the 1980s to study proton decay. That phenomenon was assumed to be so infrequent that they could only detect it if they could filter out the cosmic rays that would otherwise flood all the observations. Cosmic rays are so penetrative that you need an incredible amount of shielding to filter out their effects. Enough water would do the trick nicely, but it was more practical to use half a mile of earth."

"Yeah, I can see that. Especially when the half mile is iron."

"There's not much iron ore left, actually. Most of the rock above us is Ely greenstone. That's ancient rock, dating back almost three billion years. But it doesn't really matter what the exact substance is, as long as there's enough of it. Water would have done just fine, except that building a laboratory at the bottom of Lake Superior or somewhere in the ocean would have cost a fortune. This was expensive enough, even as it was."

"So how many decaying protons did they find?" Brisebois asked.

Richard smiled. "Not one, as it happens. Eventually they decided there was something wrong with the theory that predicted them. The whole thing would have been a bit of a boondoggle except the facility could be modified to study neutrinos and look for the postulated dark matter of most current cosmological theories." He nodded toward his colleagues. "That's what they were doing here when the Grantville Disaster happened, and their equipment picked up traces of it."

"Traces of what?"

Leo Dingley snorted. "Good question. We're still trying to figure that out. Me, I'm partial to a WIMP side effect of some kind. That's capital W-I-M-P, not slang. It stands for 'weakly interacting massive particles.' They're one of the proposed solutions for the dark matter problem." He gave his own nod toward his colleagues in the chamber. "Most of them, however, think that what we're observing will eventually be explained by some variant of string theory."

Nick held up his hands. "Folks, I'm a trash-hauler and Tim and Bruce are cops. Can you put this in layman's terms?"

Most of the scientists looked very dubious at that proposition. Morgan-Ash smiled. "You have to make allowances. They've lived their whole lives in academia. I, on the other hand, once had to be able to explain things to paratroopers. Even more valiantly"—here he puffed out his chest—"I have to explain things to a teenage daughter."

Nick grinned. "Tough, isn't it? I had two of them. Thankfully, they're now both off to college."

"So I'll do my best. You can think of what's happening this way. Our planet regularly gets hits by objects from space. Many of them are simply isolated occurrences, but many others are part of more concentrated impacts."

"Like meteor showers," said Boyle.

"That's one good example, yes. Most of these bombardments are barely noticed, beyond a show in the sky, because the objects are too small to have much effect when they hit the Earth. If they hit it at all, which most of them don't because they burn up in the atmosphere. You're with me so far?"

The three visitors to the lab all nodded.

"Well, we're looking at much the same thing. Except *these* objects seem to be oriented along a different dimensional axis. If you think of time as a fourth dimension, perhaps that one. If you believe, as most of us do, that string theory is onto something, then we could be looking at as many as eleven dimensions."

Dingley jeered. "All of which except the first four— even you admit this much—don't get beyond the string itself. Or exist in some hypothetical multiverse that we're just a tiny four-dimensional part of."

Morgan-Ash looked patiently long-suffering. "Leo, can we hold off on the debate for a moment? I'm simply trying to explain to our guests *what* we think is happening. Not *how* it's happening. The point is, gentlemen— regardless of what's causing it—the way these objects strike the Earth has most of its effects along a time axis instead of a spacial axis. Where a normal bolide from space that strikes the Earth—a meteorite or an asteroid or a comet—would expend its energy moving mass through space, these objects move it through time. They don't leave three-dimensional craters, they leave time craters."

Brisebois scratched his chin. "In other words, you think Grantville was destroyed by what amounts to a time comet."

Richard shrugged. "If it was destroyed at all. It's far more likely that it was simply carried back in time and left somewhere in our past."

"But—"

Margo interjected. "Somewhere in *a* past, he should

have said. That much we're certain of. No matter which way you calculate the problem, there's no way to account for what happens without assuming that a separate universe is created by the impacts. Or separate timelines, if you prefer. Anything else produces insoluble paradoxes."

Nick shook his head. "That's not what I was getting at. I know the old saw about time travel being impossible because you might kill your own grandfather or just do something by accident that has the same effect. What I meant was—"

But he got no further, because Harshbarger exploded.

"Wait a fucking minute! Are you telling me that Joe Schuler is still *alive*?"

"Yeah," said Nick. "*That's* what I was trying to get at."

The scientists in the room looked at each other, even more dubiously than they had before. So did Morgan-Ash, this time.

"Well . . ." he said.

Margo stood up. "I think we need to quit beating around the bush. It's not as if we haven't all been kept up nights wondering the same thing." She turned to face Harshbarger. "Tim, we can't tell you whether or not your friend is still alive. The truth is, he might very well be dead. What we can tell you—and we're pretty sure of this, now—is that the time impact wouldn't have killed him."

Harshbarger's face, flushed red a few seconds earlier, was now rather pale. "How sure are you about that?"

Margo hesitated, but O'Connell now spoke up. "As sure as we can be short of meeting the transposed people and talking to them."

Harshbarger stared at him. "Why?" asked Nick.

"Two reasons. First of all, there's no mathematical reason they should have been destroyed. As cold-blooded as it sounds, I can give you an exact mathematical explanation of why someone gets killed when he gets hit by a bullet in the right place or has a big rock dropped on him. It's just a matter of mass and energy, really."

He turned and pointed to the diagrams that were displayed on a big board toward the far end of the huge chamber. "The same is true here—and it doesn't matter which way you calculate it. The point is, whatever these bolides are, almost their entire impact is along a time axis. They're no more capable of shredding three-dimensional objects like a human body than a bullet from a gun or a falling rock is able to send someone back in time."

"Jesus," whispered Harshbarger.

"What's the second reason?" asked Brisebois.

The mathematician shrugged. "Hell, Nick, you saw it yourself." He nodded at the two policemen. "We've finally been able to identify the creature they shot. One of our . . . call him a fellow traveler, is a paleontologist at the Museum of the Rockies in Bozeman, Montana. He's a dinosaur expert. We sent him the carcass you gave us and he says it's definitely a dromaeosaurid of some kind."

"A *what*?" asked Boyle.

"Dromaeosaurid. The common name for them among dinosaur people is 'raptor.' They're one of the families in the theropod group of dinosaurs."

Boyle's eyes were wide. He gave his partner a glare. "You crazy bastard! Tim, you had us both out there in the night shooting at a goddam velociraptor. I saw that movie too, y'know? It's a good thing *we're* still alive!"

Harshbarger made a face. "Oh, cut it out. The thing was nowhere near as big as Spielberg's monsters—not to mention that it was trying to run away from us."

Margo cleared her throat. "She, actually."

The two cops looked at her.

"Well, sure, of course we dissected it," she said apologetically. "Or, rather, sent it to the museum and had them do it."

"As a result of which," Richard added, chuckling, "I don't believe our colleagues at Bozeman can be described as 'fellow travelers' any longer. Rabid converts to the cause, would be a more accurate way of putting it. And I believe you can put your mind at ease, Officer Boyle. There are—were—a lot of dromaeosaurids. The name itself is just Latin for 'running lizard.' The velociraptors and their huge cousins the Utahraptors were just two genuses among many in the family. Our expert told us the one you shot is related to them, but was probably a scavenger. No more dangerous to a human being than a very large coyote would be, in other words."

Nick ran fingers through his hair. "Okay. I see your point. Yeah, that's evidence, all right."

Harshbarger was looking back and forth between Brisebois and O'Connell. His face was starting to get flushed again. "Well, I *don't* get it. What does the critter me and Bruce shot have anything to do with whether or not my buddy Joe is still alive?"

"Hell, Tim, you can figure it out for yourself. Think about what it means to say that a bolide's impact happens along the time axis instead of the three space axes. What happens when you shoot a bullet into a body?"

Boyle grinned crookedly. "If I shoot it, the body dies."
He jerked a thumb at his partner. "If Ol' Tick-eye Tim
here shoots it, who the hell knows? The brick wall eight
feet from the target might get dented up a little."

Harshbarger scowled at him.

"I *am* the one who brought down Slavering Sue," Bruce
said cheerfully. "Not to mention that *my* scores on the target range—"

"Ah, shaddup."

Nick waited for the banter to end. Then said: "But what
else happens? Does a neat hole just appear in the body?
Does the flesh and blood vanish? Does the residue from
the cartridge vanish? If the gun you used was a .357
Magnum instead of a target .22, was the recoil the same?"

His friends still looked puzzled. "There's always a
re-action, is my point. And the reaction, just like the
action, only happens in the three spacial dimensions. Well
. . . yeah, sure, there's also a time element, but it's not
distorted from the time around it. You follow me so far?"

The two policemen nodded.

"Then figure out what happens if the impact is fourth-
dimensional. You get a reaction also—which is the residue
of whatever time period the bolide is passing through getting kicked back." He looked at Malcolm. "Is that the right
way to put it?"

"Uh . . . not exactly. Mathematically, it's more like a
loop. But keep going. You're doing fine."

The air transport specialist turned back to the cops.
"Don't you get it? If the *re*-action showed up alive and
kicking—that's your Slavering Sue, fellas—then why
wouldn't the same be true of the ones acted upon? The

bolide *can't* shred them, in three dimensions. All it can do is shift them around in time."

Harshbarger's expression cleared. And, again, his face paled. "Jesus H. Christ. Joe—all of them—they're still alive somewhere."

O'Connell winced. Before Harshbarger could get emotionally see-sawed again, Margo spoke up hastily. "We simply can't say that, Tim. I'm sorry. All we can say is that the time shift itself wouldn't have killed them. But what happened afterward . . ."

The state policeman shook his head. "Yeah, yeah, sure. They might have landed in the middle of a battlefield. But Joe and them were—are, dammit—pretty damn tough. I'm betting they can cut it."

Margo wondered if she should leave it at that. But . . .

These men weren't children. If nothing else, they had a right to know.

"No amount of toughness could have saved them, Tim," she said gently, "if they ended up in the wrong time. This—event—was a really deep one. For all we know, they might have gotten driven back two billion years ago."

Now, Brisebois winced. "Oh, hell."

Harshbarger looked at him. "What? Dammit, I don't care how big the dinosaurs ever got, I'm still betting on Joe Schuler and those men and women at Alexander."

Nick shook his head. "There weren't any dinosaurs two billion years ago, Tim. There weren't any land animals of any kind. Nothing. Not even lichen."

"Jeez," said Boyle, rubbing his face. "They'd starve. It's not like a maximum security prison has more food than maybe a month's supply."

Margo sighed. "They'd have died almost instantly, I'm afraid. That far back in time, the Earth's atmosphere was completely different. There wouldn't have been enough oxygen to keep them alive."

"Oh."

Harshbarger's jaws tightened. He looked around the huge chamber, full of scientific equipment whose design and function meant nothing to him. "Isn't there *any* way you can figure out where—when—they ended up?"

Margo shook her head. "I'm afraid not. We just—"

Karen Berg cleared her throat. "Uh, Margo, you've been out of the loop for a bit. As it happens, we now think we can. Malcolm and I have been working on that almost round the clock, and we've got a *lot* more data than we did when you left."

O'Connell looked smug. Everyone else in the chamber stared at Berg.

"Well. Roughly," she said apologetically. "It's sort of like a circular error of probability thing—and the farther back in time you get, the bigger the error factor."

"Still!" exclaimed Richard. "That's fantastic, Karen."

"*How* big?" demanded Harshbarger. He made a gesture with his hands, as if juggling a basketball. "That circular error thing, I mean."

Karen Berg was normally given to being cautious in her projections. But, seeing the so evident distress on Tim's face, she clearly decided it was a time for being as precise as she possibly could.

"They ended up somewhere—some*when*—in the Age of the Dinosaurs. We're pretty sure it was the early Cretaceous, approximately in the Hauterivian stage. Say, one hundred and thirty-five million years ago. But, that far back, the error spread is something like plus or minus eighteen million years. They could conceivably have landed as far back as the very late Jurassic, although that's not likely."

Harshbarger looked at Nick.

"Hell, I'm not sure, Tim. But I think—"

"The air was almost certainly quite breathable any time during the Mesozoic, which that period was in the middle of," said Richard firmly. "Probably thick with moisture, quite warm, and I wouldn't begin to guess what it smelled like. But your friends wouldn't have suffocated. Dinosaurs may have gotten them, but they'd have been breathing till the end."

Harshbarger slumped into a chair nearby. "I'm not worried about giant lizards. Joe and his people handle human lizards every day. Maybe not as big as dinosaurs, but every bit as mean and a lot smarter. They'll make do."

His eyes started to water. "Damn, I'll miss him. But at least I don't have to grieve."

CHAPTER
24

Terry Collins whistled softly as he walked toward the armory. Things were working out perfectly. The Indian with his sob story had been the icing on the cake. Captain Blacklock, along with over two-thirds of the guards, was gone. They were off to save the world, the silly bastards.

Collins gave a small chuckle and slowed his pace. He wanted to enjoy the night. It was beautiful. The sky was clear of clouds, giving him a spectacular view of the heavens. He had never realized how many stars there actually were. The moon was just as impressive. It was full and golden.

If he'd still been a kid he would have skipped across the parking lot, or tossed a rock at the man in the moon, just for the joy of it. He hesitated. Grinned. Bent and retrieved a rock.

But when he looked up at the sky once more, the mood was gone. There was work to do. The rock fell from his hand.

251

He knew from the shift roster, which Joe Schuler had so kindly given him a copy of, that the armory was unmanned. Almost everything was unmanned. The sixty-four guards still inside the walls had been divided up into two twelve-hour shifts—forty guards on days, twenty-four on nights. He suppressed the urge to laugh out loud. This was going to be like taking candy from a baby.

He didn't bother to look around, to check if anyone could see him. If they did, so what? He was the night supervisor, making his rounds. He was just being thorough.

He pulled a key ring from his pocket and flipped through the keys till he found the one he was looking for. Unlocking the door, he felt a twinge of doubt, but suppressed it. If Andy Blacklock stayed in charge they were going to spend their lives working like dogs, and for what? To keep a bunch of guys who weren't worth the air they breathed alive and locked up? No. It was crazy.

The prisoners needed to be released, or shot. That simple.

Oh, he had heard the arguments. If they were released they couldn't be given guns and ammo, so that meant they would starve. And those that didn't would freeze if this time and place had a winter. They wouldn't be able to build a shelter and gather enough firewood to make it through even a mild cold snap. Winter could be too close. As for prisoners being released and allowed to stay inside the prison, that was an impossibility. There weren't enough guards to keep things controlled.

Well, keeping them fed and watered till spring was *not* an option.

Everyone would starve.

This was a primitive time. Survival of the fittest, and he intended to be one of the survivors. If Andy Blacklock and Joe Schuler and Rod Hulbert were too stupid or weak to do what had to be done, that was too bad for them. He wasn't. He could do what needed doing and it wouldn't keep him up at night.

He stepped through the armory's door and closed it behind him before turning his flashlight on. He had a right to be here, but there was no sense in advertising his location. He glanced at his watch. He was well ahead of schedule. Luff had already been given his key to the cell house and a hand-drawn map. In one hour he would unlock the door and then he and his boys would remove the guard and make their way to the armory. The guard would be easy to take out. He didn't have a gun, a nightstick, nothing. Not even a can of pepper spay. His protection was a battery-operated radio whose battery had been removed twenty minutes ago.

That was another example of Andy Blacklock's stupidity. Sure, in the world they'd come from, guards didn't carry guns inside the prison. That was standard procedure. No gun meant no prisoner could take it from a guard and then be armed. Well, that might have made sense when the world was still outside the walls. But now, the rules needed to be changed.

When Joe suggested that change, Andy had shot him down. "No. That rule is there for a good reason. We can't afford to panic."

Blacklock just didn't get it. He didn't understand how much things had changed. But he would. When he got back and found his prison was now Collins' fortress, he would finally catch on.

If he got back at all. Collins wouldn't be at all surprised if he didn't. A man who couldn't figure out what to do with a prison filled with cons, sure as hell wouldn't know how to handle a bunch of marauders and wild Indians.

Collins checked the shift roster once more, just to make sure he hadn't overlooked anything. He grinned again when he saw Marie Keehn's name scratched off. Obviously, that had been done at the last minute. Hulbert must have gotten his way, and taken the little honey with him.

Collins couldn't blame him. Marie Keehn was fine-looking. Not as fine as Casey Fisher, though, whom Collins had already picked out as his own.

Andy Blacklock had left them forty women. Collins had made it plain to Luff that all forty of them were to be taken alive. Even the old, ugly ones. That had been the one and only point the bastard hadn't argued about.

He checked his watch once more. A half-hour to go.

He unlocked the doors to the cabinet, and left them standing open. He pulled out the vests and the helmets, and then took down the radios. These were C.E.R.T. radios, set to their own channel. The guards wouldn't be listening to that channel. Collins and his people could keep in touch, and no one would know.

Adrian Luff turned the key, heard the click and gave a little sigh of relief. He hadn't dared try it any earlier. Getting too anxious had caused more than one solid plan to disintegrate. Using his mirror he checked the hall to be sure the guard was nowhere to be seen.

It was clear.

He moved down the row of cells, unlocking each door as he passed it. The men inside were expecting him. None of them made a sound. Instead, they stepped out and fell into line behind him. They carried their shoes. Many of them also carried jury-rigged weapons made from whatever material they had managed to locate. He came to the end of the row less than five minutes after leaving his cell.

He passed a key to the man behind him and motioned for him to go up the metal stairs to the third floor. The rest of the men followed him to the ground level. The guard had just finished rounds, so he would be at the desk. The idiots still did their paperwork. There was no administrative aide who was ever going to read it, but they did it just the same.

Howard Earl Jameson looked up just as Luff cleared the last step. He snatched up his radio and keyed the send button, shouting a warning to the other guards. But the radio was dead, of course.

Luff waved at the guard. Three prisoners moved toward him, blocking his way to the door. The short struggle that followed didn't last long. Once it was over, the guard lay on the floor, tied up with a cord clipped from a now useless television. His keys were in Luff's pocket, his flashlight in Luff's hand.

"Let's move," Adrian said.

One of the prisoners took off down the cellblock releasing the men on the lower level. These were the men chosen for tonight, and for the months ahead. Most of them were smarter than the average con and all of them had backgrounds that Luff thought would be useful in this new world. And they included, of course, all the men who had become part of Luff's informal organization.

That was something Luff hadn't bothered to explain to Collins. He had let the man think they were being chosen because of their fighting prowess. Collins was another idiot. He couldn't think past tonight. He couldn't see they were going to need farmers and soldiers, mechanics and laborers, everything you could think of.

Collins had insisted the women be spared and Adrian had agreed. What Collins didn't know was that *none* of the guards were going to die if Luff could help it. Including the male guards whom Collins obviously expected were going to be murdered on the spot.

Not tonight, anyway. Not until he discovered who was useful and who was not. Who could make things run. Who could *build* things.

Tonight was the easy part.

The hard part was months down the road. Actually, it was years from now. Running water and sewers and baked bread with jam. Those were the things that gave life a quality Luff wasn't anxious to live without. He didn't mind doing it for a while, but he wasn't going to do it forever. Before he was busted, he had made a good living as an accountant for a manufacturing company that made specialty parts for machinery. He hadn't worked the floor. He didn't have those skills, but he knew men who could look at a drawing and two weeks later hand you a functioning machine.

And that's what he had to know about the guards they captured, before any of them were killed. Who was working this hellhole because the economy sucked, their old line of work had dried up, and they needed cold hard cash to meet the mortgage?

Once he sifted through the guards he would go through the prisoners. Some of them would be men of talent who happened to fall on the wrong side of the law. But, prisoner or guard, it didn't matter to Luff. As long as they had a skill that was usable, they could live. After he knew who was who, who had those talents and skills, then he would thin the numbers, but not one minute before he was sure.

He motioned for everyone to put their shoes on. If things went right, they wouldn't have to worry about noise from this point on. When the last man gave him a heads up, he turned the knob on the door and pushed it open.

He stopped halfway through the door, startled. This was the first time he'd been outside his cell since the Quiver. The fresh air felt good on his skin, and in his lungs. The sky was prettier than he remembered.

Then he noticed the slight chill in the wind. He had heard winter might be coming. This was late November, pre-Quiver time. Now, no one knew. Everyone just guessed and hoped.

He moved on. The weather wouldn't change anything that happened tonight. June or January, it didn't matter. Tonight he had to take the prison.

When Collins had approached him with his plan to take command, Luff had agreed. Partly because he preferred being in charge to being incarcerated, but more because he was afraid to turn him down. If Collins succeeded, he'd be the one deciding who got culled and who didn't. He might easily decide that there wasn't any use for an accountant in their new world.

So, Adrian had agreed. He'd even encouraged the fool.

He'd had to do more than encourage, soon enough. Collins really wasn't very bright. Adrian had had to baby him along. Patiently explaining what was needed, over and over. Explaining and arguing. Pushing him to make all the steps, not letting him take any shortcuts.

Walking through the grounds, moving quickly, using Jameson's keys as they came to doors that had been left unguarded, they made their way to the armory. The map Collins had given him was good. So was the route. They did not run into one guard from the time they left the cellblock until they stepped into the door of the small block building twenty minutes later.

"You're early," Collins said, frowning at his watch. "Ten minutes."

Luff nodded. "It went better than we thought it would."

"You took care of Jameson?"

"Yeah." Luff looked at the room beyond the entry area. "He won't be a problem."

"I bet not." Collins chuckled and shook his head. "Okay, the easy part's over. You and your boys are about to earn your keep."

"How many are on duty, and how many are in their bunks?"

When Collins told him, Luff gave a low whistle. "Are you sure?"

"Sure I'm sure. Everyone not on duty is beat. They've been pulling twelve-hour shifts ever since the Quiver. They're sacked out in A-block. You send a few guys in there with repeating rifles, and you'll have them before they've had a chance to roll out of their bedrolls."

"And the other twenty-four?"

"You only have eighteen left to worry about. You've already got Jameson. Marie Keehn went with Hulbert and I'm right here." He looked at his list. "Kathleen Hanrahan's on maternity; she's just had a kid. And Elaine Brown is still out of it. She's the CO Boyd Chrissman nailed. They're both in the infirmary with two of the three nurses." Collins snickered. "Blacklock left the two old crones and took the honey with him. They're both as old as dirt, and look like shit. But what the hell. I'll take care of them myself."

Luff took the roster and looked at it. "Casey Fisher, she's their guard. I take it you plan to take care of her, too."

Collins shrugged.

"Okay. You go to the infirmary. But remember, you're the one who made the rule: none of the women are to be hurt."

"Killed," Collins said.

"We'll need the nurses. I don't want any of them hurt. Are you understanding me?"

"Not a problem. I won't lay a finger on either of the nurses."

"Or the guards, or the kid," Luff said forcefully. "You have a job to do tonight. No horsing around. And I mean that. We take the prison tonight. We take it, and then we get ourselves in a position to hold it."

He saw the resentment well up in the man, resentment and suspicion. It would be just like the stupid bastard to start an argument in front of everybody. Adrian needed to defuse this, for the moment.

He gave the big prison guard a friendly clap on the arm. "Hey, man, relax. We'll party big tomorrow. You want that guard, that Casey Fisher, she's yours. Tomorrow. Tonight, we've got work to do. And the first thing we're going to do is take A-block. After that, while we mop up, you can take care of the infirmary."

Collins nodded, but Luff knew the man had no plans to wait. He was dumb as a rock. Before this night was over they might need those nurses' cooperation. Luff knew the two women in the infirmary. He had been sent to clean the clinic a few times before the Quiver, and he'd seen them work. They did a good job under pressure, but if they were scared, they'd cave. If Collins hurt that baby or raped one of the women guards in front of them, neither nurse would be any good after that for days.

Well, this was a simple problem. After Collins turned away, Luff gave Butch Wesson a small hand signal that said: *stick close; I have a job for you.*

There really wasn't any reason at all that Collins needed to stay alive any longer. Adrian was tempted to just shoot him in the back right now and be done with it. But a gunshot might alert the guards sleeping in A-block. And he was leading a bunch of cons. Even though he'd picked them personally, some of them were still a little unpredictable. If they saw the leadership fall apart right in front of them, one shooting the other, they might get their own ideas.

No, better to do it quietly. By the time most of the cons found out, it would be a done deal—and Luff's authority would be enhanced rather than undermined.

James Cook reached up for the six-inch metal bar from the small opening the health examiner required for ventilation in the cell house, that had come loose during the Quiver. He'd taken it down from time to time and had patiently filed the end to a reasonably sharp point, and then placed it back. He just wanted to make sure the sharpened bar was still loose and would come easily into his hand if he needed it. Which he figured he would, with a prisoner uprising underway led by Adrian Luff.

"Boom," he whispered into the dark, "we're trapped like a couple of bug-eyed flies on fly-paper."

"Yeah, I know. You got anything useful to say?"

Cook watched the black giant roll off the bottom bunk and press his ear to the floor. The cell house was empty. They were the only two still behind bars.

"They be a lot of blood spillin' soon. You afraid?"

Cook chewed on his bottom lip, not sure what to say. To admit fear was to admit to a weakness, a very stupid move when behind bars. But the Boom wasn't exactly a normal con. Honesty could just as easily be what the giant was after. In the end he decided on a non-answer. "Do I look stupid?"

The giant shook his head. "Nah. You be one of the smart ones." He sat up facing the bars. "Half the guards is gone. And the whole world is gone. All that's left is us and the monsters outside the walls."

Just to keep his mind off his fear, James blurted out an idle question he'd been wondering about.

"How'd a black man wind up with an Italian last name like Bolgeo, anyway?"

As soon as he asked the question, he realized what a

stupid thing it'd been to say. You never knew exactly what might set off Boomer's temper. Most of the time, the huge man was genial enough. His boys all called him "Uncle Timmy" and the only thing you usually had to watch out for was his cut-throat killer way of playing spades. But when he did lose his temper, the results were legendary. The man must be pushing sixty, but he was still hard-bodied despite his enormous size, and he was almost literally as strong as a bull.

Fortunately, the Boom just chuckled. "Well, they be two theories in the family 'bout that. One of them is that Great-grandpa Luigi was an Eye-talian. The other is that Great-grandpa was a high yeller nigger passing as an Eye-talian, who invented the name. I hold to the second theory, myself."

"Ah." That seemed safe enough.

"Now it's my turn to be nosy. What you in here for?"

"Second degree murder. I got charged with first degree, but the jury wouldn't go for it."

"You had a *trial?*"

Most convicts didn't. Their sentences resulted from plea bargaining. James' public defender had urged him to do the same, but James had refused. Stupid, probably, but he hadn't seen where he could do anything else.

"Did you do it?"

That question was so astonishing that James' jaw almost dropped. Cons didn't ask each other if they were guilty or not, because nobody except a fool would try to claim he was innocent in a prison. Didn't matter if he was or not. That was another form of weakness, and you never showed weakness.

The Boom really was an odd one. Of course, with his size and capacity for fury, he could afford to be odd.

With anyone else, James would have just issued a noncommittal grunt. With Boomer, though . . .

"No, I didn't."

"You was framed?"

James barked a sarcastic laugh. "Oh, come on, Boom! 'Framed?' The cops don't bother to frame Injuns. Or niggers, or greasers. Or poor white trash, for that matter. The prosecutor had a killing to clear off his docket, I was a handy suspect who fit the bill and didn't have an alibi, and there it was. Their case was weak enough that the jury wouldn't go for a first degree, but they found me guilty of second."

"What happened?"

"I was in a bar one night. Friday night, after work. It'd been a bad day and I was pretty much tying one on. Which was stupid, because when I'm in a bad mood like that I can lose my temper if I've drunk too much. Sure enough. Some asshole started ragging me, I got pissed, chose him out, we stepped outside and I beat the crap out of him."

He took a deep breath. Even now, he still got angry thinking about it. "But that was it. We fought, I won— hands down—he was lying on the ground with a split lip and a buncha bruises, and it was over. My hands hurt and I felt stupid as hell. So I went back into the bar, paid my tab, and went home to sleep it off."

He took another deep breath. "Which I did. The next morning the cops were at my door arresting me for first degree murder. Seems the asshole went to another bar afterward and got himself killed about three hours later.

They found him in the parking lot with the back of his head caved in. Probably from a baseball bat."

Boomer nodded. "And nobody saw you come home and could vouch for your whereabouts."

"Yep. They said they had motive, method, and opportunity." He spit into a corner. "Never mind that the motive didn't make any sense. I'd already whipped the guy, for chrissake, so why would I be seeking 'revenge'? I won, he lost, it's over. Never mind that they never found the murder weapon. Never mind that no eyewitnesses ever placed me at that other bar. Never mind that I'd never heard of that other bar and nobody had *ever* seen me there."

He shrugged. "But you know how it is. I had a juvie record. Nothing really heavy, but enough to make me look like a bad boy. I'm not white. I'm not a person of color from a so-called good family. I had no alibi. It was an easy case for the prosecutor, and he didn't give a flying fuck whether I was guilty or not. Hell, neither did my own so-called lawyer."

"That how it is." The Boom started laughing softly. "But that all behind us now, boy. We in a new world that ain't got no prosecutors. Just Adrian Luff and his goons and a buncha dinosaurs."

After a while, James started laughing too.

Lieutenant Joe Schuler lay on the narrow bunk, tossing and turning, feeling every lump of the mattress and every wrinkle in the blanket. The pillows weren't right. One was too low; two was too high. He glanced at the chair he was using as a nightstand. The small wind-up clock he'd borrowed from Woeltje showed he still had four hours of sleep-time. Too many to just call it a short night and get up.

He closed his eyes so he wouldn't have to stare at the ceiling and tried to relax. He had been asleep earlier, but it hadn't been restful. He had been dreaming in short, unrelated clips that his brain pretended fit together. The type of dream you seldom remembered. But this one had been a rerun, so he remembered too much of it. He was with Maria, before the split. They were on a picnic.

He lay there thinking about that. The two of them had never taken a picnic to the beach. Not once. He hadn't had the time, and she was just as busy. It had always been fast food, or eating at home to save money. It had been his mother who liked picnics and his father who would load everything up in the car and drive the thirty minutes it took to get the family to her favorite spot. A small park sitting next to a creek. The trees were old oaks filled with acorns, birds and squirrels. Joe and his brother, Keith, would play on the swings and monkey bars, occasionally sneaking a look at their parents lying on a blanket staring at the sky, or sometimes each other. He started drifting away, back to his dreams, wondering if Maria went on picnics with her new husband.

Marie Keehn knelt on the flat rubber roof located on the administration building's new wing. Below her were the offices that used to be payroll; above her was the sky. A portrait of infinity. She spread her bedroll out and laid down. It was just chilly enough to make for good sleeping weather. She had thought about sleeping inside A-block with the others, then changed her mind.

She wanted to be alone. She needed time to think.

Hulbert was what she needed to think about. He was in love. It showed. And she wasn't so sure she wanted that. The fact that he fell so quickly hadn't surprised her. She thought men usually did. She'd read an article in a women's magazine once, explaining how it took most men less than two minutes to fall madly in love, and she thought the article had it right.

It took most women much longer, the article had said. Many of them were actually married for a year or so before they realized just how much they loved their husbands. Women were considered the romantics, but in reality they tended to be a lot more practical with their hearts. It was men who jumped in with both feet to sink or swim.

And she liked it that way. It felt right to her. Especially now.

Her grandmother had told her once that a man had to love a woman enough to die for her. And a woman had to love the man enough to live her life for him. That had struck a cord in Marie. It suited something in her personality.

And it was why she was still single. She had been waiting for that man who would lay down his life rather than let her die. And she had been looking for someone she could wrap her life around. As her dear old grandmother used to say, someone worth giving up the *she* and becoming the *we* for.

She didn't know how she felt about Hulbert. She knew without a doubt he would step between her and death. He had already done it. Without his quick reflexes she would have been killed by that scary cat-thing. It was the other half of the deal that worried her. The giving up of the *she*. The becoming a *we*.

She knew the smart women, the ones with good marriages, had remained themselves. They hadn't become clones of the men in their lives. But the *we* had still taken first place. And if that meant changing a few things, that was fine. They made the changes. If that meant talking or raising hell till the man did something important for the *we*, then they did that too. It was work. And with the world turned upside down right now she wasn't sure it was a job she wanted to take on.

She knew Hulbert had started the trip to the field already infatuated. The physical attraction, the chemistry, had been there, drawing them together. Then the other things happened: starting a fire, finding a set of prints, skinning out, reducing meat down to its usable parts, easy to transport. And then came the talking of tomorrow and of yesterday and the working together on the today.

And Hulbert had been caught, and she was walking around the edges of it, teetering.

"What the hell, girl. Quit lying. You fell." She laughed at herself. Yeah, if she hadn't fallen, she wouldn't be on a rooftop in the middle of the night thinking about her grandmother's old fashioned sayings and wondering if the name Marie Louise Hulbert sounded right.

CHAPTER
25

Joe woke to the sound of a little shriek and a prisoner standing over the next bed.

"If I were you, I'd lay still."

In the cot across from him he could see Judith Barnett looking wide-eyed at a man with a gun pointed at her head.

The man was talking to them both. If Joe moved, Barnett died. Then—the man held the repeating rifle in a way that suggested he knew how to work it—Joe would be next.

"Easy does it, fella. We're not in a hurry to die. We're cooperating." The lieutenant slowly sat up, praying the man wouldn't panic and pull the trigger. "Just tell me what you want and where you want me."

The lights came on and Joe could see armed men in prison garb lining guards up along the east wall. There were at least ten men with guns, and a half dozen others with nightsticks. Some of them had vests and helmets. They had raided the armory.

His eyes went back to the man standing over Barnett. What was his name? The face was familiar. He wasn't one of the death row inmates. He knew each of them too well. This guy was from . . .

A-block, he thought. Yes, before they had moved the prisoners.

Joe glanced around the large room with its dozens of half walls designed to give each prisoner his own cubicle. A-block's clientele were considered nonviolent. In for robbery, if there'd been no violence involved. Maybe assault, if there'd been extenuating circumstances. But not murder, even in the second degree. They could be allowed a little more elbow room. And a little more contact with other prisoners.

He remembered the name, now. Danny Bostic, in for bank robbery. The man had hit at least four banks before he was caught, but each of the operations had been well planned and he hadn't hurt anybody. Whether that was the result of Bostic's residual morality or simply the fact he was smart, there was no way to know. But, under the circumstances, either explanation was somewhat relieving. Whatever else, he wasn't a hothead.

"Danny, we're moving slow." He motioned for Judith to sit up. "Very slow."

Bostic took a step back. Using the gun's barrel, he motioned to where the other guards were now standing. "Over there."

Barnett scrambled to her feet and rushed to the wall. Joe took his time. He didn't want to spook the man into firing. He could tell the prisoners were edgy. All of them, not just Bostic. If just one man panicked, the whole room would turn into a charnelhouse. He joined the others on the wall, hoping like hell they weren't being lined up just to be mowed down.

Then he saw Collins, and that answered a lot of questions. How the inmates had gotten out of their cells, how they had gotten into the infirmary, how they had gotten into A-block without having to bust in the doors. He should have known the second he woke up.

They'd all known Collins was a problem. But it had never occurred to any of them that the man would be so egotistically stupid as to throw in with the convicts. Did the lunatic seriously think he would survive in such a situation? He'd probably made more enemies among the prisoners than any other single guard at the facility.

"Joe, my boy, hope you slept well."

Joe didn't answer Collins. Instead, he studied the man who stood behind him. This would be the prisoner who was really in charge.

Joe recognized him immediately, of course.

"Luff and Collins," he said. "That's one for the books."

Collins grinned and Luff's eyes turned to Joe. They were cold and calculating.

"Take them to C-block and lock them up," Luff said.

Joe breathed a sigh of relief. They weren't going to be shot, at least not right away. The relief quickly turned to worry as they were herded out the door and into the night air. They had been sleeping, so no one had shoes. Most were without socks. Some of them were like him, in tees, their uniform shirts neatly folded and lying on the chair next to the bed they had been on. A few of the men had stripped down to tees and boxer shorts.

Marie woke, momentarily confused, trying to decide if she had heard a shout or if she'd dreamed it. The prison seemed quiet enough. She peered over the edge of the roof, wishing for a pair of binoculars and promising herself she would have Joe snag her a pair when day shift came on duty. The parking lot was empty. So were the areas between the buildings. The armory was dark. So was the guardhouse out by the gate.

Moving quietly, she slid across to the other side of the roof, looked over the edge and almost let out a hiss before she caught herself.

Even in the dim moonlight she could make out the prisoners leading what looked to be over three dozen guards through the exercise yard to C-block. They were armed, too.

She hunched down as much as she could and still see what was happening. Collins was not being led, she suddenly realized. He was one of the men doing the leading.

That bastard!

She squinted into the darkness. The guards were shoved through the door to cell house C. Then, the prisoners started dividing up. A few followed the guards inside the building, but most of them continued through the exercise yard, coming to a standstill outside each door. She knew what they were doing. They were going to attack the lone guards at their posts, all at the same time. None of them would have a chance.

She snatched up her radio to call a warning to them, and stopped. A warning wouldn't help anyone. There was nowhere for them to go, and nothing for any of them to defend themselves with. All she would accomplish would be drawing attention to herself. No. If she was going to get caught, or killed, she was going to make it worth something.

She watched silently as one guard after another was pulled from their post and marched to join the other guards in C-block.

Not one shot was fired.

They weren't killing the guards. *Why?* It wasn't morals; that she was damned sure of. The answer came to her very quickly. Over half the guards left behind when Andy set out to find the Indian camp were women.

"Oh no, you don't, you assholes," she muttered under her breath. "No way in hell."

She watched as Collins veered away from the others. He was headed toward the infirmary.

She made her decision. If she was going to get caught or killed, Lieutenant Terry Collins was the one she would take out first. He was the traitor. And she had the pistol she'd taken from the armory on a holster on her hip.

She keyed her way into the infirmary, hesitated, then left the door unlocked. If one of the prisoners decided to join Collins, she had just let him in. And that could be bad. But she might need a quick way out, and an unlocked door could be the difference between instant death and a chance at escape.

The baby was still wailing and she could hear several women screaming at Collins to let them out. That meant they were locked in one of the holding cells. The crash of metal on floor told her not all the women were locked away. One of them was in the examining room with Collins.

That would be Casey Fisher, she thought. She was the youngest and the prettiest, except for Elaine Brown—and given Collins, Marie didn't think he'd be attracted to a black woman. He hid it pretty well, but she was sure the man was a bigot on top of everything else.

Marie pulled out the pistol and made her way toward the room. When the women saw her they stopped yelling. Then Elaine Brown, quick-witted, began screaming with a renewed vigor. The others realized what she was doing and why, and joined her. Marie made a motion of turning a key. Caldwell shook her head and pointed toward the examining room.

Okay, they couldn't give her any help. All she could hope for was surprise.

She approached the door carefully. It wasn't closed, which meant she could see inside. It also meant she could be seen, but neither Collins nor Fisher was in sight. The sounds had moved to the storage area and were slowing down. Fisher was losing.

Marie increased her pace. She took four steps to the entry, turned right, and peeked around the corner. Collins didn't see her. As she'd expected from the noise, he was preoccupied. Casey was on her back, on the floor, with a bruise on her cheek. Probably put there by the butt of the pistol Collins still had in his right hand. He was grinning and unfastening the belt to her pants with his left hand.

Marie drew her head back out of sight.

How should she handle it? A gunshot would draw attention.

Casey screamed. Collins cursed.

She didn't see where she had any choice. It would be

insane to try to subdue Collins with blows. He was almost twice as big as she was.

Marie slipped into the room and stepped up to the two figures struggling on the floor. She'd been well trained in the procedure to follow. *Aim your gun—shout halt or I'll shoot—give the prisoner time to respond—he will—he does not want to die—*

None of which had any relevance.

Collins spotted her at the last moment. His head started to come up. That was good because it meant Casey was well out of the line of fire. Marie's pistol was six inches from his skull when she fired. Collins spilled over, flat, with just his leg still on top of Fisher.

Marie was so angry that she almost fired another shot—or three or four or five—at the body lying on the floor. Barely, she managed to restrain herself.

First, Collins was dead anyway. No doubt about it. She was an excellent shot, she'd fired at point blank range, and her pistol was .40 caliber. Half his brains looked to be scattered across the floor and there was blood splattered everywhere on that side of the room. One of his eyes had come out of the socket, connected to the skull only by the optic nerve, and his hair was smoldering around the entry wound.

Secondly—most importantly—she knew people reacted differently to one loud sound than they did to a series. One loud sound . . . could be anything. Two or three or four would be recognized as gunshots.

After a few seconds, she sighed, thumbed the decocking lever and reholstered the gun.

"You all right?" she asked Fisher.

Casey's head was turned, her eyes on Collins' corpse. "Are you sure he's dead?"

"Are you kidding?"

Casey choked. Half-sob; half-laugh. "Okay, stupid question. God, that's the most horrible looking thing I've ever been so glad to see."

"Barbara, can you give the baby something so it won't cry?"

The LPN shook her head. "We don't have anything like that."

Marie nodded. She hadn't really been all that hopeful, but she had to ask.

"All right. Kathleen, you keep that baby of yours quiet. No matter what you have to do, don't let him cry until you hit the woods." She handed Barbara the crude map she had drawn on the back of a used work order. "When you get to the river, go upstream, about a four-hour walk. Well, four hours if you're in good shape and making good time. You'll probably need longer. You'll come to a hilly area that's covered in strange-looking stones. Most of them are taller than you. Look for one that has a tree growing out of it. The tree isn't all that big, maybe six feet tall. About ten yards directly west of it will be a small cave. The opening is only about half the size of that tree I'm talking about. It'll be a tight squeeze getting in, but once inside, you'll have plenty of room. There's enough shrubbery and fallen branches in the area that you should be able to disguise the entrance."

She rubbed her head, sure there was something else she needed to say but couldn't figure it out what it was.

She looked at the map once more, trying to think. Then she knew.

"Use the moon's new position as your directional guide. Figure it's dead east and moving west. It doesn't. But that's the guide for the map."

"Okay," Barbara said. "We'll do that. But after we get to the cave, how long do we wait for you?"

"I don't know. Give me at least a day. Um. Better make it two days."

Lylah Caldwell was frowning. "Elaine and Kathleen aren't in shape for this. They're both wide open." The RN pointed to the area on the paper Marie had indicated was forested. "They'll get an infection sure as hell."

"Lylah," Kathleen hissed, "are you crazy? I'd a lot rather get an infection from tramping through the woods than catch what we would from a prisoner gang rape. If we lived through it at all."

"Same goes for me," said Brown.

"That's not what I meant. I meant we needed to take some antibiotics along, that's all. I know we can't stay here."

The six women and one baby came to a halt just inside the administration building. What had once been an area that was always staffed with a minimum of three COs, was now empty. The glass doors leading to the outside were unguarded. The small guard shack that sat a dozen yards from the edge of the parking lot was empty.

Marie nodded toward the outside. "I want you to run, don't walk, to the edge of the woods. Take off, and don't look back. And don't wait for one another in plain sight. Get inside the brush, then you can wait."

"I'm not going to make it," Elaine Brown whispered, tears welling in her dark eyes. "I thought maybe I could, but I can't." She leaned against the wall. Even in the dim light the women clustered around her could see the beads of sweat on her face.

"You have to," Marie hissed. "You have no choice."

Brown closed her eyes. With her teeth clenched tight she said, "You have no idea how much pain I'm in, girl. I can't go on. Period." The CO pulled up her blouse, exposing the bandages on her abdomen. There was fresh blood seeping through. "The walking is tearing everything loose. There's no way I can make it through a long hike in the woods."

"Oh, hell," Barbara Ray whispered. "Marie, she's right. We're going to have to slow down." The LPN looked at the others. "Better yet, you guys get going. I'll stay with Elaine. We'll catch up with you."

Brown shook her head. "No. You go with Lylah and Kathleen. They're going to need help with the baby. And you can't stay with me. One person might be able to hide. Two won't. Marie, get them out of here. I need to drag my sorry ass off someplace safe, and I don't have time for a debate."

Marie nodded. She knew what the woman wasn't saying, and she agreed with her. Elaine didn't think she had a snowball's chance in hell, anyway, so there was no reason for Barbara Ray to throw away her chance at living.

Barbara looked like she was going to argue, but didn't. Instead she took the baby from Kathleen and started toward the doors. "Don't tell anyone where you hide. If we get caught, we can't tell what we don't know."

Elaine Brown walked away as soon as Kathleen and the nurses were out the door. Neither Casey Fisher nor Marie Keehn looked in her direction. Barbara Ray's comment about not knowing where the CO hid had struck a nerve, and neither of them wanted to be able to even guess where she would be holed up.

Instead, Marie and Casey watched the women work their way across the open ground. When they disappeared behind the trees and foliage, Marie whispered, "I really don't like sending them off like that, with nothing to defend themselves with except one shotgun and three shells. They could run into some animal and . . ."

"Yeah, but we only had the three guns, and for what we have to do, we couldn't afford to give them any more than that," Casey said.

Marie nodded but didn't feel any better. She knew exactly what type of animals the women could run into. And with some of them, their death wouldn't be any easier than death at the hands of the men inside the prison. But out there, they had a chance. Inside the walls, they had nothing.

She drew her gun out of the holster. "You ready?"

"No, not really," Casey said. "But I won't be in an hour, either, and we better get started or the sun will catch us."

They made their way to the back of C-block. There was a seldom used door leading to the furnace room that Marie figured wouldn't be guarded. At least, she was hoping the prisoners were feeling safe enough they wouldn't have felt the need to post sentries at every entrance.

They were in luck. No one was there.

They made their way down the deserted corridor leading to the holding area as fast as they could, being careful to walk on the balls of their feet. They didn't want to have their heels clicking on the tile floor, announcing their presence. They came to the door that opened onto the cellblock, their hearts in their throats.

The view port was located dead center of the steel door, five and half feet off the floor. Casey was the taller of the two women and she stood only five feet, four inches tall. Marie dropped to one knee, lifting her other leg, giving Casey a platform to stand on.

Casey climbed up, looked, and then came down. "The place looks empty, except for our people in the cells," she hissed. "Where are the prisoners? Why aren't they guarding them?"

Marie shook her head. "I don't know," she whispered. "It doesn't make sense. But we've got to go with it."

She pulled the key ring she'd taken from Collins out of her pocket. Careful not to make any noise, she tried unlocking the door. She thought she'd picked the right key but she wasn't positive. The last thing they needed was for her to spend a minute out here trying out every key on a big key ring.

It was a little awkward. She was using her left hand to work the key, since she had the pistol in her right. But at least she'd picked the right one. The lock turned. Using her left hand, still holding the key ring, she pushed the door open.

Nothing. No one.

Just in case someone was hiding behind the door, she pushed it all the way flat. Hard, with her pistol ready.

Nothing. No one. The cells were packed with captured guards and no one standing watch over them.

It was crazy, but she figured somebody leading the convicts—or somebody else they'd put in charge of the task—had screwed up somewhere. And she wasn't about to look a gift horse in the mouth.

"Well, shit," said Butch Wesson, standing over the corpse of Terry Collins. "Looks like somebody else already did it for us."

Carl Yeager frowned. He was one of the prisioners who'd been standing watch in C-block. Butch had ordered all three to follow him to the infirmary. They weren't really needed at C-block, to watch over the captured guards, since the doors were solid and locked, and Butch had figured he might need some help. Collins was a big bastard, and as vicious as they come.

"Yeah, that's great," said Yeager. "But *who*?"

One of his companions, Eddie Trenton, had a jeer on his face. "Hell, I can think of thirty guys right off the top of my head with a score to settle with this shithead. Could have been any one of them, decided to take the opportunity."

Butch wasn't happy with that explanation. Sure, it *could* be true, but—

The third of the men he'd brought put his doubts into words. "Then what happened to the women?" demanded Gary Reading. "If it was just one guy, how'd he get all of them to go with him?"

"And what would he want with the old bitches any-way?" Yeager said. "Butch, something's wrong."

Wesson's jaws tightened. He'd have to report this to Luff right away, and Luff was going to be pissed as all hell. The boss was still a little mad at him for messing up the Cook business a while back.

Marie ran to the cells packed tight with guards. She found the right key on her second try and started unlocking the gates. They swung open and the men and women poured out.

Nobody said anything. They knew they had to keep silent and they knew they had to *move*. Marie's and Casey's pistols were the only weapons they had.

Marie led them back the way she'd come. Joe Schuler brought up the rear. He and three other guards took turns helping to half-carry Keith Woeltje, with his bum knee.

Back down the hall, out the door, through the exercise yard, hugging the walls, staying in the shadows. Through the double set of gates leading to the administration building.

Through the admit center and past the X-ray machines. Through the set of double doors leading to the parking lot. Toward the guardhouse, the field and the woods beyond.

So far, the guards had been moving pretty slowly, since they were trying to keep quiet. But their discipline finally started fraying, seeing safety up ahead. Temporary safety, anyway. They started hurrying toward the woods, then trotting, then running.

Joe Schuler tried to restrain them, at first, hissing orders to keep quiet. But Marie didn't really see any point to it. The terror they'd kept under tight control was breaking loose, and there'd be no holding them back.

And why bother, anyway? They'd make it to the trees long before any prisoner with a gun could get within shooting range, even if they were spotted. And, after that, who cared? Convicts could be dangerous as all hell inside the walls, even without guns. But Marie didn't think more than a handful would be worth a damn in the wilderness.

So, she was running herself by the time she passed into the trees. So was Joe Schuler, insofar as he could run carrying Woeltje piggyback. Luckily, Keith wasn't a big man, and Joe was both big and in excellent physical condition.

She stopped then, and looked back. The sun was just starting to come over the horizon. So far as she could tell, their escape had still gone unnoticed.

For a moment, she wondered where Elaine Brown was hiding. But there was no point in that. There hadn't been time to rescue her anyway. Not without jeopardizing dozens of other people.

So, she just sent her a silent mental salute. *Good luck, gutsy lady.*

Elaine Brown turned the knob of the door to the basement slowly. She didn't think there would be any prisoners inside the furnace area, but she couldn't keep her hands from shaking, or her heart from racing. She had heard voices coming from the upper level of the administration building, so she had stayed on the lower levels, wandering in and out of rooms looking for someplace she'd be overlooked. The kitchen would get too much traffic; she hadn't bothered to even look there for a place to hide. The payroll department seemed deserted enough, but with its fifteen floor-to-ceiling windows, every nook and cranny would be too well lit once the sun came up. The bathrooms didn't have any windows, but they were still useless as a place to hide. That left her nowhere to go but the dirty, moldy, roach- and spider-infested basement.

And that door was kept locked. The only people who went down there on any sort of regular basis were the maintenance crew. She went into the small room they used as an office, hoping there'd be a spare key some-where. A search through the drawers turned up a key ring with four keys, and to her relief the third key on the ring unlocked the door.

She entered the stairwell and closed the door behind her, then locked it again. She played her flashlight along the basement's interior, and suppressed a groan. There were sixteen steps and she had to climb down those stairs.

She shut off the light and shoved the flashlight into her hip pocket. Then she clutched the metal handrail with her right hand and applied pressure to her blood-soaked dressing with her left. She had a handful of butterfly strips and the supplies for one dressing change. Once she found herself a little cubbyhole, she would use the strips to stop the bleeding, apply what was left of the antibiotic salve to the wound and then cover the area with fresh bandages.

The CO gave a small whimper in anticipation of the pain, and began the long climb down.

CHAPTER
26

The floor felt hard. The light drifting in through the bars and small window was just enough for James Cook to make out the bunk beds and the combination stainless steel toilet and sink, the only things left in the room. As consciousness returned, he began checking the damage to his body. He knew he was bruised and bloodied, but he was hoping none of his bones were broken.

The cement floor felt colder than usual. As James moved his legs, trying to ease the pain in his hip, he realized he was naked. He gritted his teeth, staring at the ceiling twelve feet above him and at the single, unlit bulb behind its protective wire mesh, and allowed the reality of his situation to sink in. He could hear screams coming from a cell one row above him.

James took a deep breath, slow and long. Nothing seemed broken, at least. He forced his hands to continue checking the damage done. Half afraid, he touched his rectum. He'd taken a beating, and he was sore all over, but he hadn't been raped. At least he didn't think so. If he had been, he'd know for sure the first time he had a bowel movement.

"You be a tough bastard, that's for sure."

Startled, Cook looked to his left. The light had been so dim that he hadn't noticed Boomer in the corner. James nodded at his roommate, and immediately regretted it. The room lurched and spun out of control, causing him to close his eyes. As soon as things settled down and he was sure he wasn't going to puke, he reached for the orange coverall being offered by the black giant. "Thanks, Boom," he mumbled.

Another scream went through the cell house.

"Who's the lucky guy?" Cook asked between clenched teeth.

Boomer looked at the ceiling. "That blond kid that come in with you. Luff has a few debts, and the kid's paying 'em off. Whether he want to or not."

Cook squinted at him. "You look good, not a mark on you."

The black man shrugged. "It was your fight, not mine. They steered clear of me."

James shook his head. He hadn't expected Boomer to intervene when Butch Wesson and his buddies came into the cell. He was just surprised that Luff hadn't ordered him taken down too. Of course, they'd have had to send a lot more than the three guys who came in for Cook.

"Yeah, I understand that," he said. "I just can't figure out what Luff's doing. He's got no love for you, that's for sure. For that matter . . ."

Now that his head was clearing and he could think straight, James was wondering why *he* was still alive.

"This weren't ordered by Luff. Butch was on his own, settlin' a grudge."

Sensing James' skepticism, Boomer chuckled. "Boy, the only reason you still alive is that Luff put a stop to it. He was pissed as all hell at Wesson. Butch mighta died anyway, after you stabbed him. But Luff shot him. Three times. Then shot one of Butch's buddies just before he could cut you."

He chuckled again, with a lot more humor. "I will say I ain't seen too many sights as delightful as the look on Butch Wesson's face when you stuck six inches of steel in him. They never expected you'd have a shiv." He glanced admiringly at the cell window, one of whose bars was now missing.

James looked at it also. That was the last clear memory he had. Seeing Butch and his two buddies piling into the cell, he'd known he was in a fight for his life. He hadn't expected to survive, but he'd been determined to take as many with him as he could. He'd jumped up, grabbed the bar he'd loosened and sharpened earlier, and things had gone from there. He remembered stabbing Wesson, but that was about it.

"What happened to my clothes?"

"Luff had 'em strip you down and beat you some. But he didn't let 'em go too far with it. He said he didn't want you too badly hurt. Just softened up some, was the way he put it."

James started to shake his head, but stopped when he felt the pain that caused. "I don't get it. Softened up for what? And why would Luff stop Wesson at all? Much less shoot him? He's got no love lost for me."

Boomer looked out of the cell, his heavy face pensive. "Luff a smart one, boy. Don' ever forget that. Real smart. Only way a guy like him coulda made it to the top in here. He thinkin' ahead. After he shoot Butch and one of his buddies, he was hollering at the top of his lungs. 'Bad enough the stupid fuck let all the nurses escape. Now he wants to kill the only EMT in the place!' That's what he was yelling."

The Boom turned his head to look at Cook. "That be true? You an ambulance man?"

"Fire department, not a hospital," James said. "But, yeah, it's true." Some fragment of an earlier life's pride drove him to add: "I was damn good at it, too."

Boomer looked away again. "I believe that. I been watching you. Studying you. You be damn good at everything."

He leveraged his massive body to an upright sitting position. "You got heart, too. And you be honest. So I decided you okay with me. I told the rest of the boys."

James nodded. His kept his face impassive, though, letting no sign of his relief show.

Before the Quiver, the Boom's pronouncement would have meant James was safe for the rest of his stay here. The Boomer's gang was the smallest and in some ways the oddest of any of them. But with the Boom as its head, nobody messed with them. Not the white supremacists, not the hardcore black gangs, not the Hispanics. Nobody.

Now, he didn't know. If Luff hadn't pulled off his

uprising, things would have been the same. But with Luff running things . . .

Boomer seemed to be reading his mind. "We deal with Luff, we need to. But like I said, he thinkin' ahead. And you ain't the only con with skills. Lot of my boys got 'em. Not medical, though."

That was probably true, now that James thought about it. For all the Boom's occasionally erratic and explosive temper, being a member of his gang was a relatively sane experience compared to some others. It even had two white members. For form's sake, they insisted they were actually part something else—Puerto Rican, in the case of one; Jamaican, in the case of the other—but James didn't think anybody really believed that, not even the Boom himself. James wasn't surprised that men who'd had a life before they got sent up wound up drifting toward Boomer's people. He'd done it, himself. He knew that John Boyne, for instance—he was more or less Boomer's top lieutenant—had been a machinist before he got sentenced. And his had been the sort of crime you might get from anybody, not that of a hardened criminal. He'd caught his wife cheating and killed her lover.

Several of them were like that. Two were auto mechanics, another was a pipefitter. He thought the skinny Mexican kid they called Jalapeno had even been a computer programmer. Something to do with computers, anyway.

"You think you can make a deal with Luff?"

Boomer nodded. "Think so. I not lookin' for trouble. And I don' think he is, neither." The pensive expression returned. "'Course, in his own way, Luff be the craziest

fucker in here. He get it in his head to do something, be
hard to stop him."

James finished putting on his coverall. When he was
done, Boomer said: "Your old roomie, Paul Howard. He
be dead."

James forced himself not to show the shock. "Who did
him?"

"No one. He just up and jumped from the fifth tier."
Suicide. The coward's way out.

No. James didn't accept that. Paul Howard hadn't been
a coward. But he had been marking the days until he
could go home. He'd only had a few months left on his
sentence, and his wife had stuck with him all the way
through. He had kids who'd come to visit him also.

Now there was no going home. He must have seen no
reason to spend the rest of his life in this hellhole.

"Terry Collins also dead. Somebody blew his head off
during the takeover."

"Who?"

"They sayin' it was one of the women in the infirmary.
That's where they found his body. But they don't seem to
believe it much."

He rubbed his shaved head with a hand the size of a
baseball mitt. "Don' believe it myself, neither. Which one
coulda done it? The old ones? The one just had a baby?
The black girl with her belly cut open? And where would
they have got a gun anyway? Nah. I figure it had to have
been somebody else. But who? The guards was all locked
up and accounted for."

He gave James a sly little look. "They'd prob'bly think
you done it, 'cept they know you was locked up too. You

got 'em spooked a little, the way you don't look like much but took out Butch—hell, did it twice—and the way you don' never have no expression on your face. You wadn't an ambulance man, Luff prob'bly have a stake driven through your heart like they do in the movies to them vampires."

James didn't say anything. And didn't let anything show on his face.

"I hear you be a real Cherokee," the Boom said.

Cook shrugged. "More like one-half. But I'm on the tribal rolls and the truth is there aren't too many full-blood Cherokees left any more. Hell, any kind of Indian. We're almost all at least part white. And in the case of Cherokees and some of the other southern tribes, a lot of us are part black too. I know I am. I've seen old photos of my great-grandmother."

Boomer grinned. "Nah. She was prob'bly just sunburned real bad. Livin' out there on a wild Injun reservation."

James grinned back. That made his face hurt, some, but it was worth it. Someday, that exchange of grins might save his life.

Afterward, he realized that was probably the first expression he'd let onto his face since he'd come through the gates, and had to fight off the sadness. He could remember a time when he'd laughed a lot, and never thought twice about smiling at people.

CHAPTER
27

Adrian Luff sat behind the large desk that had once belonged to the warden, staring at the clock on the wall.

The generator had died six hours ago. There was still fuel, so that wasn't the problem. But nobody Luff could find knew how to fix whatever was wrong with it.

The second hand wasn't moving. The computer didn't work. Even the pencil sharpener sat dead and useless in front of him. Nothing electrical worked, unless it had a battery backup, and half the battery-operated equipment was down.

The world was completely, totally, one hundred percent fucked up.

He was out of his cell, but still couldn't go anywhere. And if he did decide to get the hell out of Dodge, then what? The dinosaurs outside the prison were carnivorous. They ate meat. He was meat. And since he wasn't one of those great white hunters, he was going nowhere.

Besides, there was nowhere to go. There were no

towns. There was no reason to leave. Bad as it was, the prison was the safest place that existed in this crazy new world. At least the dinosaurs couldn't get through the walls.

He hefted a small red ball he'd found in the bottom drawer of the desk. He'd spent some time earlier tossing the ball at the wall. It would hit the dark paneling with a satisfying thump, touch the floor halfway between the wall and the chair he sat in, and then bounce close enough for him to catch it without getting up. That had helped steady his nerves, which needed it.

The takeover hadn't gone as planned. They hadn't hung on to any of the guards. Worse yet, none of the nurses. They had the methane outhouses, but no one knew how to operate and maintain them. Said they didn't, anyway. Adrian was pretty sure at least one of the Boom's boys would know how to make them work. But that would require a deal and Adrian wasn't sure he wanted to deal with Boomer. He hadn't decided on that yet.

There was a greenhouse filled with dirt, but no one knew if it had been planted or if it was just sitting there, waiting for seeds. Chuck Reed was a farmer and he said he could figure it out. But Reed was half-crazy. He also said he owned a ten thousand acre cattle ranch in southern Texas and was descended from old Spanish hidalgos, when everybody knew he'd been born and raised near Mattoon and had had a hardscrabble farm that barely made him a living.

There were pills and sprays and ointments, but no nurses who knew how to use them. Just that freaky new guy, Cook. He probably knew, but that was going to take more dealing. Right now, Luff was in no mood to deal.

There were no women of any kind.

That was what most of the men were focused on right now. The women had slipped through their fingers. But Luff wasn't really worried about that. Soon enough, they'd accept the fact. A lot of them had been without a woman for so long they didn't even miss it anymore. They just liked the idea. It was a taste of normal. Whatever that was.

In a day or two, though, they would start focusing on the other stuff, and when they did he was going to have trouble keeping them in line. Things weren't the way he had envisioned. The food shortage was going to produce a crisis soon. The amount of ammunition on hand was nowhere near enough. Hell, the only thing they had going for them was the well. And even that was primitive. The water had to be dipped with a bucket on a rope, one bucket at a time.

There was equipment and tools inside the machine shop that looked as though it had been separated out for some purpose. But he didn't know for what. None of the men he had could make sense of the stack. Some of it looked like it might be farm equipment, but Reed's only contribution had been to insist the guards had been putting together a time machine so that they could escape.

Luff's only hope was that once the interview of the prisoners began he would strike gold and come up with a dozen or so who had the skills he and his men were going to need in order to survive in this new world. Then he wouldn't need to deal with the Boom at all.

He swiveled his chair a little to face the three men on the other side of the desk. They were the three he'd decided would make the best lieutenants, although he wasn't sure about one of them. That was Danny Bostic.

"How many we got?" he asked.

Jimmy Walker looked at his list. "Twenty-two hundred and forty-six prisoners, in total. Three-hundred and eighty-four of them can be shot today. They're waterheads. Totally useless. There are another hundred and thirty-one men too old to work. Most of them have been here since they were in their twenties, anyway. They wouldn't know anything useful that any con doesn't know. They could also be gotten rid of."

Luff did the math in his head. Five hundred and fifteen who could be eliminated as soon as possible, bringing the number of prisoners down to one thousand, seven hundred and thirty-one. That would cull a lot of the dead weight right off the bat, and ease the pressure on everything.

It would also set the tone. It was important to set the right tone, and do it at the start. That would prevent misunderstandings.

Luff nodded. "Okay. Start making the arrangements."

Walker started out the door.

"Jimmy," Luff called.

The man stopped.

"I don't want them shot. We can't afford the ammo. Slit their throats, hang them, chop their fucking heads off with an axe, I don't care. Just don't waste any bullets."

Walker nodded and left, closing the door behind him.

"Why don't we just turn them out?" Danny Bostic asked.

The third man nodded. That was Phil Haggerty. "Be the easiest way, Adrian. Without supplies or guns, they wouldn't last long and we wouldn't have to worry about them."

"Can't," said Luff. "They aren't all stupid. Too many of them would run right to Blacklock. And some of the others might wind up with the Indians. We have enough enemies. I'm not going to provide any of them with recruits. Those we don't keep, die. If we have to, we'll just lock them in one of the cell houses, and close the door behind us. It's not that hard. Now, give me your status reports. You first, Danny."

Bostic ran through the numbers. "We're looking at maybe a six weeks' food supply. As far as fuel goes, if we just use the fuel for cooking, we could go a little over three months. But, in the meantime, if winter comes, things are going to get chilly. Could be very chilly, we just don't know. We're going to have to use wood for heating, and that'll mean figuring out ways to make wood-burning stoves. We'll also need some pretty big wood-gathering crews."

"Those estimates were based on what? Two thousand men?"

"A little more, actually. My estimate was just about the same as what Jimmy came up with in his head count. But I figured twenty-four hundred men, just to be on the safe side."

Adrian gave him a thin smile. "Always good to be on the safe side. Which I just made safer, didn't I?" He pointed at the pad in Bostic's hand. "So now recalculate everything, starting with seventeen hundred men instead of twenty-four hundred. I just increased our margin by almost fifty percent."

Haggerty cleared his throat. "We're gonna have to figure out what to do with the bodies, Adrian. We can't just leave 'em lying around. Things stink bad enough already, just from the couple of dozen men we've got waiting to be buried. By the time Jimmy's finished, we'll have twenty times that many."

Bostic scowled. "And most of the chamber pots aren't being emptied any more. Stupid fucks. That's their idea of liberty."

"So use the backhoe. It works, doesn't it?"

"That'll take fuel," Bostic said. "And even using a backhoe, five hundred bodies is a hell of lot to bury. You make the grave too shallow, that'll be a problem after a while."

Luff was getting impatient. "Fine. Burn 'em. We can use wood for that." He waved his hand at the window. "There's wood out there. Lots of it."

"That'll work," said Haggerty. "Kill two birds with one stone, too. Put the marginal ones on wood-cutting detail. If they squawk, shoot 'em. I think we could get some of those big ass trees down and chopped up in a just a few days. That would give us what we needed to burn the bodies without eating into our fuel or food supply. The men could be worked without feeding 'em much, too. If we called it a test, a tryout, promising that the best workers would be fed better, they'd work their asses off."

Luff nodded. Haggerty was sharp. He understood the logic of the situation right off, where Bostic was still dragging his ass.

He considered Haggerty's proposal, liking it the more he thought about it. Timbering was hard work; everybody knew that. Adrian had read once that a man doing hard labor needed at least four thousand calories a day. If they fed them starvation rations, they'd drop like flies, all except the best.

"Push the motherfuckers hard," he said. "Whichever die from hunger and overwork, that's all the better. Seventeen hundred is still way too many."

He sat up straight in the chair. "Phil, you make up the list. Put anyone questionable on it. Anyone you think might be trouble. Double-check with Jimmy. Anyone that Jimmy decided to let pass but it was a close call, put him on the wood-cutting detail. However many we have tools for, we'll put 'em to work. If they can get two or three trees down before dropping dead, that'll help. And if you get a half dozen guys who are actually good at bringing them down, fine. We'll keep those and feed them better. We don't know anything about this place. Winter could get long and cold."

Bostic was staring out the window. "Who burns the bodies? We can't use our own guys, Adrian. We're going to need them—all of them, each and every one, with a gun in his hands—to keep control over the situation. Once the guys figure out you're planning to get rid of one out of four of them—"

"One out of two," Luff interrupted forcefully. "By the time I'm done."

Bostic made a face. "That just reinforces my point."

"He's right, Adrian," said Haggerty. "We gotta keep our own guys with their hands free of anything except a weapon. We only got maybe two hundred we can really count on."

Walker had figured three hundred reliables, but Luff

thought Phil's estimate was probably closer to the truth. Some of "our guys" wouldn't cut it, when push came to shove.

He thought about the problem. When the solution came to him, he smiled.

"Use Boomer's rugheads. You handle it, Danny. Put them in charge of the whole thing. Designing and building the pyres, furnaces, whatever works. Running them. Dumping the ashes. The whole nine yards."

Bostic looked dubious. So did Haggerty.

"The Boomer's crazy," Haggerty protested. "He might go ballistic at the idea."

"I didn't say Boomer himself." Luff's grin widened. "Tell him we want Cook in charge. Boomer can stay in his cell, keeping his hands clean. I want that fucking Indian running the show. Let the son of a bitch spend some time handling corpses. I figure he'll be a lot more cooperative in a week or two when I offer him a job running our new medical department."

He leaned back, shrugging. "Boomer'll go for it. He's not actually crazy. A lot of that's just a reputation he built up, and did it on purpose. He knows he and his guys are on thin ice. As long as we don't shove his own face in it, he'll accept the situation. Cook's new, anyway. It's not like he and Boomer are old buddies."

Bostic looked back at his pad. "What about hunting parties? By the looks of the freezer, that's what the guards were doing. They butchered something."

Luff shook his head. "Which of these motherfuckers would you be willing to give guns and ammo to, and a *pretty please, come back and share with us*?"

Bostic shrugged. "Want to or not, sooner or later, that's exactly what we're going to have to do. We'll have to use our own guys, of course."

"I know. But not now. Right now we need every man we've got and every damn bit of ammunition to keep the lid on. And don't forget that Blacklock and his guards will be back, sooner or later."

Bostic scooted his chair closer to the desk and dropped his voice. "That's what I'm worried about, Adrian. If I were in Blacklock's shoes, I wouldn't attack us. This place is a fortress. I'd just put a few shooters in the trees and keep us hemmed in. Eventually we'd get starved out."

Luff nodded. He had thought the same thing. He just hadn't come up with a solution yet. He'd looked at the problem from every angle he could look at it from and, so far, had come up empty. Saving the dead in the freezers, just in case, wouldn't work. Cannibalism only sounded acceptable the day before you died of hunger, and by then it would be too late. Besides, the electricity was gone. Unless they could get the generator back up, the freezers would be warm a long time before the last of the meat was gone.

Leaving the prison, moving away from the area, getting out of reach of Blacklock and his guards might have worked, but he didn't know who else was out there. If there were Indians and Spanish conquistadores, like Collins said, there could be too many of them. Or there could be other people altogether; modern people—hell, maybe even people from the future—who were well enough armed to take them out. Besides, there were dinosaurs roaming around loose out there. Real no-fooling dinosaurs. Adrian had seen one of them himself. It had walked past the prison just a few hours ago. As big as a shopping mall.

No. They had to have the walls. Whatever else, they had to stay behind the walls.

"What about hanging onto the disposable prisoners?" Bostic suggested. "Use them as cannon fodder. Force Blacklock into wasting his ammo on them. He can't have too much with him."

"Don't you understand? We can't feed them in the meantime, period. We don't know how long the guards will be gone." Luff was getting tired of Bostic. The man was smart and capable, yes, but he could be a pain in the ass.

"I heard once," Bostic said, "a man could go a month or so without eating. If we give them water, keep them locked up, they should still be alive."

Luff slammed his left hand on the top of the desk. "What! Do you have shit for brains? They wouldn't go after the guards. Every swinging dick in the joint would turn on us the second we opened the gates. No, we have to get rid of them."

Bostic shrugged. "Okay, then give me a few of our guys. Half a dozen or less. We can spare that many. I'll take them out into the woods before Blacklock can get back here. We can bring in enough meat to give us an edge. Dammit, Adrian, we need *someone* outside the walls."

Luff thought about it. He was skeptical about how much meat Bostic and a small crew of hunters could produce. Sure, Danny could find deer hunters among the cons—but how many of them had been hunting in years?

And shooting a deer was a whole different ball game from shooting a dinosaur.

But it was true that they could spare that many men from watching over the others, once things stabilized a little. And Bostic and his guys could probably turn up something. The man was sharp and hard. In fact, he was probably the smartest and most capable of the three top lieutenants. He was sure as hell smarter than Haggerty. That was the reason Adrian had picked him, despite his misgivings.

So, fine. Send him on his way playing Dinosaur Danny. Eventually, Adrian figured he'd probably have to get rid of Bostic. If that's what it came down to, he could use the time Bostic was gone to make the arrangements to do so.

But there was no reason to do it now. The man was useful for the moment, and you worked with what you had.

"Okay, fine. Put together a crew. Four or five guys including you, no more. You can leave in about a week, I figure. By then, things should have settled down enough."

After Haggerty and Bostic left, Luff looked at the unmoving clock again, his mouth a hard straight line. Their prison was still their prison.

He got up and went to the window. Things were moving too fast. He didn't know what to do. Hitler killed and disposed of something like six million Jews. You'd think a thousand or so dead cons shouldn't be that hard to arrange.

But it was trickier than it looked.

He couldn't leave them in their cells to starve and

302 Eric Flint & Marilyn Kosmatka

rot. That would draw vermin, and pretty soon they'd
have an epidemic—with no medical people except one
uncooperative redskin EMT.

He couldn't shoot them. They had to conserve as much
ammunition as possible. There was no way to replace it,
and they still had Blacklock to deal with. Not to mention
wild Indians and what sounded like wilder Spaniards and
fucking dinosaurs and God knew what else.

He couldn't just turn them out. Some of them—
probably most of them—would die, sure, but some
wouldn't. When Blacklock showed up, they'd slobber over
him like dogs. That would give Blacklock an edge. Dealing
with Blacklock was going to be a bitch, as it was.

And he couldn't feed them. Not two thousand, two
hundred and forty-six men. He figured he couldn't feed
more than a thousand or so. Actually, right now, he couldn't
even feed that many. But with only a thousand mouths
and stomachs, he thought he'd be able to stretch out the
food supply long enough to come up with alternative food
sources.

It was the only chance he had. This was really just a
simple mathematical problem, when you got down to it.
And he'd been a damn good accountant.

Still was.

Danny Bostic left the office and headed for the
compound.

Luff was crazy. He was screwing up, and Danny wasn't
going to sit on his ass and die just because the man was an
idiot.

The prison was a trap, for God's sake, not a haven.

Yeah, there were people out there. But they were people armed with rocks and spears. And, yes, their ammo wouldn't last long. But it didn't have to. All it had to do was get them on top of the heap. Then, they'd be home free. They could set themselves up as chiefs, with warriors they'd recruited from the natives to keep them on top. The same way any good gang got organized.

Danny knew some history. Not much, but enough.

Medieval times, medieval ways. Nobody started off as Duke Whoozit. They started off—their ancestors, anyhow—as the toughest and smartest barbarian gang leader around.

Walking fast, he went down the corridor in the administration building that led to the yard. Bostic knew Luff. If the man was already planning to kill five hundred people, just like that, it wouldn't take him long to decide that was the way for lots more to go. Including, sooner or later, Danny himself.

Luff was a sicko. The fact that he didn't seem to be, didn't have any of the obvious habits of a sicko, didn't mean squat. Underneath, the bastard was the scariest crazy in the whole joint.

Where would it end? Danny could already see the logic. As long as Luff was fixated on staying in the prison because he thought it was a safe haven, there'd *never* be enough food. How could there be? A prison was a fucking prison, for Christ's sake. What'd he think it was? A farm?

Cannibalism, that's where it would end. Sooner or later, in that crazy quiet way he had, Luff would decide it just made sense for the men he wanted to stay alive to eat the ones he didn't.

Danny Bostic had been a criminal since he was eleven years old. Earlier, really, if you counted petty theft and misdemeanors. He made no bones about it. As far as he was concerned, so-called "honest citizens" were just damn fools. Work their asses off their whole lives so the million-aires and billionaires they worked for could buy some more yachts, and then retire on Social Security and a measly pension—assuming the pension hadn't been shredded. Spend their last dollars paying the bill at a nurs-ing home that smelled like piss.

Fuck that. If Danny hadn't been born into a great wolf pack family, he could at least make a decent weasel.

But this was just nuts. Plain and simple nuts. Even if Luff could keep control over the situation, he didn't seem to realize he was just the captain of a ship going down fast.

Danny slowed his pace as he neared the exit, trying to keep his expression neutral. That was the reason he'd pushed, at the end, for his own hunting party. He didn't want a large band. A few men would be plenty, as long as they were well armed and well supplied. He knew the men he wanted, too. They could raid the armory, the kitchen, and the infirmary before they left. Take every-thing they needed. Leave during the night.

He paused at the entrance and looked down at the list of things Luff wanted him to do. He would do them. He had no choice. He had to do them and anything else the asshole told him to do. But a few days from now, he would be gone.

First, he had to go see the Boom about the body-disposal business.

That was another stupid move. Boomer might be crazy,

but he was crazy like a fox. On that, at least, Luff had it right—but he hadn't thought through the logic. The Boom had managed to keep his boys together for years. Word had it that his gang of misfits had even grown a lot lately. Every con not already hooked up and not full white—or who was even willing to claim he wasn't—had attached to the man.

That wasn't surprising, of course. Not long after the uprising, things had gotten out of hand for a while. Every con or group of cons with a grudge to settle had settled it, or at least tried. The big gangs had steered clear of each other, but lots of loners had been taken down. That was the reason there were twenty-three bodies piled up in the yard.

That had scared every loner in the place, and some of them had gone running to Boomer. Who—yeah, crazy, sure he was—had played that "Uncle Timmy" bullshit to the hilt.

It was *nuts*. Couldn't Luff see that Boomer and his boys needed to be kept isolated? The other gangs could be played off against each other, but Boomer's was unpredictable. They should all be locked up tight, in lots of separate cells. You put them in charge of something— didn't matter what it was—and you gave them the opportunity to start planning and working together.

And then—icing on the cake—Luff wanted the new kid in charge. Jesus H. Christ. New or not, Cook was a fucking hardass, couldn't Luff see that? With that Indian mask of a face he had, you never knew what he was thinking. Danny wouldn't put the bastard in charge of emptying kitty litter boxes.

Bostic left the administration building and headed toward D-house. One of the men he was planning to take with him was very good at making keys. A few of those passed out at the right time, and the rest would be history. The shit would come down and when it did, he would be long gone.

CHAPTER
28

At what he estimated was noon, Joe Schuler called a halt. He had to estimate based on the sun's position, because he couldn't use his watch. The watch was working, as were most watches. The problem was that they were skewed. His watch said it was 6:17 AM. Not surprising, really. It would be a little much to expect that a disaster that had sent them all back tens of millions of years in time would have maintained the same time of day. Someday, he supposed, if they could survive long enough to afford the luxury, they'd have to agree on a new standard.

This was a good place to stop anyway, since they'd finally come to the river Marie had instructed the nurses to follow north. If the women had made it—and all indications were that they had—then his band of a little over sixty men and women were less than a half-day's walk from the cave Marie had sent the nurses to. Joe sat at the edge of the stream and soaked his feet in the cool water. Most of the others joined him.

Their feet were raw and bleeding. Marie and Casey were the only ones wearing shoes. They were also among the few wearing long sleeved shirts, so they'd been spared most of the misery of the sticker bushes.

When Joe first felt the cool water, his skin crawled with the cold. But that sensation left as the icy water numbed the dull, burning ache of his feet. A few more hours and they could rest. Food wasn't going to be an option. Not tonight. But Marie had said she should be able to get enough to feed everyone at least one good meal tomorrow.

Joe thought about that, smiling ruefully. One good meal sounded good. Not so long ago, the thought of just one meal in a two-day time frame would have had him complaining to the high heavens.

He stretched back on the bank, leaving his feet in the water, and looked at the sky. A few clouds were drifting in front of the sun. He was looking forward to the shade they would give. It was the little things that mattered. So he told himself, as he closed his eyes, trying to relax. The little things: a little touch of cool, a little food, a little water to ease the pain in your shredded feet.

But he couldn't relax. Too much anger was still seething inside him. Not anger at the prisoners. They had behaved no differently than he'd expected them to behave, given a chance. Better, actually. They hadn't killed anyone or even raped any of the women. The only one who'd even tried had been a guard.

That stinking filthy Collins. That was the source and object of his fury.

But the anger faded. Collins was dead, after all. He'd gotten his just desserts and, best of all, had gotten them almost right after his betrayal. Certainly before he could enjoy any of the fruits he'd expected from his treason.

Mostly, Joe knew, he was just mad at life, at that thing that could throw you for a loop no matter how hard you tried.

But that was pointless, too. Collins was dead and life was what it was. Joe was in charge of this group and he needed to stay in focus.

When they'd left the prison, at his command, they'd gone away from the cave and the nurses. If they were tracked, he didn't want to lead the prisoners to the women and the only baby on the planet. He still thought that had been the right decision, although he hadn't anticipated the price their feet would pay for it.

One day out, and now one day back.

He sat up and pulled his feet out of the water, drying them as best he could on a handful of torn-out ground cover. He could only hope the ground cover wasn't something like poison ivy or nettles. Whatever it was, it certainly wasn't grass. Jeff Edelman said that grasses hadn't evolved yet. Oddly enough, the plants that Joe would have assumed were the most basic and ancient were actually among the most recent.

The lack of the kind of ground cover grass usually provided would have been simply a curiosity except that, today again, they'd been forced to continue on barefoot. Without a single meadow anywhere to give their feet any relief. He'd already decided that before they went any farther than the cave, they'd have to come up with some sort of foot covering. Leaving aside the pain, they were just asking for funguses, worms, you name it. He looked at the scratches and skin tears, grimacing a little when he saw a spot on his heel that was bruised and swollen. That was going to hurt for days, every time he took a step. Maybe even weeks.

He sighed and pulled himself up. He needed to make sure everyone was all right. Some of the guards were too old for the hike they had just made. Others were too overweight. Some looked fine, but he knew they were out of shape. He planned for a one-hour rest, but then they would have to move on. He hated pushing so hard. It worried him. The memory of Greg Lowry's heart attack was too fresh. But he didn't feel he had any other option. He wanted to make sure they were at the cave before sunset.

He did a head count out of habit. Each time he did one he came up short and his stomach would churn. Then he would locate the missing person and he wouldn't feel any relief. Instead, the dread would double. Dread of the time the numbers really wouldn't be right, and the missing person wouldn't step from behind a tree or a bush or from behind a person just large enough to hide him or her from view.

This time the missing person was Willa. He started looking around. Then he spotted her, talking to Hope McDaniel. Her face was creased into a frown. The same frown she had been wearing for over two weeks. The first time he saw her mouth turned down and her forehead creased, he had been shocked. Willa didn't do that. She laughed and smiled. Sometimes, if she was concentrating on something, she would develop an almost blank look. But never a frown. He imagined that had changed forever, that the woman would wear this new look clear on up till the day she died.

Moving around the clearing he was once again struck by the sounds of the forest. He had always thought of cities as noisy and the country as quiet. But he'd been a country boy in the well-settled and secure Midwest of the late twentieth and early twenty-first centuries.

He knew differently now. "Quiet" was in the ear of the listener. When you were in a real no-fooling wilderness trying to spot dangerous animals, the woods were a cornucopia of never-ending sounds. Constantly changing, constantly . . .

A slight rustling in some nearby brush drew his attention. Then, he froze. A pair of eyes was staring at him from the brush, less than ten feet away.

Dredging up the nature documentaries he had watched on TV, he tried to remember what to do when you encountered a large animal in the wild at close range.

Did you make eye contact or not? With male gorillas, you didn't, he remembered. They'd take it as a challenge. Instead, you acted submissive.

But gorillas weren't carnivores. Whatever this thing was, it wasn't a gorilla. Did you do the same thing with lions or bears? Did you stand your ground or run?

Stand your ground, he was pretty sure. Running would almost certainly trigger off a carnivore's hunting reflex. Fine if you could outrun it, but he wasn't an antelope.

What *was* the damn thing? From what little he could see of it through the branches, it looked like a bear, but it wasn't any bear he was familiar with. About the size of a black bear, as near as he could determine, but it was the wrong color. The fur was grayish blond, with a white band around the eyes, as if it were wearing spectacles.

Fear was making it hard to think. He wanted to shout a warning, but didn't. He was afraid the noise would spook the thing, make it attack. He couldn't shoot it, because he didn't have a gun. They only had two guns among them. Marie always kept hers, because she was the best shot. Casey's was passed around to whomever was standing guard at the moment. Right now, that was Frank Nickerson.

If Joe turned his head he would be able to see Frank, and if he shouted, Frank would certainly hear.

But Frank was a good thirty yards away. And a pistol, even a .40 caliber, wasn't a rifle.

Out of the corner of his eye, Joe saw Karen coming out of the bushes a little downstream. He watched as Stacey stood up. She was stretching, getting ready to walk away from the river, toward the bushes. The women had been going in and out of them, one at a time for the last ten minutes. Then Stacey spotted Joe and stopped. The way he was standing stock still must have puzzled her.

Oh, hell. Now she was moving toward him, calling out, wanting to know if something was wrong.

The animal turned toward the noise, emitting a low, soft growl. Joe could see enough of its body to tell that it was now hunched low to the ground, as if it were getting ready to spring.

He shouted out a warning. Not a word, just a roar of sound, the only sound his brain could force his vocal cords to produce. He roared and then roared again, springing forward like a madman. Getting between the beast and the woman.

The creature charged him, rising up on its hind legs. With it erect, Joe could finally see it clearly. It was a bear, sure enough, although he still didn't know what kind. A little shorter than Joe, obviously heavier, but nothing even close to the size of a grizzly or a brown bear.

They slammed together with a thud of flesh. They grappled like wrestlers, clutching tight. The beast had Joe's chest in a bear hug and his hands were on its throat. Whatever else, he had to keep the teeth from closing on him. The canines weren't as huge as those of most big carnivores, but those teeth would tear flesh easily.

They swayed. Twisted. Back and forth. He could hear Stacey and Karen screaming for help, but didn't pay them any attention at all.

He couldn't. God, the thing was strong! Joe could feel the air being squeezed from his lungs. Suddenly, the bear roared and drew back its paws, then smashed them into Joe's torso. He thought he felt some ribs go. One, at least.

He staggered, but he didn't let go of the throat. The gaping maw was what terrified him. The bear roared and slammed him again, with that double blow. Then went back to the bear hug.

They tumbled to the ground. Joe shifted his grip, searching for a hold that would let him strangle the creature, not just hold off the teeth. He dug his fingers through the creature's fur, feeling the beast's hot breath on his face, arching his neck to stay away from the jaws.

He was desperate now. His vision was blurring. He'd been hurt badly by those blows, and knew it. He only had a few seconds before his strength would go, and he couldn't for the life of him find anything under the thick fur and muscle that he thought would do any good to squeeze.

BOOM!

Up close, the sound of the pistol going off was like a cannon shot. The full weight of the animal pressed against him, knocking what little breath there was in his lungs from his body.

BOOM! BOOM!

Then the beast was gone, hauled off. Cool air covered him and he could almost breathe. When his vision cleared, he saw Frank Nickerson leaning over, deep concern on his face.

"You okay?"

Like an idiot, macho reflexes took over. "Yeah, sure," he gruffed, extending a hand. "Help me up."

But when Frank started pulling him up, he screamed. It felt like knives were being driven through his chest.

Hastily, Frank let go of his hand and Joe collapsed back onto the ground. That impact sent the same knives through him, and he screamed again.

He saw Marie's face now, also full of concern. Dizzy with pain, he tried to smile. He couldn't. He had to cough. When he did, he cried out in pain and sprayed blood onto the hand he had used to cover his mouth. Not much. Just a little.

Marie knelt next to him, looked at the blood, and squeezed his shoulder.

"It'll be okay," she said. "It'll be okay. Just take it easy."

Joe thought about telling her to close her eyes the next time she lied, but was hit with another wave of pain and dizziness. When the wave peaked, he passed out.

He came to sometime later. At first he was confused by his whereabouts. Then he realized he was lying inside a cave, covered with a shirt that had been warmed somehow.

They must have made it to the cave, carrying him all the way. Joe thought about crawling to the entrance, but knew he didn't have it in him. It took everything he had just to breathe. He brought his hand up to feel his chest. It had been wrapped.

That surprised him. He knew they didn't wrap broken ribs any more. They said it could cause pneumonia. But maybe the monster's claws had cut him.

Feeling his body preparing to cough again, he instinctively braced himself for the pain. The cough was pathetic sounding, no more than a whisper, but the pain from it caused him to moan.

"You're awake," Lylah Caldwell said. She entered the cave on one hand and two knees. The other hand held a small bowl of steaming liquid.

"You wrapped me," he whispered. "Why?"

"I had to. You didn't just crack your ribs. I'm sure at least one of them was snapped loose. I didn't want it to do any more damage than it already had. A couple of the women who had blouses donated their T-shirts for material." She held the bowl to his mouth and he took a sip.

It was some kind of meat broth. It tasted wonderful.

Lylah smiled crookedly. "It's bear soup."

The smile went away. "I would normally tell you to breathe deeply and do plenty of deep coughing. But I don't think that's the way we need to go with this." She offered him another sip.

"No more. Man, that hurts."

"I know. But, hurt or not, you have to drink a little. It's good for you. Besides, you can think of it as revenge." She put the bowl back to his lips, tipping it, forcing him to swallow or wear it. Three painful sips later she pulled it away, allowing him to rest. "We made it out of whatever that thing was that jumped you. Marie showed us how to skin it and use the brain to tan the hide. She has people working on making a sort of moccasin for our feet."

Joe's head still felt muzzy. "How long have I been out?"

"Almost two days, off and on. You came back to consciousness a few times, but you probably don't remember."

Out for two days. That was . . . scary. More to take his mind off his fear than any real curiosity, he tapped the plastic bowl she'd use to feed him. It was odd-looking. "What's this?"

"Karen's on her monthly. It's her pad-case. She had it in her pocket."

That made him laugh, unfortunately. The pain made him stop. He wondered what they were using to heat the soup in, but was afraid to ask. Another burst of laughter might kill him. Or, worse yet, make him just wish he were dead.

He was too tired, anyway. He drifted off to sleep seconds later.

Marie dropped another thin twig onto the small blaze. She had been feeding the fire since sundown, one stick at a time, even though she wasn't sure making a fire was the right thing to do. The fire might be spotted by cons out looking for them.

But Marie didn't think that was likely. The fire wasn't that big, after all. They were well into the wilderness here, and if you didn't know the route to the cave it would be like finding the proverbial needle in a haystack. For the sort of men likely to be prisoners in a maximum security prison, anyway. There might be a mountain man type among them, but she doubted it. Alexander's inmates had come from all over the state. Most of them had been residents of Chicago or one of the state's other cities. She figured they weren't going to leave the security of the prison's walls to wander miles into a wilderness filled with wild animals up to and including dinosaurs. Not even looking for women. And for all they knew, by now the escaped guards had hooked back up with Andy Blacklock and his people, who were well armed.

No, it was the dinosaurs she was worried about. She'd made the fire because in the world she'd known, a fire at night was a good way to keep off predators. But those were animals she knew. Probably more importantly, they were animals that had generations upon generations of evolution to teach them that humans were dangerous and a fire was likely to mean humans.

But was that true of dinosaurs? For all she knew, a fire might draw them like moths to a lightbulb.

So, she'd had to guess, and she hated guessing. In the end, what had tipped the scales was a simple fact.

Twice now, she'd encountered dangerous animals out here up close. The first had been the cat-thing that

Hulbert had shot before it could attack her. Jeff had told her later it was a Smilodon of some sort. What they called a "saber-toothed tiger" but wasn't really a tiger. In fact, it wasn't closely related to modern cats of any kind.

The second was the bear that had injured Joe so badly. That it wasn't any bear species she knew didn't mean anything. It was some kind of bear, for sure.

Mammals, both times. Not dinosaurs. The fact was, although they'd seen dinosaurs, they didn't seem to be plentiful. Not big ones, anyway. Since escaping the prison, she'd seen a few creatures that were either dinosaurs or some kind of ancient reptiles. But none of them had been big, and none of them had been threatening in any way. In fact, most of them had run away as soon as they became aware of the humans approaching.

That wasn't surprising. It was what you'd expect, unless the Quiver had transported them into some kind of fantasy world. In the real world, big animals were scarce. Wilderness or not, it didn't matter. That was true of herbivores, and it was even more true of carnivores. They couldn't be plentiful, because there wasn't enough food to support them. Even the huge bison herds of America's past hadn't really covered the plains. It just looked like it, when you were in their vicinity. But most of the plains, at any given time, had been empty of any big creatures.

So, she'd decided to take their chances on the dinosaurs. She was more worried about something less exotic. Granted, the mammals of this time didn't have the same ingrained instinct to avoid humans. But she was still hoping they'd stay away from fire.

And all of that was probably beside the point. Everybody was exhausted and scared half out of their wits. Whether making and keeping a fire through the night was the right thing to do or not, it helped settle everyone down.

Including her.

"Mind a little company?" Frank Nickerson sat down next to her.

"How're you doing?" she asked, not taking her eyes from the orange, red and blue flickering light. "That toothbrush you took in your leg did some damage."

"It's been a while now. It seems to have healed pretty good."

"The nurses look at your stitches?"

"Yeah. They're going to take them out in a few days." After a short pause, he said: "They told me what you did at the infirmary. I still feel bad that I wasn't there when that bastard came in. They sent me to A-block just six hours before the shit hit the fan."

"What could you have done anyway, Frank? You didn't have a gun. Collins would have just shot you as soon as he came through the door."

"Marie, what you did . . ."

"Let it go, Frank. I wasn't being a hero. I was scared spitless. I can't even remember the details of it now. It's just a disjointed blur."

She tilted her head so she could see the stars. They were as beautiful as they had been the night before and the night before that. She didn't think she would ever tire of looking at them or ever get used to how plentiful they had become. There was no light pollution at all in this new world. Unless the moon was out at night, the darkness was like nothing she'd ever imagined.

She dropped another stick on the fire. "I wish we had a radio so we could just call the others."

Frank shook his head. "It wouldn't do any good. They didn't take one with them. They were going to be out of range after just a few hours."

"I hope they're all right." She had to work at keeping her voice steady. For her, as for all of them, the greatest fear was that something bad had happened to Captain Blacklock and the rest of the guards. As long as Andy and Rod were out there somewhere, safe and sound and with well-armed people around them, things would eventually work out okay. But if they were gone . . .

He nodded. After a while, he said: "No one talks about what happened to the rest of the world. It's like it never existed."

Marie didn't answer. She wrapped her arms tight against her chest. There was a feeling—an ache—that left her feeling hollow each time she thought of home. She knew why no one ever mentioned it. It hurt too much. And everyone believed his or her pain was the worst. Kathleen, with her new baby—and her husband and three other children gone. Barbara, with her four-year-old grandson at a babysitter's. She'd been the boy's mother, for all intents and purposes. Her daughter and son-in-law had been dead for sixteen months, killed in a car wreck. Marie herself, with her sister living just a mile away and her two nephews waiting for her to take them to the movies next weekend like she promised.

They had all been ripped away from family and friends.

She knew most of the stories, including Frank's. He had lost his wife—a bride, almost. She'd been nineteen years old, a few years younger than he was. They'd been married exactly one month to the day when the Quiver turned the world upside down.

They couldn't talk about it. Not yet. Maybe the not knowing would make it taboo forever. Were they the only ones ripped away? Was there just a hole where the prison had stood? Or had everything and everyone been caught up in a hurricane and dropped at random, scattered across time and the universe, dumped here and there like litter blown on the wind?

Or maybe the unthinkable had happened. Everyone else in the world had been destroyed in the disaster, and they were the only survivors.

"Luck for us," she whispered at the sky.

Joe woke during the night, shivering with fever, his skin clammy with sweat. Casey Fisher was leaning over him, soothing him, using a dampened rag to cool his forehead.

"I need you to . . ." The pathetic little cough came, followed by racking pain. "Go tell . . ."

The effort to talk was just too much. It exhausted him, sending him back to a sleep plagued by giant ants carrying off a picnic basket filled with his wife and sons.

Barbara lay listening to Fisher moving around. She wanted to get up and help her, but couldn't. The last of her energy had left several hours back. Now all she could do was lie in the dark and wish for a sleep that wouldn't come. She had always been a bit of an insomniac, but since the Quiver, she hadn't been able to get more than a few hours sleep in any one stretch. While inside the prison, that hadn't mattered. She would sleep three or four hours, work about eight hours, then do it again.

Out here, that wasn't going to work.

The cave's floor was made up of a finely ground sand, something she had seen in a few of the cave tours she had taken when the kids were little. It was also dry and free of animals. When they first found it, she had been afraid it would be full of bats. She hadn't wanted to enter, but Kathleen had insisted. The CO figured a few rodent type creatures were a lot easier to deal with than the men at the prison, and she had been terrified they were being followed.

They weren't followed, and there weren't any bats or rats. Barbara hadn't even found any insects. That had also surprised her. She'd been sure the place would be infested with spiders. It had seemed a perfect hiding place for creatures like that.

Kathleen and she had handled the trek better than she had hoped. It was Lylah Caldwell who'd had the most trouble. The RN's legs had swelled and turned black. She had popped a dozen or so veins on the walk. Barbara knew Lylah had the beginning stages of congestive heart failure. She also had a touch of emphysema. They had talked about it on several occasions. The woman had intended to work just six more months and then take an early retirement. She'd planned to sell her house and move in with her sister, a widow living in Arizona. She'd been looking forward to moving. She and her sister were close and they both liked to sightsee. They had a long list of places they intended to visit.

Barbara rolled over. Joe, twenty-eight women, and one baby had filled the cave to capacity. There hadn't been room for the others. Most of the women and all of the men except Joe were sleeping beneath an overhang about fifteen feet from the opening. Christopher Jordan, armed with one of the pistols they had and a whistle Marie had made from a reed, was standing guard right now.

She could tell by the sounds around her that sleep was coming hard for quite a few of them. And after she dropped the bombshell she was going to drop tomorrow, it would come even harder.

They were going to have to send Marie and Frank on ahead, while the rest of them stayed behind. They couldn't travel as a group to find Andy Blacklock and Rod Hulbert. That had been the plan, but she could now see that the plan wouldn't work.

First, they didn't have the supplies. A lifetime of never being more than a half hour's drive from a grocery store had simply never prepared them for the reality of what life was like when you had no food and were stranded in a wilderness. Abstractly, maybe, but not in their guts.

Joe had been attacked, and because of that they were going to eat for a few days. But a few days probably wouldn't be long enough. It might take weeks to find the others and they couldn't forage as they traveled. None of them had that level of skills, except Marie and maybe Frank Nickerson. And the two of them couldn't possibly feed seventy people while on the move.

But it didn't matter anyway. There was a second reason

the plan wouldn't work. Too many of them simply wouldn't make it if they tried to cover even ten miles a day, which is what Marie said was a good average for a hike. Much less do it day after day after day.

Joe Schuler would die if they tried to move him even a mile. Lylah Caldwell would die if they had to travel more than a day or two at the pace they'd been traveling. Stacey White would last a little longer, but not much. Her asthma was acting up. Barbara had seen her sneak off to use her inhaler a half dozen times already. And the woman wouldn't have a refill once it was gone.

There were others. Not in that bad a shape, but bad enough. They wouldn't survive too long either, in any trek through a wilderness that lasted more than a few days.

She wondered how long she'd survive herself.

Probably too long. Long enough to bury the only friends she had left, and then either get captured by prisoners or eaten by a predator.

She lay there thinking about all the ways she had made sure she stayed in shape: the good diet, the vitamins, the exercise. She'd never smoked and used liquor very sparingly.

She thought of the genes passed down to her by both her parents and grandparents, who'd all lived into their late eighties or even nineties.

Strong bones. Good hearts.

The tears started coming, and then came faster and faster. She finally fell asleep shortly before the sun came up.

CHAPTER
29

Marie shook her head forcefully.

"No, Barbara. Absolutely not."

If the cave had been tall enough and hadn't been so crammed with people, her anxiety would have had her on her feet and pacing around. "I agree that someone has to go for help. I know we can't move Joe. Or Lylah, or some others. And if the rest of us leave them behind, we might as well just shoot them now."

She shook her head again. "But there's no way both Frank and I go. Except for me, he's the only one here with any real outdoor skills. One of us has to stay behind or the rest of you don't have a chance of surviving until we bring back help."

"I've done some fishing . . ."

Barbara broke off, grimacing. "Okay, I always needed somebody else to bait the hook. But I'm sure there are enough of us who know enough, pooled together, that we can make it without the two of you."

It would be tempting to let that argument sway her, but Marie knew it was wrong. A number of the men and a few of the women in the group thought of themselves as outdoorsmen. But their experience with "roughing it" was a commercial campground with all their gear, up to and usually including either a trailer or a camper shell on a pickup. At a minimum, they'd had a tent and sleeping bags.

Hunting deer and fishing was as far as their experience went—either in a public forest or someone's private land. In the twenty-first century, in the middle of long-settled and secure North America. That bore about as much relationship to what they faced now as one of those stupid video games did to a real gunfight or a real battle.

The one and only really useful skill they had was that all of the COs could shoot. Some of them were even good at it.

Swell. They had exactly two pistols among them, with a handful of rounds left. And one shotgun with no rounds left. They'd already used the three rounds it had once had to bring down some game and provide desperately needed food.

No, the only way they were going to survive was if someone went out there and found Hulbert and Blacklock. Or maybe the Cherokees, if they turned out to be friendly.

"Someone" meant either her or Nickerson. Frank probably didn't have her level of skills in the outdoors— he certainly didn't have Hulbert's—but he'd been in a military unit that had gotten a lot of training along those lines.

She rubbed her ankle and tried to think things through.

The Spaniards were out there too, somewhere, and they were definitely not friendly. She had seen for herself what they did to prisoners. The Cherokee, Stephen McQuade, had been in bad shape when she found him.

De Soto would think the small band of guards was easy pickings, and he would be right. They weren't armed except for the pistols. They couldn't possibly protect themselves against a small army of conquistadores.

Or the prisoners, if they showed up.

No, the equation was hard and clear. Everyone else had to stay here in hiding, because that posed the least risk, while someone went and found Blacklock and the rest of the guards. And the rest was just as clear and hard also.

Joe coughed. His face turned white with the pain. "She's right, Marie. Have to go, both of you," he whispered.

He had spiked a fever during the night and it never went back down. Lylah Caldwell had told them he had developed pneumonia and was starting to dehydrate. If he drank something, it came back up in under three minutes, upsetting his electrolyte balance even more than it already was. Between the dehydration and the infection he wasn't going to last much longer. As for the few antibiotics she had snagged from the infirmary, they weren't going to help. The man was bleeding internally.

Marie didn't wait for him to finish what he was saying. He needed to save his strength and he'd already told her a half dozen times what he wanted.

"Joe, we can't do that. You know we can't."

"Can't go alone. Too dangerous." His voice was weak and she had to lean close to hear what he said.

He was right, as far it went. The first rule of surviving

in a wilderness was not to be alone. Even something as simple as a stumble and a bad fall on a trail could kill you, if you were alone.

Read any of the manuals, and they'd tell you the same thing. But none of those manuals included a provision that you had to leave dozens of people behind with just two pistols and without any of the skills *they* needed to survive.

Not knowing what else to do, she patted Joe's arm gently. "Even if we're all together, we aren't safe. We were all there when the bear got you."

"Be dead, if alone."

Marie had to fight off the tears. Joe Schuler was already dead. He just hadn't died yet.

He would, though. Barbara and Lylah thought Jenny Radford might be able to help, if she could be found. They had developed a lot of faith in the woman in a very short period of time. Jenny, even more than Blacklock and Hulbert, was who they really wanted here.

But Marie knew it was too late. It had always been too late. It had been too late five seconds after the attack started. The creature had broken him apart inside. Only Joe's size and strength and excellent condition had kept him alive at all through the attack and for this long afterward. A fully staffed hospital with all the bells and whistles might not have been able to save him.

"I know," she said. "But we can't risk both of us leaving."

Barbara decided she had to end the argument. She still didn't think Marie was right, but what she knew for sure was that the argument itself was taking a terrible toll on Schuler. It had to end or he would.

"That's enough, Joe. After thinking about it, Marie's right. We can only afford for one of them to be gone. So, Marie can stay with us, and Frank can go for Andy and the others."

"No," Marie and Frank said simultaneously. Marie, forcefully; Frank, wincing apologetically.

"Marie goes and I stay," he said. "We don't have any choice."

He motioned to his bruised and swollen feet. "I've been sitting here thinking. And the only thing that comes into my head is a damn poem. It's the one about the one-penny nail getting lost. Do you remember it? A horse lost its shoe because of it. And because of that the horse was lost, and then the message. And because of that a battle was lost. And because of that a war was lost." Now he laughed bitterly. "Well, I've lost both shoes."

Barbara looked at his feet and almost cringed. Not so much at their condition but at her own cowardice. She knew he was right—had known it even when she made the proposal. It was just that if only one of them could stay behind, she wanted it to be the short brunette with the upturned nose and the light scattering of freckles. Small or not, female or not, Marie made her feel safe. Frank Nickerson didn't. He was probably good at surviving—maybe just as good as Marie—but the woman had saved dozens of people, not him. Nickerson was just one of those she'd saved.

But now, looking at the angry red streaks beginning to creep up his legs, she knew he was a patient, not a guardian.

Joe coughed again, then moaned. "You win," he whispered. "Go get Andy."

Barbara Ray, relieved the argument was over, snatched up a damp rag and began washing Joe's face and neck, trying to cool him down. She used her head to motion for them to leave so she could do what needed doing. The LPN's refusal to give up was the only reason the lieutenant was still alive. She had spent hours keeping him cooled. And more hours tapping his back to knock the phlegm loose, then holding him tight as he coughed it up. When she got too worn out to continue, Casey Fisher would spell her for a while.

"He *has* to rest," she hissed.

Marie looked at the pistol, longingly. "Keep it. It might make a difference."

"What about you?" Nickerson asked.

Marie, using Joe's pocketknife to trim the walking stick she had snagged the day before, shrugged. "I'm taking three days' food. I'm not planning to stop for anything. No hunting, not even fishing. And the truth is, I'm less likely to be hunted by something than you are. There's only one of me. There are lots of you. Every carnivore within ten miles knows you're here by now. And if the prisoners find you, you're going to need everything you can lay your hands on. Two pistols isn't enough as it is."

She sat on the ground, loosening the laces to her shoes and then retying them. "If I don't get back by the time the food runs out, send someone hunting. But I'd start by trying to spear fish in the creek. For that—"

Frank waved his hand. "Yeah, I know. Thin blades, two or three, tied onto the shaft. And cut little barbs in the end or the fish will squirm loose." Smiling a little, he hefted the makeshift spear in his left hand. They'd made over a dozen of those, by now. They were just sharpened poles with fire-hardened tips. "These won't hardly do."

Marie nodded. "If a dangerous looking animal comes around, pile everyone into the cave. Stay there even through the night, even if some of you have to sleep standing up." She looked at the spear in his hand. "Except for maybe a giant dinosaur, no predator's going to try forcing its way into a cave past a dozen of those sticking out. Even if it does, you can probably kill it."

She hadn't been looking at him while she talked. Now, her shoes tied, she stood up and did. She looked him right in the eyes. "The last thing. Frank, you and I both know that Joe's probably not going to make it."

Frank sighed and looked away. But he didn't argue the point.

"Okay, then. If and when Joe dies, take care of the body right away. Don't leave it in the camp, whatever you do. You couldn't bury it deep enough to do any good. And you sure as hell don't want to burn it. The smell would attract everything for miles. Get him at least a mile away from here."

Nickerson nodded, his jaws tight.

She tightened her own jaws. "And now comes the worst part. Don't take the time to bury it. It's not worth the risk. You'll be running enough risk just carrying the body. Not too much, I don't think, if you do it right away. But if you leave it lying while you take the time to dig a grave deep enough that scavengers wouldn't just pull it up, it'll start to go ripe in this heat and moisture. Don't forget that most predators are also scavengers."

Frank was holding his breath. Suddenly, he let it out in a little burst. "Shit," he said. But it wasn't an argument, it was just a pained acknowledgement of the truth.

"Just pick your spot, dump the corpse, and then hightail it back here. We can make up some kind of memorial for Joe later."

She knew Frank would have already thought of everything she was saying. But telling him what to do made it easier for her to leave, somehow.

She handed Nickerson the knife. "You may as well take this too, I guess."

But Frank shook his head. "Not a chance, Marie. It's the only real tool and weapon you have. Not much of the first and even less of the second, but it's something. It might save your life, and I can't see where it's critical for us one way or the other. If we need cutting edges, there are stones around we can use to sharpen belt buckles."

She decided he was probably right, and tucked the knife away. She was on the verge of giving Frank some more advice, but stopped herself. At this point, she was just jabbering at the man.

He and Barbara Ray went with her to the creek. Once they got there, she knelt and soaked her T-shirt in the water, then rolled it loosely and wrapped it in some big leaves they'd found from a plant that looked tropical but wasn't any plant she knew. That was the closest thing to a water bottle they could manage. She should be able to find enough water along the way to keep it water-logged.

She started to get up but Frank pointed at the creek. "Not so fast. You need to hydrate as ~~much~~ as you can before taking off."

He was right. She was just feeling nervous and wanting to get on with it.

"Thanks." She dropped to the ground and drank as much as she could hold. The water would bring her body temperature down, and that would mean she would have to burn extra calories to warm back up. But for now, the calories were something she could spare more than she could the risk of searching for water along the way. Water drew animals and animals drew predators.

"Marie," Barbara said, tears in her eyes. "I would go if I thought I could do it."

"I know, Barbara. I'll be fine."

"Do you think you can find Andy and Jenny?" The nurse looked toward the cave entrance. "I wouldn't even know where to start."

"Rod told me where they were going. It's about a two-day journey from here, I figure."

"Will the Indian camp still be there?" Nickerson asked.

"It doesn't matter. If they've moved on, I'll be able to follow them. They couldn't have gone too far. According to Stephen McQuade, there were about three hundred people in his Cherokee group, many of them elderly or children. They'll be moving slowly enough for me to catch up with them."

Barbara gave her a hug, "God bless you, girl."

When she was out of sight of the cave, Marie stopped to look around. She wanted to make sure she could find it again. Even though she had a knife, she couldn't mark a trail on the trees as she went. Blazing trees was as obvious to pursuers as to the pursued. She needed something the prisoners or Spaniards would miss if they decided to track her.

She'd use twigs, stones, and patches of downed grass. She found a branch that was small enough to go unnoticed but large enough it would take a significant wind to move it, and laid it against the base of one of the trees. She placed it on the side facing the setting sun. Her next marker would face sunrise. Rotating her marks was one of the little tricks she had learned as a kid, but it was something that would be missed by anyone but the most experienced tracker.

She started walking. About an hour later she came across an old set of prints.

She shivered a little. They were big enough that she could almost lie down in one of them if she curled up.

Well, not really. But they sure looked that big. She tried to imagine the size of the creature that had left the prints and then broke off the exercise before she scared herself into running back to the cave.

Besides, she didn't think the tracks had been made by a predator anyway. As big as they were, they had to be dinosaur tracks, and she'd gotten a lesson in basic dinosaurology from Jeff Edelman. She'd paid very close attention.

In the Cretaceous, big land predators belonged to the theropod group of dinosaurs. From giant multiton tyrannosaurs down to velociraptors the size of a big turkey, they were all theropods. At least, so far as Jeff knew. That meant they were all two-legged, walked something like birds—and, more to the point, all had birdlike feet.

She looked down at the tracks. No bird in the world

had left those tracks. They looked more like something a gigantic elephant might have left.

So, feeling a little better, she continued on her way.

The better feeling faded soon enough, though, as other alternatives came to her.

First, they only *thought* they were somewhere— somewhen—in the late Cretaceous. But even Jeff, whose theory that was, had admitted that some of the creatures they'd seen belonged to much earlier periods.

She tried to remember the names of the earlier periods in the Earth's evolutionary history.

Permian was one of them, she remembered. What did giant *Permian* predators look like? For all she knew, they looked like gigantic elephants with fangs instead of tusks.

The second alternative was even worse, though, in a way. At least if she got caught and eaten by a predator, there'd be *some* sort of purpose to her death. Even if it was just the primitive purpose in the tiny brain of a prehistoric monster. But she could also imagine herself being squashed flat by a giant herbivore, simply because it didn't notice her at all.

That was a really creepy thought. It wouldn't happen in the daytime, sure. Unless she'd been hurt in an accident and couldn't move, she was certain she could get out of the way of a dinosaur just lumbering along.

But what about at night, when she was asleep? She'd have to sleep sometime.

She and Frank had already considered the possibility of her sleeping in the trees. But neither one of them thought that was really such a good idea. First of all, because they had no idea what lurked in the trees. Even in the world they knew, some big predators could climb trees. And once you were in a tree, you were pretty well stuck there if something came after you. You might not have much of a chance of running away on land, but at least you had some.

The biggest problem, though, was the simplest. Sleeping in the trees sounded great in adventure stories, but in the real world people tossed and turned in their sleep. Marie knew for sure she did. She'd never been married, but she'd had several boyfriends. Two of them had lived with her for a while. Both of them had made wisecracks about waking up to find Marie sprawled every whichaway on the bed.

That was fine on a queen size bed whose mattress wasn't more than hip-high off the floor. Not fine, perched in the fork of some tree branches thirty feet off the ground.

And they had no rope she could use to tie herself down. Tying together strips of cloth was another one of those things that sounded great in stories but Marie had her doubts about. And they didn't have enough suitable cloth anyway, unless they stripped somebody of the one and only suit of clothing they had. Which was skimpy enough as it was, since most of them had been caught by the prisoners while asleep.

No, she'd have to sleep somewhere on the ground. She was hoping she could find a cave, or at least a decent-sized rock overhang.

On the bright side—so she told herself, anyway— the tracks were leading in the same general direction she needed to go. She decided to follow them on the supposition that an animal that big probably scared away other animals, added to the hypothesis—very dicey, this one was—that an animal that big would also find it hard to turn around. And both of which were irrelevant anyway, since she could tell that the tracks were at least three days old.

But . . . at least it gave her an orientation. She'd be less likely to just get lost.

After she'd traveled perhaps another two miles, however, her heart skipped a beat. The tracks she had been following were now covered by the tracks of another creature. Creatures, rather. These tracks were smaller, but they were obviously made by a pack and were just as obviously tracking the larger beast.

Abstractly, Marie knew that what she was seeing was old news, at least three to four days old. She also knew the pack animals weren't following footprints. They would be following a scent trail. That was the one trail every creature left and any creature but man could follow.

Her father's words from the past came back to her. *If you're ever in the woods unarmed and on the run, pray like hell you're running from a human. They're easy. A bear or wolf pack is a lot harder to beat, but if you use your head and haven't pissed off lady luck, you can even beat them.*

"Yeah, maybe," she whispered to his memory. "But does Lady Luck help with monsters?"

Days old or not, she wanted nothing to do with whatever creatures had left those tracks. Those *did* look like something giant birds might have left. She angled off to the north. The big tracks had been starting to veer a little too much to the south anyway.

She didn't find a cave, or a good overhang. But she did find something she hoped would be just as good if not better. A huge old tree, dead now, struck by lightning. But the lightning or maybe a series of lightning strikes had hollowed out the interior. It was a bit like a tall and narrow teepee with walls made out of thick wood instead of hide.

It was a squeeze getting through the opening, and the interior was just barely big enough for her to stretch out. She was very tired, by now. Not exhausted, exactly, but pretty close. She'd been pushing hard since she left.

She had enough energy to eat and drink. Then she lay down and tried to sleep.

Normally, Marie slept easily. But she couldn't keep her mind from pondering a question. How strong was the trunk left by even a huge tree, once it was dead and hollowed out? And how much did a really huge dinosaur weigh? If it was big enough, it might just topple over the whole tree, blundering around in the dark.

It was a stupid thing to worry about, and she knew it. First, because really big animals were diurnal, not nocturnal. She couldn't think of a single really big animal that moved around at night. Living by night posed problems that could only be solved at a price, evolutionarily speaking. And if you were big enough, who cared what saw you in daylight?

Second, it was stupid because the real danger she faced was that of a nocturnal predator who was not much if any bigger than she was, and could fit through the opening.

Still, she couldn't help brooding over the horrible

ignominy of ending her life as an accidental byproduct of a damn animal's clumsiness. *Here lies Marie Keehn. Look close and you might spot a little crushed bone or two mixed in with the bark and wood splinters.*

But, eventually, she fell asleep. She even slept through the night, and slept well. When she woke up in the morning, she found herself sprawled almost ninety degrees from the orientation she'd had when she lay down.

How had she managed that, in this tight a space?

She almost giggled, then. She was pretty sure Rod Hulbert would prove to be a light sleeper. If she did survive all this—and he did—she was probably looking at a lot of mornings filled with wisecracks.

CHAPTER
30

Through the mob, James Cook could see the front gate. But it was too far away, even if Luff hadn't positioned men at the gate itself. In the two seconds it took him to make that calculation, he could see that four more prisoners had been shot down trying to rush the gate.

James spun around, looking for an alternative. His foot struck something. Glancing down, he saw that he'd accidentally kicked a man in the head.

Well, no. He'd kicked a head. The body it had once been attached to was nowhere in sight.

The head must have belonged to one of the men Luff had had decapitated a short while ago. The heads had fallen into a barrel positioned below the execution platform. In the chaos that erupted after the Boom blew his stack, somebody must have upended the basket. The heads had spilled out, and they'd been kicked all over the yard ever since by hundreds of frantically milling men.

"What do we do?" asked John Boyne. He and the

rest of the men in Boomer's gang who were still alive, clustered around James.

Boomer wasn't one of them. His body lay in front of the executioner's platform. Shot to pieces by Luff's goons.

James felt a moment's sharp pang. But there was no time to grieve now. The only reason he and his group were still alive was because Boomer's charge at the execution stand and the firing squad response had triggered a mass rebellion by over fifteen hundred prisoners gathered in the yard. The fact that Luff's men were the only ones with guns gave them the edge, but it still wasn't easy. Some of the cons were crazy and plenty more who weren't had been driven crazy over the last few days. They might not have guns, but they were old hands at makeshift weapons and some of them weren't afraid to die.

So, for the time being, Luff and his goons were pre-occupied with staying alive. But it wouldn't be long before the tide turned. Then it would just be a slaughter—and James didn't have any doubt that Boomer's people would be at the top of the list.

Hearing shouts, he glanced over. Luff's men must have finally driven off the first frenzied assault. Now, they were concentrating their fire on the center of the crowd. There were already at least a hundred dead or dying between X-row and the front gate. He couldn't really estimate how many men had been killed trying to rush the gate itself. Their bodies were piled up too high. At least two dozen.

When the riot started he'd been surprised, but he hadn't been unprepared. Some things you could predict, even if you couldn't predict when they'd happen. Having the freedom to work together over the past few days, even if the work itself had been grisly, Boomer's boys had been able to do a lot. All of them had shanks now—good ones, usually made of sharpened pieces of steel. Better still, they'd been able to bribe a few key-holders and James now had copies of a number of the prison's keys.

James checked to see if the men were still with him. Those still alive were, and that was almost all of them. As far as he knew, besides the Boom himself, only three of their guys had been killed so far.

He was their anchor now. Somehow, in the days during which he'd organized the death detail, he'd emerged as the gang's second-in-command. Boyne probably would have contested that, eventually, but he wouldn't any longer. His instincts and attitudes were those of a subordinate. Now that Boomer was dead, he had no inclination to be the leader—as long as he could stay the lieutenant. In four short words he'd just made that clear. "What do we do?"

No reason he couldn't stay the lieutenant, so far as James was concerned. Boyne was a solid man.

The question itself remained. *What do we do?*

And he only had seconds to decide. This was rapidly turning from a rebellion into a massacre. Most of the prisoners now were just trying to get away from the killing ground at the center of the yard.

That provided at least part of the answer. If they were moving with the crowd, Luff and his men wouldn't be able to spot them. If they were even trying to, which James doubted. Boomer's eruption and the riot that followed had obviously caught Luff by surprise too.

Which way, though?

A slight thinning of the crowd gave him the answer. He

thought they could make it into the admin building. Luff and his usual bodyguards wouldn't be in there. They'd been on the execution platform. It doubled as a speaker's podium. Luff always gave a little speech after each morning's killings.

He led the way, ready to knock aside any con who impeded them. But he didn't have to. Before he'd taken more than a few steps, he heard Boyne say: "Get in front of him and clear a path, Dino! You're the biggest." A moment later, Dino Morelli strode past James and did as he'd been told.

Morelli was built like a basketball player, not a football player. But even a slender man who stands six feet, seven inches tall packs a lot of weight. Especially if he pumped iron, which Morelli did religiously. And just his height was intimidating by itself.

So they got there more quickly than James would have believed possible, and easily enough that he had time for a wry thought along the way.

Leave it to Boomer. Morelli's insistence that he was really a Puerto Rican with an Argentine great-grandfather, not a goddam Eye-talian which wasn't much different from a white man, was as transparent as you could ask for. Privately, the Boom made jokes about it himself. But James knew that when Morelli had approached him, a few days back, asking for a place in the gang, Boomer hadn't blinked an eye.

James would miss Boomer, he surely would. He'd been a giant in more ways than one.

Once they were through the door and into the admin building, the cool calm of the dark empty rooms seemed to hit the men like a hammer blow. Most of them sank to their knees gasping for air. James leaned against the wall, his heart pounding in his chest. They needed to rest, but he knew they couldn't. It wouldn't be long before Luff's killers started searching this building along with all the others.

He moved a few feet to peek out of one of the windows that opened to the outside and overlooked the front gate. But there was still no solution there. The area between the prison and the woods was a kill zone. The small group of men Luff had positioned at the gate must have finally been overwhelmed, because there were prisoners pouring through. But other goons on the walls were firing at them. Some of them would make it to the woods, sure, but most of them wouldn't. Bodies lay everywhere.

"Where to, boss?"

James turned away from the window and studied his new lieutenant for a moment. John Boyne was a middle-aged man who was very thick-bodied and strong-looking but was so short the top of his head barely reached Cook's chin. Despite the man's name, he looked Hispanic rather than Anglo. James had never asked about his ancestry and the Boom had never told him anything.

Not that he cared. James didn't share the Boomer's animosity toward white people, as such. As far as he was concerned, Boyne could be every bit as Irish as his name sounded. He was dependable and solid as a rock.

Where to, boss?

James thought fast. After his transfer to the clinic he had spent a lot of hours in this building. This is where he'd come for cleaning supplies. He knew it very well—and he could only hope that one of the keys he'd paid bribes for would open the critical door.

He pointed down the hall. "Move everyone that way. We'll see if we can get into the basement. Almost nobody ever goes there. I think we can hide until things settle down. Then we'll try our break after the sun goes down."

No one needed coaxing. They were on their feet and moving as soon as James finished speaking. The guns were still going off in the exercise yard and men were still shouting and screaming as they got butchered.

The one critical piece of luck they needed came through. The fifth key James tried unlocked the maintenance door leading down to the basement. He almost thought it wouldn't, since the lock was stiff from lack of use. But a little jiggling had done the trick.

The basement was cool, dark and damp, and smelled of mold and rats. James hated rats. He'd grown up in a roach- and rat-infested housing project. It had been hell, but it was better than a reservation. At least that's what he'd been told. He didn't know for sure. He had never set foot on a reservation.

A con—he didn't see which one—opened the drain valve on a water tank and another one was passing out water in a curved piece of scrap metal someone found. James gulped the liquid and then handed back the makeshift cup so someone else could get a drink. The water tasted of iron and rust, but it was water. It was the first drink they'd taken since early this morning.

The tank looked plenty big, too. They'd need to take water with them when they make their break into the woods.

"Look around and see if you can find anything that'll hold water," he told Boyne. "Anything one man can carry by himself will do."

While Boyne set about that task, James pondered the problem of food. They had nothing with them, and there was no chance at all of finding food in the basement. Whatever scraps a maintenance man might have left down here would be long gone by now, eaten by rats.

There'd be food upstairs in one of the rooms in the admin building. There was a refrigerator in a small lunch room on the second floor, and even if the refrigerator didn't work something would be up there. Luff and his top goons had used the building as their own headquarters, after they took over. Luff was not a man to go without his lunch handy.

But he didn't dare send anyone to look. The search could start any minute. It was better to go hungry than run the risk of being spotted. James was fairly certain none of the goons would do more than rattle the door leading down to the basement to make sure it was locked—and he'd been careful to lock it behind them. The goons wouldn't have a key to open it anyway.

Luff would, of course. But James was even more certain that none of his underlings would risk triggering off his temper right now by pestering him for a key, just to open a locked door that no fleeing con could have gotten through anyway. Not an underling low enough on the totem pole to be sent searching a building, anyway. Luff wasn't hot-tempered in the usual sense of the term, but the man could go quietly crazy when one of his plans didn't work.

And this one hadn't worked, big time.

James leaned against the wall, finally allowing a bit of his grief to wash through him. He knew perfectly well what Luff had been doing. So did the Boomer, because they'd talked about it.

The killings had started the day after the uprising. Just ten men, that first day. All of them complete crazies that nobody would miss.

That was the same day the execution stand had gone up. Luff had given a little speech, as he would do every day thereafter. The only difference was that in the days that followed he'd give the speeches after the killings.

The charges Luff had leveled against the ten condemned men were completely ludicrous. None of them were competent enough to do what they were accused of, even if they'd wanted to. Three of them had been in the psych ward, practically catatonic. One of them had been hauled to the noose in a straight-jacket.

The next day he'd hung fifteen, also crazies. The charges had been every bit as ludicrous, but they'd gotten vaguer. "Plotting with the guards" had become "treason against the people."

The third day there'd been twenty-five men hung. And, for the first time, some of them hadn't been waterheads. Just . . . old.

The fourth day there'd been thirty. Half of them . . . just old. And by then the standard charge had become "uncooperative with the new order." Which was about as good as it got, in the could-mean-anything department.

By then, too, the timber-cutting details were well underway. And it hadn't taken more than two days for every con in the prison to figure out that being chosen for the details was tantamount to a death sentence. The men hung weren't the only dead bodies that James and his people had had to dispose of.

He grinned a little, thinking about that. There was even a trace of humor in the grin.

The ovens had been Boomer's idea.

"Tell 'em you need ovens to burn the bodies, boy."

"Why ovens? Be easier to just burn them on piles of wood."

"You not thinkin' straight. Wood be wood. Ovens gotten be built. To work right, they need doors. Doors need latches and you can't make no latches wid'out steel." The big grin had appeared. "You follow me now, boy?"

How could a man that smart have just blown up? James wondered. He *knew* the Boom understood what Luff was doing, because he and James and John Boyne had spent hours talking about it—and just as many hours talking about how to handle the situation.

The executions, the life-draining work details, the sporadic food and grotesque water rituals, the lack of exercise, it was all part of an age-old practice of divide and conquer. Start with the outcasts and the weak, whom nobody would stand up for, just to get everyone accustomed to the killing. Then, broaden the scope, but always give people the hope that they might be spared.

Give them shit jobs to do, and make believe if they did what they were told they would live. Let them know if they didn't they would die.

Rub their noses in it.

Set up a kangaroo court and let those on the jury know the only acceptable verdict was guilty.

Hold court daily.

Have only one penalty.

Make the executions public. In fact, require everyone to attend. Make it plain that the people were being killed for a reason. They had done something wrong. Whatever it was. Something the rest of the population could avoid doing and thus be spared. If you didn't understand what could get you killed, at least you knew what wouldn't. Being "cooperative" with the new regime. Sucking ass.

Destroy the will of the ones you wanted to control. Grind them into the ground. Break their spirit.

But Luff screwed up. He was too much of a bookkeeper, not enough of a psychologist. He went too far, too fast. The killings were too methodical, too transparent. The guards hadn't been gone much more than a week and already the prison population had been cut by almost two hundred. The promise of *do as you're told and you'll be okay* wasn't believed any longer by too many people.

It wasn't just the public executions. In some ways, the timber details had been worse. Even men being deliberately worked to death shouldn't die in a few days. The goons didn't feed them badly; they didn't feed most of them at all—and then shot dead anyone who slacked off from the heavy labor of cutting trees and turning them into firewood. Given that most of the men picked for the timber details had serious medical problems to begin with, it wasn't surprising that they started dropping like flies almost immediately. Two men had died on the first day from heart attacks. They'd both been in their late fifties.

By the time the rebellion erupted, James didn't think many of the prisoners outside of the two or three hundred who were tight with Luff thought they would survive another week, the way things were going.

And through it all, as cold-blooded and calculated as Luff, Boomer had held them steady. "Just be good boys. Do your job wit' the bodies. Stupid fucks are leaving you alone, mostly, so you can do the things we done talked about. Time ain't right yet, but it will be soon enough."

The night before, the Boom had even told James and Boyne that he thought it was about to blow. "Just take a little spark now, that's all. Just one spark."

He'd been right, too. But he'd never said anything about being the spark himself.

James sighed. That hadn't been planned, he knew that much for sure. Somewhere inside Boomer, somewhere inside that giant with no education beyond the sixth grade but a mind as sharp as any, something was broken. Probably broken long ago, when he was a kid. The same thing that had landed him in prison over thirty years earlier. When something did set off the Boom, he just went nuts. Plain berserk.

James didn't know exactly what had set off that crazy streak this morning, and he'd never know. But he thought it was probably the guillotine. Today was the first time that had showed up. Luff must have decided hanging was too slow, too inefficient, so he'd had some of his men design and build a crude version of the device.

That would be just like the bastard. He had a crazy streak buried inside a lot wider than the Boom's, even if it didn't manifest itself as spectacularly.

The moment Boomer had seen the thing, his eyes had never left it. He'd stood there, stiff as a rock, while one man after another was dragged up and had his head chopped off.

He'd lost it at the eighth man. *"Fuck you, Luff!"* he'd bellowed—and a Boomer bellow could be heard all over the yard. *"We men, you motherfucker! We ain't sardines!"*

And he'd charged the stand. Armed with absolutely nothing but his fury and three hundred pounds of meat and muscle.

He'd gotten almost all the way there, too, before the bullets finally brought him down. And the rebellion erupted.

Boyne appeared at his side. "Boss, I found something. But you better take a look just yourself."

He was speaking in a whisper. Why? Puzzled, James pushed away from the wall and followed the short, stocky man into a far corner of the basement, mostly hidden by some sort of old retaining wall.

The wall created something in the way of a big cubbyhole in that area. The lighting was very dim.

"There," Boyne said, pointing.

Cook peered into the darkness, not seeing anything at first except two odd reflections. Then, suddenly, he realized he was looking at a pair of eyes staring back at him.

"What the . . ."

He stepped closer until he could see clearly. On the floor was a small, dirty makeshift mattress. Not a mattress, really. Just some kind of folded-over . . .

Something. Probably an old blanket a maintenance man had had down here when he took a nap.

On it, covered with nothing more than old newspapers

and spread open old magazines, was the young black CO he had seen in the infirmary just a few days before Luff had taken over. He knew she had been knifed and was in bad shape.

She was staring at him, saying nothing.

James was sure she was petrified. She must have been hiding here for more than a week, ever since Luff took over the prison. She'd managed to get water from the tank, the same way they had. He could see a big tin can next to her, with the shine of water coming from it. But she probably hadn't much if anything to eat.

Worst of all, he could only imagine what she must have been thinking all these days. One woman—young and pretty, too—trapped inside a prison with more than two thousand convicts on the loose. The only surprising thing was that she wasn't just gibbering.

What was her name? He had to think hard; those days seemed so long ago.

Then he had it. "Ms. Brown," he whispered. "Elaine Brown, if I remember right. We're not here to hurt you. We didn't come here looking for you in the first place. We're just trying to do what you're doing. Stay alive. Nothing more."

He waited. She just stared at him.

"Do you understand what I'm saying, Ms. Brown? Please. I'm an experienced emergency medical technician. I need a response."

Abruptly, she nodded. Once.

Okay, she hadn't gone nuts. That was something.

"Now I need to ask you some questions. First, where are the other guards?"

She stared at him. Belatedly, James realized the question might seem like an interrogator's, hunting the guards.

He waved his hand. "Never mind. You don't have to answer that. I just asked because—"

"Gone. I'm the last one." Her voice was low, barely above a whisper.

Cook didn't know if he should believe her. If there were others, she probably wouldn't say so. She would want to protect them, and maybe save herself by giving them a chance at surprising the escaped prisoners.

The woman shook her head. "I'm not telling you where they went, so don't bother asking." Unlike the first two sentences she'd spoken, her voice almost quavering, that came flat and hard and final.

Boyne chuckled. "Girl's got guts, for sure."

James smiled. That, she did.

He squatted next to her, reached out and laid gentle fingers on her forehead. Wanting to touch her more than check her temperature. Just to make sure she was real, maybe. He didn't know what to do, but whatever he did, he wanted to make sure it wasn't something he'd regret for the rest of his life. Touching her seemed to steady him, somehow. That was instinct, probably.

She flinched from his fingers, but relaxed when she realized he wasn't doing more than touching her brow.

Her temperature seemed fine. He tried to figure out what to do. Not even that, yet. Just figure out the right way to talk to her.

This wasn't a gangbanger, or a tough street whore playing the percentages. She was just a young woman, badly hurt and scared, wanting to do the right thing and not knowing what that was.

"Lady, the shit jumped off less than an hour back. Luff and his thugs are killing men left and right. You must have heard all the gunfire even way down here."

She nodded. He took his fingers away from her brow.

"We're just trying to escape. That's why I asked about the other guards. After we get out of this prison, if we want to stay alive, we have to find Captain Blacklock and his people. We have a common enemy, in the here and now, and I figure what's past is past. That makes us allies."

Elaine Brown chewed her bottom lip. Her eyes moistened a little but her voice remained steady. "Prove it, then. Take me with you. There are enough of you. You can carry me out. Take me with you and I'll show you the way to the captain."

James hesitated. All of his instincts told him to agree, but he wasn't sure it was even possible.

"*Please*," she said. "If you found me, how long until someone else does? And I don't think I can make it much longer even if they don't. I'll starve. Worse yet, I'll get so weak I can't keep scaring off the rats when they sniff around me. The last time I went upstairs at night to steal a little food was two days ago. I can't make that climb up the stairs again. I could handle the pain but I'm not strong enough any more."

James reached out again; and, again, Brown stiffened and pulled back a little. "I'm just checking," he whispered. Gently, he removed the newspapers covering her abdomen, then lifted her blouse. The I.V. he remembered was now gone, but the bandages were still in place. Her breathing was rapid and a little irregular. The basement was too dark for him to see if that reaction was due to fear or infection.

He touched the bandage itself. It was dry. That made her proposal . . .

Well, possible anyway, without just killing her. She wasn't a big woman. Never had been, even before a bad injury and a week without much food shrank her weight down even further. If James and his men could escape at all, they could carry her easily enough.

And, being completely cold-blooded about it, having Elaine Brown with them when and if they finally found Blacklock would work in their favor. James could make bold statements about "being allies," but the fact remained that Blacklock had well over a hundred well-armed guards and James had a little over twenty convicts armed with nothing more than shanks. He could easily see where Blacklock might decide that locking up his new "allies"—or just shooting them—was the appropriate measure.

Harder to do that, though, if those same cons were the ones who brought out alive a female guard whom the other guards had left behind to die.

Alive, and unhurt. In any way.

James pondered that for a moment. The problem was that he didn't really know all of the men in the gang that well.

Once again, Boyne showed how good a lieutenant he was. It was a little uncanny, the way such a dull-looking man could seem to read his mind.

He squatted next to them and said: "Won't nobody hurt

her, boss. Don't think any of them would anyway, but I'll see to it." His grin split the gloom. "Just to make sure, I'll have Kidd watch over her. Be her personal bodyguard. Goofy bastard'll get a kick out of that."

James chuckled.

Elaine's brow wrinkled. "What's so funny?"

"Geoffrey Kidd's as queer as they come, lady. He's also six feet tall, weighs well over two hundred pounds, and hospitalized the last man who tried to make him his bitch. That was . . . what, John? Before my time."

"Four years ago." Boyne stood up and looked down at Brown. "Just relax, girl. Won't nothing bad happen to you. Not from us, anyway."

The moist gleam in her eyes turned into a sudden flood. Her body was wracked with sobs. Quiet ones, though, very quiet. Even now, she was trying to maintain her control and self-discipline.

Hoping it wouldn't be misconstrued, James slid right next to her. Half-sitting and half-lying down, he put his arm around her shoulders.

This time, instead of drawing back, she leaned into him. Started to clutch him, in fact, before the pain brought by the motion made her pull the arm back.

"I've been so scared," she whispered. "Never thought a person could get so scared. Or stay so scared for so long."

He felt a lump in his throat. Ancient instincts were getting stirred up, no doubt about it. For the first time, her good looks registered on him.

Big time.

He needed to bring that under control, for damn good and sure. The effort to do so made his mind veer off to something that made him laugh. Not chuckle, laugh outright.

"What's so funny?" she asked again.

His initial reaction was that an honest answer would *certainly* be misconstrued. But something in the way she looked up at him, her head resting on his shoulder, made him think otherwise. There was something very steady about this woman, as young as she was. He didn't think she rattled easy.

"It's just that, when I was a kid, I used to have this daydream. Like in the comic books or the movies. Someday I'd rescue a beautiful princess from dire peril."

He laughed again, more softly. "You're good-looking enough, that's for sure. But I'd been figuring I'd find the princess in a fancy castle somewhere. Not . . ."

He waved his hand at their surroundings.

Brown laughed softly herself. And then, to his complete surprise, nestled into him. "I was born in a bungalow, not a castle. And the closest I ever came to being a princess was being runner-up—second runner-up, mind you—in a stupid beauty contest my mother made me enter when I was sixteen. *Junior Miss Alexander County*, I would've been, if I'd won. Oh, whoop-de-do."

She looked up at him again. Her dark eyes seemed bigger than any eyes he'd ever seen. That was a trick of the dim lighting, of course.

"What's your name? I remember seeing you now, once or twice, in the infirmary. But I never knew your name."

"Cook. James Cook." He smiled. "Not the sort of fancy name any knight in shining armor would have, is it?"

"No," she said calmly. "But it's the same name as that

famous captain. The great explorer. The one who sailed all around the world and discovered almost everything, way back when. More'n two hundred years ago, I think."

James knew who she was talking about, of course. His crazy damn father had named him after that captain.

He chuckled, harshly. "Yeah, I know. And wound up, in the end, being killed by cannibals."

"I like the name."

Oh, Lord. The lump was back in his throat and James had a feeling it wasn't going to get dislodged any too easily.

A little noise made him look up. He was a little embarrassed to discover that the whole gang had quietly gathered around, peering into the cubbyhole.

He cleared his throat. "Uh, boys, this is Elaine Brown. Ms. Brown, these are . . . ah . . ."

What to call them? They'd always just been "Boomer's boys."

Boyne cleared his throat. "Boss, I been thinking we should probably have a name. I mean, now that Boomer's gone."

He was right, and the name came to James immediately. "We do have a name. We're the Boomers."

The men murmured among themselves for a little while. It didn't take more than a few seconds before Morelli said: "Hey, I like it," and everybody else nodded their agreement.

Geoffrey Kidd pushed forward and knelt on one knee in front of Brown. As big as he was, he seemed to dwarf the little woman. That wasn't just his height and his weight. Kidd had figured out right from the start that the best way for a gay man serving a life sentence in a maximum security prison to survive on his own terms was to outdo the cons at their own dominance games. Being almost as black as the proverbial ace of spades helped, but he'd gone the whole nine yards. He lifted weights until he looked like Arnold Schwarzenegger, shaved his head bald, and had tattoos all over. The four knuckles on his left hand spelled out F-U-C-K. The ones on his right spelled out Y-O-U-2.

"Pleased to meet you, Ms. Brown," he said. "I've been assigned the task of watching over you, it seems."

Kidd had a good sense of humor, and was obviously amused by the situation.

"Pleased to meet you as well, Mr. Kidd." Her little hand came out from under the newspaper and magazines to shake his great big tattooed one.

"Well, isn't this touching?" said a hard voice from somewhere in the rear. "Move aside, girls. *Move,* I said."

Startled, the gang members at the rear skittered away, letting a man come through.

No, not one man. There were four others standing behind him. Each and every one of whom was holding a rifle or a shotgun and had a pistol holstered to his hip.

A couple of pistols, in the case of the one in front. One holstered on his hip and one shoved into his waistband.

Too late for it to do any good, James realized that the interest sparked by finding Elaine Brown had drawn everyone away from watching the door.

His fault, his fault. He'd been too damn sure that no con searching the building would have a key to the door leading down to the basement.

He'd been right, actually, as far as it went. The man in charge of this squad was no minor underling. It was Danny Bostic, one of Luff's three top lieutenants.

Specifically, the one Luff had put in charge of handling the daily executions. And who'd done it very efficiently, day after day after day.

CHAPTER
31

"Hold this for me, Fritz," Bostic said, handing his shotgun to one of the men behind him. That was Arthur Fritz, another con who went back with Luff a long ways.

He then shrugged off the heavy backpack he was carrying, as all of them were, and set it on the floor. His hands now free, Bostic pulled out the pistol in his waistband with his right hand and, from his back pocket, a flashlight with the other.

The beam of the flashlight played across the cubbyhole, settling quickly on Brown. Her eyes shut against the light. After this many days in near darkness, the flashlight must have seemed blinding.

"And will you look at this? One mystery solved, anyway. Boys, we've discovered the whereabouts of the missing Elaine Brown. You remember her, I'm sure. That little black honey made such a stir when she started working in the joint."

Elaine's lips tightened, along with her eyes. "You'd

better stay away from me. I've got AIDS. Was diagnosed right after I started. They were planning to fire me."

Bostic smiled. "Nice try, girl. Relax. We didn't come down here looking for pussy."

One of the men behind him said: "Yeah, sure. But now that we found her, why not bring her along? A day into the woods, and pussy sounds real good to me. Especially that one."

By now, James was standing up. Since the flashlight was aimed at Elaine instead of him, he could see Bostic. A little wash of expressions went over the man's face at that suggestion. There was maybe a trace of lust there, but most of it seemed calculation.

James didn't really know Bostic. But he knew he had a reputation for being a cold-blooded bastard, even by the standards of a maximum security prison. He didn't think Bostic himself had the inclinations of a rapist. But if Bostic decided it was a good idea to haul Elaine along to provide his men some entertainment, he'd do it without thinking twice.

There was only one way to handle this. Straight ahead.

"You don't take the girl, Bostic. Just forget it."

Bostic's lip curled. "And what exactly are you going to do to stop me, Cook? What you got? A shiv? A sock full of batteries?"

He hefted the pistol. "Meet Mr. .40 caliber. Full clip. Not to mention our good Dukes Twelve Gauge standing right behind me."

"Fuck you, Bostic. We're at close quarters and there are twenty of us. Stop flapping your mouth if you want to start killing and do it. But we'll take down at least two or three of you. We all got shivs and they work just fine at six-inch range."

He jerked his head, indicating the floor above. "You aren't here on Luff's business, are you? No, you're looking to do the same thing we are. Get the hell out before the lunatic takes everybody down. Am I right?"

Bostic made no reply, but something in his face made the answer obvious.

"Thought so. Well, figure it out, then. It oughta be easy, unless you got the brains of a carrot. Even if you kill all of us and don't get a scratch yourselves, how many rounds will you have to fire? Twenty, rock bottom minimum. Be more like fifty or sixty. You think that won't draw attention?"

He waited, just long enough for that to sink in. "And then what? You gonna hold off Luff and his men with a few pistols and shotguns? Just having used up half your ammunition?"

He could sense their hesitation.

The same shithead who'd proposed taking Elaine spoke up again. "He's bluffing, Danny. They ain't got the guts."

That was the wrong thing to say. Really, really, really, the wrong thing to say. The truth was, James wasn't sure if he was bluffing or not. He had no idea what the other Boomers would do, if the shit hit the fan here.

But the one thing you didn't ever do with cons—sure as hell not anyone who made it into Boomer's good graces— was suggest he didn't have balls.

The flaming gay one, especially.

Kidd came to his feet, with a grin on his face that was really a snarl. "You're a dead man, Williams." A steel shank came into his hand from somewhere. "I guarantee I'll get to you."

All of the Boomers were shifting their stances, now. And Kidd's wasn't the only hand holding a blade. At least a dozen were.

"*Hold it!*" Bostic half-shouted. "Everybody. Just hold it."

He turned his head slightly, not taking his eyes from James. "Williams, if you say one more word, I'll kill you myself."

"Won't have to," muttered Fritz. He had his shotgun pointed more at Williams than at any of the Boomers, now. "Shut the fuck up, you stupid bastard. Shut. The. Fuck. Up."

Williams seemed to deflate like a balloon.

James and Bostic stared at each other.

"It's your call, Bostic," he said. "I'll give you ten seconds to make it."

Danny knew he wasn't kidding. The Indian might well be bluffing, as far as what his men would do. Probably was, at least until Williams opened his fat mouth. But he wasn't bluffing about what he'd do. Cook hadn't bluffed since the day he walked through the gates.

Danny made a quick note to himself to get rid of Williams. He hadn't been sure about him to begin with. He was only along because he was the one who'd had access to the armory.

Concentrate, you idiot.

Three things made up his mind.

The first was that James Cook was just plain scary. It

was that goddam wood Indian face of his. You never knew *what* the fucker was thinking. He'd be hell on wheels at a poker table, if he could keep track of the cards and knew the odds.

The second was that, on balance, he didn't think taking the girl was a good idea anyway. At first it would please his guys. But then what?

He'd sneered at Luff enough times, privately, because of the man's inability to think in the long run. So Danny had better not make the same mistake himself.

What happens to a group of five men—four, soon— with one hot-looking woman among them?

Nothing good, for sure. And there were plenty of other women out there. Indian women, from primitive tribes. Maybe they were scraggly looking and stank, but that could be fixed. A little soap and combs went a long way. Most things could be fixed, if you were running the show and weren't stupid.

Finally, and simplest, rape didn't appeal to him. Not at all. And that it would have to be rape, with Elaine Brown, was obvious. Even when he got his hands on a native woman, he wasn't planning to force her. In the long run, that was stupid, and he wouldn't enjoy it in the short run. He wanted his women willing. Better yet, eager. And, unlike Williams, he hadn't been in prison for so long that he'd forgotten how to manage that.

"Ease up, Cook," he said. "I'm not looking for a fight." He put the gun back into his waistband. "As you figured, we just want to get away from Luff."

He turned his head; again, keeping his eyes on Cook. "Boys, we're all just going to stay calm and peaceful while we wait it out here for nightfall. Keep your guns ready, but that's it. You understand?"

"Yeah," said Fritz. "We do. Don't we, guys?"

All of them murmured agreement. Including Williams.

"Okay, then," Danny said. He gave Brown a smile and a little salute with the flashlight. "Nice to see you again, lady. By the way—I'm just curious, that's all—who *did* kill Terry Collins?"

She cleared her throat. "Marie Keehn. She stayed behind, but her boyfr—ah, Lieutenant Hulbert—had her name crossed off the list so she wouldn't have any set post."

Danny laughed softly. That really was pretty funny. That asshole Terry Collins, Mr. Swagger and Strut—plugged by a woman who didn't stand more than five feet, two inches tall.

"Wish I'd seen it."

"It was pretty horrible," the girl said, wincing. "She shot him right in the head. At close range. One of his eyes came out."

She was telling the truth, then. Danny had heard about the popped-out eyeball, from one of the men who'd seen the body.

He grinned. "Still wish I'd seen it. I despised that prick."

While he and Elaine had that little exchange, James had been thinking quickly. An idea had come to him.

Risky, though. Not because it might not work. That was a given. But it was still a lot better chance than their existing plan of just rushing the gate after nightfall.

The real problem was what would happen if the idea *did* work. Afterward, they'd be at Bostic's mercy. There'd be no tight, confined space that partially neutralized the mismatch between guns and shanks.

"How smart are you, Bostic?" he asked abruptly. "Smart enough to make a deal and stick with it?"

Bostic looked at him. "Depends on whether I think it's a deal worth making. But, yeah, I am. 'Ain't no honor among thieves' is bullshit. Your word is all you got, when you're outside the law. If you cross a man, he ain't gonna run to find a cop or a lawyer. He'll come after you."

"He might not get you. You might kill him."

"Sure. That's why a lot of stupid crooks pull double crosses. Sometimes they even work—but now you got a reputation as a double-dealing shithead." He shook his head. "It's amazing how many idiots don't know the word 'tomorrow.'"

Bostic's curiosity was aroused now. "And why are you asking? Have you got a deal to propose?"

"Yeah, I do. I know a way we can all get out of here, if we work together. It's not fool-proof, but it's better than what we were planning. Or you, I'm figuring." Again, he nodded his head, indicating the floor above. "You're planning to try to bluff your way out, come nightfall, aren't you?"

"Yeah." Bostic said. "It oughta work. I'm one of Luff's big men and everybody knows it. Me and my guys walk up to the gate right after sundown, tell the guards that Luff's sending us out on an errand, they won't argue the point."

"Won't they? What's the errand? Why would Luff be sending you out after dark?" He paused, for a second.

"And now that I think about it, why are you going to wait until dark anyway? Why not just do it now, while everything's still confused?"

Again, he nodded above. "The gunfire's dying down a lot. It'll be killing from now on, not a fight. I'm willing to bet the yard's almost empty. So just walk out now."

"What I said earlier," Williams muttered.

Bostic swiveled his head, glaring at him. "Yeah, I know you did. That's why I'm the leader and you ain't. Right now, everybody up there is jumpy as hell. Can you say 'trigger-happy,' you dumb son of a bitch? I'm not taking the risk. There aren't enough of us to scare the guards at the gate. By now, Luff will have a dozen of them standing watch there. Come nightfall, we got a better chance of talking our way through."

"I know a way you *can* scare away the guards at the gate," James said. "And do it right now. Twelve or two hundred. It doesn't matter. They'll scatter like rabbits."

Bostic sneered. "Forget it, Cook. No way I'm giving any of you some of our guns. And it wouldn't work, anyhow. Even if twenty-five of us charged the gate instead of five, it's too dangerous. Some of us would make it, but too many of us would get killed. I'm not taking the risk. My plan might have some holes in it, but that one's Swiss cheese."

James gave him a smile. The thin one he'd perfected by now, that never reached the eyes and was never a tell. "Do I look stupid? Of course that wouldn't work. But my plan will."

He explained what it was. After he was done, Bostic scratched his jaw for a few seconds, thinking it over.

While he did, Boyne brought up the obvious objection.

"Boss, if it works"—he jabbed his shank in the direction of Bostic and his men—"we'll be easy meat for these guys. They could just shoot us down."

Bostic's hand came down. "Fuck that," he said. "If I agree to this, we'll keep the deal. And why wouldn't we? Some of you would make it into the woods before we could get you—and then I'm looking at sleeping in the woods having to keep an eye out for a con slipping up to cut my throat as well as dinosaurs."

He shook his head. "No, once we get out—*if* I agree, which I haven't yet—we'll keep our end of the deal. The only thing you've got that we'd want anyway is the girl and"—he looked over and gave Elaine a jaunty grin— "meaning no offense, Ms. Brown—she's not *that* good-looking. No woman is."

He gave Williams another glare. "You hear that, Williams? You want pussy, I told you I'd get it for you. But we do it my way, not yours. And if that takes a while—if it takes a year or two years or three years—then that's the way it is. You'll survive. You been in here for years. You know how to jack off."

By the time he turned back to James, he was grinning again. That same jaunty grin he'd given Elaine.

"All right, Cook. I'll hand it to you. It's a good plan. We'll do it. But there's one condition."

"What's that?"

He pointed to Elaine. "You go with her. Not with your guys. We'll wrap the two of you up together."

James frowned. He'd be completely helpless, then, which he didn't like at all. "Why?"

"Don't be so modest. By now, Cook, whether you know

it or not, you're too well-known. You make too many guys twitchy. They see you in the group, some of them will start thinking. They probably still wouldn't do anything, on their own, but there's a good chance somebody would insist on checking with Luff. That's the one big weakness in your plan. If Luff gets involved, it goes up like smoke."

He nodded at Boyne. "Whereas if he looks to be in charge of the detail—meaning no offense again, John—it won't be a problem. Nobody disrespects Boyne, but he doesn't make people jumpy, either."

"He's probably right, boss," said Boyne.

James still hesitated. There was nothing in the world he hated more—even more than rats—than feeling helpless.

A soft voice came from the pallet. "I'd feel a lot better if you were with me, James," said Elaine. "I really, really would."

Bostic's grin seemed fixed in place, damn the bastard. "How can you resist a plea like that, Cook?"

Well. He couldn't.

"Okay, Danny. We'll do it your way."

CHAPTER
32

Bostic didn't wait any longer than it took to make the preparations. And that didn't take long at all, because he didn't face the problem Cook and his people did of having to stay hidden in the basement and scrounge up whatever they could find. That might have taken forever, since there probably wasn't enough in the basement for the purpose to begin with.

He just marched back upstairs with Williams, locked the door behind him, and went through the admin building until he found what they needed. Which didn't take any longer than finding the first linen closet.

The admin building was still empty, except for six men they found in the hallway almost as soon as they came out of the basement. They were all carrying rifles and shotguns.

Bostic knew all but one of them and gave them a wave from the other end of the corridor. "Don't bother, guys! We already searched the place. Ain't nobody here."

Kinsey, the con in charge, nodded and led his squad back out into the yard.

The best thing about this new plan was that it was taking place right now, in broad daylight, while everything was still chaotic. Waiting until nightfall had always been a weakness in Danny's original plan, and he'd known it. He just thought the alternative was riskier.

And he hadn't counted on the riot. He'd planned to leave on a quiet night. What a laugh that was, now. The guards Luff would have back at the gate would be edgy as all hell. Especially after contemplating the corpses of the first detachment Luff had put at the gate, who'd been overwhelmed in that big rush right after the killing started. Anything coming toward them that looked even remotely like a threat would be likely to set them off.

But the riot had done one thing for him. At least he didn't have to worry that Luff might show up at an awkward moment. Luff would stay in his hole for hours today. He wouldn't stick his nose out until well after sundown.

Luff really did suffer from megalomania, in his quiet accountant's way. That was the reason Luff wasn't in his usual office in this building today. It wasn't fear—you had to give it to him; the guy didn't have a nerve in his body— it was delusions of grandeur.

On the very next day after he'd led the prison rebellion, Luff had decided he needed a "war room." That was exactly what he called it, too. *War Room.* Like he was some kind of president or four-star general.

The warden's office in the admin building wouldn't suit the purpose. No, of course not. Too humdrum. He needed someplace that *looked* like a "war room." As best as he could manage, anyway, in a prison.

And that's where Luff would be right now. He'd have made a beeline there as soon as the crap hit the fan this morning. Probably cackling with glee—not openly, of course; he was almost as hard to read as Cook—that he finally had a chance to use it properly.

Danny grinned. Which meant he was almost all the way across the prison from the front gate, and would stay there for hours. Holed up in a corner of the machine shop, with his stupid diagram of the prison spread out across a work bench, pretending he was General Patton at the Battle of the Bulge. If he'd ever found some toy soldiers in the prison, he'd be pushing them around all over the diagram.

What a lunatic. If he lasted long enough and stayed in charge, Danny wouldn't be surprised if Luff wound up setting himself up with a little camp a mile or so into the woods, to which he'd retreat from time to time. He might even call it Camp David.

Williams found the linen closet. "How about this, Danny? Will this stuff do?"

Danny went over. It was a big closet. Not quite a full walk-in, but almost. And every shelf was piled high with sheets and pillowcases and thin blankets.

"Perfect. We'll take a dozen of the sheets. And . . . one blanket."

"Just one?"

"Yeah, one's enough to let 'em breathe."

In a perfect world, he'd have made it all blankets. In the long run, blankets would be far more useful. But sheets would do better for the short run. They could be wrapped tightly, where blankets couldn't.

He spotted a roll of masking tape on the top shelf. A full roll, and it was the big tape, three inches across. That'd be perfect. Icing on the cake.

He grinned again as he reached up and took it down. Cook would absolutely hate it. But he couldn't possibly object.

Once they had the stuff piled up on the floor, Danny studied it for a moment. It'd be a load, but he could handle it all himself. This was the best place he could think of, given that he saw no reason to postpone the matter.

He pointed at some of the pillowcases on a far shelf in the closet. "Better get a half dozen of those, too. We might need something smaller."

Williams started into the closet. Behind him, now, Danny drew the gun from his waistband. It was one of the prison's double action pistols. He didn't need to work the slide like he would with an old-style automatic.

As soon as Williams was all the way into the closet, Danny shot him in the back. A quick double-tap, extending the gun so it was inside the closet too. That made a lot of noise, where he was standing, but he didn't think anyone outside the building would hear the shots.

Even if they did, he didn't think it'd be a problem. There were still plenty of guns being fired in the prison. Not the fusillade that had been happening earlier. These were the sounds of executioners at work, coming once every two minutes or so.

Just to be sure, he waited in the corridor, listening.

Nothing. He was sure the building was still empty,

except for the people in the basement. And whenever someone finally did come in, he'd be long gone by the time they got here.

He looked back into the closet. Williams hadn't died yet. But he was unconscious and would remain that way until he did. Which wouldn't be all that long. Danny had been careful not to shoot him in the head or heart, because he didn't want to risk a big blood spill. Instead, he'd shot Williams in the spine, low down. Either one of the shots would have been fatal. And he wasn't bleeding that much.

Quickly, Danny stooped, set the gun on the floor, grabbed a blanket from a lower shelf and pushed it around Williams' legs and feet, after shoving the one foot sticking out back into the closet. That should sop up whatever blood did come.

He stood up and closed the closet door. There was no sign at all that a body was inside.

He touched the pistol with the flat of his hand. The muzzle wasn't too hot to shove down into his waistband. It would have been a pain in the ass having to perch the pistol on top of a big pile of blankets and sheets and carry them all the way down two flights of stairs to the basement.

As it was, the stack was awkward to handle. But a little labor—you couldn't even call it hard labor—was worth getting rid of a problem immediately and neatly.

"Where's Williams?" asked Fritz, after Danny dumped the pile of bedding next to Brown.

"It turns out he won't be coming with us after all." He

had no expression on his face when he said that. He might have been talking about a slight delay in traffic.

There was a moment's silence in the basement. Then Fritz smiled, very thinly, and gave the other two men in Danny's group a quick, meaningful look.

Those three and Danny himself were the inner circle. Fritz had never wanted Williams in on it at all.

"Too bad," he said. "And after all the talking he did about getting some pussy."

He gave Brown a glance. The girl's eyes, big at any time, looked like saucers. Apparently she wasn't as naïve as she looked.

Danny's eyes were on Cook. "Is there a problem, officer?"

The Indian gave him that creepy smile he had. The one that would scare a crocodile.

"Not at all. I'm glad to see everything's working out for you."

Danny nodded. "Fine." He pointed at the girl on the pallet. "Time, then. Make like Hansel and Gretel."

"Get the fuck away from it!" Danny shouted at the ten men standing guard at the gate. There were three sets of gates, actually, but since the uprising Luff only kept the inner one closed.

Joey Enders was in charge of the detail. He frowned, looking at the weird big bundle that was coming toward him and his men, perched on top of a makeshift litter being carried by eight men shuffling forward. A dozen other men came behind them. Two of them were carrying shovels.

"What's going on, Danny?" Nervously, he hefted the rifle in his hands. But he wasn't pointing it at anything.

Danny came forward, skirting widely around the litter.

"I'm telling you, Joey, you guys *don't* want to get close to this." He jerked his thumb over his shoulder, indicating the litter. "It's Koppler. Him and his bitch Inglewood."

"You shoot 'em? What for?"

"Fuck no, we didn't shoot 'em. We found 'em in Koppler's cell. Deader'n last year's garbage and looking a lot worse. They both got these big purple spots all over 'em. They're oozing something, too. Pus, blood, who knows? Luff thinks it might be plague or something. He wants these bodies buried deep, at least a mile into the woods."

Enders sidled back from the oncoming litter. Since Danny had spoken plenty loud enough for all the guards to hear, all of them started sidling away. Within a few seconds, the gate was clear.

It was still locked, of course.

"Open it up," Bostic commanded.

Enders was nervous, obviously, but some shred of being in command held him a little steadier than the others. After taking that first two-step backward sidle, he hadn't moved any farther. His eyes came away from the litter and went to the men carrying it, and the ones coming behind them.

"What you got? The whole damn burial detail? Why?"

Bostic was right next to him, now. "Why d'you think?" he growled softly. "Do *you* want to let these guys back in, after they've handled bodies full of plague?"

Enders eyes widened. "You gonna shoot 'em all?"

"Jesus! Where were you when they passed out the brains, Enders? Taking a dump? Of course we're not going to shoot 'em. They know how to get rid of bodies and there's likely to be more. Figure it out, fer Chrissake. It didn't take me and Luff more'n two seconds."

Enders really wasn't too bright. So Danny went ahead and spelled it out for him.

"It's simple. First, we shot Cook."

"You shot Cook?"

"Jesus *and* Mary. Of course we shot Cook. We would've shot him anyway. Luff wants Boomer's boys broken, finally. Cook had to go, especially with this plague shit coming up."

He nodded backward. By now, the litter was only twenty feet from the entrance. "We let Boyne live. He's enough to keep them under control, and he won't get ideas. But that's also why he's one of the ones carrying the litter."

Joey Enders looked. Sure enough, John Boyne was one of the two men in front, on the left, holding up one end of the two poles. Except they weren't poles, they were just ten-foot-long two by fours. Strips of linen tying the two boards together formed the rest of the litter's framework.

Boyne was looking distinctly unhappy. So were all of his men, especially the ones carrying the litter.

Enders looked back up at the litter. Up close, he could see the forms of two human bodies in the big bundle on top. The bodies themselves were invisible, all wrapped up in sheets the way they were. The sheets had been tied down tightly by long strips of masking tape, too.

But those were bodies; they couldn't be anything else.

The shapes weren't very distinct, as many sheets as they had wrapped around them, but they were distinct enough. One of them looked awfully small, but that made sense too. Inglewood had been a little guy.

He couldn't see the faces at all. The area where the heads would be was wrapped around with a blanket.

Enders started to wonder why. When the answer came to him, he held his breath. They didn't want to take any chance that something in the corpses' lungs might get through a thin sheet.

"Oh, shit," he said. Then, realizing what he'd done, took a quick breath and held it. He wasn't breathing again until that *thing* was gone.

"'Oh, shit' is right," hissed Danny. "These guys don't come back into the prison. They stay out there, unless we need to haul out another body. That's why I'm taking out all of them, and that's why me and my guys are hauling these big damn backpacks. We gotta stay out there for a while too, watching 'em. We'll let just enough of 'em back in to do that job. And nobody who's handled a body directly ever gets back in, even for that. That's why Boyne's in this first crew of body-handlers."

He gave Enders as evil-looking a smile as he could manage. Which was very evil-looking indeed. "Hopefully, we won't need to run through more than Boomer's boys. But if we do, I'm sure we can find suitable replacements somewhere. Now. Are you opening that gate? Or do I have to go get Luff?"

Still holding his breath, Enders pulled a key ring out of his pocket. "You do it," he croaked. Not letting any air out at all.

CHAPTER
33

"You okay?" James whispered. With everything piled on top of their heads, he was sure the soft sound couldn't be heard by anyone else. Especially since Bostic—he didn't know whether to curse the bastard or heap blessings on him—had wrapped the two of them so tightly together that his mouth was pressed right against Elaine's ear and her mouth wasn't much farther from his.

"A little stuffy. But, yeah, I'm okay."

"How about your wound?"

"Hurts some. But no worse than usual."

At least Bostic hadn't argued the point when James insisted that he had to be lying on the side opposite Elaine's injury, when they were wrapped up together. Whatever else he was, Bostic wasn't dumb. He'd understood immediately that if James was pressed against the wound, Elaine was likely to twitch at some point. At the wrong time, that could blow the whole thing. Corpses don't twitch.

James was trying not to twitch himself. He could feel every curve in her body, from her shoulder down to her toes. And it was a very curvy body, as small as it was.

Worst of all, he'd gotten a curve himself. And the damn thing was showing no signs of going away.

He was sure she knew it, too, since his groin was pressed right against her. He felt like a jackass, but he just plain couldn't help himself. His body was paying no attention to the fierce commands he was sending down.

She hadn't said anything, though. Hopefully, he could just keep pretending it wasn't happening.

It was a crazy reaction, as well as an embarrassing one. Here he was, in one of the most dangerous situations he'd ever faced, and all he could think about was the girl pressed against him.

But that was instinct again, he supposed. He'd read somewhere that the imminence of death tended to make people get really horny. At the time, he'd thought that was weird and hadn't really believed it. But he believed it now.

Trying to take his mind away, he listened to what was happening outside their cocoon.

He couldn't really tell. They'd stopped, very briefly, half a minute or so back, but they were moving again. The blanket and sheets around them didn't block off sound, as such, but they muffled everything. He could tell that people were talking to each other, but he couldn't make out the words.

Was that the sound of a gate being opened? He thought so. He wasn't positive, but he thought so.

"I think it's working," Elaine whispered.

"Yeah, me too."

"Tell me when you think we're through. And nobody can possibly hear us. I got things I want to say. Without worrying about having to be so quiet."

"Sure, lady."

"That's the first thing. Don't call me that."

"Sorry. I didn't mean—"

"I know that. I just don't like it because it's so formal." She issued something that sounded like a suppressed giggle. "Which is really silly, given the situation."

They *were* through. There was a sudden little high-pitched metallic squeal. One of the gates always squealed like that, when it was about halfway open. A slight dent in one of the hinges, probably.

"Okay," he whispered. "We're through. But wait a couple of minutes. We still have to get through the holding area before we're all the way outside. There might be a guard in there."

There were four guards stationed in the holding area, as it happened. But none of them were there any longer. Not with Danny Bostic ranging ahead, spreading the word. All four of them were now in the guardhouse, watching through the window. And standing about three feet back from the window. Just in case.

"No, dammit!" Luff snapped. "I'm not worried about the fucking gate. Use your brains, Haggerty. We musta shot, what? Fifty guys there? Won't be nobody we're looking for stupid enough to try another break. They're all hiding somewhere. I want 'em rooted out."

He leaned over the diagram spread across the big workbench in the machine shop. "Now pay attention. Since Bostic's off somewhere, I'm putting you in charge of Operation Caduceus."

"Cadoo . . . what?"

Luff's lips tightened. Where the hell *was* Danny Bostic? At least the man had read a book or two.

"Never mind, Haggerty. Operation Double Snake, how's that?"

He took one of the triangular carbide tool bits he'd found in a drawer near the lathe and moved it across the big diagram to the location that marked the infirmary. "This is Larrocha's squad. They should be done with A-block by now. They search the infirmary. Top to bottom. And tell 'em to be on their toes. I think Cook's probably in there with the rest of Boomer's boys. It'd be a natural hiding place for him."

He moved another tool bit next to it. "That's Ollie and his guys. They're backup. If Cook's there, I want him shot dead on the spot. But don't kill any of the others unless you have to. Especially don't kill Boyne. Without the Boom and Cook, we can control Boyne—and we're still gonna need those fucks to get rid of bodies for us. In fact, they'll be doing a landslide business. So if they're there, and after they're rounded up, Ollie and his guys march them back to their cells and stay there, watching them. Got all that?"

Haggerty nodded.

"Good." He took a third tool bit and moved it to the infirmary also. "And that's Zimmerman's squad. They are to watch Larrocha while he and his guys search. I catch anybody stealing shit from the infirmary, the blade's coming down. Make that clear to everybody."

Luff stood up straight, studying the whole diagram. "It's going pretty damn well. The best thing about today is that it finally gave us a chance to get rid of all the gang bosses. Cook's about the only loose end left. By this time tomorrow, we'll be in complete and total charge. Some sanity can be established."

"We're clear," James whispered. "By now, we're at least thirty yards out into the open. But keep it quiet, just to be safe."

"I would anyway. This is between you and me. First, I got a question."

"What is it?"

"Why'd you get sent up?"

He thought about telling her the truth. No, she'd think it was a lie. Better—for now, anyway—to just say it . . . Neutrally, so to speak.

"Second degree murder. I got in a bar fight and the guy died afterward."

"A little more detail."

He sighed. "He provoked the fight, not me. But if I hadn't been drunk, I would've just walked away before it got that far. I got a problem with my temper, sometimes, when I've had too much to drink. But even after the fight started, I wasn't trying to do anything more than whip him."

She was silent, for a few seconds. "Okay. I can deal with that. I just wanted to make sure it wasn't something, you know . . . Sicko."

He almost chuckled. "Uh, lady—Elaine. Second degree murder's not exactly considered a misdemeanor."

"Yeah, sure. But it's not sicko. My cousin Eddie almost did the same thing. He got lucky, because the other guy didn't die. Not quite. But he's still serving time."

Her body shifted a little. By now, they were both suffering from long immobility, and she had an aching wound to boot. But Elaine was still being careful. No one outside the wrappings would have noticed the slight motion—and their bodies were shifting back and forth anyway, because of the swaying of the litter.

"I'm not a fairy-tale princess, born and raised in Disneyland. My family's just one generation away—thanks to my dad, who got a decent factory job and then worked his ass off—from dirt poor Cairo black people. That's not Karo syrup, neither. It's Cairo, Illinois. You ever been there?"

"No. I know where it is, but I've never visited."

"Don't bother. Unless you got a thing for rusted out old cars and cheap trailers on cinder blocks."

This time, he did chuckle. "Not much chance of that, these days."

"Tell me about it. That leads to my next question. Do you have a girl?"

"In *prison*? Look, whatever you may have heard, not all convicts—"

"I didn't mean it that way. Sorry. What I meant was, did you have . . . Is there anybody you're pining after, so to speak? You know, the girl you left behind."

He couldn't figure out where she was going with all this. "No. I broke up with the girlfriend I had—well, she broke up with me—not long before the fight. Part of the reason I was in such a bad mood, that Friday night."

Again, her body shifted a little. Impossibly as it seemed, she was pressing against him even more closely.

"Good. That makes everything easy. Well, James Cook, you got a girl now. And I'm giving you fair warning. I catch you fooling around with any other woman, you'll wish you'd never been born."

He stared at nothing. There was a little open shell around their faces, but the blanket wasn't more than an inch or two away at any point. Bostic had wrapped the entire thing around their heads. It wasn't quite what you'd call pitch dark, but almost.

That was too bad, because he really wanted to be able to look at her face. Badly.

"You don't even know me, Elaine."

"That's true. But if we survive, I'll have plenty of time for that. Right now, I'm concentrating on the basics."

James didn't know what to say. For one of the very few times in his life—the only time, actually, that he could remember—he was literally struck speechless. He didn't even entertain the possibility that the woman might be joking. He didn't know Elaine Brown, either, but somehow he knew she wasn't kidding at all.

Which . . .

Was pretty basic knowledge, now that he thought about it. In a world full of rampaging felons, conquistadores and giant reptiles.

"I spent eight days down there," she murmured. "The worst eight days of my life. Not even that. Days that were worse than anything I could have imagined, before it happened. I never really thought I had a chance, all that time, but I just set that aside. And every day—every hour—I promised myself that if I did survive, I would never again, not ever in my life, waste a single moment on bullshit. And I was never much of one for bullshit in the first place."

He still didn't know what to say.

She giggled. And didn't try to suppress it, this time. "Speaking of bullshit, are you really going to tell me that's a gun in your pocket? I might even believe it, almost. Seeing as it's now been solid as a rock for longer than any hard-on I ever saw. Or even heard about from my girlfriend Sara, who saw a lot more than I did."

Incredibly, he felt a stab of jealousy, at the thought of her and another man's—

Was he going as nuts as the girl?

"Well. Answer me." There was something relentless about the little woman. "*Is* it a gun in your pocket?"

He probably flushed. And, for a very brief moment, was thankful for the darkness.

"No, it's not. But look, lady—Elaine. You can't make . . . I mean, I've been locked up for . . ."

He was fumbling all over the place. And the more he fumbled, the more he realized he was fumbling in bullshit. He'd *never* had this reaction to a woman. Not even when he'd been a teenager with his tongue hanging out at every pretty girl who walked by and had gone without sex for a lot longer than he had since he got in trouble in the bar brawl.

"I intend to stay alive, James Cook. Do my very, very best. And help anyone else I can to do the same who deserves to. I've got no time any more for fooling around. I need a man, in a world full of monsters. I want a man. And you're him."

"You don't know me—"

"It doesn't matter. It doesn't matter whether you're the perfect man for me. You probably aren't. I can tell you right now I'll ride herd on you about the liquor. I'd hate liquor even if my church wasn't against it. I've seen way too many people get fucked up that way."

That wasn't a problem. James hadn't had a drink since the fight. And had promised himself he never would again, either. He'd seen way too much of that himself, starting with his father and two of his uncles. All of whom had spent some time in prison, and always for something involving booze.

"But it doesn't matter what faults you have, James. We all have faults. As long as there isn't anything just plain twisted inside of you—that's why I asked the first question, just to be sure—I'll deal with whatever else I have to."

"I don't actually have too many faults, I think. No more'n usual, anyway. My temper's fine when I'm sober." Honesty made him add: "Okay, I'm probably too jealous. That's why my girlfriend broke up with me, and . . . Well. She had at least some right on her side."

"Won't be no problem. I never played around even as a girl. And I get pretty possessive myself. Now, in this world . . ."

He could feel her head shake a little. "You really don't understand, James. I don't think anyone could, who didn't go through those eight days. It wouldn't matter if, tomorrow, I did meet my 'perfect man.' The handsomest man in the world, smarter'n Einstein, sunnier than the sun, you name it." She nuzzled him softly. "All the things you aren't, exactly."

He would have chuckled, except the nuzzle paralyzed him. Sent a spike right down from his skull to his toes.

She shook her head again. "They still wouldn't be the man who came down to hell and got me out. No man ever will, except you, even if I live to be a hundred. Which I might, if the dinosaurs don't get me. Women in my family live a long time, if they stay away from liquor."

From the feel of her head, he thought she was looking at him. He couldn't wait until he could finally look into those dark eyes again. The feeling was almost scary.

Except it was too exhilarating.

"You ever hear where little ducklings—or maybe it's chicklets—get imprinted by the first thing they see when they come out of the shell? Whatever it is, that's momma."

"Yeah," he said. "Don't know if it's true."

"Well, it's true with me. Like it or not, fella, you done went and imprinted yourself on me, down in that basement of hell. James Cook. My man. Way it is. Get used to it."

He laughed outright, then. They had to be far enough away from the prison, by now. And he couldn't possibly have contained it anyway.

Danny Bostic was genuinely fascinated, by the time they got well into the woods and could stop to set down the litter. Had Cook managed to get *laid* in there?

It sounded like it, between his laughter and the happy little noises the girl was making.

Apparently not. At least, when they cut away the tape and unwrapped the sheets, all the clothes seemed to be in order. And he'd forgotten about the girl's stab wound. As passionate as she might be, there was no way she'd have been able to have sex. Not and be smiling at the man like that afterward.

Still, it was impressive. For at least twenty seconds after the blanket was removed, the two of them just stared each other in the eyes, both smiling from ear to ear, as if they'd met for the first time and fallen instantly in love. Cook's smile was the first honest-to-God expression he'd ever seen on the Indian's face. And Brown's smile . . .

He had to look away. The temptation to break the deal and snatch the girl got almost overwhelming, for a moment.

Because he looked away, he saw the expressions on the faces of Boyne and the other Boomers. They were staring at their boss, with their eyes almost bulging. Who would've guessed he was this much of a ladies' man?

"Does anyone know the location of the nearest jewelry store?" Brown asked brightly. She finally took her eyes off Cook and looked up at the other men standing around. Still smiling from ear to ear, even if the smile didn't have the same laser intensity. "We need engagement rings. Mr. Cook proposed to me in the course of our little journey, and I accepted."

"Well, Jesus," said John Boyne. "Jesus H. Christ."

He shook his head, as if clearing away confusion, and looked at Cook. "Is that true, boss?"

Cook was still looking at Brown. "Yeah," he said.

Then, like a startled rabbit, he looked up at his lieutenant. "By God, it is true."

With Cook, of course, sentimental moments couldn't be expected to last long. Less than a minute later, he was back on his feet. Back in charge, with that inscrutable Injun look on his face.

He and Danny studied each other for a moment.

"Which way are you going?" Danny asked.

"I don't know." Cook looked down at the girl on the litter. "Elaine?"

She seemed uncertain. "Well, it's hard to explain easily. The directions I have are a little complicated."

"Never mind the complications," Danny said. "Which way *now*?"

"Oh." She pointed a finger at one section of the woods. Which didn't look any different from any other. "That way."

"Fine. Then I think it's best if we head the other way. We don't have a specific destination in mind, so it really doesn't matter." Danny gave Cook a little salute and started to turn.

But a stray and ridiculous thought bloomed into focus.

Maybe not so ridiculous.

He hesitated. What the hell. If nothing else, it was a little funny. Not much, but a little. And while it had seemed like a good idea, at the time, to bring a back-up pistol, he was loaded down heavy as it was. With each step he took, the idea seemed less and less bright.

He drew the pistol from his waistband. With his left hand, not his right. Then, he shifted it so that he was holding it by the barrel instead of the grip. No point in setting off tight nerves at the very end.

"Here, Cook." He extended the gun, butt first. "Take it. It's got a full clip."

Cook came over, and took the gun.

"Why?" he asked quietly.

"First, a deal. Give us ten minutes before you leave. I'd just as soon know we're well out of sight. It's not that I think you're a double-crosser, it's just . . ."

"I understand. 'Good fences makes good neighbors,' as they say." Cook nodded. "No problem. You can have twenty. It'll take us that long to adjust the litter so it's comfortable for Elaine on a long trip. Second?"

Danny shrugged. "To be honest, I'm not sure. But you never know. We might meet up again someday. If and when we do, remember this."

For a few seconds after he was gone, James stared at the pistol Bostic had left behind.

Boyne came over. "Funny damn thing for him to do."

"He's thinking ahead, John," James said, almost musingly. "Way, way ahead."

He understood, he thought, Bostic's plans. He wasn't thinking like a con. Most cons would go out there figuring to rob. Bostic was figuring to rule. Find some tribe of primitive Indians, kill or intimidate the existing leaders, and take over.

So far, most hardened criminals could have followed the logic. But Bostic parted company with them here. He knew that a tribe—call it a gang, call it whatever—needed rules. They might be tough rules, for the ones on the bottom, but they were still rules. Not caprice, not whimsy, not just whatever struck the Big Man's fancy come Tuesday morning or a spot of indigestion.

Rules. Then, give it some time, he wouldn't have to watch his back every night and day. He'd have men doing it for him, because they damn well thought it was the right thing to do. He was the chief—maybe, someday, even the king—not just a thug running things until a tougher thug could do him in.

In the end, it had been that as much as James' threat that had kept him from taking Elaine. Whether the man understood it consciously or not, he'd sensed that starting his new life by breaking the rules would send him off at a tangent.

The same reason he'd given James the gun. He didn't really need it, the Boomers sure as hell did—and he'd just laid the basis, maybe, for an alliance someday. A truce, at least.

"Smart man," James murmured. "Hard and cold as nails, but smart. Even ethical, in his own way, if you're willing to stretch the term. Too bad he wasn't running the show instead of Luff."

Boyne looked skeptical. "I dunno, boss. For all his fancy talk about honor among thieves, he double-crossed Williams, didn't he? In a heartbeat. I betcha he shot him in the back, too."

John was wrong, but explaining why would be difficult. It was a subtle matter, and James could only grope at the edges himself. That Danny Bostic had his ethics, he didn't doubt any longer. But they'd be razor thin, without any of the plush and comfortable padding that people in a law-abiding society gave each other. That was mandated by law, in fact.

The way Bostic looked at things, Williams had double-crossed *him* when his lust and stupidity had almost triggered off a deadly brawl. The moment he did that, Bostic would have removed the man's protection. He'd gone instantly from *one of my loyal vassals* to *a problem to be removed.*

James smiled thinly. Removed his lord's grace, you might better call it. Yes, it was too bad that Bostic hadn't been running the show instead of Luff. But James still wouldn't want to live under his rule. It'd be like walking on thin ice from dawn to dusk, and egg shells through the evening until the lord went to bed.

But there was no point debating the matter with John. Not now, for sure.

He shoved the pistol into his waistband. Later on, they'd have to figure out who was the best man to carry it. That wouldn't be James himself. He'd never been into guns, the way some people were. He knew how to use one, but that was about it. One of the Boomers was bound to be good with a pistol.

He was a little startled, then, when he realized that he'd given no thought at all to keeping the gun just to make sure his authority wasn't challenged. He didn't need to. That was just a fact, by now. So thoroughly engrained that he hadn't even thought about it.

He looked around, at his men. Three of the Boomers were fussing over Elaine, giving her water, asking her how she was. But it was the actions of loyal men tending to the lady, not guys angling for her themselves. He realized that he also hadn't given any thought at all to how the Boomers would react when they realized that the one and only

woman among them had just been separated out—and by
the boss himself.

That could have easily triggered off deep resentment.
Instead it had done the opposite. It seemed to settle them
down a little.

He knew his uncle had been wrong. There were lots of
men behind bars, hiding the fact beneath animal masks.
Boomer had known it too, on some level, and known how
to select them. These were men who, deep down, wanted
nothing so much as a place of their own. Being part of a
society again instead of a pack of wolves that you had to
watch every moment. You might sleep alone, at night, for
a while. But at least you could sleep.

This might be the best day of his life, he realized
suddenly. Between Elaine and this . . .

It was sure as hell the best day since three cops showed
up at his apartment one morning, with handcuffs and an
arrest warrant. He'd forgotten what it was like to look
forward to the future.

Okay, it had dinosaurs in it too. Big fucking lizards.
Who cared?

He clapped his hands, quite cheerfully. "Okay, guys,
listen up! In twenty minutes, we're gone."

He pointed at Elaine. "And we're going to need all
twenty of them to get her ready. Her, not just the litter.
She has to be completely wrapped back up in the sheets.
Head to toe, with just her face clear."

He hesitated, torn between new-found anxiety and
common sense. "Well, that's a little much. We should
leave her hands and arms free too. And then we're going
to have to move her very carefully, all the way along,

making sure she doesn't ever get spilled out of the litter. We'll spell each other, carrying it, so nobody gets worn out."

He looked at the ground cover he was standing on, which was nothing he recognized. "We've got no idea what's down there."

Elaine frowned. "James, I'm not a porcelain doll. Okay, I'm not in great shape, but—"

"I'm not worried about breaking you, sweetheart. I'm worried about infection. That wound hasn't really healed yet, I don't think. I'm not positive and I can't be, without taking off the bandage. Which is the very, very last thing I'm going to do. Right the way it is, it's the best protection you've got."

"Oh." After a moment, she smiled up at him. It was a great big smile. "Thank you for thinking of that, James. I knew I could count on you. Sweetheart."

He wondered if a throat lump could be surgically removed. Probably not, as fast as it seemed to be growing. He'd just have to get used to it.

CHAPTER
34

Margo Glenn-Lewis sat at the large conference table in the center of the underground site's main chamber and silently berated herself for being an idiot. Worse still, a confused idiot.

That she was an idiot was now a given. It was the confusion that annoyed her this afternoon. She was fifty-two years old, for Pete's sake, a highly respected and well established physicist. So you'd think that if she found it damn near impossible to concentrate on the discussion in a critical meeting because she kept finding herself thinking about one of the men around the table, she'd at least know the reason *why*.

Did she really find Nicholas Brisebois that attractive?

Answer: she *still* didn't know.

Well . . . That was nonsense. Twaddle produced by a confused and befuddled brain, such as had no business residing inside the skull of a teenage pom-pom girl, much less a woman who'd been able to make a successful career—no, even a quite distinguished career—in a notoriously male-dominated branch of science.

Of course she found Nick attractive. Very attractive, in fact. If she didn't, she wouldn't be fidgeting like this in the first place.

The problem was that in the course of the week he'd spent in the research facility in Minnesota, she'd gotten to know him well enough to understand that any relationship with Brisebois would not be a casual one. Assuming any relationship got started at all, of course. She still had no idea if he found her attractive. The man was very self-contained, in some ways.

To start with, he was a devout Catholic. Not ostentatious about it, but he was. Margo was a devout atheist. True, not ostentatious about it, either. She'd never do something like sue a school board or a city because their Christmas pageantry included scenes from the Nativity. Who cared? If the dolts wanted to wallow in their tribal superstitions, let them. Any kid who wanted to figure out things for herself could do it easily enough, when she got a little older. It wasn't as if you had to pry loose anything from the government using the Freedom of Information Act to figure out that any creed that thought a Being capable of creating an entire universe gave a rat's ass whether you ate lobster or fish with scales was no more sophisticated than hunters and gatherers somewhere who refused to eat rats because rats were their totem.

That'd be a problem. On the other hand . . .

She also knew Nick well enough by now to know that he was extremely good in the mind-my-own-business department. For that matter, so was she. If they had kids, the religious thing would become an issue—and she couldn't believe she was scatter-brained enough to even be thinking about stuff like this at a critical professional meeting—but that was a moot point. She'd never wanted kids, was too old now to have them anyway, and Nick already had plenty of his own. Five, no less.

Besides, he'd said once, in that slightly sardonic way of his that she found very attractive, that it would take a direct intervention by God with the divine finger pointing right at him to get him to go through child-rearing again.

That brought up problem number two.

"—what we've tentatively concluded," said Leo Dingley. He turned away from the display on the far wall. "The time spike isn't simply stuttering and wobbling as it keeps driving back in time, it's reverberating. That's what we've decided to call the effect, anyway, for lack of a better term. If you want the math, Malcolm can give it to you, but prepare to have your eyes glaze over. Me, I like to think of it in acoustical terms. The spike is emitting time bongs like a bell every time it stutters—and every time it does so, the time effect sends an echo ahead of it."

"Excuse me, Leo," said Esther Hu. She was one of the paleontologists who'd come to the conference. She wasn't connected with the museum in Montana, though, as most of them were. She had a faculty position with SUNY and worked on the side as the expert adviser for the man she was sitting next to at the table. That was Alexander Cohen, a New York financier who'd nurtured a lifelong interest in paleontology through a foundation he'd sent up that dispensed grants.

"Yes, Esther?"

"Is this still *happening*? You keep speaking in the present tense. What I mean is—"

"I understand what you mean. And it's a good question, too." Leo looked at the display on the wall and puffed out his cheeks, then blew the air out and said: "The answer— yes, I know you're probably getting sick of it—is that we simply don't know."

"Leo's fudging," said Malcolm O'Connell. "It's true that we don't *know,* but the math really only allows for one solution that I can see." He pointed to the display. "What we're facing here is the chronoletic version of the uncertainty principle that's been bedeviling particle physicists for over half a century. We can analyze the raw data that comes in across only one axis, so to speak. We can tell you *when* it is—where it stopped, so to speak—or we can tell you where it's reverberating, or we can tell you where it's stuttering, or where it's wobbling. But we can't put all four of them together without removing the first axis."

Cohen had a trim beard much like the one Morgan-Ash favored. And, like Richard, he had a habit of stroking it. He was doing that now. "Yes, I can understand that. But what would it look like from the viewpoint of someone inside the phenomenon?"

He nodded toward Tim. "Let's posit, for the moment, that I'm Officer Harshbarger's friend Joe Schuler. What would I be seeing? Or have seen?"

Leo looked uncertain. Margo leaned forward a bit and said: "Again, we're not positive. But the likelihood—

the great likelihood—is that for anyone caught in the radius of the time spike's effects, everything would happen simultaneously. And, for all practical purposes, instantaneously."

She gave O'Connell and Morgan-Ash a gleaming smile. "I will leave it to these two mathematicians—later, gentlemen, later—to debate the issue of whether the word 'instantaneous' has any real meaning. For a lowly physicist like myself, it means way faster than I can flag down a cab in Manhattan, and if that were an Olympic event, I'd have a real shot at the gold medal."

Nick Brisebois took advantage of the round of laughter to study Margo, rather than having to pretend he wasn't.

And, as had now happened many times over the past week, his resolve to let the matter slide because it obviously wouldn't work flew south for the winter. And, as so often, it was the smile that did it. That quick gleaming smile with the crinkled and intelligent eyes above it that made telling himself he could just walk away seem utterly ridiculous.

As the conference returned to business, he chewed on his thoughts. He had to leave the day after tomorrow, since he'd almost used up the week he'd taken from his vacation time. So he'd better start nailing down whatever conclusions he could.

Conclusion number one. He could live with her political attitudes, even if some of them set his teeth on edge a little. Like almost all military officers, active duty or retired, Nick was politically conservative. In his case, as with many if not all, that was not due to any attachment to any particular political party. He simply had a deep skepticism about the human race's ability to do more than muddle through, and was generally of the opinion that the old maxim "if it ain't broke, don't fix it" applied in politics just as much as it did anywhere else.

On the other hand, he wasn't oblivious to the fact that whether something was broken or not was often in the eye of the beholder—and the beholder's viewpoint was heavily influenced by where they stood. From the standpoint of many people at the time, Jim Crow worked just fine. So it wasn't as if the issues that Margo would occasionally express pungent opinions about weren't real issues. He could even see—quite easily, in fact—her side of the matter.

The problem was the attitude that usually lay beneath, for him. He'd found most people with liberal or radical political views to be glib and cavalier in the solutions they advocated, and it was that more than anything else he found so irritating about them. Measures and policies that seemed clear and simple in a Manhattan cocktail party were not clear and simple at all, if you were the poor bastard in the trenches who had to carry them out.

On the gripping hand—he was a science fiction fan, and particularly liked Niven and Pournelle's *The Mote in God's Eye*—it was difficult to imagine Margo at a Manhattan socialite's cocktail party. She'd been born, bred and raised on that most peculiar of America's islands, and in most ways shared its inhabitants' unique mix of hyper-sophistication and abysmal insularity. But there was nothing flighty about her at all.

As he brooded and pondered, giving only half his attention to the discussion at the table, Margo flashed the smile at some jest made by Karen Berg.

Nick, quit stalling. Just ask the lady out. If you leave without even giving it a shot, you'll be cursing yourself the rest of your life.

Everything finally came into focus.

That left the problem, of course, of where you went out on a date in an iron mine.

"—world they'd be in would be predominantly early Cretaceous, but there'd be elements from every time and place the spike stuttered and wobbled—including, of course, their own—and every place in time periods still earlier where what we've called the reverberations struck."

Cohen paused in his summary, for a moment, and stroked his beard. "You'd have everything in that mix, from modern plants and animals and people to animals and plants from—possibly, at least—as early as the Devonian. Am I right?"

"Yes, Alex, you are." That came from Morgan-Ash.

"How big would the geographical area be? What I mean is, at whatever time the spike finally stopped and . . . dropped everything off, how's that?"

A little laugh went up. "At that specific place in time— let's assume for the moment that the center of the estimate is valid and they wound up in the year one hundred and thirty-five million BP—how big would the area be in which this incredible time jumble applied? I'm assuming, at least, that it couldn't possibly cover the entire planet."

"Oh, God no." Dingley looked startled, for a moment. He'd obviously not considered this aspect of the problem. "I have no idea what sort of energy figures you'd need to carry through a complete time jumble that covered the whole surface of the planet, but . . ."

He looked at the display. "Karen, go back to image ten, would you?"

After she did so, he studied the new display for a moment and shook his head. "Not a chance, Alex. Even with almost all of the energy striking along the time dimension, that sort of energy would have left a crater in southern Illinois the size of . . ."

He peered at one of the paleontologists from the museum, Fred Gibbs. "What's the name of that damn thing in Yucatan?"

Gibbs smiled. "Chicxulub. The best way to learn to pronounce it"—here he gave Margo a theatrically apprehensive look—"but make sure there aren't any radical feminists around—is 'Chicks Who Lube.' If you say that maybe ten times in a row accompanied by any serious use of your visual imagination, I guarantee you'll remember how to pronounce it."

That brought a big round of laughs; Margo's, louder than anyone else's.

Once it died down, Leo shook his head. "I'm afraid— again, alas—that we can't give you a precise answer. But I figure the radius of the . . . okay, guys, what do we call it?"

"Blast zone," said Brisebois. "Call it that, why not? I'm sure from the standpoint of the people caught in the spike, that's what it must look like."

The somewhat grim note quieted everyone for a moment. Then, Leo nodded. "'Blast zone' it is."

He pursed his lips, studying the diagram. "I figure the radius of the blast zone has to be at least fifty kilometers.

At the upper limit . . . figure two hundred kilometers. If I was placing a bet, though, I'd probably plunk it down on a radius of somewhere between seventy and eighty kilometers."

"And—assuming you were in position to explore at all—if you traveled beyond the perimeter of the blast zone," said Cohen, "you'd find yourself in the normal conditions of the early Cretaceous."

"That's right."

The elderly financier leaned back, his hands on the table. "I have to tell you, I am deeply impressed with the work you've done here. It exemplifies, I believe, the reason I've been so devoted to the pursuit of science my whole life." A wry smile came to his face. "Perhaps some of that is compensation, I suppose, for a lingering feeling of failure. You'd think someone who can play the stock market as well as I do would have managed to get better than a 'D' in high school math and a 'C-minus' in physics and chemistry."

Another little laugh went up. It was a bit hushed, though. All of the scientists around the table, if not perhaps the policemen, understood that they were on the verge of that precipice that all scientific projects were forced to skirt. The great yawning chasm called "money."

Cohen understood it also, of course. He smiled serenely. "I think I can spare us all a lot of awkwardness at the cocktail party you've gone to such lengths to organize this evening—no small feat, I imagine, in such an isolated area. I will have my people running the foundation start funneling every dime we can manage to The Project. We do have many existing commitments, of course, which I feel obligated to sustain. But I'm quite prepared to tap deeply into the foundation's capital, if necessary, not just use the interest and dividends."

The scientists at the table seemed frozen. That would be their way of maintaining decorum. Otherwise, they'd be leaping around the room making war whoops and whatever pitiful attempts they could at dancing. The Cohen Foundation had a *lot* of money.

"There are some conditions, though. The first and most important is that I want someone running this show. I mean no offense, but the sort of relaxed and collegial way you've managed The Project's work thus far simply won't do any longer."

The scientists were not entirely pleased with that, of course. But they'd half-expected it, assuming Cohen had proved interested.

"Yes, of course," said Morgan-Ash firmly. "That sort of funding needs careful handling and accounting for."

"I'm not particularly concerned about that," said Cohen. "Yes, obviously, we'll need serious bookkeeping and accountability. But I've done quite a few inquiries since I arrived. One of the things I discovered—not to my surprise—is that every scientist attached to The Project undoubtedly suffered some damage to their career prospects as a result of it. I hardly think people who'd do that voluntarily are people I need to watch like hawks to make sure they don't pilfer the till."

He shook his head. "The problem lies elsewhere. As much as I'm fascinated by the science involved, my personal attitudes are far closer to those"—he nodded at Harshbarger and Boyle—"of the policemen sitting at the table." Grimly: "I also think a crime is being committed here. And quite possibly more than one. As I'll explain in a moment."

He looked at the display. "The point is, I want someone in charge who isn't quite as . . . detached, so to speak. And, even more importantly, has a completely different mindset. I believe The Project is the most important—critical, at least—scientific project since the Manhattan Project. I will let you scientists choose your own equivalent of Oppenheimer. But I want my equivalent of General Groves."

Nick Brisebois shook his head. "Alex, I think you're going way over the top. I'm not sure I even agree with Tim that you can call the government's policies with regard to these time events a 'crime' in the first place. National security run amok, sure. But that's not the same thing."

"Isn't it? I believe I can make a good case that, in a democracy, what you call 'national security run amok' *is* a crime."

Cohen waved his hand. "Leave that aside for the moment. It's public knowledge that I am sharply critical of the current administration. They have no love for me; nor I, for them. But, being fair about it, it's not as if I think the previous administration would have handled the problem all that much better. Some, yes. I believe they would have, at least, avoided the absurdity of labeling the Alexander Disaster a terrorist incident—and, by the way, I can tell you from my sources that they will soon be announcing that they have finally concluded the Grantville Disaster was *also* a terrorist attack."

"*What?*" said Margo.

"Oh, yes. Wait and see if I'm not right. But don't put money on it, betting against me. My sources are very good. Yes, it turns out that Grantville was Osama Bin Laden's test run, so to speak, for 9-11. And if that strikes you as risible beyond belief, you will soon be part of a club numbering in the billions."

Nick was the only one not joining in the sarcastic laughter. "Look, I'm not going to defend blithering stupidity. Believe me, I've seen plenty of it, after spending my whole adult lifetime in the military and the Defense Department. I still think you're overreacting. Dealing with a government abusing its authority—and doing it stupidly, to boot—is not the same thing as being at war. The Manhattan Project was a wartime project. And we're not at war."

"Aren't we?" said Cohen, lifting an eyebrow. "You may well be right. But I think you're overlooking something."

He turned to Karen Berg. "Go back to image seven, would you please? I think that's the one I want."

When Karen did so, and the results were displayed. Cohen shook his head. "Sorry, my memory was amiss. I need the one before that. Image six."

The display that came up was the final—so far, at least—plotting that The Project had done of the time spike's chronoletic trajectory. It showed, in three-dimensional relief, every stutter and wobble and reverberation.

"Thank you. Now please zoom in at the top. I only want the details of the spike's trajectory while it was still traversing historical times. Human history, I mean."

Karen did as he asked. When the image settled, Cohen turned to Tim Harshbarger.

"You grew up in the area, I understand?"

The policeman nodded. "Yup. Born there, lived there all my life."

"Are you familiar with the area's history?"

Harshbarger shrugged. "Pretty well." He hooked a thumb at his partner, sitting next to him. "Bruce here's more familiar with the subject. For a while, back there, he even did some civil war reenactments."

"For three years, that's it." Boyle shook his head. "I enjoyed the reenactments, but I got tired of the traveling involved. The closest big battle was Shiloh, and even that's a little bit of a haul."

"There were no major civil war battles in southern Illinois?" Cohen posed it as a question, but it was obviously a rhetorical one.

Boyle chuckled. "Oh, hell no. I was born and raised in the area too, just like Tim. The truth is, southern Illinois falls into the category of a nice place to live—if you can get a job, anyway—but a lousy place to visit. I mean, honestly, there's not much there and never really has been. The reason we make such a big deal about the Trail of Tears and the Mounds people is because those are about the only big events, you could say, that ever happened in the area's history."

"There was one other, actually, although I'm not surprised you overlook it. The man's exploits—using the term loosely—are more often associated with Florida, Arkansas and Texas. But Hernando de Soto passed through the area at one point, in the course of his famous expedition. The exact date is unknown, but it would have been sometime in the year 1541."

He turned his head, examining the display. "Only three dates, then, of any real significance in the history of southern Illinois. Using the term 'date' a bit loosely. Going backward, the late 1830s, when the Cherokees were forced onto the Trail of Tears and passed through the area on their way to Oklahoma. The year 1541, when de Soto came though. And a period that can't be defined anywhere nearly so closely, when the Mounds culture was at its peak. But we can use the dates 800 to 1200 as a benchmark."

He paused a moment. "*Now*, consider that image. The spike stutters very abruptly at some point between the fall of 1838 and the spring of 1839. Stutters again, very sharply, somewhere between the spring of 1540 and the summer of 1542. There's a wobble at that point also, as if it shifted a bit geographically. As you've noted, the farther back the spike goes, the larger becomes the uncertainty. Then there's a big stutter somewhere in the decade between 1185 and 1195. Followed by a series of short stutters—accompanied by a lot of wobbling—all the way back from there to around the year 600. And then there's nothing, until it reaches the early Pleistocene."

He looked around the table. The two policemen and Brisebois were frowning. All of the scientists looked like statues. And Richard Morgan-Ash's face was starting to get pale.

"So, ladies and gentlemen. Please tell me again that we're looking at random accidents produced by a mindless natural catastrophe. If you want my opinion, this looks about as random and accidental as a housewife going through a supermarket putting together the makings for a fancy salad. 'Let's see. I'll take some Cherokees on the Trail of Tears. That'll be nice for pathos. Hernando de Soto, of course, to add some spice. The Mounds builders, for bulk. And . . . yes, let's grab a bunch of primitive villages while we're at it, for croutons. Now, what for a nice lively salad dressing? Oh, I know. Let's pour a maximum security prison full of criminals over everything.'"

"Jesus H. Christ," whispered Leo Dingley.

Cohen leaned over, looking at Morgan-Ash. "You're the statistician here, Richard. As I explained, I almost flunked high school math. So maybe I'm crazy. But you tell me, as a statistician, what the likelihood is that something like this would happen by accident."

Morgan-Ash's eyes were riveted to the screen. Abruptly, he shook his head. "I'm not an historian. We'd need to bring in an historian—several, probably—"

"Yes, I agree," said Cohen. "In fact, that was going to be my next condition. I want historians and anthropologists added to the project. But I think you're quibbling, Richard. You might need the expert advice of historians to fine tune your analysis, but I believe you can give me the gist of it right here and now."

"It's impossible," he said. Then, again, shook his head abruptly. "Well, no, not exactly. But the probability that something like this could happen by accident . . ." His eyes became unfocused, as he did the calculations in his head.

Then, almost irritably, he waved his hand and reopened his eyes. "Oh, blast it. I'm just twiddling. For all practical purposes, it's impossible. If I were to calculate the odds against this happening numerically—as you might do by saying, 'a hundred to one,' the number I'd have to substitute for 'a hundred' would be bigger than the estimated number of galaxies in the universe. Possibly even the number of stars in the universe, and conceivably even the number of subatomic particles."

He looked around the room. "He's right, people. He's absolutely right."

Still leaning over the table, with one hand stretched out a bit, Cohen now looked at Brisebois.

"Nick, it is quite true that I detest the current administration. But as stupid as I think they are, I don't think they're *that* stupid. I don't think, as most people here seem to, that the explanation for all of their absurd and grotesque attempts to keep the Grantville and Alexander disasters under wraps are simply due to their usual secretive reflexes. I think they *are* genuinely worried. Scared out of their wits, actually. Because I think they found something in Grantville—and probably, now, at Alexander—that has led them to the conclusions I've come to."

He leaned back, grimacing. "And, of course—here is where the nature of the administration does come into play—naturally it never occurred to them to bring the matter forthrightly before the public and enlist the resources of the nation to ferret out the truth. Instead, as is their habit, they slapped everything under national security and are conducting whatever investigations they're conducting in complete secrecy. And making it as difficult as possible for anyone else to uncover the truth.

"So, Nick. To go back to where we started, I think we may very well be at war. With what enemy, I have no idea. What their purpose might be, I have no idea. But it's a big universe out there. Who's to say it doesn't have its equivalent of Al Qaeda? Or, perhaps"—he grinned here—"knowing my tendencies toward paranoia, which are pretty much inevitable when you swim with the Carcharodons in the stock market, we're simply looking at collateral damage, so to speak. Perhaps these bolides or spikes aren't aimed at us at all. They're some sort of bizarre weaponry being used against each other by alien species at war, and we're just unfortunate enough to be getting caught in the crossfire."

He shrugged. "And I can think of other possibilities. There are any number of them. Perhaps an incredibly advanced species has its equivalent of nasty children who like to torment ants. Perhaps we're the subject of some sort of bizarre experiment. Or an even more bizarre religious rite. Who knows? What I do know is that, first, I want to find out. Second, I have absolutely no confidence that the government will be of any help whatsoever. Certainly not under this administration. We'll have to see what the next one is like. Indeed, I expect that if they find out what we'll be doing they will try to impede us. And, third, to go back to where I started, I want this thing run by someone like Leslie Groves. No offense intended to all you splendid scientists, but I want a military man in charge."

Karen frowned. "But who? We don't know any military people." She glanced at Morgan-Ash. "Well. I guess Richard . . ."

Richard shook his head. "I was a lieutenant commanding a small unit of paratroopers. What Alex wants is someone with at least field grade experience. Preferably someone who has coordinated major and complex operations."

"Precisely," said Cohen. "And my dear Karen, it's absurd to say you don't know any such person. You have one sitting right here at the table."

He pointed a finger at Nick. "Him."

Nick stared at him. Everyone else at the table stared at Nick.

Cohen smiled serenely again. "I told you all, I have very good sources. And I have them in many places."

"I'm a trash-hauler," Nick said.

"Please. You were one of a handful of men in the Pentagon who coordinated the entire logistical effort for the first Gulf war." He cocked an eye at Brisebois. "Yes?"

"Well . . . yeah. But . . . for Pete's sake. Groves was a *general.* I retired as a major. Didn't even make the cut to lieutenant colonel."

"True. Perhaps the fact that you explained, much too bluntly, some logistical realities to a three-star general notorious for his vindictiveness had something to do with it, though."

Nick scowled. "How the hell—"

"I told you. I have very good sources. And a staff that is even better at compiling information for me. But leaving that aside, Nick, I was only using the Manhattan Project as a model. An example, if you will. Even with the influx of money I'll be providing The Project, the scale of its operations won't come even close to the scale of the Manhattan Project."

He leaned all the way back in his seat, his hands folded over his stomach. He looked very complacent. "I think a major with extensive managerial experience who was willing to tell off a three-star general—*and* who is already familiar with The Project—will do quite nicely."

Nick didn't know what to say. Cohen said: "Do this much for the moment, would you? Call your office and tell them you need to take another week of your vacation time. That way—I'm planning to extend my own stay here for at least another week—we'll have time to discuss the matter at length and in detail."

"Well . . ."

"Please don't tell me you've used up your vacation time. Or, if you insist, let's make it a bet. I'm willing to bet you're the sort of fellow who has more vacation time piled up than you know what to do with."

That wasn't . . . entirely true. When Laura and he had still been together, and with the kids, Nick had used all of it every year. But since the kids grew up, and the divorce . . .

"Well, yeah."

Margo gave him that gleaming smile. "You can borrow my cell phone, if you need to."

The smile did it. "Okay, fine. I'll make the call."

CHAPTER

35

Andy Blacklock sat next to the Cherokee chief, Geoffrey Watkins, comparing him to the Indians in the western movies he'd seen. The results were . . .

Disorienting, from head to toe. Literally, from head to toe.

Watkins' hair, to start with, wasn't long and black and tied up in braids. It was reddish-brown and cut almost as short as Andy's own. He wore pants, not leggings; boots, not moccasins; and his torso was neither bare nor covered in war paint. He was wearing a shirt and a vest. There wasn't a feather anywhere in sight, much less a feather bonnet—and his English was fluent, colloquial and idiomatic.

That was the first half of the discrepancy between reality and the Hollywood version. The second half was more subtle, but was in some ways even more disorienting.

Watkins' hair was cut short, but the style was different. Parted at the top instead of the sides, like the hair in some old nineteenth-century sepia photos Andy had seen. The shirt and pants and vest had the same vaguely antique flavor about them, and the boots even more so. It wasn't that they were crudely made. In some ways, they were obviously better-made garments than mass-produced modern ones. Andy was genuinely envious of the boots. But they weren't quite as uniform as modern garments were, in some way Andy couldn't quite discern.

Finally, and most of all, there was the English. Fluent, yes. Andy and Watkins had had no difficulty understanding each other. Colloquial, yes; idiomatic, yes—but the colloquialisms and idiom weren't the same. Except when they were, and that was probably the most disorienting thing of all. Just when Andy thought he had a handle on Watkins' idiom—he'd figured out quickly that "bean't" meant "isn't" or "weren't"—Watkins would toss in a reference to the President of the United States, Martin Van Buren, as a "fucking asshole."

It turned out, apparently, that whatever else changed in a language, its fundamental profanity was deeply conservative. Andy was rather amused, thinking of all the little perorations he'd heard in his life bemoaning the growing coarseness of public speech in twenty-first century America, to discover that people from the early-mid nineteenth century swore like troopers. At least, if acculturated Cherokees and mostly-immigrant U.S. soldiers were a valid sampling of the populace. He suspected they probably were.

There was one difference, though. The Cherokees and the soldiers would use the notorious four-letter Anglo-Saxon words without hesitation. More so, even, than most modern

Americans. But he'd yet to hear any of them use any of the religious varieties of cursing. The distinction between profanity and blasphemy, which had been all but erased in the America he'd come from, was still alive and well in this one.

So, while Martin Van Buren was a fucking asshole, he was a "Gol dang" fucking asshole, and was surely condemned to tarnation in the afterlife.

Andy had already quietly passed along the word to his people to try to hold down on their own unthinking use of expressions like "goddam" and "Jesus Christ." He'd noticed, on several occasions, a Cherokee or one of the soldiers frowning a little when they heard that.

He found their religious attitudes a bit peculiar, overall. That these people, Cherokees and soldiers alike, had a deeply religious attitude on at least some level, was obvious. Even those Cherokees—a large minority, so far as he could tell—who had not adopted Christianity, at least formally, were quite respectful of it. If for no other reason than that, he'd discovered, it had often been white Christian missionaries working among the Cherokee who'd been among the few Americans to raise vehement public protests against the policies of the U.S. government toward the southern tribes.

But there was very little formality involved. In the world Andy had come from, anyone who called themselves a Christian almost invariably belonged to a specific denomination—and could not only tell you exactly what it was, but could more often than not explain why their brand of Baptism or Methodism or whatever was distinct in XYZ ways from other denominations. With these people, so far as he could tell, being a Christian and joining a church were almost completely different things. Watkins, for instance, clearly considered himself a Christian. But he'd mentioned to Andy, on one occasion, that his recently deceased wife had pestered him for years to join the church and he'd steadfastly refused; although, privately, he'd decided he'd do it just before he died, to placate the woman. Of course, he'd expected she'd probably outlive him, which she hadn't.

Looking away, he could see Jenny. She was holding one of the Cherokee babies and talking to its mother. Several other women sat nearby, their own children playing in the dirt a few yards away. It all looked very serene, and on one level it was. There'd been no trouble of any kind from the moment Andy's people found the Cherokee town and established contact with them. But he knew the Cherokees—from Watkins down to small children—were watching every move made by every member of his party.

So were the small group of soldiers. If anything, even more intently. Andy wasn't sure, yet, what their attitude was. At least so far, the leader of the soldiers—that was Sergeant James Kershner—had been taciturn whenever Andy or Rod had tried to engage him in conversation. It didn't help any that with Kershner, they had to plow through a thick German accent along with the different idiom. If it was even a German accent at all, as such. From a remark Kershner had made on one occasion, he apparently considered himself a Swabian, whatever that was, more than a German.

The tentative conclusion Andy and Rod had come to, though, was that Kershner and his men had been in the middle of working out their own accommodation with the Cherokees when Blacklock and his people showed up— and were now very uncertain how to handle this new complication.

Of course, the same could be said for all three parties involved. Andy himself, as much as anyone.

The greatest disorientation was also the biggest. Without really thinking about it, Andy had assumed that he'd be more or less riding to the rescue of a bedraggled group of downtrodden Indians, all but on their last legs due to the double hammer blow of the Trail of Tears and the Quiver.

So much for stereotypes. Perhaps even, he'd guiltily wondered, some residual racial prejudices on his part. Well, not "prejudices." That was too strong a term. Andy wasn't a bigot, had never been, and despised bigotry. Still, any society imparts its subtle attitudes to its members, and those are shaped by its history. The Indians of Andy's world had been the product of centuries of victimization, which had been almost as complete as that suffered by any people in history.

These Cherokees, on the other hand, were almost— not quite, but almost—a people still in their prime. They were quite self-confident, certainly. And all Andy had to do was look around the small little town—that was what they called it, anyway, although Andy would have probably used the word "village"—to see that they had plenty of reasons to be. The simple and plain truth—Rod Hulbert had commented to this effect at least a dozen times, and always with envy—was that the Cherokees were far better equipped to deal with the realities of this new world than

Blacklock and his people were. In fact, if it hadn't been for the military threat posed by de Soto's conquistadores, it would be the Cherokees who were in position to give aid to the modern Americans, not the other way around.

They weren't lying awake at night trying to figure out how to feed themselves. Or how they'd clothe themselves when their store-bought garments wore out. Or what to do when and if winter came.

It wasn't easy for them, no. Not in the least. One of their men had already been hurt badly in the course of hunting some smaller herbivorous dinosaurs. They'd been deer hunters in their own world, not mammoth hunters, and were having to learn from experience and make adjustments. But they obviously had no doubts that they'd manage.

They didn't plan to hunt the really big dinosaurs, of course. And they were clearly worried about how they'd handle an attack by one of the big predators. But that's what the one really huge theropod they'd seen at a distance had been for them—just a very big, very dangerous, predator. They certainly weren't jabbering to each other about the Great God Lizard and wondering what sort of offerings or magic rituals or sacrifices might placate the being. Just how to kill it in the event they had to.

They were actually more concerned about the agricultural situation than they were about the dinosaurs. Predators were predators, and meat was meat. Simple enough. But so far as the Cherokees had been able to discover, none of the food plants they were accustomed to growing had come through the Quiver. The one and only exception was a small patch of corn they'd found—which their men were guarding like hawks and upon which their women were lavishing tender loving care. They'd located the town, in fact, right next to the patch, even though the location was far from optimal in many other respects. Nourishing that small patch of corn and turning it into a staple overrode everything else.

But there was nothing else they'd always depended on. No squash, no beans. No acorns.

Jeff Edelman said that was because almost every edible plant that human beings had domesticated in their history had been what he called angiosperms—and the angiosperms apparently hadn't evolved yet. That enormous group of flowering plants that had come to dominate the Earth by the time humans beings showed up were simply absent here, so far as he could tell, except an occasional little patch like the corn. And that was obviously a transplant produced by the Quiver.

There weren't even any grasses yet. Some variety of fern usually provided the ground cover.

Jeff had fretted over the problem. According to him, the angiosperms *should* be here. They'd emerged in the late Mesozoic and by the end of the Cretaceous had come to dominate the world's vegetation. They should *certainly* exist in a world that had tyrannosaurs in it.

The solution Edelman had finally come up with was, from Andy's point of view, simply to change his terminology. It turned out, he explained, that they were actually in an earlier stage of the Cretaceous than he'd thought originally. And what he'd thought were tyrannosaurs were actually allosaurs, their somewhat smaller ancestors. They didn't look much different, after all.

"Well . . ." He'd scratched his chin. "Probably they're something in between allosaurs and tyrannosaurs. Allosaurs are a little too ancient, really. Their heyday was the late Jurassic, and I don't think we've gone back *that* far." Apologetically, he added: "The fossil record really is pretty spotty. The truth is we have no real idea what creatures might have lived in great big chunks of geologic time."

Andy had smiled. "Has it occurred to you, Jeff—I'm not arguing the point, mind you—that your new theory isn't too different from insisting that a personnel department is really a human relations department?"

"Smart ass." Jeff's eyes ranged over the landscape of the Really New World around them. "The problem is that there's something fundamentally screwy about this universe. We've got too many things from too many different periods all mixed together. What I'm *hoping* is that we'll eventually discover the effect is geographically restricted."

"Meaning?"

"Meaning that the Quiver scrambled time for a relatively small area of southern Illinois—insofar as you can use the expression 'southern Illinois' to refer to that area of the globe all through geological history." The gaze he now bestowed on the horizon was a longing one. "You know, if I could take a few guys with me and explore maybe fifty or a hundred miles away from here, I'm willing to bet everything would settle down. I could tell you then, for sure, if we're in the late Cretaceous or the early Cretaceous or some part of the Jurassic or what."

"Forget it. Look, Jeff, in the end it's really an academic question. Call them tyrannosaurs or allosaurs, who cares?

We've still got to figure out how to deal with them, if they come after us. And we can worry about what to call these plants around us after we figure out which ones we can eat."

Jeff scowled. "Yeah, fine. But have you contemplated the alternative, if the effect *isn't* geographically limited? That would mean that we're in a universe that apparently has no logic at all, at least for a geologist and a biologist. Hell, for all we know, the Aztec winged snake god Quetzalcoatl might come flapping over the horizon tomorrow. Or dragons instead of whatever-you-call-ems."

"I'd settle for a field of wheat, whether it's got winged snakes or not. The Cherokees would be ecstatic if some squash turned up—and they'd take the dragons in stride."

They were now in a world of conifers, ferns, horsetails, cycads and gingkos. The Cherokee women were fuming. Generations of practical learning and lore and skills—gone with the wind.

Not really, though. The specific skills might be gone, but the generic skills that underlay them were still there. Yes, the women groused incessantly, and the curses they rained down on the new plants they experimented with would have made sailors' blanch. But they'd already figured out how to grind up something that looked like big pine nuts into a sort of gruel that they could use to make a cornmeal substitute or fried flat bread. They called it "nutmeal." The stuff needed to be leeched, since the raw taste was very bitter, and the end result didn't have much taste at all. But it had become their staple food—and, lately, they'd found some herbs that brightened it up a lot. Andy didn't have much doubt that, given a little time and peace, they'd eventually produce a full diet that, along with the meat and fish the Cherokee hunters brought in, was nutritious and plentiful enough that people could live on it indefinitely.

Including Andy's people, whose skills in these critical areas were far more primitive than the Cherokees'.

But that still left the problem of "time and peace." Both of which, unfortunately, were in shorter supply than food.

He figured it was time. Watkins liked to ponder a problem, and Andy respected that. But he'd pondered it enough.

"Have you decided, Chief?"

Watkins smiled. "And when did you start being formal, Captain? If I remember right, it was 'Geoffrey' less than an hour ago."

But he knew the reason for the sudden formality perfectly well. He looked away and, after a moment, finally started talking.

"The proposal is attractive in many ways, certainly. Each party provides the other with what it lacks most. We provide you with food, eventually clothing, those sorts of things. And you"—he glanced at the pistol holstered to Andy's hip—"provide us with the firepower we will need to deal with monsters. Human and otherwise."

He looked away again. "All the more attractive because the disparity is so great on either side. Our muskets and bows and spears are fine for hunting, but if this Spanish man de Soto's army is as large as you say, they bean't enough. The Spanish will have muskets too. Maybe not as good as ours, but good enough. I used a matchlock as a boy. Clumsy fucking thing, but it worked. Their crossbows and swords will easily match our bows and spear and war clubs. Worst of all—"

He glanced at the town. "—I don't have that many warriors. Not more than thirty-five, really, and even that is . . . what's your expression?"

"Stretching it. Or pushing it."

"Yes." He smiled again. "On the other side, the disparity is every bit as great. Meaning no disrespect, but except for your Lieutenant Hulbert I don't think any of you out here in the wilds can . . . what's that really delightful expression? The one Hulbert uses so often?"

"Find our ass with both hands."

"Yes." His smile widened. "Astonishing, really. What sort of superstitious savage doesn't understand that a big bug is food?"

Andy laughed. The reaction of the modern Americans—any creed or color; it didn't matter in the least—when the Cherokees had passed around a big platter of roasted grasshoppers at the first welcoming feast, had been a sight to behold.

His, too. He still thought it was yucky.

But he'd eaten the stuff. That night and ever since. The grasshoppers—that Jeff insisted really weren't grasshoppers but an earlier species of Orthoptera, as if that made it any better—had become a staple of the Cherokee diet only slightly less important than the meat and fish the hunters brought in and the nutmeal. Every Cherokee child had been assigned the task of hunting and catching the big insects. Which they did gleefully. For them, it was a great game.

The nineteenth-century U.S. soldiers in Kershner's

squad refused to eat the bugs at all. But by anybody's culinary standards, those men were Neanderthals. So far as Andy could tell, they were firmly convinced that the only food fit for human consumption was salt pork and potatoes sauced in hog lard, and were deeply aggrieved that the Really New World didn't seem to have a single pig or potato in it.

"So what's bothering you, Geoffrey?" Andy asked quietly. "I understand why you'd have hard feelings toward the United States, believe me. I was born almost a hundred and forty years after the Trail of Tears, but it's something that's still remembered. And with a great deal of guilt, now. But—at least for us, if not you—that was a long time ago. The attitudes of Americans in my day has changed enormously since then."

Watkins made a little motion with his hand, as if waving something down. "That's not really the problem, Andy. Yes, it's very fresh for us still." He took a long, slow, almost shuddering breath. "My wife was killed by that Trail of Tears, and she died not more than a few weeks ago. And she wasn't the only one in my band of people who died on the Trail. Many did."

He nodded toward the town. ".Walk through there and talk to any Cherokee, and you will find a similar story. And for them, as for me, it happened just a few weeks or months ago. Not a century and half."

He made the same little hand motion, but much more peremptorily. "But we're not little children, who can't react to anything except emotionally. Even during the Trail of Tears, we were constantly dickering and bargaining with the Americans over the details—and sometimes we got what we wanted. Even from that fucking asshole Van Buren. Or at least some of it. Many more of us would have died otherwise."

He fell silent. Brooding, maybe, it was hard to know. Watkins was certainly not what you'd call "inscrutable," but he did come from a somewhat different culture. Andy had had to remind himself of that more than once. You simply couldn't assume that you were interpreting facial expressions and so-called body language quite the right way.

So, he waited again. After about a minute, Watkins stirred.

"I'm not worried about the past, Andy. And it bean't necessary for you to keep reassuring me that the America you came from had changed its attitudes. That's obvious to anyone but an idiot. All I have to do is turn my head right now and contemplate the fact that about half of the people you have with you carrying those marvelous guns have black skins. In my day, black people were slaves—for us as well as the whites."

He chuckled, rather harshly. "All things considered, it's probably a good thing that the Cherokees you encountered here were my band. Not that mine was the only one that favored traditionalism, by any means. If you'd run into John Ross or any of the bands of rich Cherokees, I can imagine things would have gotten tense."

Andy scratched his chin. "Yeah, they probably would. I can just imagine Brian Carmichael's reaction—worse still, Leroy Ingram's—when they saw a dozen black people being used as slaves."

"Speaking of Carmichael," Watkins said, "will you tell him to please restrain himself a bit? He's starting to annoy the older people. Well, the most traditional ones, anyway."

Andy made a face. "Yeah, I'll speak to him again. Won't be easy, though. Brian's a very nice guy, but he's firmly convinced now that the Quiver was God's way of telling him he'd been slacking off."

Carmichael really was a nice guy. Easygoing, friendly, genial, good-humored, everything you could ask for. He'd been popular among the guards since the day he started working at the prison. Even a lot of the cons had liked him, at least the black ones.

The problem was that he also belonged to a fundamentalist church that took missionary duties seriously—and he'd had a bad conscience for years that he hadn't really done his fair share of that work. So, now, he was making up for it with a vengeance.

Thankfully, he wasn't patronizing in his attitudes. It might be that Brian saw himself as bringing the word of God to heathen Cherokees—the fact that most of them were already Christians didn't matter, since they weren't the right kind of Christians—but he wasn't at all snotty about it. In fact, he considered them what you might call a high-class clientele. His church had done most of its missionary work in the slums of East St. Louis. Brian was preachifying to stalwart and upright folk, compared to gangbangers. At the very least, he didn't have to worry about getting mugged.

Still, it could get annoying, simply because the man didn't know when to quit. Having even the nicest and friendliest person in the world jabbering at you endlessly about the need to save your soul gets tiresome after a while. If anything, the Cherokees had been more patient with Brian than people from Brian's own time would have been. They were used to missionaries jabbering endlessly.

The real problem, Andy suspected, was one aspect of the overall problem—that he was pretty sure Watkins was still circling. Part of the reason the Cherokees were patient with jabbering missionaries was that they'd put them to *work*. They could jabber all they wanted—as long as they also set up a school and taught the children how to read and write.

But how do you make a schoolteacher out of an armed man who belonged to what amounted to a military force, instead of a church? An *alien* military force, to boot. Maybe not hostile, but still alien.

Andy was pretty sure, by now, that that was the core of the issue, for Watkins. Not Brian Carmichael, by himself, but the problem he embodied.

He decided to just bring it all out in the open, since Watkins still seemed reticent. They really didn't have much time. He'd been willing to spend days negotiating, but he wasn't willing to spend weeks. More to the point, he couldn't, whether he wanted to or not. Leaving aside the threat posed by de Soto, he couldn't leave less than seventy guards back at the prison to watch over thousands of convicts for much longer.

"You want me to give you people. Or swap them."

Watkins eyed him sideways. "People—and some of your guns."

They'd been sitting together on a log. Now, Watkins swiveled to face Andy more squarely.

"Yes, that is the problem. Not the past, but the future. It doesn't matter what a people's attitudes are. Well, it matters, but it's not enough. Power also matters. In the end—we chiefs all knew this, had known it for two or three generations—the real problem we had with the Americans of our time wasn't their attitudes toward us." He barked a laugh. "Ha! Trust me. I can name ten Indian tribes whose attitudes toward us were just as bad if not worse. The real problem was that the Americans were powerful enough to simply push us aside. It wasn't even a fight. A squirrel can't fight a buffalo. When the Red Stick Creeks tried to fight, Sharp Knife crushed them."

Sharp Knife was their term for Andrew Jackson, Andy had learned. When they weren't referring to him as a fucking asshole.

Slowly, Andy drew the pistol out of his holster and looked at it. He had it in the palm of his hand, not held by the grip.

"Geoffrey, our power over you today—if we exercised it, which I have no intention of doing—would come entirely and simply from this. And the rifles, of course. And the fact is, this is a very finite resource. That's a lot of the reason I want to make this alliance and go after de Soto. Now. While we still have enough ammunition. By this time next year . . ."

He shrugged, and slid the pistol back into the holster. "This gun and all the others will just be so much scrap metal. Fancy-looking, but still scrap. We have no way of making new ones. We don't even think we can make new ammunition that they could use. Maybe a little, but certainly not enough to rule anyone unilaterally. That's one of the reasons I lie awake at night worrying about the prisoners. I hate spending any ammunition on de Soto, with two and half thousand convicts to keep under control. But I figure I don't have any choice. De Soto's on the loose, and at least the convicts are locked up behind bars."

Watkins shook his head. "You are being too shortsighted, Andy. It may be true—I'm not questioning your statement—that you can't make new guns like that. But your people will still start outpacing my own, when it comes to such things, as time goes by."

He waved his hand at the town. In some indefinable manner, the gesture included everything, not just the buildings. The meat being smoked, the nutmeal being made, the little patch of corn, even the children Andy could see in the distance, eagerly picking their way through some short horsetails looking for grasshoppers.

"We are very good at this," Watkins said softly. "Much better than you are. But you have things we don't, and they go much farther than guns."

Andy made a face. "I suppose. But—"

"What is this thing you call a 'machine shop'?" Watkins asked abruptly.

Andy began to explain. And, as he did, finally began to understand what the Cherokee chief was getting at.

"You see?" Watkins said when he finished. "Even in one of your *prisons*—a place you put the worst people you have—you have the means to work with metal and make complicated machines. And I can tell you more, because I have spoken to many of you and listened very carefully when you told me things that you yourselves did not even think about. For here is what else you have."

He started counting off on his fingers. "Even in one of your *prisons*, you have a library. Even in one of your *prisons*, you have what Jenny Radford calls an infirmary. Even in one of your *prisons*, you have vehicles that make the fanciest carriages in the Washington D.C. of my time look like a child's toy."

He grinned, then. "Speaking of which—I know you have at least one, so don't pretend you don't—I will insist as part of any bargain that we get all the ones called a 'Cherokee.' Call it a penalty for being presumptuous."

Andy laughed. "Okay, fine. I think we've got three of them, if I remember right. That belong to the prison, anyway. Some of the guards might have one as a personal vehicle out in the lot. You'd have to dicker with them about that. But I'm warning you, Geoffrey. They won't run for very long. We're very low on gasoline."

"Then you will make gasoline." He held up his hand in a peremptory gesture. "Don't tell me you won't. If not gasoline, something else. Rod Hulbert told me the vehicles can also run—some of them, at least—on what he calls 'biofuel.' As I understand it, that's a sort of whiskey."

He lowered the hand. "Now, do you see the problem? What you propose is to provide us with protection, and we will provide you with food. From which you will make— or we will make for you—this whiskey you will use to ride across the land as warrior kings. While we remain working your fields and bringing you meat. That we gather with hoes and bows and arrows.

"No, Captain Blacklock. That is not a bargain I can accept. I can accept it this year and next year. I cannot accept it for ten years. A century from now—less, even—

we would be walking another Trail of Tears. A people's attitudes are important. But I am not an idiot like those warriors of Tecumseh's, who thought his magic would protect them from bullets. I would much rather have unpleasant attitudes, if need be, and an equality of power, than have splendid attitudes—today—if they come with a complete disparity of power. When a wolf offers to lie down with a sheep, the sheep can only agree if the wolf offers to share his teeth. Or, sooner or later, he's just mutton."

He looked away, sighing. "You were not there, Andy. I was. To you, it is ancient history; to me, it happened weeks and months ago. I have listened to you and your people, as you apologize to us for the Trail of Tears. And swear it cannot happen again, because you are not the wicked people your ancestors were. And it is all a lie, not because you lie, but because you do not understand your own ancestors. You do not understand, not really, that your ancestors were not wicked at all."

He shrugged. "Not most of them, anyway. The Georgians were horrible, true, and some others. No different from the worst convicts in your prison or de Soto. But the rest . . ."

He nodded his head toward the town. "No different from James Kershner, whom one of my nieces is already plotting and scheming to get for a husband. No different from his soldier John Pitzel, who is the object of the plots and schemes of Susan Fisher's niece. If Van Buren is a fucking asshole, Winfield Scott is not. The very general the Americans placed in charge of the Trail of Tears tried to stop it. And Winfield Scott is not alone. Others are still better. Attitudes? You could not ask for a better attitude than Sam Houston's. Who has lived among us, was married to one of our women for a time, speaks our language fluently, and has always been a friend of our nation.

"And what did it matter, in the end? We still walked the Trail of Tears.

"Even Andrew Jackson, whom some of you seem to think is the arch-devil in the business, bean't a monster. I know him myself, Andy. I fought with him at the Horseshoe Bend, and I visited him years later—twice—with some other Cherokee chiefs at his home at the Hermitage. Many Indians visited Sharp Knife at his home, over the years. The man's wife was distant and aloof, but he was friendly and cordial. The truth is, I enjoyed the visits. He did not force the southern tribes off their land because he was filled with hatred for Indians. He adopted a Creek orphan for one of his sons—a boy he'd made an orphan himself, in his war against the Red Sticks. He's simply doing what he thinks best for his own people."

He lifted his leg and straddled the log, now looking at Andy squarely. Then he grinned. "Jackson's still a fucking asshole, you understand. But that's my point. You can expect people to be fucking assholes, from time to time, if they think their interests are deeply involved in something. So the trick is to make sure that, when they act like assholes, they really can't do very much harm. But that brings us back to the problem of power, which is where I started."

Andy scratched his head. He understood what Watkins was saying, and the simple fact that he kept referring to the history involved in the present tense drove it home more sharply than anything.

"I can give you some of our guns right now, easily enough," he said, although he really didn't like the idea. Not because he was worried about what the Cherokees would do with them, but simply because that would mean fewer guns to deal with the convicts in the prison.

Watkins shook his head. "I'd want a few of the rifles, and some ammunition, but that's just to deal with the immediate threat of the big lizards. In the long run, the rifles are almost nothing more than a symbol. It's the rifles and everything else."

Andy kept scratching his head.

Watkins raised his hand again. "Never mind, Andy. I bean't raising this to get an answer right now. Truth is, I don't think there are any simple answers. I'll agree to the alliance. But I just want to point out that we're going to need to keep dickering. For years."

"Oh." Andy finally stopped scratching his head. "That's no problem."

Watkins grinned.

Belatedly, it occurred to Andy that Cherokees had a reputation for being good at dickering, if he remembered his history correctly. And prison guards didn't.

CHAPTER
∽∾36∽∾

Lieutenant Rod Hulbert, using a pair of field glasses taken from the storeroom the day of the Quiver, watched the people inside the small circle of huts sitting two dozen yards from the edge of a small creek. He had counted thirty-three adults and twelve children. During his briefing prior to leaving the prison, he had been told there was a possibility of running across any group of people who had ever lived in southern Illinois. The most famous and the most plentiful of these ancient groups were the Mound Builders. But Rod was certain these men, women and children were not members of that ancient tribe. They might be their predecessors, or maybe a nomadic people who happened to be in the wrong place and wrong time when the Quiver hit. But their technology was wrong for that group, judging from everything the prison guards had been able to put together about the Mounds people. Which was quite a lot, actually. Living in the area, several of the guards had wound up, one way or another, knowing a fair amount about the subject.

No, these were definitely a pre-Mounds culture. Their clothes were made from animal skins. The Mound Builders of southern Illinois had been expert weavers who decorated their brightly dyed clothing with beads made of quills, bones and shells. They were also an artistic people who decorated their pottery and tools. The equipment he was seeing scattered here and there inside the village appeared to be well made, but didn't seem to be anything more than functional. The decorations that did exist on their pottery and baskets—the ones he'd seen, anyway—were simple and rudimentary.

Gary Hartshorn, another one of the guards, was next to him. Robert White and Kevin Griffin—the two Cherokees whom Chief Watkins had assigned to come on the expedition—were perhaps ten yards away.

All four of the men in the expedition knew the people they had been watching—they were too few to call a "tribe"—were no threat to anyone. Except, perhaps, people on the same cultural level. They were simply too poorly armed. Spears and knives and bows that looked pretty flimsy.

They hadn't been in the area long, either. That was obvious by the look of their camp. There were no paths leading to and from their huts. No gardens, and no garbage. It looked as though the huts were freshly constructed, too. And there seemed to be a certain clumsiness about the way they were built. Rod was pretty sure that was because the villagers had been forced to use materials they weren't familiar with. In the world they'd come from, they'd probably built those huts using a lot of grass. No grasses in this world.

Hulbert scanned the horizon with his field glasses, and then returned to watching the villagers. He wasn't supposed to make contact. The captain wanted to play things safe. He didn't want Hulbert to risk spooking a bunch of people into a fight. And with the Quiver just one day short of three weeks behind them, and de Soto's bunch on the prowl, he was afraid the language barrier would tip the scales towards bloodshed.

So, they were on a mapping and fact-finding mission only.

He put away his glasses and worked his way toward the others. They'd done all they could, within the parameters given for the expedition. If they headed back to camp sometime within the next few hours, they would reach the Cherokee town a few hours ahead of schedule. Andy had given them forty-eight hours to explore the region. It wasn't much, but it was all he felt they could afford.

Rod had agreed with the captain. He wanted to get back to the prison as fast as he could. Things hadn't felt right when they left, and as each day passed he found himself worrying more and more about Marie.

"Time to go," he said quietly to Gary. Hartshorn nodded, pulled back slowly and got to his feet. A few seconds later they reached the Cherokees in their position.

"Time to go," he repeated.

The two Cherokees obviously heard him, but they didn't take their eyes off whatever they were looking at in the distance; which, whatever it was, was considerably to the west of the village.

"Look over there," said Kevin. "With your binoculars. We think that's smoke."

Rod pulled his glasses from their case and scanned the western horizon. He took his time. And, sure enough, he saw smoke. There was a thin line of dark-white haze blending into the darker smoke and steam released by the volcano further out. It was very faint, so much so that he hadn't spotted it earlier.

Someone was burning wood, was the most likely explanation.

Just to be sure, Hulbert watched the area for a full three minutes. Okay, it wasn't a forest fire and it wasn't a thermal vent. It was definitely confined, not growing, and was most probably manmade. A campfire was the most logical explanation.

He did the calculations in his head. Two miles out—a couple of hours for observation—two miles back: It looked like they would be eating a cold supper again tonight.

It also looked like they would be late reporting in.

"Fucking bastards," Hulbert muttered. They were lying on their stomachs watching the Spaniards. They were close enough to hear what was being said, if it was said loudly—and the Spaniards were being loud. Quite obviously, they were not in the least bit concerned that the noise they made might alert somebody. De Soto's name had come up once or twice. Another name that kept cropping up was Moscoso. And that was the bastard he was talking about.

Hulbert's Spanish was weak. He had what he had been exposed to on the job, plus the two years he had in high school. That was it. And these guys had one hell of an accent. And most of the words being said made no sense. The parts that he thought he did understand made his blood run cold.

There looked to be about three or four hundred well-armed Spaniards all together. Between bits and pieces in the prison's library and the history that a few of the guards remembered, they'd been able to put together the basic facts about de Soto's expedition. So, Rod knew de Soto had started his trip through North America with almost seven hundred men. He also knew only three hundred and eleven survived to make the trip home. Disease had taken a large number of them out, including de Soto himself. But most of those who died had done so in battle with the Indians. For three and a half years, the Spaniards, unable to carry enough food for their trip, robbed every village they came to. They also enslaved the people they captured, and took anything that might be of value when they retuned home.

Most of the men Hulbert watched were dressed in bold colors. Their shirts were made of a combination of cloth and leather, and some of the shirts were padded at the shoulders. Most of their pants were short breeches that were flared and stuffed. They wore long, tight-fitting stockings and thigh-high boots. He didn't think much of their taste in clothes. A lot of it was stupid and impractical for traipsing through a wilderness.

But the things they covered those clothes with were not. Most of the footmen wore morions—multi-peaked, steel helmets with short, down-turned brims. They also wore padded vests called *escaupil*, a sort of armor made of nothing more than cotton, yet could stop an arrow.

Other footmen wore the brigandine vests. These were the precursors to the prison's own bullet-proof vests—sleeveless shirts with steel plates riveted in place to protect vital organs. Each horseman wore a helmet and a cuirass to protect his chest, abdomen, and back. Some wore arm and leg armor. Others wore chain mail and gauntlets.

They were well armored and well armed. They carried steel swords, matchlock guns, crossbows, and lances. Hulbert was a crossbow enthusiast and knew the damage the weapon was capable of. These men would not be easy to defeat, and Rod didn't think for a minute it would be possible to negotiate anything with them. The bastards had a couple of hundred Indians roped together by the neck, mostly women and young girls, being marched through the tangle of trees and brush. Each of the prisoners carried a basket filled with food, tools, blankets, and everything else the marauders thought they might need. Another, much smaller group of male Indians worked at keeping a small herd of pigs from wandering away.

That would have been a tough job under any circumstances. With the pigs the Spaniards had brought with them to America, it was almost impossible. They seemed half-feral and had probably been selected for their endurance more than anything else. They certainly didn't look much like the pigs Rod was accustomed to seeing at county fairs.

One of the pigs had gotten away and escaped into the brush. The man called Moscoso had apparently decided the Indian closest to the animal was responsible and needed to be punished. He began cursing and beating him savagely with a quirt, until the Indian was writhing on the ground pleading for mercy. Even then, Moscoso didn't stop for at least half a minute. This went well beyond even the harshest notions of discipline. It was pure and simple cruelty.

Throughout, Hulbert ignored the Indian and studied Moscoso, making sure he could recognize the man anywhere he saw him, in any kind of reasonable lighting. When the time came, he'd see to it personally that Moscoso was a dead man.

"We can't just leave those Indians the way they are. We have to do something to help them," Hartshorn said.

Hulbert glanced at the man and shook his head. "We'll help them when we can, Gary. But not today. We're outnumbered almost a hundred to one."

Hartshorn looked ferocious. "Sure, not today. But what about after the sun sets? We can go down and untie them. Man, what I wouldn't give for a half dozen grenades. These sonsabitches are worse than anything we have behind bars inside the prison."

"We can't," Hulbert said between gritted teeth. "There are too many of them, and too few of us. I don't care if it's noon or midnight. If you want to save lives, Gary, we do nothing. We have to get back to the captain and Watkins. They have to be warned." He started crawling back the way they had come. Just a few feet down the hill he stopped and whispered, "The Cherokee town isn't far off from the creek the Spaniards are following. They outnumber the Cherokees even if you include all the women and children and old men. Watkins only has three dozen or so warriors. These guys are all warriors. They'll find the Cherokees and destroy them. And when they're done, they'll move on like a swarm of locusts. Eventually, they'll run across the prison."

Hulbert forced himself to take several slow steady breaths. It was time to get the hell out of Dodge. He was not going to risk being seen. Too much depended on them coming home. They had to start moving now. He knew he could get back to the town before de Soto could get close enough to be a threat to the Cherokees. A group as large as the Spaniards, and driving slaves, wouldn't be able to travel more than a few miles a day through this type of terrain. Ten, at most. If he pushed, and he intended to push damn hard, they should be able to get back in plenty of time to warn Blacklock and Watkins.

For a moment, he considered trying to warn the villagers they'd been observing. But that just wasn't possible in the time they had. The language barrier would make communication impossible in any period short of several days, and for all he knew he could wind up frightening them right into the arms of the Spaniards. He could only hope they were maintaining their own scouting parties and would spot the Spaniards in time to escape into the wilderness.

No. The four of them would report back to Blacklock and Watkins. They were in charge, and it would be their decision.

CHAPTER 37

Andy Blacklock shook his head. "Rod, we can't go back to the prison. Not yet. The way I understand it, another village is about to wiped off the face of the planet. *This* planet, not the one we came from. *This* planet, that doesn't have very many villages to start with. And we have to rescue those people already enslaved, too. You said yourself most of them were women and girls."

Lieutenant Hulbert set his jaws. "Look, I understand your reaction. Believe me, I had the same reaction myself—and then some—watching those thugs brutalizing people. But you're not looking at the whole picture, Andy."

They were sitting in the cabin the Cherokees had provided them. Rod nodded toward the door. "Since tying up with Geoffrey's people, we have women and children and old people. Damn it, we could lose them. And if we do, we will never have it again. We will never see an old man or old woman and a baby on the same day. There's more at stake here than just us. Andy, it's like you've said a hundred times, our future—who we will be—is on the line. We have to pick our battles, and make sure we win them. We can't risk a loss. If we die trying to help that village, then there won't be anyone to protect this town or the people we still have at the prison."

He stopped, and took a deep breath. Obviously, trying to keep his temper under control. This was the first time since the Quiver that Rod and Andy had had a serious disagreement, and neither one of them wanted to risk escalating it into a shouting match.

Andy took a deep breath himself and looked away.

"Okay, Rod. But you're the one who's not looking at the whole picture. This isn't simply a moral issue. It isn't even simply a strategic or tactical issue, in a narrow military sense. It's quite possibly a matter of life and death for every human being on the planet. Not now, but generations from now."

Rod frowned. "That seems awfully melodramatic, Andy."

"No, it isn't. We've got a problem—and you can spell that with a capital P—that I hadn't even thought about until Jeff raised it with me privately, the same night you left on your expedition. And it's about as crude and simple as problems get."

He looked at Edelman, the third man in the cabin. "Tell him, Jeff."

"Rod, I'm worried about the genetic pool."

"Huh?"

"Genetic pool. Breeding population. There are various terms for it. But what they all come down to is that if the numbers of a species drop too far, that species is doomed.

It either goes extinct quickly, or it starts developing such serious genetic problems that its chances of survival get really dicey. That's why population number is the key benchmark they use to declare a species endangered."

By the time Jeff was done, Rod had his eyes closed. Andy understood the reason. He'd done exactly the same thing when Jeff had raised the issue with him earlier. Closed his eyes and did the math himself.

The arithmetic was pretty damn stark. A little over two hundred guards and nurses, the majority of them male. And of the females, a good percentage were no longer young enough to have children. Certainly not more than one child. Two thousand plus convicts, all of them male—leaving aside any other consideration, such as the fact that some of them were psychotic. Somewhere between three hundred and seven hundred Spanish conquistadores. All of them male. A small number of U.S. soldiers. All of them male. About three hundred Cherokees, evenly divided in terms of gender but with a number of the women beyond child-bearing years.

"Well, aren't we screwed?" muttered Hulbert.

Jeff chuckled humorlessly. "Probably a poor choice of words, given the circumstances. Aren't we *not* screwed would be a lot closer."

Rod blew out some air and rubbed his face. "We needed this like we needed a hole in the head." He thought about it for a moment. "Okay, then. What's the magic number? How many *do* you need?"

Edelman shrugged. "Nobody really knows, is the only honest answer. The minimum, of course, is the Biblical two. Adam and Eve. But even in the Bible, their sons found wives somewhere else. Where'd they come from? Even the Lord Almighty doesn't seem to have known the answer. We sure as hell don't."

Hulbert glared at him. "Will you puh-lease stop being such a damn academic? Give me a ballpark figure, Jeff."

"Sorry. Can't even do that. The problem is that the number seems to vary, from species to species—and nobody's ever put it to the test with human beings."

Hulbert's glare didn't fade at all. Jeff sighed. "Look, I can put it this way. Leaving out of the equation for the moment whatever number of Indians are out there other than the Cherokees, I figure we've got somewhere around two hundred females, all told, who are capable of having children. Please note that I'm being wildly optimistic, in that I'm presuming that each and every one of them is capable of bearing a child and is willing to do so. I've already told Andy that if and when the time comes that we have to declare a public policy, I'm ducking behind the podium and letting *him* tell Bird Matthews that she's gotta start screwing guys."

Rod laughed. One of the guards, Bird Matthews, was a confirmed and I'm-not-kidding lesbian. She was cheerful about it, not belligerent, and she wasn't a "militant" in the usual sense of the word. In fact, she was quite popular with the other guards, of either sex. But she'd made clear the I'm-not-kidding part by organizing a small motorcycle club that called itself *Dykes on Bikes*. They even had the logo on their motorcycle jackets.

"Okay, point taken. But let's assume the two hundred figure is valid. What then?"

"Well, like I told Andy, I'm not positive. But I'm pretty

sure that's not enough. Not in the long run. It's not a simple matter of arithmetic. Obviously, if two hundred women each have two daughters, and those daughters each have two, etc. etc., you wind up with a problem of overpopulation faster than you might imagine. But people are complex packages of DNA, on a genetic level, they're not numbers. If the original breeding stock is too low, you run into what's called a bottleneck problem. That won't just apply to us, either. Any of the animals that came through in small numbers, such as the horses, are looking at a bottleneck too.

"Even something as random as genetic drift can screw you up. All it takes is one or two bad mutations and you can find yourself dying off. It's not so much an arithmetical problem as a statistical one. Theoretically, a species could survive with an initial breeding stock of one male and one female. It's just that the smaller the pool, the worse the odds get."

He looked at the small fire in the chimney they were sitting by, for a moment. "On the other side of the coin—again, with the caveat that this is really just an educated guess—I think that two thousand females would be enough."

"Oh, swell. We're screwed, then." A bit grumpily: "And don't lecture me about my choice of words. We're still not even in the ballpark."

"Not . . . necessarily. We have no idea how many little Indian villages or hunter-gatherer bands are out there. But I can tell you this much. I think it has to be a fair number."

"Why?"

"Because the Quiver—whatever it was; which we don't know and I doubt we ever will—wasn't just a temporal phenomenon. It was also a spacial phenomenon. And it looks to me as if the spacial dimension involved in its effects—call it the radius—got larger the farther back in time it went. Or maybe it started way back in ancient time and came forward, narrowing as it went. Either way, if you were to plot the Quiver in three dimensions, it would look like a cone rather than a cylinder."

"Run that by me again."

"Think about it, Rod. Who got taken in our day? Just us. The prison, and a little bit of territory around it. Go back almost a hundred and seventy years, and who got taken among the Cherokee? I've asked, and the answer is interesting. Chief Watkins and his people weren't all gathered together in one small area when they got snatched by the Quiver, the way we were. They were strung out along a trail—and the soldiers were riding point quite a ways ahead. Still, most of them got snatched. The only ones who didn't, in his band, were a group that had been bringing up the rear a long ways behind, and the soldiers who were with them. Which was most of them."

"Ha. I'll be damned. I hadn't even thought about that."

"Don't feel bad," said Andy. "Neither had I."

"Jeff, have you tried to figure out—"

"Don't teach your grandmother to suck eggs. Of course I've tried to figure out what the radius must have been. As near as I can tell, at least a half a mile and maybe even a mile. The problem is that nobody knows exactly how far back the group that didn't get taken were lagging. The soldiers were a good quarter of a mile ahead, though, according to Sergeant Kershner. So no matter how you slice it, the territory involved was a lot bigger than the prison area."

Idly, he picked up a stick and fed it to the fire. "Okay. The next group of people who got snatched, that we know of, were de Soto and his army. Please note the use of the term 'army.' Fine, a small army—but you don't cram even a small army into a small space. Not when you're on campaign, for sure—and every report we've gotten about the Spaniards seems to indicate they're foraging constantly. What little we've been able to squeeze out of the one Spaniard we captured seems to confirm that. No matter which way I look at it, I figure it has to have been a lot bigger radius than the one the Cherokees were in, much less us."

Another stick went into the fire. "I get the same results when I look at the animals, except it's even more extreme. We haven't seen more than four deer—and yet, between us and the Cherokees, we've seen three allosaurs. There's no way to explain that ratio *without* presuming a steady increase in the radius of the Quiver as it went further and further back in time."

"Uh . . . sorry, I'm not following you."

"That's because you're not a biologist. One of the laws of biology is that predators are always outnumbered—a lot—by prey, and the bigger an animal gets, the scarcer it gets. Especially predators. That's because big predators need a very big hunting range."

It didn't take Rod, with his extensive outdoor experience, more than a second to grasp the point. "Jesus. What's the hunting range of something like a grizzly bear or a tiger?"

"Tigers, I don't know. And I don't remember the specific numbers for big bears. It's different anyway, for male and female bears. But I do know the numbers, from the lowest to highest, are all measured in square kilometers. *Hundreds* of square kilometers."

"Gotcha. And a big bear weighs what, approximately? Half a ton?"

"Not quite, although a few individuals get even bigger that that. The biggest are the southern Alaskan brown bears. If I remember right, the males average somewhere around four hundred kilos. Call it nine hundred pounds."

Hulbert nodded. "What do you figure an allosaur weighs? And spare me the lecture about variation. I know that. Ballpark figures, Jeff, ballpark figures. For right now, that's plenty good enough."

Edelman smiled. "They're at least three times bigger than a large male Alaskan brown bear. Probably closer to five or six times bigger, on average, and I wouldn't be surprised if some of them got up to four or five tons. Which would make them eight to ten times bigger."

"Four deer and three allosaurs . . ." Rod mused. "Yeah, I see your point. There's simply no way you could have found three allosaurs in an area the size of the prison, or even that stretch of trail the Cherokees were on."

"Not unless they were having a convention or a rock concert. No, by the time the Quiver reached the Cretaceous, the radius had to have been something like fifty miles. Probably more, and maybe a lot more. We have no reason to think that the three allosaurs we've seen or heard about are all there are."

Rod pondered the matter, for a minute or so. "In other

words—this is the gist of it, stripped down to the essentials—the future of the human race in this world depends ultimately on the most primitive people in it. Those pre-Mounds Indians out there, in their villages."

"Yup. Just like the Bible says. The meek shall inherit the Earth."

Rod scratched his cheek. "Andy, since you're the big shot, I do believe I'll follow Jeff's example. When the time comes, I'm ducking behind the podium while you tell an assembled crowd of prison guards and prehistoric hunter-gatherers that they've got to start dating."

All three of them laughed. When the laughter died down, Edelman shook his head. "It won't have to come to that, thankfully. This is a generational problem, not something measured in years. And while I don't know nearly as much history and anthropology as I do biology and geology, I do know one thing. There has never been a time recorded in human history or told about in myths and legends, when two groups of human beings met for the first time, that they didn't start screwing each other." He leaned back on his stool, looking very complacent. "Besides, that's what adolescence is for. Let our teenage descendants deal with it, the snotty worthless brats."

Rod sighed and ran fingers through his hair. "But we can do what they can't. Keep those Indians alive to begin with."

"Yeah, that's right," said Andy. "Look at it this way, Rod. We had a job to do in our old world, and all that seems to have happened is that we're picking up the same job in this one. Protecting people against the worst people."

Rod chuckled, softly and without much humor. "I don't

think the term 'correctional officer' was ever intended to be applied to Spanish damn-the-bastards conquistadores. But, okay, I see your point. When do we leave tomorrow?"

CHAPTER
38

Susan Fisher sat down next to Jenny. She didn't say anything, just sat on one of the stools positioned in front of the stone bowls the Cherokee women used to grind the nutmeal.

Jenny nodded at her, her mind still distracted. She and Andy had had a very heated, whispered argument this morning. She hadn't been happy at all that he wasn't taking her along on the expedition to fight the Spaniards.

But, in the end, she had agreed. Andy was right, and she'd known it all along. She'd just had a fierce emotional reaction to the idea of being left behind. Especially to the idea of being separated from him.

In the type of battle that lay ahead, her supply level made her skill level almost useless. She could do more good staying behind than as a field surgeon. Which, given what she had available, wouldn't mean much more than amputations—and the Cherokees had their own people who knew how to do that.

Andy had made the alliance with Watkins, but he figured it was still shaky. If not for Watkins, for many of the other Cherokees. And Watkins' authority as their chief was very far from absolute. The Cherokee power structure wasn't exactly what modern Americans would call a democracy, but that was mostly a matter of formalities and custom. It was far closer to a democracy than a dictatorship. For that matter, it was far more democratic than any number of supposedly democratic institutions in their own society.

Andy thought Jenny could play a key role in solidifying the alliance. Leaving aside the fact that the Cherokees respected her medical knowledge, Jenny was the most experienced person in the group when it came to dealing with other cultures.

So, she stayed behind. And did her best to control the knot in her stomach.

The first order of business was not to be rude. Susan Fisher would have come here for a reason.

"Can I be of help, Susan?"

She forced herself to turn her head from looking at the horizon where the expedition had gone to the woman next to her.

She had to look down, too. Fisher was a tiny woman, although Jenny was sure she would be strong as an ox. In her endurance, at least. She'd watched the woman—her, and several other Cherokee women—working a mortar and pestle for hours, grinding the nutmeal. Her knarled hands were wide and calloused. Her hair, still black, framed a face that was at least fifty.

She was obviously a woman who had worked hard all

her life, and it showed. But her voice was soft. Almost musical.

"Eat, first. You ate nothing this morning." The medicine woman handed Jenny a small piece of some sort of food. "It is not much for taste. It should have dried berries in it, but we haven't found any berries. It will fill you, though."

"What is it?" Jenny asked, curious. She really couldn't tell what the stuff was. Dried meat of some kind, obviously, was one major ingredient. But it didn't feel like jerky. She took an experimental bite. Didn't taste like jerky, either.

"Pemmican. I'd say it was the Cherokee version of it, but that's probably silly. There's not a single thing in it we would have used back home."

Pemmican. Jenny knew what it was, theoretically, but had never eaten any in her life. Never seen any, so far as she could remember. It was a concentrated food that, in one form or another, had been used by many tribes in North America. And then, later, adopted by European explorers, trappers, and fur traders. It was a mixture of rendered animal fat, dried meat, and berries. Grains and seeds could be added too, if she remembered correctly.

The combination sounded a little gross, especially the rendered fat, but pemmican was a concentrated food supply that would last without spoiling for a long time, and was quite nutritious. It would be a valuable addition to their resources.

As for the taste . . .

Best not to go there.

"It's good," she said.

"It's fucking terrible. We need berries. And the fat's not right. You want bone marrow fat for good pemmican, and there's not enough in these lizards. So we had to make do. The meat . . ." The little woman shook her head. "Lizard meat. Deer would be much better. But it'll do, for the meantime."

Jenny nodded, forcing herself to continue chewing. Food was important to a people. They were emotionally attached to their diet and took offense when foreigners criticized their eating habits. But she had a feeling the pemmican was going to be one of those things she would have a hard time getting used to, even if Susan and the other women found berries or a substitute.

But maybe not, if the fat were different. She thought it was the rendered fat that gave it that rather nasty taste. Perhaps fat taken from mammal bone marrow would be different.

After all, she *liked* the grasshoppers. Because of the years she'd spent in South America, Jenny was far more cosmopolitan in her culinary tastes than the prison guards; most of whom, like Andy himself, had been born and raised in southern Illinois or nearby. There were any number of good things to be said about the men and women from small towns and cities in America's heartland. An adventurous spirit when it came to food was not one of them.

As she'd already figured out from watching Fisher in the various discussions that had taken place, the little woman was not one for idle chit-chat or beating around the bush.

"The captain. Andy Blacklock. He is your husband?"

Jenny gave a small sigh. Women always wanted to know who you were paired with and how tight that bond was. It didn't matter what race or what religion or what part of the world they came from. She forced herself to give Fisher a smile. She knew it was a pathetic imitation of the real thing. But it was the best she could do. She knew why women asked. It was because at some instinctual level women knew it was important. It was what kept the human race going.

"No, he isn't. I'm a widow. My husband died almost three years ago. Andy and I . . . We just met very recently, right after the Quiver. Ah, the Great Wind." That was the Cherokee term for the disaster. "And things have been so hard-pressed since that we haven't been able to decide . . . Well. To be truthful, we haven't really even talked about it."

They hadn't even had sex yet. Partly because of the pressure; partly because there'd been so little privacy; but mostly, she thought, because both she and Andy understood that once they took that step everything would lock in. She didn't think Andy was nervous about that. She certainly wasn't, she'd come to realize at least a week ago. Still, it made both of them a bit cautious. The bar had been raised very high, so to speak.

She regretted it now. If she'd known Andy would be leaving to fight a war, she'd have ended the dilly-dallying. She might never see him again.

Fisher nodded. "Smart woman. Three years is a good time to wait between husbands. I waited three years after my first husband died before I went and got another."

Fisher sat quietly for a while, watching the children trying to coax a small, furred creature down from a tree. The creature was having none of it.

"How did your husband die?"

Normally, Jenny would have resented the blunt question, coming from someone who was almost a complete stranger. But the medicine woman wasn't prying; she was trying to get to know her. And the only way to know who a person was today was to know what things had happened in their past.

"My husband was a doctor, and we were working in Brazil, down in South America. We'd been there for a little over two years. We were scheduled to stay until the end of the third year, but we became infested with one of the local parasites. As soon as we realized what was wrong, we came home, back to the states. But it didn't help. There was nothing anyone could do for him. He was gone in less than four days. I was sick for months, and off work for a year."

"You had no children?"

Jenny shook her head.

Fisher took her hand and gave it a squeeze. "Stephen McQuade has explained to me that the world you came from was very different than our own. I am curious. He says a nurse in your time is not the nurse of my own."

Jenny started to laugh. "Oh, heavens. Yes, he's right. Things have changed a lot. I still give baths, and help a patient to the bathroom, but I do a lot more than that. I've probably had more education than the best physician working in the most modern hospital in the eighteen hundreds."

Fisher nodded. "Hospitals are where the whites go to die."

Jenny knew that wasn't prejudice. Fisher was right. Until very recently, historically speaking—certainly in

Susan's stretch of the nineteenth century—hospitals were death houses. To start with, they were usually filthy. The care was frequently worse than no care at all, since it consisted of things like bleeding that often made the patient's condition worse.

A person actually had less of a chance to survive if they entered one than if they stayed home and weathered it with nothing but the help of a friend or family member. And the death rate in childbirth of wealthier women who used doctors was far worse than that of poorer women who just used the help of a midwife.

"You do not make your own medicines, though, he said. That seems strange to me."

"No." She decided not to try to explain, right now, all the complexities of a modern medical and pharmaceutical industry. "In my day, that was specialized work. It was done by doctors called 'pharmacists.'"

The American Medical Association would scream bloody murder if they heard that. But the AMA wasn't here and Jenny's opinion had always been that a good pharmacist was worth ten mediocre doctors anyway.

"I know a few of the old remedies, but not many. And"—she waved at the woods around them—"those I do know, I don't know how to find."

Fisher nodded. "Yes. It is the same for me. I know some of the old ways, but not all. And the plants I used are now gone."

They sat silent, grieving for their losses. Fisher for her small herb garden, and Jenny for her telephone and pharmacy.

"If there is fat left over after making the pemmican I

will make an oil to keep away the insects. I do not know if it will work with these strange bugs, but I will try just the same. This place is so different from home, but it is also the same in many ways. There is a bog not too far away. A half-day's walk from here. It will be very useful."

Jenny's estimate of the little Cherokee woman's medical skills went up steeply. It would be foolish—really foolish— to underestimate Susan Fisher.

Because she was right. Bog-water and moss were the two most sterile things on the planet now. Her mind was racing. A bog was the first step. It would give them sterile dressings and an antibacterial rinse. Her thoughts twisted and turned.

"Sea water. Do you know how far we are from the ocean?" In a pinch seawater would work as an I.V. solution for short-term stabilization of a patient. Doctors, caught in the middle of battle without their usual supplies had resorted to ocean water. It hadn't worked as well as whole blood or plasma, but it had saved a lot of lives. Salt water had also saved more than one burn victim.

Fisher shook her head. "We have not seen the ocean. Not even any big lakes."

"That's okay. There has to be an ocean. In fact, Jeff Edelman says the world today probably has a higher sea level. There was even a big sea some of the time, he says, in the center of—"

Luckily, she caught herself before she said United States. In Fisher's time, the United States ended at the Mississippi River—and the land beyond it had been promised to the Cherokee. Another promise that would eventually be broken.

"In the middle of North America. If it's there, we'll find it sooner or later."

Jenny stretched, feeling her gloom vanishing. "Most medicines from my time still came from plants and animals. If we put our heads together, I bet we could get some of them back. We will just have to experiment a little."

CHAPTER
39

"Stay low," James Cook whispered to Boyne. He used his left hand to wipe the sweat from his brow. The sun had set an hour ago, and a small fire flickered and glowed in the darkness. From the small rise he and John were hidden behind, they could just see down into the clearing below them. There were a half dozen strangely dressed men sitting around the flames. They were wearing some kind of body armor too. It looked like metal.

"Did you see the shape they left that couple in?" Boyne made the sign of the cross. "Man, they're worse than the animals back at the prison. Jesus, Mary, and Joseph. That poor woman was raped and mutilated. And her man, he died even harder. I think they were trying to get him to tell them something. God knows what. Those people didn't look like they had a pot to piss in."

James didn't answer. Boyne was hissing between clenched teeth and the sound was barely traveling to him, but he still wished he would shut up. He needed to think.

He'd thought the men in the camp were Mexicans at first, but Boyne said they weren't. They had the wrong accent—the "s" sound was almost a "th"—and he could make out most of what was being said. The men were Spaniards and they were following somebody they called de Soto. Apparently, they weren't happy with his leadership, but they weren't willing to buck him.

James tried to figure out what to do. The easiest and simplest answer was just to leave. The six men sitting around the campfire weren't maintaining any guard. That seemed strange to James, since there was always the risk of huge predators even if they weren't worried about people. But everything about the way those men carried themselves exuded arrogance.

Whatever the reason, the Boomers could avoid them easily. Except for him and Boyne, the rest of the group was waiting about fifty yards to the rear. All he and John had to do was slip back, collect the others, and they'd be on their way. There was a partial moon, which gave enough light to see. They could travel through a good part of the night, even carrying Elaine, and be a mile or two away by sunrise.

On the other hand . . .

James *really* wanted their weapons. Sure, they looked like antiques, but those were still guns. They had swords, too, and some sort of odd-looking spears with big blades on the end. Odd-looking or not, though, they were obviously far superior weapons to the spears the Boomers had jury-rigged. Those were nothing more than sharpened branches or poles with shanks attached to the ends—and not too well attached, at that.

He knew they'd been lucky, so far. In the two days since they made their break from the prison, they had only encountered one large predator. And that wasn't a dinosaur or anything nearly that big. It was just a big, chunky-looking cat of some kind. About the size of a lion and scary enough, with its huge canine teeth. But they'd stood their ground with the half-assed spears they'd made, and after growling for a while the cat went on its way.

The problem was that while the men at the campfire seemed arrogantly careless, James didn't have any doubt at all that they were tough and experienced fighters. All of them had their swords readily available, and all but one still had their guns in their hands. Even caught by surprise, this could be chancy. All the Boomers had was the pistol Bostic had given them.

True, it was a good weapon. A Glock Model 22 with fifteen rounds in the magazine. Still, it would be one gun against six.

Then, there was a third factor, that he was sure wouldn't have bothered Danny Bostic in the least but bothered him a lot. The Spaniards had three captives. Children, a boy and two girls, the oldest of them maybe ten and the youngest maybe six. They were probably the children of the couple that had been murdered. James had wondered what they'd want with such young children. It was conceivable they were keeping the girls for sexual pleasure, even though the youngest was no more than eight years old. But although the kids looked bruised up a little, they didn't seem to have been harmed otherwise.

John Boyne cleared up the mystery for him. "They're planning to sell them into slavery when they get back to the coast," he whispered. "I guess the stupid fucks haven't figured out yet that the Caribbean isn't there anymore."

That made sense. James knew from stories he'd heard from his grandfather that the Spanish had enslaved Indians when they first stumbled across the New World. They didn't start bringing black slaves from Africa until later.

"Oh, screw it," he muttered, more to himself than Boyne. "John, slip back and get Kidd up here. I need the expert's opinion."

Boyne flashed a smile, quite visible in the moonlight. "Okay, but I can tell you what it'll be."

Geoffrey Kidd arrived soon. As dark-skinned as he was, James didn't spot him until he was less than five yards away. The man moved almost silently, despite his size.

Boyne came up behind him. When the two of them were squatting next to James, just out of sight of the men in the clearing, James explained the situation.

"If we fight, you'll have to do most of it, Geoffrey," he concluded. "You've got the pistol."

Kidd had wound up getting the pistol because the general consensus of the Boomers was that Kidd was the best gun-handler among them. It turned out the reason he was serving a life sentence was because he was a contract killer for whichever set of gangsters met his price. He'd been charged with only one first-degree murder, though, after he was finally caught, even though the police suspected he'd done at least five. He still might have gotten the death penalty except the prosecutor didn't really care that much. Everybody Kidd had murdered had been a gangster also. Life without parole was good enough.

Kidd didn't say anything, for maybe a minute, as he studied the men sitting around the campfire.

"Don't need anybody but me," he said. "But I'm warning you. There won't be too many rounds left when I'm done. With that armor they're wearing, I'll have to double-tap all of them." He smiled thinly. "'Course, I'd do that anyway."

James wondered if he was bragging. Probably . . .

Not.

The fact that Kidd was openly gay convinced him he wasn't boasting. James had never hung around with gangsters and didn't really know that much about them. But what he did know was that being macho was pretty much a given in that crowd—so it stood to reason that a gay man who could make a living at it was probably every bit as good as he claimed to be.

"Okay, then. What do you want the rest of us to do?"

"Boyne's already here. Bring up Dino and Elroy. All three are real good with shanks. Them and you can follow me in and cut whatever throats need cutting. I probably won't need 'em but I might, and by then I may have run through the magazine. But—I'm stressing this, so pay attention—make sure you don't move until I holler. While I'm shooting, I don't want anything around me but targets."

"Be careful of the kids."

Kidd curled his lip. "I ain't worried about the kids. They're off to the side, tied up to that tree. I'm worried about Injuns rushing in. Crazy Injuns, like the kind that would threaten a man holding a gun with a pitiful little shank. Down in a fucking basement, where the ricochets would get anyone the shooters missed."

James smiled. "Okay. We don't move till you tell us to."

He turned to Boyne. "You heard him, John. Get Dino and Elroy."

By the time Dino and Elroy got there, Kidd had disappeared. He'd just taken a few steps and vanished.

"How soon?" Morelli asked.

"Hell if I know." James' headshake was a rueful sort of thing. "I was an EMT, remember? Don't ask me how contract hit men go about their business. I never even had to clean up after one. I did get plenty of shootings and knifings, but they were just hothead stuff."

"Just wait," Boyne hissed. "Won't be that long. Kidd's probably set already. He's just waiting to give you two a chance to get here."

About a minute later, it all broke loose.

James didn't even see Kidd coming out of the darkness until he'd already shot the first Spaniard. The first thing he saw were the gun-flashes.

The gunshots didn't sound like much, really. *Bang-bang* and one Spaniard went down, gushing blood from his neck. James was sure he never saw the man who'd killed him.

Bang-bang. Another Spaniard down. Some of the blood spouting from his neck went into the fire and started hissing.

Bang-bang. Another down. The same neck wound. James was a little surprised. He'd thought Kidd would go for head shots. The men still had their body armor on but they'd taken off their helmets.

Bang-bang. Another down. This was the first man who'd started reacting before he got shot. The other three had been killed so quickly that James didn't think they'd had any real idea that they were in danger, beyond— starting with the second man—a completely unconscious rush of adrenaline.

But even the fourth man hadn't managed to do more than start getting one leg under him.

The fifth man had good reflexes. Instead of trying to get up like the other one had, he just grabbed his gun and flung himself to the side.

Bang-bang. The man screeched and clawed his leg— but still didn't let go of the gun.

"Well, fuck you too!" Kidd snarled. *Bang-bang.* And that was that.

The last man was on his feet, bringing up that big clumsy rifle. No, it was probably a musket.

Kidd moved quickly, circling to the man's right, making it awkward to bring the musket around.

James was expecting the same double-tap, but Kidd shot the man in the leg instead. Right about mid-thigh.

That was enough to stagger him, even if he somehow managed to stay on his feet. But he dropped the gun.

Kidd almost shot him then. It would have been an easy kill, given his deadly marksmanship with a pistol. The Spaniard wasn't more than fifteen feet away.

James could see Geoffrey struggling with his training and instincts. But, after maybe a second, he lowered the pistol a little, strode up, and sent the man sailing onto his back with a tremendous cross-step sidekick.

"Come on down and cut his throat, guys!" he yelled. "I only got but two rounds left. That one bastard made me miss. Worthless motherfucker."

James was still trying to figure out if they wanted to keep the Spaniard alive for questioning when Elroy made it all a moot point. He'd gotten so used to the Boomers that he sometimes forgot just what a murderous crew they could be.

The first thing he did when he got down to the clearing was go over to the children. They watched him coming, wide-eyed and obviously petrified. He made what he hoped were reassuring gestures and sounds—that's all his words would be to the kids; just sounds—and started untying them.

The knots weren't too hard to get undone, fortunately. He hadn't wanted to pull out his shank to just cut the ropes, figuring that would terrify the poor kids even more.

After he untied them, he rose and stepped back. They stared up at him, still wide-eyed and still saying nothing.

Suddenly, as if they had a single mind, the three kids lunged to their feet and raced into the woods.

"Oh, hell!" James exclaimed. He was an idiot. He should have realized the kids would be as scared of the Boomers as they were of the Spaniards. They obviously belonged to some sort of primitive Indian tribe. The boy, not more than eight years old, already had decorative tattoos on his face. Not many—nothing compared to the tattoos that had adorned the corpse of his father. But not even lifers in a maximum security prison tattooed their faces that way. The older girl had had a small tattoo also, on her chin.

God only knew what they made of the firearms. Geoffrey's murderous gunplay must have seemed like black magic to them.

Boyne came up. "Do we go after 'em, boss? Maybe

we oughta. They won't last long in the woods, just by themselves. Not with dinosaurs and who-all knows what else roaming around out there."

James hesitated. That had been his immediate inclination also. But the children would just think they were being pursued, and would race still further into the woods.

"No. That'd backfire, I think. Let's just make camp here, and hope the kids will come back eventually."

By the time the Boomers got Elaine there, on her litter, James had been able to move the bodies to one side of the clearing. But that was about it. He didn't know what to do with the corpses, though. Digging a mass grave would be a lot of work for people who were already tired from a long day's march. Even if they had shovels, which they didn't. Gathering enough wood for a big funeral pyre wouldn't be much less work. They didn't have axes. Those weird-looking half-spear/half-axe things of the Spaniards didn't really look like they'd serve too well for the purpose. They were obviously designed to chop flesh, not wood.

When her litter was set down, Elaine stared at the small pile of corpses. Then, stared up at James.

"Did you . . . ?"

"Well, no. Not exactly."

Kidd came up, grinning. At least, "grinning" was the technically correct expression. Personally, James thought that grin would send a great white shark racing for deep waters.

"I shot 'em," Kidd explained. "It's what I do, girl. Well. Did, anyway. But it's like riding a bicycle. Once you learn, you never forget."

Amazingly, the grin widened. By now, the great white would be looking for an underwater cave to get away from the monster.

Elaine might have swallowed. It was hard to tell, in the dim and flickering light thrown out by the campfire. But all she said was, "Yeah. I guess."

Geoffrey turned to James. "Me and John found a decent sized creek just a little ways off. Probably why they made camp here."

"Good. We need water."

Boyne came up in time to hear that. His grin wasn't much better than Kidd's.

"Better get what we need now, then. Pretty soon, that creek's gonna be where these bastards sleep with the fishes. You won't want to be drinking from it after that, I guarantee you."

"Huh?"

"Think about it, boss. With all the damn critters running around, we can't just leave the bodies here. And there ain't no way we're digging a big grave. We got no shovels. Come morning, there's likely to be some huge dinosaur chomping on 'em—and not being any too particular whether what he chomps is dead or alive."

"It's a big creek," Kidd chimed in. "Not big enough to carry the bodies downstream, but at one spot nearby there's a good sized pool in it. We weight the bodies down with some rocks—we can use the same rope they used to tie up the kids—and they should all wind up sinking below the surface. Maybe not more than a few inches, but we'll be gone soon enough that shouldn't be a problem."

It was a grisly proposal, but it seemed the most practical.

And it wasn't as if James had any sentimental attitude about the corpses. Those men had been as vicious as they come. Serve them right to wind up as fish food.

James looked over at the corpses. "Okay, fine. But I want to save the rope, if we can. Rope's likely to be useful. I think we can just loosen that body armor they're wearing, stuff some rocks in, snug 'em back up, and that'll be enough."

"We don't want the armor?" asked Boyne. "Boss, that's a lot of steel. We could make stuff out of it."

"With what?" demanded Kidd. "We ain't got no tools that'll work metal."

He shook his head. "Fuck the armor, John. We can't do anything with it and just the way it is, as armor, you saw how much good it did them. I got some great big dinosaur chasing me, the last thing I need is to be hauling around thirty-forty-fifty pounds of steel on my body. I bet I can dodge a dinosaur, if I have to—but not wearing that crap."

James was doubtful that dodging dinosaurs was all that easy. But Geoffrey did have a point. It wasn't likely any dinosaur's jaws would be slowed down all that much by the armor. Whatever it was called. He thought the term might be "cuirass," but he wasn't sure.

"Okay, let's do it. As far as the steel goes, John, if that creek's not big enough to carry bodies downstream, it sure as hell won't be carrying any steel armor either. If things work out right, we can always come back and get it out later."

Carrying the six bodies to the creek took about ten minutes. Loosening the armor and weighting the corpses with rocks stuffed inside took at least twenty minutes. They had to hunt around for suitable rocks. But, eventually, it was done—and into the creek they went.

Fortunately, Geoffrey's estimate concerning the pool's depth was about right. They had to shove the bodies around a little bit with one of the spear things. What Morelli said was called a "halberd." But it didn't take long before all of them were submerged.

Before they pitched them in, of course, everybody drank their fill and they topped off the leather pouches the Spaniards had possessed in the way of canteens. Nobody wanted to drink from that creek afterward, not even upstream.

That night, again, James slept alongside Elaine. He insisted on keeping her wrapped up in the sheets. Between that and her wound, there wasn't going to be any sex involved, of course. Still, they could cuddle and kiss plenty well enough.

It was frustrating, maybe. But James was just as glad that, willy-nilly, they'd have some time to get to know each other better. Mostly, they talked about their former lives.

Elaine chuckled, at one point. "I think you're supposed to go out on at least one date first. You know, before you get engaged."

When Morelli woke him up before sunrise, to take his turn standing guard, the tall convict was grinning.

"Take a look," he said, pointing to one side of the clearing.

James looked over and couldn't help from laughing.

The children had returned sometime during the night.

All three of them were bundled up under one of the Spanish blankets with Geoffrey Kidd.

"Guess they figure he's their magic protector," said Dino.

"Yeah, some. But I think it's more the tattoos. Black or not, he must seem like something a little familiar."

Kidd's eyes opened. He stared at James and Dino, without moving a muscle otherwise. If he had, at least one of the kids would have been dislodged. They were pressed as close to him as puppies.

"It's a strange world," he observed, and closed his eyes again.

CHAPTER
～～ 40 ～～

The weeping willow stood tall in the midst of weeping cherry and dwarf apple trees, its long tendrils stretching to the ground in a curtain of green.

"How the hell . . ."

Hulbert looked at Jeff Edelman. "Can you explain *this*? We haven't seen anything since we left the town except ancient vegetation."

Edelman shook his head. "I have no idea, Rod. But this isn't the first time I've seen something like this. Whatever the Quiver was, it seems to have moved some other pieces of land besides the one Alexander sat on and scattered them all over the place. Nothing very big, though, not even close to the size of the prison's area." He pointed a finger. "Look at the terrain. It's not just the trees that are out of place. That land doesn't really match the surrounding landscape either. It looks tilted a little, and you can see where that stream undercutting the bank is recently formed."

"Will they bear fruit?" Andy asked.

"The dwarf apples should. I'm not sure about the weeping cherries. Some do, some don't. Whatever fruit they do bear won't be very big, though, and probably won't taste that good."

"Who cares? That's what the word 'horticulture' is for." Andy smiled wryly. "Not that I know much more than that about the subject. But what I do know is that if we have something to start with, we can eventually breed fruit trees that will bear good fruit."

"Take a few generations," Hulbert said doubtfully.

"And what else have we got?"

Andy was half-tempted to leave some people behind, to guard the small grove of precious fruit trees. But he didn't want to run the risk of weakening their forces before the upcoming battle with the Spaniards. He still didn't know exactly how many men were in de Soto's expedition. They might be outnumbered as badly as three to one.

"Too bad they're not maples," said Rod. "I love maple syrup."

"And what would you pour it over?" asked Jeff. "No wheat, remember? No pancakes."

"Don't be silly. If that corn the Cherokees found survives, you can make pancakes using cornmeal. That's how the Mexicans do it, usually. Except they call them hotcakes instead of pancakes. I've had some. They're not bad. *If* you've got maple syrup."

"So we'll make corn syrup instead," Andy said, a bit impatiently. "That's assuming we live past tomorrow. Speaking of which, let's get moving again."

He almost said "let's get the column moving again," but

refrained out of a lingering sense of embarrassment. He was hardly William Tecumseh Sherman leading the march to the sea. Andy had served a tour of duty in the Marines, but he'd never been in combat. He hadn't been old enough to join until the first Gulf war was over, and had left the service before the second one started. By one of those odd quirks of fate that seemed to be inseparable from military service, he'd wound up spending half his time in the Corps guarding the U.S. embassy in Paris. Boring as hell while you were on duty, sure—but once you were off duty, you were a young man in gay Paree.

"And you can have your maple syrup," he said. "Me, I wish I was back in Paris chowing down on a croque-monsieur. God, I loved Paris."

"What's a croque-monsieur?" asked Jeff.

"Grilled ham and cheese sandwich, basically. It's the French equivalent of a hamburger, except it's maybe eight times better."

Hulbert looked sour. "I don't like the French."

"Have you ever met a single Frenchman in your life, Rod? They're pretty thin on the ground in southern Illinois."

"No. So what? I know what and who I don't like."

Even if they hadn't been on campaign, there would have been no point to pursuing the debate. Andy liked Rod, but like most survivalists Hulbert's political attitudes tended to be somewhere to the right of Genghis Khan, insofar as Hulbert was interested in politics at all, which he generally wasn't.

Still, Rod knew the basics. Liberalism was the work of the debbil, the right to own guns was maybe second to godliness but a long way ahead of cleanliness, both coasts were dens of iniquity inhabited by wimps and fops— never mind that one of the men on the extraction team came from Oakland originally—and the French were the ultimate source of the world's wickedness. Well, the world's liberalism anyway, and the difference couldn't be pared with a razor.

On the other hand—such are the quirks of human nature—Hulbert didn't have any problem with abortion, and had serious doubts about prayer in school.

"Let's get going," Andy said.

Hulbert nodded, and turned his head. "Form up the column!" he bellowed. "We're moving out!"

He didn't have any qualms about playing soldier.

Barbara Ray's name tag said she was an LPN, but for the last five days she had been doctor, nurse, councilor and mother to sixty-three worried, frightened prison guards, a downed lieutenant, one newborn baby, and an overworked, ill RN. And at this moment she was playing the role of pastor, praying with two COs whose faith had been shaken by all that had happened.

Frank Nickerson watched her and sent a short prayer of thanks of his own. Without the woman's calming effect things would be a lot tougher to handle.

She had been the one who patched him together after that bastard Taylor got him with the toothbrush. As she sewed him up, she had done a good job calming his nerves with jokes about the scar's location and the stories he could tell. An occasional gentle pat had let him know that she was genuinely glad it wasn't any worse than it was. She was old-school, tough—a thing to be proud of. But everyone had their breaking point, and Frank was guessing she was getting pretty close to hers.

Marie Keehn was another woman who was old-school tough. But a lot of the guards were newbies, including Frank himself. They were getting anxious from the wait. They had too many hours on their hands and too many worries on their minds. They needed something to do.

The truth was, so did he.

Nickerson crossed the clearing; it was time to check on the guards posted at the camp's perimeter. Judith Barnett would need to be relieved. She wasn't old-school. She was too busy grieving to be reliable for more than a short stretch, and that pissed him off to the point he hated to talk to her. And he sure as hell didn't want to look at her. She hadn't stopped crying since Marie Keehn left. It was like the plumbing in her eyes had let go and she had a leaky faucet. Drip. Drip. Drip.

Frank wasn't natured up like the LPN. He was more like Lylah Caldwell. Barnett's wet face, bloodshot eyes, and snotty nose made the RN mad every time she saw the CO. He had pretty much the same reaction. Barnett was driving him nuts.

He was grieving too. He'd lost a wife who was barely more than a bride. They were all grieving. There was no one here who hadn't lost someone. There was no one here who hadn't been torn away from everything that meant something to them. But letting yourself collapse wasn't going to accomplish anything.

And neither would being short with the CO, he reminded himself, trying to restrain his temper.

It was hard, though. Especially when Frank thought about Joe Schuler.

Now there was a man who was not only old-school tough, he was a real leader. Here the lieutenant was fighting to take every breath, and what was he worried about? Everyone else. He wanted to know how the food was holding out, if there were any signs of the prisoners, if there had been any signs of wild animals. He wanted to know how everyone was holding up to the pressure. If he had been told about Judith Barnett's steady stream of tears, he wouldn't be impatient. He would simply be concerned about her.

Nickerson increased the length of his stride. A middle-aged guard with short hair and a wide face turned toward him as he approached the outer edge of the clearing. He watched as a tear rolled in slow motion from her right eye, slid down the side of her nose, dripped from her top lip to her bottom lip, and then down her chin. The drop of salty liquid fell to her shirt in what seemed to be the same slow pace it had used to travel the length of her face. He reached out and patted her shoulder. Gently, he said, "I'm your relief. Try to get some rest, Judith."

But what he thought was: *Marie, hurry up and get back with Captain Blacklock. I'm not cut out to be the boss-man.*

"Lylah," Lieutenant Joe Schuler whispered.

The RN moved close enough to hear what the man had to say.

"How is everyone doing?"

Lylah Caldwell shrugged. "They're okay. A little antsy, but they'll get over that."

"I'm cold."

"It's the fever, Joe. My guess is you're at about a hundred and three." She wet his forehead with a damp rag she had made by ripping her undershirt.

Using his good hand he reached for her hand and the water-soaked rag. "You said there was a stream. Does it have rocks in the bottom of it, or is it sand or mud?"

She gently pushed his hand away and said, "A little of each. Some sand, some mud, and then a lot of rocks."

"Are the rocks good sized?"

The nurse nodded.

"Throwing size, like a baseball?"

"Yes, I think so. A lot of them are bigger than that, and some smaller. But there would be quite a few that size." She waited a couple of minutes for him to continue; when he didn't say anything more she asked, "Why did you ask?"

He closed his eyes and said, "It might be a good idea to stack some of them in piles around the camp . . . in case wild animals . . ." He gave a small cough and grabbed the nurse's hand. "Damn, this hurts."

Five minutes later his grip on her hand relaxed, and his breathing slowed slightly and became a little deeper.

She waited until she was sure the lieutenant was asleep and then crawled out of the cave. Marie had put Frank Nickerson in charge, so he was the one she would tell about the rocks.

Marie Keehn spotted a tree the size she was looking for and jogged toward it. It was about eighteen inches in diameter; plenty big enough to hold her weight, and tall enough she could get fifteen to twenty feet off the ground.

That was high enough the mosquitoes wouldn't follow her. Best of all, it was the first tree she'd spotted in the last two hours that had the right spread of branches, creating a sort of hollow cup in the fork that—she hoped—would be big enough and deep enough for her to sleep in without falling out of the tree.

She needed the rest. Badly. And as much as she didn't like the idea of sleeping in a tree, she didn't think she had a choice any longer. The terrain she'd been passing through for the last two days was flat. She hadn't seen anything close to a cave and didn't expect to.

She'd been traveling for five days and, except for that first night, had not slept much. The only "caves" she'd found hadn't been much more than rock overhangs. She'd only been able to sleep fitfully under them, waking up constantly at the sound of anything.

She hadn't slept at all the night just past, since she hadn't even been able to find an overhang and was unwilling to sleep out in the open. As stupid as it might be, that nightmare image of being accidentally squashed in her sleep by a passing dinosaur had never gone away.

She'd had little to drink for the last twenty-four hours, and nothing to eat in the last forty-eight. She couldn't afford the time to hunt and process the food while she traveled. Besides, she had nothing to hunt with but her walking stick. And so far she hadn't seen anything small enough to club to death with it that wasn't too fast to catch.

She shuddered. She'd seen some *big* animals, though. Four times. They'd looked to be the size of eighteen-wheelers, although she knew that was probably a trick of her imagination. They certainly couldn't be as heavy as a fully loaded tractor-trailer.

Luckily, they were all herbivores. None of them seemed to mind her walking past them. In fact, only one of them had seemed to notice her at all.

That hadn't reassured her any. In fact, it made her nightmare scenario seem less irrational. If the dinosaurs she'd seen were oblivious to her presence in the daytime, while she was moving, they'd pay no attention to her at all at night while she was sleeping.

She'd look like a pancake. No, worse. A squished little bug on a windshield.

Better to fall out of a tree.

Using the branches like rungs on a ladder she made her way up the trunk of the tree. When people starved, they tended to sleep more. It was a way to charge their battery. She knew she was a long way from starvation, but the lack of food combined with the intense exercise she had endured over the last few days was enough to sap her energy. Even a couple of hours napping would help. And if she were lucky, the wind would pick up a little so when she climbed back down she wouldn't have to fight off the swarms of mosquitoes she'd encountered once she entered the lowlands.

Who ordered mosquitoes in Jurassic Park, anyway? she thought sourly. You'd think dinosaurs would be enough.

Mosquitoes could—and did—kill. She'd heard from her father about elks in Alaska being drained down to skin and bones by the bloodsuckers. That would have been enough to make her wary, all by itself. But once, while in Canada, she'd seen a young deer lying on its side, covered in mosquitoes, too weak to get on its feet. That memory was enough to scare her silly.

According to what Hulbert had told her, and her own best guess, she was not much more than a day's walk from where the Cherokees were supposed to be. She was hoping like hell that Hulbert and Blacklock were there. If they weren't, she hoped whoever it was she found was friendly because she needed food, water, and rest.

The water was the most important thing. She'd managed all right, at first, when it came to finding water. But once she reached the lowlands, she hadn't done so well. Unarmed, she was unwilling to risk getting near any large bodies of water. Leaving aside the danger of predators, most of those bodies of water were surrounded by treacherous-looking soil. Her nightmare about being squashed by a dinosaur might be a new one, but she had other nightmares that went back a long ways. Even as a kid, the thought of getting caught in quicksand had been frightening. Drowning, she could handle. Drowning in mud was a little much.

She was dehydrated enough she had started to run a fever. And her reflexes had slowed considerably. And she was starting to get dizzy spells.

She settled into the fork of the branches. As she'd hoped, the cup they formed was big enough to hold her. She leaned back against the trunk and looked toward the sky. She ached all over. The day before, while working her way around an area of steaming, sulfur-laced geysers, she'd taken a tumble. She'd managed to crawl out of the hollow easily enough, but she knew she'd been lucky. She was scraped and bruised, but not broken.

She was so tired. She wasn't sure what she was running

on now. She figured it was stubbornness or habit. It didn't matter which one, though. When a person got down that low, they either got help soon or they didn't make it.

Where are ya, my fella? I need ya. Ignoring strange sounds coming from somewhere in the distance and the occasional tear of exhaustion that dripped down her face, she tried to picture the way Hulbert looked when he left the prison. A moment later she was asleep.

CHAPTER
⸙ 41 ⸙

Jerry Bailey hissed between gritted teeth. A little over two weeks back, the soft-spoken guard hadn't so much as twitched when Hulbert, Carmichael and Keehn used him as bait when they were hunting. But today, looking across the open area toward the pre-Mound Indian village, his face was pale and he'd broken into a sweat. The village was less than a hundred yards from where he and Rod lay hidden. And even though things were quieter now, the screams of the children and the sobs of the women could be heard too well.

The Spaniards had beaten them to the village.

Hulbert didn't bother answering or use the binoculars tucked into a leather case attached to his belt. They were close enough he could see every gory detail of what was happening. The smell of burned flesh was heavy in the air, mixed with the stink of whatever the Indians had used to make their huts instead of grass. Two of the huts were burning fiercely. De Soto's men must have tossed the

488

bodies into the huts and set them aflame, as a quick and simple way to get rid of them. Knowing the bastards, Rod was sure they hadn't bothered to make sure everyone they tossed in was dead already.

Now, the same bastards were busy ensuring the people they had captured would remain docile slaves. They'd only kept alive the younger adults and the children, to begin with. Old slaves—even middle-aged ones—were of no interest to them. It looked as though they'd beaten all four of the males with whips, and at least one of the women. The six women had been separated out from the rest of the captives, who were all tied together with ropes around their necks. They'd be providing entertainment for the conquistadores that evening, presumably.

"We need to move, Rod," Bailey said. "Now. Those people can't take any more."

The lieutenant shook his head. "No. We wait for the signal. They've stopped whatever killings and atrocities they were carrying out because they're getting ready to leave. But it'll be at least twenty minutes before the Spaniards start moving out."

Andy Blacklock had divided his forces in half and placed one group—they were calling them platoons for lack of a better term—under Rod's command. Hulbert and his platoon had been ordered to stay in place, just out of sight behind the screen of trees surrounding the clearing where the village was located. They were to hold their fire until the captain signaled.

Privately, Rod thought Andy was being too cautious, but he hadn't put up an argument. Right or not, the man was the boss, and these were battlefield conditions.

Still, he thought his own platoon could have handled the situation by themselves. They had modern repeating rifles and Rod knew from personal experience just how slow and clumsy matchlocks were.

Besides, leaving aside the weaponry, the more Rod saw of these famous conquistadores, the lower became his opinion of them—militarily, not simply morally. They might be tough as nails individually, sure, but they seemed no more disciplined than a street gang. And even less well organized. The one group of Spaniards milling around closest to Rod numbered about sixty or seventy men. They seemed to be under the command—if you could use the term at all—of a committee of four or five sergeants. And the sergeants seemed to spend most of their time arguing with each other.

Arguing about what, it was hard to know, given the crude nature of the operation. Probably arguing about whether to rape the women now or wait until nightfall.

Hulbert, realizing he was holding his breath out of sheer anger, forced himself to resume his normal slow, easy breathing.

Andy, where the hell is that signal?

Blacklock had gone one way, off to Hulbert's left, and Watkins and his Cherokees and the U.S. soldiers off to the right. The two leaders were working partway around the big clearing, far enough to encircle it as much as possible without running the risk of getting into a crossfire.

The plan was simple enough. Andy figured—with Watkins' smile confirming his guess—that the Cherokees could get in position faster than his own people. So, once Andy was ready, he'd give the signal.

The signal would be as simple as the plan. Blacklock and his platoon would just start shooting.

No warning, nothing. Whatever lingering thoughts any of them might have had about negotiating with the conquistadores went up with the flaming huts. Even Andy, with his incredible self-control, had reached the limit.

"I want all of them dead," he'd said quietly. As even-tempered as the man was—he was something of a legend, that way, among the prison guards—there was no mistaking the fury lurking beneath the words. "As many as we can manage, anyway. And we're not taking any prisoners, either. We never did get anything worth getting out of that one shithead we caught."

Rod had spotted Watkins' expression, when Andy said that. The Cherokee chief seemed to be suppressing a smile.

Ross didn't have any trouble figuring out the reason. Not knowing what else to do, Andy had decided to leave the prisoner in the town when the expedition set off.

Stephen McQuade was still back there too. The man's wounds were healing, well enough, but he wasn't in good enough shape yet to participate in any battles. On the other hand, he wouldn't have any trouble using a knife.

For that matter, neither would Susan Fisher, on a trussed-up prisoner. Between the two of them, had Rod been in that Spaniard's boots, he'd have much rather faced McQuade. There was something implacable about the little Cherokee medicine woman.

By the time they got back, McQuade and Fisher would have discovered whatever it was that Spaniard knew. Their notions of suitable interrogation methods were decidedly nineteenth-century frontier. Rod was quite sure of that.

He was just as sure that the man would be dead. He'd come to like the Cherokees, as he'd gotten to know them. But he didn't much doubt that under that sophisticated surface, at least when it got provoked, there was a spirit just about a savage as any Apache's or Comanche's.

A fusillade erupted, coming from the area where Blacklock had taken his people. An instant later, the gunshots sounding much deeper, came a fusillade from the Cherokees and Sergeant Kershner's men.

"Fire!" Bailey shouted.

Rod had told Jerry to give the signal. He didn't want to be distracted from his own immediate task.

Moscoso was there. Rod had spotted him almost at once. Not hard to do, since he was one of the arguing sergeants.

Hulbert had never stopped tracking him with his rifle since.

He was tempted to gut-shoot the bastard, as angry as he was. But he didn't break training and habit. The sniper's triangle was his target.

The shot took Moscoso right above the breastbone, rupturing the aorta. Blood spouted everywhere as he went down.

He was *still* tempted to gut-shoot the bastard. But that was pointless. Moscoso was dead and they didn't have ammunition to spare.

In the distance, maybe a hundred yards from the village and over two hundred yards from Hulbert's position, there was a man on horseback surrounded by several other horsemen. That might be de Soto himself. It was worth hoping for, anyway. Rod had kept him under surveillance also.

He went down. Then, the horseman next to him. Then, the one on his other side. Shooting from a prone position with a rifle at this range—about two hundred and twenty yards—Rod Hulbert might as well have been called the Grim Reaper.

He took down two more of the horsemen in that center group before the rest scattered. Thereafter, it was slower work.

Hulbert concentrated on the horsemen he could see at a distance, ignoring the bulk of the Spanish troops milling around outside the village. The closest of those soldiers weren't more than a hundred yards away, and the farthest not more than two hundred. Any guard could hit that target, especially as bunched up as they were.

Hulbert did take a moment to survey the battle, to see how it was going.

"Battle, my ass," he muttered. "This is a turkey shoot. I *knew* we could have handled it on our own."

"Quit bragging," said Bailey. He aimed and fired again. "Even if you're right."

Rod estimated there were somewhere between four and five hundred Spaniards in the little army they were facing. That meant the numerical odds were worse than two to one, abstractly. But that was reckoning "numbers" by a crude head count. Once you factored in the force multiplier that the repeating rifles gave the prison guards, the odds switched drastically. In the same time it took a conquistador to fire and reload one of their matchlocks, a guard could go through a ten-round magazine—aiming every shot, not just blasting away. Measuring by firepower instead of men, the advantage was actually five to one in favor of the prison guards. That wasn't even counting the Cherokees and the U.S. soldiers, who were also firing.

Much better than five-to-one, actually, since you also had to factor in the much greater accuracy of the modern rifles. A sixteenth-century matchlock wasn't accurate beyond fifty yards, if that far. A number of shots had been fired by the Spaniards since the fighting started, but Rod was sure that if anyone on his side had been hit, it was pure bad luck. They were all sheltered behind trees and logs, and the Spaniards were out in the open.

At least one person in charge over there seemed to have finally realized it, too. Out of the swirling chaos of hundreds of conquistadores caught completely by surprise, somebody was managing to bring some order and discipline to a group of about thirty of them. And then— ruthless bastard, but smart—he was moving the group behind the tied-up villagers, using them for a shield.

Several of the guards were now yelling at the captives to lie down, but those poor people were even more frightened and confused than the Spaniards. Most of them were children. Besides, throwing yourself to the ground when you were tied to the person next to you by a rope around the neck was a good way to get strangled unless everybody did it in unison.

"Fuck," Rod hissed.

Bailey was looking off to the right, where Watkins and the Cherokees had taken position. "What the hell . . . Rod, what are they *doing*?"

Hulbert looked over. Sergeant Kershner and his squad had moved out into the open area surrounding the village, and were forming up into a line. Then, at a shouted command from Kershner, they started marching around to the side.

"They're going to get behind the Spaniards, so they can't use the villagers for a shield. Jesus. Talk about raw guts."

Seven men against perhaps thirty—and Kershner's men were armed with muzzle-loading muskets, not semi-automatic rifles. As firearms, shot for shot, their Harpers Ferry Model 1816 flintlocks were considerably superior to the Spaniards' matchlocks. But they couldn't be reloaded all that much more quickly. Once those U.S. soldiers fired a volley, they'd be dead meat if the Spaniards charged. All they'd have to counter the Spanish halberds and swords would be nineteen-inch bayonets. Rod's low opinion of the conquistadores as a military force did not extend to sneering at their ability to use edged weapons at close range. In that situation, they'd be murderous.

"Come on," he said. He rose and waved his hand at the rest of his platoon. "Follow me!"

He started trotting. Not directly toward the looming confrontation between Kershner's men and that one group of Spaniards, but in a looping route that took him around the still-milling mass outside the village. He thought he and his men could get there before the Spaniards charged Kershner after that first volley was fired.

But it soon became clear his crude flanking maneuver wasn't going to work. The problem wasn't any shrewd countermove on the part of the enemy, it was just the sheer chaos of the situation. Ragged groups of conquista-dores were peeling away from the big mob in the center—that was just a killing zone by now—and heading toward the shelter of the trees. Some of them were confused enough to run toward Rod and his men instead of away from them.

"Oh, *fuck*." Rod stopped and gestured for his platoon to come to a halt. They were going to have to fire what amounted to their own volleys just to clear a path.

Kevin Griffin gave Geoffrey Watkins a sly little smile. "I *told* you he'd be strong-headed."

Watkins didn't respond. He was chewing on his lower lip, trying to decide what to do.

On the one hand, he didn't have that many more men than the Spanish group Kershner was going at. And the muskets they had weren't much better.

On the other hand . . .

"Let's go," he growled. "I don't want to have to listen to my niece yelling at me for the next year or two."

Griffin chuckled. "She yells pretty good." He stood up and waved the Cherokees forward.

Andy Blacklock was trying to decide what to do also. His battle plan had worked just about the way he'd hoped it would, until those Spaniards started using the villagers for a shield. Now, what had been a completely one-sided fight—not even a battle, so much as huge firing squad in action—was likely to become a hand-to-hand melee. Up close, he was quite sure the Spaniards would be a far deadlier opponent.

But he didn't see where he really had much choice.

So, he too rose and waved his people forward. Then, when they were more or less lined up, they advanced on the enemy in a formation that wasn't much better organized than the shattered Spanish army. The training that prison guards got did not include battlefield tactics. It sure as hell didn't include precision marching.

"*Go, Salukis!*" Brian Carmichael shouted. Within two or three seconds, more than half the guards in Andy's platoon were shouting the same slogan. Then many of the guards in Hulbert's platoon started doing the same. Just before they stopped, more or less lined up, and started firing into the mob of Spaniards at close range. And most of them kept shouting the slogan as they fired.

"This is nuts," Andy muttered to himself. But the shouting was contagious, and it impelled everyone forward at a much quicker pace.

"Go, Salukis!" he shouted. "Go right at 'em!"

Whether it was the strange slogan—which couldn't have made any sense at all to de Soto's men—or simply the sight of dozens of guards in blue uniforms charging at them after they'd already seen half of their own forces gunned down, or whether it was Hulbert's platoon's deadly close-range fire coming from another angle, Andy would never know.

Nor care. All that mattered was that the Spaniards broke. Not more than a dozen shots were fired from their matchlocks, and they were off and running. A goodly number of them threw their heavy guns away as they ran.

"Halt! Halt!" he shouted. "Goddamittohell, come to a screeching fucking-STOP! Right now!"

After a second or two, his people obeyed him. Andy pointed at the fleeing Spaniards. "Shoot them. Now. While they're still in range."

That was just murder, really. Andy had read a little military history and knew that what he was doing came under the euphemism of "pursuit," even if his people were standing still and just shooting. But what the term really meant was *kick 'em when they're down and keep kicking until they're meatpaste.*

It didn't occur to him, until the shooting had almost stopped because there weren't any enemies still in sight, to wonder what had happened to Kershner and his squad.

"I knew they'd break," Kershner told Watkins calmly. "These men might have been soldiers once, but they're nothing but killers now. One good volley taking down three or four of them, and they ran."

Geoffrey still thought the youngster was probably a lunatic. But . . .

The Spaniards *had* broken. By the time Watkins and Griffin and the Cherokees arrived to save Kershner and his men, they didn't need saving. They'd just been reloading their muskets.

He looked at the villagers. By now, they'd managed to get themselves all on the ground, out of the line of fire. So far as he could tell, not one of them had been shot. That was a minor miracle, in itself.

"Cut them loose, Kevin."

Griffin nodded and trotted over to the villagers. They flinched, when they saw him pull out his knife, but relaxed once they realized he was just cutting the ropes away.

"Now what?" asked Kershner.

Watkins surveyed the scene. The open area around the village was piled with bodies. Piled high, in some places. You could literally walk across it stepping only on Spaniards, except for a few clear patches here and there.

This had just been butchery—and it wasn't over yet.

"Captain Blacklock said he doesn't want any prisoners. But I don't think he's really got the stomach for it. Do you?"

Kershner's blue eyes scanned the field. "I'm Swabian, you know. Wasn't born there, but I know all the stories. For centuries, men just like these slaughtered and murdered and pillaged and raped back and forth across my people's lands. Any time some villagers got their hands on some of them, they didn't take any prisoners either. So, yes, I've got the stomach for it."

He turned to his men. "You heard him, boys. This is what bayonets are for."

Watkins had always thought those bayonets were a little silly-looking. After watching for a couple of minutes, he changed his mind.

CHAPTER
∽ 42 ∽

"Hulbert, look. Can you believe what you're seeing?" Jerry Bailey's voice was gruff, but filled with humor. Then the man laughed aloud. "Man, oh man, how good can it get?"

Confused, Hulbert looked. Bailey was pointing to an area between two of the huts.

Ten brown and tan puppies, no longer than a man's palm, squirmed and whimpered as they tried to get their mother to care for them. The mother couldn't. She'd been hit by a bullet during the battle. But the puppies were fine. Alive and well.

His brows drew into a frown. The dogs the Spaniards had were vicious creatures trained to maim and kill on command. A number of them had been shot in the battle, several of them while trying to attack the oncoming prison guards. He wanted no part of those dogs. It'd be like trying to keep half-tame wolves.

But that was mostly because of the way the dogs had

been reared. And these dogs might have belonged to the villagers anyway. They looked like they might be part coyote.

Starting with puppies . . .

He thought of Marie Keehn and had to swallow hard in order to control his emotions. Marie liked dogs. If he could bring her a puppy, she would feel like she had been given a little piece of home.

"Come on," he said. "Let's get us a pair of hunting dogs before the women scoop them up for pets."

Bailey's grin was as wide as Hulbert's. "The dogs at the prison have all been fixed. I thought that meant the species was probably a goner." He followed Hulbert, just one step behind. "They won't be as tame as what we're used to."

"It doesn't matter what they are, they're close enough to dogs for me. We can always breed out the undesirable characteristics, and work towards the good ones." Rod knelt down in order to get a better look at the pups.

Jerry squatted next to him. "What are we going to call it?" he asked.

"Call what?"

"What's happening to some of the animals we're running across?" Bailey pointed at the pups. "When the last of something dies out, we say it's gone extinct. But, if something from the future dies out, it's not extinction. It can't be. I mean, how can a species die out before it evolves?"

Rod shook his head. "That's Edelman's department. Or Carmichael's, I guess, if you don't believe in evolution." He rolled one of the whimpering pups onto its back and rubbed its belly. "You found them, Jerry. You get pick of litter."

It didn't take the CO long to choose. The brown and black, chubby little female whimpered then growled when he picked her up, but quickly settled down and sucked and nipped at his pinky finger. "Uh-oh, Hulbert. It looks like we've been spotted. If you want one of these, you better hurry. Marilyn's headed this way and she looks like a woman on a mission."

Marilyn Traber was wearing the exact same grin Bailey wore. "Don't even think of hogging all of them, guys. I'm warning you. Don't go there."

Grin or no grin, she looked downright threatening.

"Yeah, sure, Marilyn. Pick whichever one you want. Except—" Quickly, Rod made his choice. Jerry had picked a female, so he'd pick a male. That way, between them, they'd have a breeding pair. "This one."

"And now a mystery must be resolved," said Watkins. "Who or what is 'saluki'?"

Andy Blacklock smiled. "Well, it's a little embarrassing. It didn't even occur to me we might need a battle cry. Luckily, somebody improvised. A saluki is a type of dog. More to the point, it's the mascot SIU chose for its sports teams."

The Cherokee chief got a long-suffering look on his face. "And who is Essayeyou?"

"Oh. Sorry. It stands for Southern Illinois University. The campus at Carbondale is the closest university to us. Was the closest, anyway. Most of the guards rooted for them."

"They dug up roots for them? Why? They were paid *that* badly as guards?"

Andy got a long-suffering look on his face.

Marilyn Traber found a reed basket inside one of the Indian huts. The ten small puppies were tucked inside it and covered with a swatch of cloth cut from a cape worn by one of the Spaniards.

The pups were very young; not all of them had their eyes open. Traber was not so young. Life had opened her eyes a long time back. And she knew too well that dealing with the horrors of this new world would probably open them a little more. But none of that mattered. Not right this minute. Now, nothing mattered except these ten, warm, squirming fragments of normalcy.

She lifted a corner of the improvised blanket and took another peek at them. Looking at them made her feel good. She then flashed a grin at the two COs standing nearby. Winnfield and Sharps were taking their orders to defend the small creatures seriously. They scanned the forest almost continuously, determined neither man nor beast would be allowed to hurt the ten small canines.

Three of the pups were promised out. She, Bailey, and Hulbert had already staked their claims. But the other seven were up for grabs. There was going to be a lottery when they got back to the prison, and seven lucky winners would become the owners of the seven unclaimed pups.

The puppies would survive. She knew there was a case of canned milk at the Cherokee Indian camp. It had been packed in with their other supplies. There was another case of the stuff back at the prison.

There was also an eyedropper in Jenny Radford's emergency bag.

"We did not kill all of the Spaniards," Watkins said "We're not even sure the horseman Lieutenant Hulbert shot was actually de Soto. None of us knows what he looked like."

Andy nodded, accepting the Cherokee chief's assessment. He'd never really expected they could kill all of the conquistadores. Not with just one battle. This one had gone as well as you could ask for, but things would get a lot harder from now on. They'd had the huge advantage of catching the Spaniards completely by surprise. De Soto and his men hadn't even known of their existence until the prison guards started firing.

Now, they did. And there were still at least two hundred of them alive. Most of them were still armed, too. With swords and halberds, if nothing else. They'd run out of ammunition quickly, though. The Spaniards had abandoned all of their pack mounts and supplies except whatever they were carrying on their persons when they were routed. The one cart they'd had was also now in the possession of Blacklock's people—and it obviously carried most of the expedition's powder and shot.

Still, it was going to get hairy. Having a couple of hundred murderers running around loose with swords was bound to get hairy.

De Soto finally rallied his men, once they got perhaps a mile and a half from the slaughter at the village.

"Rallied," at least, in the sense of getting them to stop running. There was no possibility of getting them to return to the battle. The carnage there had been incredible.

Whoever those blue-uniformed strangers were, their muskets were deadly beyond belief.

De Soto knew, because he'd been able to watch the entire battle from behind shelter. He'd dismounted and gone into the shrubbery to relieve himself, just before the ambush took place.

He'd been lucky. If he'd still been on his horse with his top lieutenants, de Soto didn't doubt at all that he'd have been the first one shot instead of Hernandez. Whoever had been the sniper targeting the expedition's commanders, his marksmanship was satanic.

Moscoso was dead, too. De Soto was sure of that, even though he hadn't seen him killed. He'd sent Moscoso to bring order to one of the companies of his army, and that had been the company that received the worst casualties. Only a handful of the men in that company had come out alive, and Luis had not been one of them.

At least de Soto had kept his horse. He was now one of only three men in his expedition still on horseback.

He glared down at his men. They glared right back at him.

The first thing to do was to reestablish his authority, of course. But de Soto was not particularly concerned about that. He was very good at establishing authority.

"We will have our revenge!" he shouted, drawing his sword.

"What do we do with the bodies?" Edelman asked. He grimaced, looking over the field.

Andy had been considering the matter himself. The bodies of the dead Spaniards had been stripped of everything. Clothes as well as the armor, tools, and weapons they'd had on them. Any and all of that stuff could prove useful in the future, and they'd been able to round up enough horses to haul the stuff back on the travois the Cherokees had made. The pack mounts were already fully loaded.

That left the bodies themselves, piled naked in horrid stacks.

Andy didn't much like the answer he'd come up with, but he could live with it. The most important thing was to get back to the Cherokee town as soon as possible—and then, back to the prison. By now, the COs he'd left behind to guard the convicts would be nearing exhaustion.

"Nothing, is what we do," he said harshly. He moved his head in a little circling motion. "There'll be scavengers out there who'll do the work for us."

He took a deep breath. "Except Yost and Littleton, of course. I don't want to bury them here, though. Even in this heat and humidity, we can get their bodies back to the town in time for a funeral there."

Hulbert looked a bit skeptical. "Well . . . yeah. But forget any idea of carrying them all the way back to Alexander."

They'd lost two of the guards in the battle. Both from gunshot wounds, both of which were obviously stray shots. The two men had been killed before the charge started, while still behind shelter. But the Spaniards had gotten off a lot of shots in that first minute or two, and it was only to be expected that a few of them would hit something they'd been aimed in the general direction of, even if only by accident.

Perhaps ironically, the Spaniards had fired many fewer

shots once the charge started. By sheer happenstance—
Andy certainly couldn't claim the credit for it—the charge
had caught most of the Spaniards while they were still
reloading their guns. A half dozen other guards had
gotten wounded then, mostly by edged weapons when
they got too close. But only Steve Adams had been hurt
badly enough to require being carried on a stretcher, and
his injury wasn't life-threatening as long as they could
keep it from getting infected.

The casualties had been much fewer than Andy had
expected, actually. But they were still a blow. Yost had
been a new guard, whom nobody really knew. So while his
death was a matter of concern, it didn't cause anyone any
personal grief. Ted Littleton, on the other hand, had
worked at the prison for years and had been well liked.
Andy himself had spent more evenings than he could
remember having a beer and a pleasant conversation with
the man after work.

Watkins didn't say anything, but his opinion was
obvious. It wouldn't be fair to say the Cherokee chief was
callous, as such. But he had a very thick hide and wasn't
given to fretting over indignities suffered by his enemies.
Certainly not dead ones.

"The much bigger problem," Edelman said, "is what to
do with the captives we freed."

Andy had been skirting around that problem. They'd
rescued twenty-three of the villagers. Thirteen of them
were children.

No babies or very young children, though. The
Spaniards had butchered those. Apparently, they'd only
wanted children big enough to make the march to the

coast. To have a chance, rather. Some of them would have died along the way, even if there'd still been a coast to reach at the end of the forced march.

After Andy saw a baby in one of the huts whose skull had been crushed by a musket butt, he stopped having any qualms about the work Kershner and his men had been doing. For a moment, he'd just had a fierce wish that the rifle he was carrying was equipped with a bayonet.

And he stopped second-guessing himself about whether or not he should have tried to parlay with de Soto. From now on, as far as he was concerned, the only good conquistador was a dead conquistador.

That still left the problem of the captives. If they simply left them here, he didn't think they had much chance of surviving. Not most of the kids, for sure. Andy's experience with the Cherokees had taught him not to underestimate the survival skills of so-called "primitive peoples," but these Indians were on a much lower cultural level than very sophisticated and often literate Cherokees. They were in a world they didn't know at all, and had just lost everyone in their village old enough to have really known very much. Even the adult captives were young, no older than their early twenties.

On the other hand, Andy wasn't sure at all how the captives would react if the guards simply started marching them along. There was a complete language barrier, for the Cherokees as much as for the modern Americans. Watkins and his people had no idea what language the captives were speaking. It wasn't any Indian language they knew, although Kevin Griffin thought some of the words sounded like garbled Choctaw.

Andy wished Jenny were here. She was the only one of them with any experience at all when it came to dealing with a situation like this.

"Why you get paid the big bucks," he muttered.

"I'll see what I can do," he said, and headed toward the captives. They were still huddled together in a group.

They watched him come, all of them down to the littlest and youngest child. They were obviously apprehensive, but Andy had no idea if they were scared of him, or by him—or perhaps simply scared that he might leave them.

When he reached the group of captives, he turned and pointed in the direction of the Cherokee town. He didn't accompany the gesture with any words. Words as such were pointless, and he'd just feel stupid doing another recitation of poetry.

Then, he made a circling gesture that, more or less, indicated the entire group of guards and their Cherokee allies. He felt stupid as it was. Then, made a *really* stupid sort of gesture that—he hoped—would get across the idea that all of them were leaving now, headed for the town.

Finally, he half-bowed and made a gesture with both hands that—he hoped—would convey the idea that the captives were welcome to join. Without—he hoped—implying any sort of coercion.

Apparently, he was something of a genius at jury-rigged sign language. It didn't take the adult captives more than twenty seconds to look at each other, jabber something back and forth, and then start nodding at him.

It didn't occur to him until much later that maybe a headnod wasn't a human gesture that meant the same thing to every group of people who'd ever lived. But, by then, it was a moot point. Clearly enough, it meant the same thing to *this* group of people.

If there was any point at which a corner was turned, Marilyn Traber provided it. After they'd marched maybe two hundred yards, she said: "Put the kids on the cart. I bet they'll get a charge out of that."

And so they did. In fact, before the first minute was up, they were squealing gleefully. They couldn't all fit at once, of course, so pretty soon Marilyn was having to arbitrate whose turn it was. She managed that pretty well, given that she and the kids didn't speak the same language.

If Andy remembered right, the inhabitants of the New World hadn't ever used wheeled transport until the Spanish and Portuguese arrived. It was obvious that this group of native Americans had never seen wheeled transport. It took a lot longer to coax the adults onto the cart. One of the young women just flatly refused, and never relented until they reached their destination. Then, with the cart safely unhitched from the horses, she climbed up on it. But she only stayed there for a few seconds before hastily clambering down.

The poor horses having to haul the cart looked long-suffering. The Spaniards had loaded the cart heavily to begin with, even before the human cargo got added.

But Andy wasn't worried about that. The horses that de Soto's expedition had brought with them were on the small side, true. But they were obviously hardy. Carmichael and Hulbert said they were some sort of jennets, and then fell to arguing about whether they were more like modern Sorraias, Spanish Barbs or Andalusians.

Horse enthusiasts. Andy thought they probably suffered from a mild form of mental disease. A variant of obsessive-compulsive disorder, maybe.

The horses looked still more long-suffering when Kershner and his men insisted on piling the four pigs they'd caught onto the cart, too. Trussed and bound. They were taking no chances that their culinary future might get jeopardized by escaping into the wilds.

Which was where they belonged, in Andy's opinion. Those had to be the ugliest-looking pigs he'd ever seen. Long-snouted and looking as tough as wild boars.

Salt pork and potatoes sauced in hog lard sounded bad enough to begin with. He could only imagine what it would taste like with pigs like this for the main entrée—and he didn't even want to try to imagine what sort of substitute Kershner and his soldiers would eventually turn up for potatoes.

To each his own. Andy had thought that was a good motto to live by even in the world he'd come from. In this new one, it was pretty much a necessity.

A pack of twenty troodontids broke off their stalking of a nearby herd of hadrosaurs and looked at each other.

There was a new scent in the air. A very powerful scent, too. It was an unfamiliar odor mixed with one they knew well, the smell of blood. Something—or some many things—had been killed recently.

They were hungry. Confused, too. The hunting had changed and they were trying to adapt. Out of desperation, they'd even started stalking the hadrosaurs, although their prey was much larger than anything they were comfortable attacking. None of the troodontids weighed more than two hundred pounds. Even the smallest hadrosaur calf was much bigger than that.

They didn't recognize the new scent, except for the blood. But they didn't recognize many scents any longer. And one thing was clear. Whatever was producing that scent, it possessed the most prized trait of all prey.

It was already dead.

The oldest female sniffed the air once more and then turned north. The others followed her lead.

CHAPTER
∽∽ **43** ∽∽

Marie Keehn looked at the smoke rising in the distance. She was too numb to cry. Instead she took off her shoes and socks and looked at her feet. She had blisters on both heels and her right foot had blisters on three of her five toes. Her shoes, fine for an eight- or sixteen-hour shift at the prison, weren't suited for a long trek through a wilderness.

She had thought she would find Alexander's staff and the Cherokees today. But that wasn't going to happen. Ten minutes back she had spotted smoke from what should be their camp. The location wasn't exactly where she had been led to believe it would be, but it was close. It was also about three miles away. On a good day, she could walk that distance in less than two hours, even across rough terrain, but today was not a good day. She was moving at a snail's pace. She guessed she still had a three- to four-hour hike ahead of her, and the sun was less than ten minutes from setting.

At least she'd found a cave to sleep in tonight. More

like a horizontal crevice in a short cliff than a cave, really, but it'd do. Especially since it was a steep twenty foot climb to reach it. That climb had used up her strength, for the moment. She could only hope it would look too chancy for any would-be nocturnal predator.

Of which she hadn't seen any signs, anyway. Not once during the whole trek. So far as she could tell, all the dangerous predators in this world seemed to hunt by daylight. Whatever night hunters there might be were probably too small to see her as suitable prey.

It didn't matter. She'd rather deal with nocturnal predators than risk sleeping in a tree again. She'd almost fallen out of the tree twice during that horrible night—and when she finally woke up in the morning discovered that she'd somehow wound up twisting herself completely around in the fork. Her head was where her feet had started.

How she'd managed to do that *without* falling out of the tree was a complete mystery. The first and only case of possible divine intervention Marie had ever seen.

Once she reconciled herself to another night alone, though, she started feeling better about the situation. True, she hadn't eaten in days—she wasn't even sure how many, any longer—but it had been long enough the hunger was gone. And she'd come across a small creek early in the day, so she'd had plenty to drink and had managed to refill her improvised canteen.

That meant, come dawn, she'd still have the reserves to get to where she was going.

"In the morning, babes," she whispered, as the last rays of sunlight disappeared.

CHAPTER
44

"Don't shoot, Nickerson. We're not looking for trouble."

Hearing the soft voice coming from somewhere in the woods close to him, Frank Nickerson froze for an instant. Then, quickly, he crouched and began scanning the area, his pistol ready.

"I said, 'don't shoot.' And we're over here."

The voice was accompanied by a rustling branch. Frank's eyes could see it moving, when he pinpointed the location of the voice and the noise. But he still couldn't see anyone.

Another voice came from a different part of the woods, about four o'clock from the rustling branch and the first voice.

"I can take him if he tries anything, James."

"Don't *you* get trigger-happy either, Geoffrey."

A laugh came from the area when Frank had heard the second voice. "I don't never get trigger-happy. Pulled too many triggers. The thrill is gone."

The first voice spoke again. "You don't have to put the pistol away, Nickerson. But lower it a little, will you? Once you do, I'll come out."

Frank's mind was racing. These had to be convicts speaking to him. He was trying to remember which of the convicts were named James and Geoffrey. The problem was that he'd been too new to the prison to know most of the inmates by name.

He did recall one Geoffrey, though. The man had been pointed out to him by another guard. Geoffry Kidd. One of the more notorious inmates. Not because he ever gave the guards trouble, but just because of who he was and what he looked like.

He hoped to God it wasn't *that* Geoffrey. Or that if it was, he didn't have a gun.

But he had a bad feeling he was going to be out of luck, on both counts.

Seeing nothing else to do, he lowered the pistol. Doing that much didn't bother him, since Frank was very good with a pistol. He could get it back up almost as quickly as he could pull the trigger. The man named James probably understood that himself. He'd just wanted to make sure no triggers got pulled by reflex when the pistol was pointed at him. All things considered, it was a reasonable enough request.

Then, with a considerably greater mental effort, Frank made himself stand up straight. There really wasn't much point to staying in the crouch, he figured. If these convicts didn't have guns, the crouch would be worse than standing up in case they attacked him with blades. And if they did have guns, they could have ambushed him before he even realized they were there.

The brush moved again and a man stepped into view. A convict, sure enough. The reason Frank hadn't been able to spot the distinctive orange coverall was because the man had it covered with a blanket.

He even recognized him, although he wouldn't have been able to attach a name to the face except the other convict had called him James. It was that new prisoner who'd been working in the infirmary.

More to the point, from what Frank had heard, the one who'd gotten into trouble with Adrian Luff. Under the circumstances, that was a relief.

The man completed his name. "I'm James Cook." He hooked a thumb toward the bushes behind him. "What's left—most of 'em—of Boomer's boys are with me. We escaped the prison three days ago. A rebellion started against Luff, he went berserk and started a slaughter, and we figured it was time to bail."

Boomer's boys. Frank knew who they were, too, although he didn't know most of the individuals in the gang. The other guards had told him about Boomer.

That was another bit of relief. Boomer's gang never caused the guards much trouble. Not even Boomer himself, whenever his temper blew, because his fury was always targeted on some other inmate. Restraining him was something of legendary task, though, by all accounts.

Since Frank couldn't think of anything better to say, he asked: "What do you want?"

"Well, that's partly up to Captain Blacklock. At a minimum, we want full paroles. But we actually think some kind of alliance would make more sense. At least, if you plan to take the prison back."

Frank had no idea what to say in response. He had no authority to make any sort of deal with convicts.

Cook must have understood that, because he nodded. "Yeah, I know. It's above your paygrade. So how about you just go get Blacklock?"

"I can't. He—ah—well . . ." Frank didn't want to say too much. Not to men like this, when he had one of the only two pistols in the group of nurses and guards.

"He'll be back soon," he finished lamely. "Just went out for a bit."

The second voice chuckled. "Yeah, sure he did. Went down to the 7-11 to get some soda pop. Damn, boy. You want to get ahead in life, you gotta learn to lie better."

There was another rustle and the man connected to that voice came out of the woods some thirty feet away from Cook.

Sure enough. It was Geoffrey Kidd. And, sure enough, he had a gun in his hand. The same prison-issue model that was in Frank's own hand.

The big, heavily tattooed convict smiled at him. "Tell you what. Now that you've shown me yours and I've shown you mine, how about we tuck 'em back into our pants?"

That seemed . . . like a good idea, all things considered. Not easy to do, of course.

With another mental effort, Frank forced himself to shove the pistol back in his waistband. He wished he had a holster, but if need be he could get the gun out of his pants pretty damn quickly.

Of course, he was sure Kidd could do the same. But the convict had his own gun tucked away, and what was done was done.

"Where *is* Blacklock?" Cook asked. "And please spare us any more bullshit."

Frank said nothing. He wasn't about to let these convicts know that there were dozens of almost unarmed guards and nurses nearby.

Cook shook his head. "I'm not stupid, Nickerson. If Blacklock isn't here—and given how jumpy you are—that means you never hooked back up with him. So it's just you and the nurses and the guards that Marie Keehn and Casey Fisher freed from the cages. Which means the only guns you've got will be the one stuck in your pants and whatever happened to the other piece."

How the hell did he know all that?

Cook shook his head again. "I told you we weren't looking for any trouble. I can even prove it."

"How?"

Cook turned his head. "Okay, guys. Come on out. And bring Elaine with you."

Elaine . . .

The only Elaine whom Frank could think of was Elaine Brown, the injured CO who'd been left behind in the prison. But everyone who'd seen her at the end seemed to be sure she was dead by now. They didn't talk about it much, though. Abandoning Brown was something that obviously preyed on them a lot.

Had she survived after all? And, if by some miracle she had, were these bastards now holding her hostage?

It was Elaine Brown, sure enough. But when she came out of the woods, she came out in a stretcher—more like a jury-rigged litter of some kind—and she was smiling in no way he could imagine a hostage smiling.

"Hi," she said. "You're Frank Nickerson. We never really met except in the infirmary and I was in bad shape at the time."

By now, Frank was confused more than anything else. He had no idea what to do.

"Who's in charge, Frank?" she asked. "It probably wouldn't be you, as new as you were."

He scratched the back of his neck. Pressed to the wall, he decided honesty was probably the best policy. Certainly the easiest one.

"Well, actually, I am. Sorta. Marie Keehn left a few days ago, to see if she could find Blacklock and the others. They're supposed to be with the Cherokees. She left me in charge because I'm the only one besides her who really knows anything about getting by in a wilderness."

In for a penny, in for a pound. "Lieutenant Joe Schuler's with us, too. But he got hurt badly by an animal and he's not in good shape."

"Is he in good enough shape to talk to us?" asked Cook.

"I don't know, to be honest. He sort of comes and goes."

Elaine spoke up. "Frank, just take us to him, will you? And the others. There won't be any trouble."

Her hand reached out and held Cook's. The clasp was easy and intimate.

"Oh, what the hell. Okay. Follow me."

Frank was worried about how the guards would react. But Cook seemed plenty smart enough to figure out that might be a problem. So he made sure that the first convicts coming out of the woods were himself and a stocky guy named John Boyne, carrying Elaine between them on the litter.

That did the trick. Elaine caused so much of a stir that by the time the guards fully digested the fact that they had almost two dozen convicts in their midst, things were fairly relaxed. Especially when they saw that the inmates had brought three kids with them—and the kids seemed attached to that scary Kidd like barnacles.

Luckily, Casey Fisher had the other gun at the moment, and she was the first guard who spotted Brown.

Her face turned pale. For a moment, Frank thought she might even drop the gun.

"Elaine?" she gasped.

Brown waved her hand, very cheerily. "Hi, Casey! How's tricks?"

"Elaine!"

That shout drew everyone's attention. Barbara Ray had just come out of the cave. Her mouth fell open. Then she started yelling—*Elaine's here! Elaine's here! She's safe!*—and before they knew it they were being mobbed.

Cook and Boyne set down the litter. Boyne stepped back, but Cook came down on one knee next to her.

"Dammit, keep your hands off!" he half-yelled. "I'm not taking any risk with infection, not after all she's been through. And where are the nurses?"

"Here," said Barbara Ray, pushing herself through the little mob. She came down on her knees and surveyed the way Elaine was wrapped up in what looked like at least a half dozen sheets.

"You're James Cook, right? The new inmate who's an EMT?"

"Yeah, that's me."

She placed her hand on Elaine's forehead. "How long has she been wrapped up like this?"

"Since we got her out of the basement in the admin building where she'd been hiding. I made sure she stayed wrapped up, too. Well, except when she had to go to the bathroom. So to speak. But she managed that on her own, and didn't take off more than she had to. I insisted. No peeking at the wound."

"Even at night," Elaine said, smiling. Again, she reached out her hand and took Cook's.

Barbara looked at the handclasp, then up at Cook. "She doesn't have a fever."

"Yeah, I know. She hasn't run a fever once."

"Any other symptoms?"

"No. Not any. I think the wound's probably healed, but I didn't want to risk taking off the bandages to look."

"Good."

"Hey, I feel fine!" Elaine said. "Except I'm dying to get out of this stupid mummy wrap."

Barbara Ray and James Cook gave her the identical sort of look. Frank almost laughed. Two medical pros, not about to listen to a damn ignorant civilian telling them their business.

"Well . . ." Barbara Ray shrugged. "I'm tempted to wait until Jenny Radford gets back. But that could be a while. If Elaine's survived this far and doesn't have any bad symptoms, we should probably get her unwrapped and take off the bandages so we can see what kind of shape she's in."

Cook frowned.

The nurse chuckled. "You can't keep her wrapped up forever, you know. Don't worry. We were able to get some medical supplies out of the infirmary before we made our break. The worst that happens is that I just put on some antiseptic and wrap her back up again. In fresh, clean bandages, right out of the original package."

"Okay," said Cook.

"You'll have to let go of her hand, young man."

"Oh. Yeah."

But when he tried, Brown wouldn't let him.

"Not just yet. Barbara Ray—everybody—I'd like you to meet my new fiancé, James Cook. We got engaged three days ago, as we were on our way out of the prison." She giggled. "It's quite a story, actually. But it's way too long to tell it now. I really, really want to stop playing mummy dearest."

"Well, hell," said one of the guards.

"What do we do?" Casey Fisher asked, that evening. She and several of the guards had gathered around Frank at the campfire, along with Barbara Ray and Lylah Caldwell.

For his part, Frank really, really wanted Joe Schuler to come out of his state of near-unconscious. So much so that he'd had to restrain himself mightily from asking the nurses to wake the lieutenant up.

But they would have refused anyway.

So. That left Frank in charge. Whether he wanted to be or not.

"I don't know," was his sterling contribution to leadership principles.

One of the older guards glanced dubiously at the area where Boomer's gang had set up for the night. Elaine Brown was with them. She'd insisted. And now, she was lying under a blanket with James Cook. With nothing but a small bandage in place of the wrappings she'd had on. Even that bandage, according to the nurses, was more of a formality than anything else. They were quite sure that Elaine had recovered fully from her injury.

"Sexual relations between guards and convicts are strictly forbidden," he said. "They'll fire you for that in a heartbeat."

"That is possibly the most asinine statement I've ever heard," Barbara snapped. "Josh Edwards, use your head. First, you *can't* fire Elaine Brown. She doesn't work for the Illinois Department of Corrections anymore, for the good and simple reason that it doesn't exist. Second—"

Lylah Caldwell interrupted her. "Just drop it, Josh. Leave aside everything else. That wonderful young man has kept me from having nightmares for the rest of my life." Her eyes gleamed wetly in the firelight, and her next words came in a whisper. "I thought I'd never be able to forgive myself. For the way we left her behind."

That caused a moment's silence.

"Me neither," said Casey quietly. "Or me," added Barbara Ray.

"Yeah, I agree," said Frank. "It's a moot point. Period. It just is."

He looked over at the couple under the blanket, then looked away when he saw the blanket was moving in . . . interesting ways. The funny thing was, he was pretty sure that if anyone under there was putting up any resistance, it was Cook and not Brown. He'd been her guardian for so long he was probably struggling to let go of it—and she was gleeful that she was finally free of her wraps.

Edwards wasn't going to give up that easily. "Fine," he said, almost snarling the word. "What do we do about the rest of the cons? Dammit, those men are *dangerous*. Kidd's an out-and-out cold-blooded killer."

"Kidd . . ." said Lylah, as if she were musing over a strange word. "Isn't he the one with the three kids wrapped around his neck?"

Edwards glared at her.

One of the other guards spoke up. That was Renfrew Smith, who'd been working at the prison longer than any of them. He was related to Frank, although the relationship was distant. Some sort of second cousin. Maybe even third cousin. Frank never had been able to figure out the difference.

"Just let it go, Edwards. They're not threatening anybody. And I never had any trouble with Boomer's people anyway." Renfrew gave the other guard a sharp glance. "Neither did you, for that matter."

"Frankly," said Casey, "I'm a little relieved to have them here. Between Kidd's gun and those matchlocks they've got, I figure we don't have to worry as much about predators."

Edwards looked mulish. Frank was coming to the conclusion he didn't much like the man. And he was remembering something Captain Blacklock had said to him, shortly after he was hired.

Frank, we are guards. Our job is to protect society from these men, and protect them from each other. We are not

*juries. We are not judges. Just prison guards. And, believe
me, that's a hard enough job as it is, without trying to play
God in the bargain.*

He'd thought it was good advice at the time. Now, he
was sure of it.

"Drop it, Edwards," he commanded. "When Captain
Blacklock gets back—or if Joe Schuler's in good enough
shape—they can make any final decisions. For now, we're
just going to accept the situation as it stands. They're here,
and at least for the moment we're on the same side."

A little later that evening, Frank decided he'd better
follow his own instructions. He went over to Kidd and
squatted next to him.

"I'm only asking because I need to know what we've
got in case predators come around. What I mean is—"

"Two rounds," said Kidd. He put an arm around one of
the Indian girls, who was cuddled against his chest and
half-asleep. "I had to use the rest to take care of the
Spaniards who had 'em."

The fact that the news Kidd only had two rounds left
worried Frank instead of relieving him was as good a sign
as any that the world had definitely changed. Again.

He eased himself out of the squat into a comfortable
sitting position.

"Tell me what happened. It sounds like one hell of
story."

Sure enough, it was.

Frank got the whole story, too, starting from the prison
rebellion where Boomer got killed. Finding Elaine in the

basement, the confrontation with Bostic, the escape, the whole works.

After Kidd finished, they didn't talk for a while. Then Frank asked, "What are you going to do with the kids?"

"Adopt 'em, I guess. Don't think I got much choice. It's either that or shoot 'em—and, like I said, I only got two rounds left. Count 'em. Three kids. I might have the heart to shoot all of them, but I couldn't possibly pick which ones."

After another silent moment, he added, "That was a joke, Nickerson."

Frank nodded sagely. He'd been pretty sure it was a joke.

Kidd's scary grin flashed in the campfire light. "And I'd have to pick two to keep alive, anyway. Seeing as how I always double-tap my targets."

There was another silent moment.

"That was a joke, Nickerson."

"I knew that."

CHAPTER
45

The first person Marie saw when she came upon the Cherokee village was the prison's newest nurse, Jenny Radford. Marie caught her breath at the familiar sight of the woman. Jenny was sitting outside a big, very long log cabin checking a dressing wrapped around an old man's forearm.

Marie Keehn looked around for the others, for Rod Hulbert and Andy Blacklock. They were the ones she needed to talk to. But after a moment, she realized the village seemed half-deserted. All she could see were women, children, and old men.

There being nothing else to do, she start trudging toward Jenny.

The nurse saw her coming and her jaw dropped; then, hastily finishing with the old man's dressing, she rose and hurried to meet Marie.

"Dear God, Marie, you look awful. What happened?"

"Long story. Where's Rod? Where's Andy?"

"They left two days ago. With Chief Watkins and his

men. They went to find the Spaniards and . . . Well. Deal with them."

"Oh . . . hell." Marie felt suddenly dizzy. Only a quick grasp by Jenny kept her from falling down.

"You need to get some rest, girl. Right now."

"No." Marie tried to push her away, but she felt as weak as kitten. "Got to tell somebody . . ."

That was as far as she got. The dizziness just seemed to suck her down.

Rod Hulbert woke her up the next morning. Once she realized who was hugging her tightly, she hugged back. Some small part of her brain, gauging the light coming in through the open door of a log cabin, realized that it must be close to noon. She'd slept almost around the clock.

"Lemme up, Rod," she mumbled. "Need some water."

"What are you *doing* here?" he asked, getting up and moving toward a table in the corner. There was some kind of tall, narrow basket there. Cherokee-made, she assumed. But when Rod picked it up and brought it back, she realized it was a water container.

She was too thirsty at the moment to try to figure out how somebody could make what looked like a reed basket waterproof. But that same small part of her brain made a note to find out. However it was done, it'd be a handy thing to know.

After she got her fill and handed back the water pitcher, she wiped her mouth. "Get Andy. I need to talk to both of you."

"I'm here," came Andy's voice. Marie turned her head and saw the captain standing in the doorway. Where

Rod's expression was a mix of happiness to see her and confusion, Blacklock's face was simply tight with concern.

"There's all hell to pay, guys." She glanced at Rod. "You were right, thinking that Terry Collins was up to no good. But it was way worse than anyone could have imagined. He cut some kind of deal with Adrian Luff. Between the two of them, they engineered a mass breakout of the cells."

"Oh, *shit*," snarled Hulbert.

Blacklock, as usual, kept his self-control. From the expression on his face, you might think he was just considering a serious problem with his car engine.

"How bad?" he asked.

"As bad as it gets. A complete takeover of the prison."

"Complete?"

She nodded.

"Fuck!" Rod rose and started pacing, his face bright red. "Fuck!" He ran his left hand through his hair; his right hand was balled into a fist.

"How many are dead?" Andy asked, his tone still level and even.

"Well, that's the good news. Nobody got killed that I know of—except Collins. I blew that shithead's brains out myself. I caught him trying to rape Casey Fisher in the infirmary. Then I was able to get his keys and let the rest of the guards out of C-block, where Luff was holding them."

Rod stopped pacing. "You did? That's my girl!"

His momentary glee almost made Marie laugh. But she didn't, because she had to pass on the next bit of news.

"That I *know* of, guys." She took a deep breath. "Elaine Brown's probably dead. We had to leave her behind when the rest of us got out. Her injury was too bad for her to move. She was going to try to find a hiding place somewhere in the prison."

"A hiding place. With over two thousand convicts running loose." Blacklock took his own deep breath. "There's something else you haven't said. Something bad. I can tell by the look on your face."

"Joe Schuler's in bad shape. Real bad. He got attacked by some kind of bear after we made it into the woods. Mauled him before we could shoot it."

Blacklock nodded. There was still no expression on his face beyond that general look of concern. Marie thought that same expression would probably be on Andy's face if he found himself plunging down into a pit full of sharpened stakes. The man really was a little eerie, the way he could keep his cool when nobody else could.

Like Rod, for instance. Who, once again, was up and pacing about. This time, slamming his fist into the palm of his other hand. "Those fucking sonsabitches!"

Andy turned his head toward him. "Rod, please calm down a little. We need to think."

"Calm *down*? Andy, those fucking—"

"*Calm. Down. Now.*"

Rod shut up. Marie almost giggled. Andy Blacklock was about the only person she could think of who could have squelched Hulbert that way. The captain was normally such an easygoing boss that you tended to forget how iron-willed he could be in a crunch.

Another voice came from the door. Jenny Radford's. "How bad is Joe?"

She must have come in just in time to hear Marie's last words.

"Pretty bad, Jenny. To be honest, I don't think he's going to make it. He might even have a rib flail. For sure, he's got at least one rib broken loose and internal injuries. And . . ." She made a little shrug. "We managed to get some supplies out of the infirmary before we ran, but it's not really that much. Not for something like that."

Jenny turned to Blacklock. "Andy, I *have* to get back to the cave. As fast as possible."

"We all do. Rod, please see to getting everybody organized. We need to be out of here as soon as possible."

Hulbert went out the door. Andy came to one knee next to Marie, who was still lying on the narrow bed she'd woken in. It was the lower of two bunk beds. There were three other bunk beds in the room, two on each side.

"Okay, Marie. Now tell me everything that happened. Don't leave anything out."

Marie started talking. By the time she was done, Jenny was crying softly onto Andy's shoulder. But Blacklock's expression never changed at all.

That was a little disconcerting, in a way. But Marie didn't mind. She knew that the person who'd eventually get really disconcerted was a certain Adrian Luff.

After Marie finished, Andy rubbed his temples. The headache he'd had in the first period after the Quiver had blessedly gone away. But he sensed it waiting, ready to return. "How sure are you the prisoners didn't follow you and the others to the cave?"

"I'm not. They weren't there when I left. That's all I can guarantee."

Geoffrey Watkins came into the cabin. "I just got the

news from your lieutenant Hulbert. These prisoners, they are a danger?"

Andy nodded. "Yes, they are. Potentially, a much worse danger than de Soto and his men. For one thing, there are a lot more of them—well over two thousand. For another, they're armed with modern rifles and they have access to the prison's machine shop."

"So, my people are still at risk."

"I'm afraid so, Chief."

"Hulbert tells me you're prepared to fight them. Two hundred against two thousand."

"We don't have any choice. If they get out of the prison, they'll rampage over everybody. Us, you, every Indian village out there. The Spaniards too, most likely, not that I care about that. Most of those men were put in prison for a very good reason. And those in charge will be the worst of the bunch."

"It seems our alliance remains, then. We will go with you."

Jenny hissed in a breath. "Geoffrey, you *can't*. The Spaniards are still out there. You told me yourself that at least two hundred of them survived the battle. If you leave the town unprotected, there'll be nothing to stop them from taking it. And kill or capture everybody here."

The Cherokee chief chuckled. "Susan Fisher told me of an expression you explained to her. 'Don't teach your grandmother how to suck eggs.' It's a nice saying. I will add, 'don't teach your grandfather how to run a town.' I have no intention of leaving anyone behind. We'll all go with you to this cave you talked about, and set up a new town there."

Jenny looked out the door. "But . . ."

"It's just work, girl," Watkins said gently. "That's all a town is. There was nothing here when we started. If the Spaniards come and burn it, so what? We'll build it again. It will hardly be the first time a Cherokee town was destroyed. I'm much more concerned about the corn. But I don't think the Spaniards will destroy the corn, because they'll want it themselves. And Susan says she can uproot some of it and maybe replant it near the cave. Who knows? It might even work. She has a way with plants."

"We could certainly use the help," Andy said softly. "My thanks, Chief."

Jenny Radford was gone within an hour. She wanted to get to the cave as soon as possible, to look after Joe Schuler, and it was obvious that if the Cherokees planned to move as a group, there'd be no way to leave until the following morning.

Rod Hulbert went with her, along with Brian Carmichael and Jerry Bailey. The only other men he took were Sergeant Kershner and his squad of U.S. soldiers.

Marie was dubious. "For Pete's sake, Rod, all they've got are those antique muskets."

"Antique or not, they're .69 caliber, Marie." He held up his own semiautomatic rifle. "These things are great for taking down men. But you want to try taking down a Tyrannosaurus Rex with a .223 round? I sure as hell don't."

He gave her a big smile. "Besides, I know 'em and you don't. I like those boys, especially Kershner. The guy's solid as a rock. If a dinosaur shows up, he'll just form a line and give it a volley. Cool as that. I'm not kidding."

"Well . . ."

"I'm telling you. They're *good*. Enough so's I'm even thinking about trying that salt pork sauced with hog lard they keep raving about, whenever they can put together the makings."

Marie puffed out her cheeks, mimicking someone trying not to barf.

Rod laughed. "It does sound horrible, doesn't it? But I swear I'm gonna try it, when the time comes."

Mostly, though, Marie was just sorry that Rod was leaving. She'd been looking forward to sharing a bed with him that night. To hell with fooling around anymore. Life was too short—something which the Cretaceous never let you forget.

After Jenny and Rod left, Marie went back to sleep. She was still feeling exhausted, and since the rest of them wouldn't be leaving until dawn, she figured she'd take advantage of the time to get some more rest.

She was awakened at dawn. The sun hadn't even come fully over the horizon yet. A tiny Cherokee woman was busily removing the door to the cabin. When Jenny sat up and stared at her bleary-eyed, the woman just nodded and kept about her work.

"Cabins are easy to build," she said. "Even the long-house isn't too bad. But good doors are a lot of work and they're not too hard to carry. Go back to sleep, woman."

Marie tried, but a stray thought just wouldn't go away.

"How in the world do you make a basket that'll hold water?"

The little woman stopped her work at the door and peered down at her.

"Do you want me to adopt you?"

"Huh?"

"Adopt you. Only way you'll find out. Basket-making is a woman's secret, and every family has its own methods. Passed down from mother to daughter."

Marie thought about it.

"Sure. Why not? And what's your name, while we're at it? I should probably know, if I'm going to become your daughter."

"Susan Fisher. We'll do the ceremony later, when there's time. Now listen to your mother and go back to sleep."

Marie was asleep in seconds.

She might have thought it was all a dream, when she woke up, except that Fisher came into the cabin and started ordering her around.

Marie didn't mind. It was kind of nice, actually. Reminded her of her own mother. Whom she missed a lot.

"You did *what*?" asked Blacklock, an hour later.

That was worth it, all by itself. The only time Marie had ever seen Andy look completely surprised.

"You heard me. Is there some law against it? If so, it's null and void. That stuff's regulated by the states, and Illinois is sayonara. In case you hadn't noticed."

She pointed a finger at the guards, who were all lined up by now and ready to go. "And aren't you supposed to be doing something besides worrying about my family affairs? You know. Take off your hat and wave it around and holler 'head 'em up! move 'em out!'"

CHAPTER
〰️ **46** 〰️

Alexander Cohen finished presenting his offer. "So, Major Brisebois. Does that seem acceptable to you?"

Nick smiled. The financier wasn't usually given to formalities, he'd learned. The sudden introduction of titles was probably his way of adding a little edge to his negotiations.

He didn't need it, though. Nick had spent his whole life working either for the military or the Defense Department, leaving aside odd jobs he'd had as a teenager. So his yardstick for measuring pay and benefits was a world removed from the pay and perks that seemed to be taken for granted in Cohen's very different circles.

Leaving aside the fact that he'd come to feel strongly about the matter involved himself, he'd have to be crazy to turn down the offer. The pay was three times what he'd been making, the benefits were gold-plated—hell, even the pension Cohen was offering was way better than what he'd get from the DoD. And he'd still be able to collect his military retirement pay.

That left one possible sticking point. "The terms are fine, Mr. Cohen. But I can't start right away. The job I have is not something a responsible man can just walk away from. I'd need to give them notice, and it might take a few weeks. I'm coordinating a lot of things that—"

Cohen waved his hand. "Yes, yes, of course. I wouldn't want you to do otherwise, in any event." He smiled thinly. "Despite my reputation in certain quarters, Nick, I *am* a patriotic citizen. I simply have an American conception of the term 'patriotism,' instead of the Tsarist one that seems to inhabit official circles in Washington these days."

He gathered up the papers he'd spread out on the desk and stuffed them back into the manila folder. "I'll have one of my assistants prepare a proper contract. How about we officially start your employment with the Foundation on the first day of the coming month? That'll give you three weeks to get your affairs in order"—again, he waved his hand—"and if it winds up taking you more time than that, that's not a problem. If nothing else, you'll need more time to sell your house and relocate. But your salary will still date from the beginning of next month."

He gave Nick a keen-eyed look. "One question, though. Do you foresee a problem with your security clearance?"

Nick shrugged. "I'll lose my current clearance as soon as I quit, of course. I'll still be obligated by the usual keep-your-mouth-shut provisions, but I can't see where that's an issue. Of course, down the road a ways, somebody in officialdom might try to *make* it an issue." He gave Cohen a smile that was even thinner than the one Cohen had given him. "But I'm quite sure there's never been a word said, in any oath I ever took, that forbade me from investigating something that happened over a hundred million years ago."

"Indeed." Cohen put the folder back in his briefcase. "And now, if I can ask, how do you plan to proceed?"

Nick had given that matter quite a bit of thought over the past few days, naturally.

"Well, I figure the physicists and mathematicians here can pretty much run their own show. I wouldn't have the faintest idea how to direct them, anyway. And the same's pretty much true with the paleontologists. Especially given that you've decided to leave Esther Hu here in place."

Cohen chuckled. "The decision wasn't exactly mine. I'm quite sure Esther would have simply quit if I'd told her otherwise. At least, that's the not-so-veiled threat she gave her university if they didn't allow her to take an immediate sabbatical."

"What I really plan to focus on is organizing what you might call the popular input into the project."

"Meaning?"

"You saw it yourself, Alex. Tim Harshbarger and Bruce Boyle left here steaming mad. You think they're the only ones who feel that way, down in those southern Illinois counties? Not on your life. I've already talked it over with them. Give us a few months—a few weeks, even—and we'll have a network organized down there that'll start running circles around the siblings. They *can't* keep everything hidden. Not if there's a well-organized effort to dig up the truth, right there on the spot by local people."

He leaned back in his chair. "Then, I plan to do the

same in and around Marion County, West Virginia. That'll take more time and be a lot harder, since the Grantville disaster happened years ago. But we'll turn up some people, you watch and see if we don't. *Somebody* down there will know something."

The financier frowned. "You think so? I'd have imagined they'd have spoken up by now, if they did."

Nick studied him for a moment. Alexander Cohen was a wizard in the stock market, by all accounts. But he'd started off wealthy to begin with. He'd been born with the proverbial silver spoon in his mouth.

Nick's father, on the other hand, had been a steel worker in a mill in southern Ohio. Nick's life in the Air Force had broadened his horizons a lot, of course, but he still knew and understood how working class people looked at the world, especially those born and raised in the nation's smaller towns.

"No, they wouldn't. Alex, meaning no offense, but you've taken for granted your entire life the fact that you had influence. As you grew older, a lot of influence. I don't think you really understand how differently things look when you grow up assuming you have no influence at all. The 'guv'mint' is just something way over there, powerful and immense and unyielding to any personal leverage you might have. Sure, once every two or four years you get to vote, but that's just so you can pick which big shot sits on top of the pile. You still don't have any leverage yourself."

He leaned forward and planted his hands on the table. Stubby-fingered, thick-palmed hands, the sort you'd expect to come attached to the son of a steel-worker. "No, trust me on this. Anybody who knew anything, once the lid came down and it was made clear that lid was lead-plated and wasn't budging, would have just kept their mouths shut. If the press had kept digging, things might have been different. But they didn't. We'll turn something up. See if we don't."

Cohen nodded and stood up. "I leave it all to you, then. I'll appreciate periodic reports from you. And, at least on occasion, reports you give to me personally in New York. But I'll keep my nose out of the daily affairs of the project. I am not in the least bit inclined to be a micromanager."

After Cohen left the iron mine, Nick took stock of his immediate situation. He'd have to leave himself in two or three days.

Silly to waste them. Two or three days could last a long time, if fortune smiled.

He found Margo Glenn-Lewis in her usual laboratory. At least, "laboratory" was the word Nick used, even though he suspected it was probably technically inaccurate.

"Is there a good place to eat anywhere around here?" he asked. "If so, can I buy you dinner?"

She looked up and gave him the smile that—he'd be a damn liar to deny it—had partly influenced his decision. "Three, actually. At least, if a radius of forty kilometers falls within your definition of 'around here.'"

"I'm a former pilot, Ms. Glenn-Lewis. I sneer at paltry klicks."

"Ha! You forget that I'm driving. We'll see how long that sneer lasts, once we get there. I learned to drive on

Manhattan, dealing with cabbies. I sneer at the paltry laws of motion and inertia. Are you in the mood for steaks?"

"Sounds good."

She glanced at the clock on the wall. "Fine. We'll leave at five o'clock."

When they arrived at Freddy's Steak House, at her insistence, he showed her the sneer.

It was pretty pitiful, actually.

But the steaks were good, and the rest of the evening kept getting better.

CHAPTER
∽∾ 47 ∽∾

Andy didn't let any of it show on his face, but he was furious. His guards had been driven halfway across the country barefoot. Without food or water. They had been attacked by animals. And now he had a good friend dying inside a cave.

Jenny, Lylah, and Barbara were in the cave with Joe. They were working on him, but Jenny hadn't held out much hope. Her biggest concern was making him comfortable. Without narcotics that was almost impossible. Kevin Griffin had handed over a flask of whiskey when he heard about the need. It wasn't a lot, but the whiskey would help.

Joe had even managed to make a joke about it. The label on the bottle was no brand of whiskey any of them knew, but it was dated 1836. "This ought to be aged well," he'd said.

Afterward, when Andy asked about Joe's chances of surviving, all three of the nurses had looked away. Finally it was Barbara who answered him. "Sometimes," she said, "all you can do is hope for a miracle and pray."

"Hulbert and Edelman have a plan they believe will work?" asked Watkins.

Andy nodded. It wasn't really a plan. Just part one, with part two to be decided on at a later date. A half dozen guards and the K-9 unit would get as close to the prison as they could under cover of darkness. Their goal was espionage. They would find out how the prison was being guarded. Once they returned, they'd figure out what to do next.

In the meantime, the rest of the Cherokees and the guards should have arrived. Andy and Watkins and a handful of others had come ahead.

"Who are you sending?" the chief asked.

"Hulbert, Marie, and the entire K-9 unit."

Watkins sat watching the flames, chewing on the end of a thin twig. "You're letting your anger guide you. That's stupid when so many are depending on you."

"Explain."

"First, you should take at least one Cherokee. Kevin Griffin would be the best. Hulbert thinks he's very good in the woods, and . . . well, he's not bad." Watkins smiled around the twig. "But he's no Cherokee."

The chief took the twig out of his mouth and used it to point to a group of men—and one woman, and three children—camped a small distance to the side. "Then, you need to settle with them. If you can do that, you should send a couple of them also. They know the situation better than you do."

Andy's jaws tightened. He still hadn't figured out how to handle *that* problem. All he needed, on top of everything else!

But . . .

He thought about it for a while. On the minus side, about half of the convicts in Boomer's gang were hardened and habitual criminals. Geoffrey Kidd was an out-and-out contract killer. Dino Morelli had committed his first armed robbery at the age of fifteen.

Their leader, on the other hand—both of them, actually, since you had to include Boyne in this category—weren't really criminals. Just men who'd let their temper slip once, and let it slip too badly.

That was assuming that Cook was even guilty in the first place, about which Andy had his doubts. After he and Joe Schuler had taken Jenny's advice and started reading the convicts' files, James Cook's had been one of the first Andy had read. His curiosity had been aroused by Cook's deft handling of the Luff problem he'd developed.

Cook might have committed the murder he was convicted of. But what Andy knew for sure—anybody with half a brain could figure this out—was that Cook's trial had been a travesty. If he'd had a competent lawyer he'd have been acquitted. The case against him was the shoddiest kind of connect-the-dots sloppy logic. There'd been no eyewitnesses, no fingerprints, no physical or material evidence, nothing. Just so-called "it stands to reason" that he must have done it. And a gullible or lazy jury.

Andy had always known—all the guards did, except a few thickheaded ones—that at least some of the men they guarded were perfectly innocent of the crimes they'd been convicted of. Not most of them, of course. But there were some. Andy had seen over a dozen men exonerated and released in the time he'd worked at the prison—two of whom had been on Death Row.

Cook might be another one. Then again, maybe not. And, in any event, there was no question about Kidd's guilt, or Morelli's—or Boyne's, for that matter. All three of them had pleaded guilty to get a reduced sentence. Which, in Kidd's case, saved him from the death penalty.

On the plus side . . .

Well, for starters, there was Elaine Brown. The one time an officious guard had taken it upon himself to lecture Brown on her duty to associate with the other guards instead of the convicts, her response had been short, blunt—and, when they heard about it, had reduced the nurses and Casey Fisher to tears.

"Let me see if I've got this straight, Edwards. You think I should leave the men who rescued me from that prison in order to hang out with the people who left me there? Fuck you."

Leaving aside the mix of powerful emotions involved, and trying to be as cold-blooded as possible about it, Andy had to admit—even that hardass Rod Hulbert had to admit—that the Boomers' rescue of Brown gave them genuine bona fides. For that matter, so did their rescue of the three Indian kids. And if the principal agent of that rescue had been a contract killer, well . . .

Andy rose to his feet. "You're right, Geoffrey. I'll see if we can work out a deal."

He headed toward the Boomers. Seeing him come,

Cook made a little gesture and several of the other convicts moved aside a bit, giving Blacklock room to sit down by their campfire.

Andy didn't see any reason to beat around the bush.

"All right, Cook. You tell me what you want and I'll tell you what I want, and we'll see if we can meet somewhere in the middle."

"Full and complete parole for everybody in my group. No exceptions. And you might as well call it a 'pardon' instead of a 'parole,' because there's not going to be any bullshit about reporting to parole officers. We're free and clear of all past crimes committed. Each and every one of us."

He shrugged. "I'm not asking for a free pass, Blacklock. Any crimes committed from this day forward will be a different story."

"Uh-huh. And who, exactly, will see to that? In case you hadn't noticed, we don't have a police force. No judges and juries, either."

"For the time being, I will. Eventually, we'll need to set up our own justice system. But that'll take a while." He gave Andy a somewhat eerie smile, that was impossible to interpret exactly. "Don't worry about it, Captain. You'll probably have more trouble keeping the peace than I will. My boys are right law-abiding, these days. That's because if any of them cross the line, I already told them I'd just have Geoffrey shoot 'em."

Geoffrey Kidd. Now employed in law-enforcement, no less.

"Strange world, isn't it?" Cook's smile got some actual humor in it. "But I'll keep my end of the deal. Now, what is it you want?"

"We need to take back the prison. Until that's accomplished, you and your men have to be under my authority or the authority of anyone I delegate. And no bullshit about it. I can order men shot too. And I will, if I have to, in a combat situation."

"And what else?"

"For the time being, that's it. Afterward . . . To be honest, I don't know. But I don't know about what we'll do with regard to anything, in the future a ways."

He nodded toward Watkins, still sitting and chewing on his twig. "The Cherokees, for instance. Will they decide to set up with us, or will they want to keep their own town? I'm figuring the latter, but who knows? And assuming they do keep their own setup, what relationship will they have with us? I have no idea. And I'm not losing any sleep over it, either. First, we've got to get the prison back from Luff and his thugs."

"Luff and his crazies, better way to put it," chimed in John Boyne. He looked at Cook. "Sounds like a deal to me, boss."

"Yeah, me too. But we'll put this one to a vote." He stood up and motioned for the other Boomers to gather around. Once they'd done so, he said: "Captain Blacklock is offering us a deal. He'll agree to—"

He cocked an eye at Andy. "Pick the term."

Andy shrugged. "You may as well use 'pardon,' I guess. I'm short of parole officers anyway. Haven't got a one."

"Right. Okay, boys. Here's the deal. The captain gives us—all of us, each and every one—a full and complete pardon. No strings attached. In return, we put ourselves under his military authority until such time as the prison is taken back from Luff."

He waited for a few seconds. "Any discussion?"

Kidd spoke up. "Yeah. Can I shoot Luff myself?"

That brought a low laugh from everybody, including Andy.

Cook shook his head. "Whatever Blacklock says, is the answer. But I imagine there's already a long line for that assignment. Any other discussion?"

He waited for a few more seconds. "Okay, then. We'll take a vote. All in favor, raise your hands."

He and Boyne started to count hands, and then stopped. "Let's do it the other way," said Cook. "Anybody opposed?"

Not a single hand went up. Cook nodded and sat back down.

"Okay, Captain. You've got your deal. On our side"—here he actually grinned; a no-fooling, nothing-hidden grin—"it was unanimous. Don't know how well it'll go on your side, though."

Andy grinned back. "I don't need to take a vote. For the time being, anyway, I'm still the boss."

"Figures. Leave it to convicts to have to introduce democracy into the Age of the Dinosaurs."

"I'll take Kidd and Cook himself," said Rob Hulbert. "They're the two cons in that group I can trust to stay level-headed."

Andy scratched his jaw. "Cook, yeah. But . . . Kidd?"

"Sure, he's a cold-blooded killer. But that's the whole point, Andy. In this situation, the operative term is 'cold-blooded.' Look at it this way. Kidd was in our custody for a little over eight years. How many times did we have to take him down in that stretch?"

"Not once. The two times he got into it with another con, it was over before we even knew about it."

"Right. How many times did he get in a confrontation with a guard?"

"Not once. Okay, I see your point. I just . . ."

Rod smiled. "Relax, Andy. The truth is, I'm more comfortable with this deal you cut with the Boomers than you are. Look, we both knew—so did Joe Schuler, because we talked about it once—that sooner or later we were going to have to start freeing some of the inmates."

"Yeah, fine, but I was thinking in terms of the ones convicted of nonviolent crimes. Or something like manslaughter. Not murderers in the first degree, for Pete's sake."

"There's first degree murder and there's first degree murder. The law may not make that distinction, but I do—and so do you. You know perfectly well that the reason the prosecutor went for a plea bargain with Kidd is because the only people he ever killed were thugs themselves. We're living in a world that has dinosaurs in it, not to mention saber-toothed tigers and God knows what else." Hulbert shrugged. "I can live with it. What I can't live with are the likes of Adrian Luff—who was *not* convicted of murder, remember—and his stooge Phil Haggerty. Now there's a piece of work. Who, I remind you, was convicted of a nonviolent offense."

Andy made a face. Haggerty had been convicted on charges of state-tax evasion. That was the only way the police could get him behind bars. Even though they knew perfectly well he'd been guilty of at least three brutal hijackings, which had left one person dead and several others badly injured. The fatality had been a fourteen-year-old boy run over by the getaway car and left to die, bleeding and mangled in the street.

"All right, point taken. Cook and Kidd. You got 'em."

Rod's negotiations with Kidd were more complicated.

The first part went well enough. "How many rounds you got left?" Hulbert asked him.

"Two."

"You'll need more. You *might* need more—but keep in mind that we're just trying to do a reconnaissance. If all goes well, not a shot will be fired."

He rummaged in his pack and came out with two magazines for Kidd's pistol. Fortunately, all the firearms in the prison had been standard issue. They didn't have to fiddle with matching a lot of different calibers to different guns.

"Thanks." Kidd stuffed the two magazines away in a pocket he'd jury-rigged. "Now we got to deal with a different problem."

"What's that?"

Kidd pointed. "Them. The three kids. They're already anxious, figuring something's up. As soon as they see me leave, they'll start hollering like you wouldn't believe."

"Jesus H. Christ," Rod muttered. "When did baby-sitting get added to my job description?"

Kidd chuckled. "When did it get added to *mine*?"

Rob scratched his head, considering the problem. After

a while, he said: "I'll talk to Hanrahan. She's good with kids, and she misses the three she left behind."

In the end, that worked out pretty well. The three kids were still unhappy at Kidd's departure, but by the time he left, Kathleen had them ensnared in a fairy tale. How she managed to get the meaning of the story across without sharing a word in common was and would remain forever a mystery to Rod Hulbert. Even in the Cretaceous, "earth mother" was still not part of his job description.

CHAPTER
48

Jenny stroked Joe's feverish forehead. He had pneumonia and was bleeding internally. She planned to open him up and see what she could do, but she didn't have a lot of hope. The small amount of pink-tinged froth he coughed up every few minutes scared her. The same thing went for his color. He was as white as a sheet and too weak to even sit without help. She was amazed he was still alive.

She gave him a sip of the whiskey the Cherokee Kevin Griffin had given her, about a half a swallow. He had to hold it down or they wouldn't be able to do anything for him.

"What are they going to do about the prison?" he asked. "We can't leave Luff in charge. The man's crazier'n a loon, under that mild-mannered exterior. I can't imagine what's happening to those poor bastards still inside, the ones he has it in for."

"Chief Watkins and his people, plus the army personnel that were with them, say they'll help us take it back."

He nodded and the slight motion caused a wave of nausea to engulf him. A jaw-clenching minute later, he mumbled, "Sorry," rolled to his side and vomited. He didn't lose much, but only because he didn't have much to lose. Once his stomach was empty, the dry heaves continued for almost three minutes.

Jenny wiped his forehead with a damp cloth. "It's okay," she lied.

"I'm dying," Joe said, matter-of-factly. "You can't stop it from happening."

Jenny knew he was right, but didn't like the idea of just sitting on her hands doing nothing. It felt wrong. This wasn't an old man who had lived his life. Joe was young and strong. He should live another thirty or forty years. Maybe even fifty, as healthy as he'd been.

"Joe, it's up to you. I can try to operate, and if we're lucky, I might be able to do something."

"You said the left lung was collapsed."

Jenny nodded. There was no air going in or coming out of the left side of Joe's chest. No lung sounds. The right lung was doing it all, and it was damaged. She could hear the sounds—much like crackling paper—that indicated more trouble than she could fix. She knew if the situation had been reversed, if the right lung was silent and the left filled with fluid, he would have already been gone. The slight difference in lung size, one side to the other, was all that was keeping him alive. And that difference wasn't going to be enough to let him survive much longer.

"If you can't fix it, just sit with me. I'd rather not die that way, cut open and out of my head. And I also don't want to die alone."

"Are you religious, Joe?"

He gave his head a slight nod. "Nazarene."

"Would you like me to pray with you?"

"Too late now," he whispered. "I have to go on my record and hope I got it right." He coughed then moaned. "Man, this hurts."

Jenny stroked his face.

He reach up and took her hand. "Don't leave me."

She looked at him and then at Barbara Ray and Lylah Caldwell. The two of them were looking at her, their eyes filled with tears. They were waiting for her to do something, anything that might help him. Part of her wanted to say *to hell with it* and dive in. She wanted to at least try.

But she couldn't do that. Joe had the right to refuse. It was his death; he should be able to decide how he would do it. "Sure, Joe. Of course we'll stay with you."

"I heard about the little girls," he said. "The ones that Geoffrey Kidd rescued. What a twist that is."

Jenny nodded and told him about Hulbert and Bailey's pups, and laughed aloud when she saw the sparkle in his eyes. She squeezed his hand and whispered, "This place is horrible, but we're going to make it. And it's going to be a real world, a real home."

She kept talking after that, about anything that came to mind. Occasionally his eyes would close, but if Jenny quit talking they would pop open filled with panic. So she talked. She told him about the trees and the bog and the medicine woman. She even told him about the tools the Cherokees had.

Using cloths that Barbara and Lylah kept moist with frequent trips to the river, she did her best to keep him cooled as she talked. The day was long, drifting by in spurts and stops as he struggled to breathe.

"How will we destroy the prisoners?"

Jenny didn't know the answer to that one, so she gently adjusted the makeshift pillow behind his back. She then took a fresh cloth from Barbara and applied it to the back of his neck. The cool water felt good on her hands, and she knew it felt good on his fevered flesh.

Suddenly, his eyes seemed to focus on her face. "You said we have keys. Which ones? Can we get into the supply house?"

Jenny nodded. "Marie had a complete set. We have keys to every lock inside the prison."

"You mean that, literally?"

"Literally," Jenny answered. She placed a fresh cloth over his eyes and forehead and the two of them sat silent. The only sound was the lieutenant's labored breathing. Several minutes passed and then Joe tried to sit up.

"No, Joe. Lie still," Jenny told him.

Joe reached out and gripped her upper arm. "Okay, but you tell Andy about the supply house. There's . . . stuff . . . for bombs. Little bombs . . . but it would be enough to . . . make them surrender."

"I'll tell him, Joe." She wondered how long this stage of the dying would last: the mental confusion. He was bleeding internally and his lungs weren't functioning properly. That meant his brain wasn't getting enough oxygen. It was no wonder he was talking a little crazy. And it would probably get worse.

"Please, Jenny. Tell him."

"I will, Joe. I promise I will." She would, too. Even

though she knew there were no bomb parts hidden inside the prison, not in the armory and not in the supply rooms. Still, she would tell Andy everything his friend said and did before dying.

"Paint, cleaners, bleach, and ammonia." His breaths were labored. "Tell him!"

He rolled over, his body shaking with the effort of coughing and dry heaves. Minutes passed. When it was over he moaned and said, "Glass jars with lids. Tell Andy about the jars and the nails. And gasoline. And tell him to ask the Boomers about it." He coughed again; it almost sounded like a laugh. "If there's . . . anyone in the world knows how to jury-rig a weapon, it's a con."

"I will," Jenny said. "I will. Now you have to rest."

But Joe didn't. He struggled to a sitting position. "No. I can't. You can't. You have to tell him now," he whispered, his eyes dancing with fever. "Now."

Barbara Ray moved from the cave entrance over to where Jenny sat. "Go on, tell Andy what he's saying. I'll stay with him."

Jenny reluctantly moved toward the small opening. She was afraid to leave, afraid he would be gone before she could return. Just as she got to the cave's entrance, Joe called out, his voice weak and raspy, but his eyes focused and determined. "I need to talk to him. And to Edelman. We might even . . . have what we need to gas them."

He coughed a deep, body-wrenching cough. He moaned and held his ribs. He then whispered, "Catapults. I bet the Cherokees could build them. Tell them we can do it. We can take the prison. Hurry. I need you to hurry."

Eric Flint & Marilyn Kosmatka*

Jenny stared at the man lying on the cave floor and then at Barbara Ray who was holding his hand. The lieutenant's eyes were clear.

"Catapults. Homemade bombs. Gas them," Joe whispered.

Andy was easy to find; he was sitting next to the fire, talking to Chief Watkins. Edelman wasn't much harder to locate. He was asleep under the ledge, curled between two other guards, soaking in their body heat and snoring loudly. When she said his name he came instantly awake, and scrambled toward her. It took less than three minutes. But those minutes were long and Jenny was scared.

Andy Blacklock and Jeff Edelman stayed with Joe Schuler until he became unresponsive and his breaths changed to the silence, followed by short rapid breaths, common to the dying. Joe had talked in soft whispers for twenty minutes. The two men had knelt beside him, their ears almost on his mouth in order to hear. Occasionally he would stop his labored whispering and cough up the red-tinged froth that was everyone's reminder that they had to hurry. Several times Edelman would ask a question, or Andy would say, "You have to talk a little louder, Joe." And the man would take a labored breath and say one or two words loud enough to be heard by everyone inside the cave, but then the low whisper would return. At times the men were forced to hold their breaths in order to hear his words. It was a struggle. But they did hear, and when he finally fell silent, they understood what he meant.

When the last rays of sunlight began fading away and the cave was almost dark, Joe took his last labored breath. Moments later, Barbara, Lylah, and Jenny left the cave. They didn't say anything to those who watched them crawl out of the small opening; instead they sat next to the fire and quietly cried. Andy Blacklock and Jeff joined them, dried-eyed but looking haggard.

After a while, Andy and Jeff got up and walked over to the Boomers. Without asking for an invitation, they sat down next to John Boyne.

Andy got right to the point. "Before he died, Joe Schuler told us he thought there was enough stuff in the supply house at Alexander to make bombs. Maybe poison gas, too. I think he may be right, but it's not something I really know a lot about." He hooked a thumb at Edelman. "Neither does Jeff. Show him a rock and he can tell you what it had for breakfast two centuries ago. But he says he doesn't know much about what you might call practical chemistry."

He stopped, and waited.

Boyne tugged at his ear. "And you think we do."

"Yeah. I figure you do. Some of you, anyway."

Boyne smiled. "Captain Blacklock, if I didn't know you better, I'd think you was implying we have criminally inclined tendencies."

"God forbid. Come on, John. You got your pardon. Everything that happened in the past is a wash. But that doesn't mean it didn't happen—and I'm damn sure some of you know what I'm talking about."

"Probably. I don't, myself. But . . ."

He turned his head and gestured to one of the men sitting a ways back. "Front and center, Leffen."

A bit reluctantly, a wiry man in his early fifties sidled up to the campfire. He had a wizened face and skin color like really old coffee with cream. Gray-brown, almost.

"Yeah," he said. "I heard. I guess I might know a thing or two."

"Cut it out, Carter," said Boyne tonelessly. "They nailed you for aggravated assault, but you know and I know and every alley cat in the south side of Chicago knows that you really made your living as an arsonist. Burning down tenements for slumlords looking to collect the insurance."

Leffen looked alarmed. "Hey! I never hurt nobody."

"Didn't say you did. I said you burned down buildings. Even managed to make the fires look like an accident."

Andy had wondered about that. There had always been rumors that Carter Leffen was a professional arsonist, although the police had never been able to pin anything on him.

Leffen looked mollified. Even a bit self-righteous. "Well, yeah. But I never hurt nobody. You can't, you wanna get a good reputation in the trade. A fire's a fire. The firemen put it out, the owner collects the insurance, and what else are insurance companies good for? But somebody gets killed . . ." He grimaced. "There's all hell to pay. Got to be careful not to set a fire so bad it'll kill a fireman, neither. Even hurt 'em. Then there's really hell to pay."

Under the circumstances and all things considered, Andy decided this was not the time and place to get into a discussion of ethics with an arsonist.

"Can you do anything with that stuff?"

"What's in there, exactly? You guys always kept the supply room locked tight."

"You bet your sweet ass, we did. I'm not sure of everything. But I know there's paint, and cleaning solvents of various kinds. That includes bleach and ammonia."

Leffen's eyes closed, as if he were falling into a trance. After a minute or so, he said: "Yeah, I can manage something." His eyes popped open. "This ain't gonna hurt my pardon, is it?"

"To the contrary," said Edelman solemnly. "You will have the thanks of your nation."

"We a nation now?"

That was a very good question, actually. One that, if they survived the next week or two, Andy thought they'd probably be spending the rest of their lives trying to answer.

CHAPTER
⟨⟨⟩⟩ 49 ⟨⟨⟩⟩

Marie shifted her pack. It was almost empty now, so walking was easy. Later, if things went well, it would be loaded. The two-day return trek though the rough terrain would be more difficult.

Hulbert hadn't really wanted her to come along. The truth was, she hadn't wanted to join the mission herself. Her body still ached from the punishment it had taken over the last week. She hadn't been able to take the time she needed to build her energy stores all the way back up. But since she was one of the few capable of the type of shooting they might need, she'd understood Captain Blacklock's reasoning—and so had Hulbert, even if he was even less happy about it than she was. And got a lot unhappier when Frank Nickerson caught up with them and told them there was a change in plans.

This wasn't going to be just a reconnaissance after all.

Silently, Marie cursed her father and brothers for insisting she got good with a gun, and pushed herself to walk faster.

Just after nightfall the next day, they reached the prison. Carefully, making as little noise as possible, they circled around until they were facing the prison's armory. The small brick building located outside the prison walls was shrouded in darkness. Using a night scope he'd luckily thought to bring along for the expedition against the Spaniards, Hulbert spotted two convicts posted outside its door.

Luff was overconfident. He should have had four men posted there. He did have four convicts posted close to the front entrance to the prison, but they were far enough away that, in the darkness, they shouldn't notice anything unless someone shouted or a shot got fired.

That would have been hard to manage against four sentries. Against two, it was possible.

Given who Hulbert had available, at least. Frank Nickerson had been trained by the army for this sort of thing. And while Kevin Griffin had never had any formal training, his life's experience probably made him even better. The American frontier in the early nineteenth century had been a world of raids and ambushes, and Rod knew Kevin had done his share of it.

Best of all, those Luff did have posted were only armed with pistols, and they had the pistols in their holsters. They should have been standing guard with rifles in their hands.

He wondered why they weren't. Probably because Luff was keeping the powerful semiautomatic rifles restricted to his inner circles. For this kind of boring sentry duty, he'd probably figured any convict would do.

That was also a stupid decision. But . . . Luff might not have had much choice. Given the situation Cook and the Boomers had depicted, it was quite possible that Luff felt he had to keep everyone he could rely on ready at hand in case of another rebellion. Not standing outside the prison watching for a less immediate threat.

Rod turned, pointed to Frank and Kevin, and motioned them forward.

He let the two men survey the situation themselves for a while, then whispered, "If we're going to get into the armory, we need to take those two guys out. Silently. I figure the two of you are the best we've got for the purpose. Can you handle it?"

"I can take one," Griffin said immediately. "Frank?"

Nickerson nodded. "Yeah. If they'd kept a clear fire zone around the prison like they should have, it'd be tricky as hell. But the lazy bums even let the ground cover grow."

He pointed a finger toward some trees that were near the armory, and had a thick growth of ferns between them and the prison. "That way, I think, Kevin. Once we're at the wall, we can sidle along it until we're close enough."

"Same thought I had. Let's do it."

Immediately, he started moving toward the trees in a low crouch, making no noise at all that Hulbert could hear. Rod wasn't surprised. He'd always considered himself an expert woodsman. But his experiences over the past period with the Cherokees had driven home to him that there was a huge difference between survivalism and surviving. Truth was, in the end, all of his skills were basically a product of play-acting taken very seriously. For men like Kevin Griffin, the skills were what had kept them alive.

Nickerson made a little bit of noise, but not much. And even the big black man—he was half again Griffin's size—couldn't be heard after he was a few yards away.

Rod turned, pointed to Marie, and summoned her forward.

"One of us keeps the scope on the sentries, and one of us is ready to shoot at any time. In case something goes wrong. You got a preference?"

"I'll shoot. You're a better shot than I am, but at this range it doesn't matter. And I'm not comfortable with the scope. Only used the damn things twice in my life."

Rod nodded. He brought the scope up and focused it on the sentries. He was tempted to use it to follow Griffin's and Nickerson's progress—or try to, anyway—but that would have been a stupid indulgence. They'd either pull this off, or they wouldn't. Nothing Rod and Marie could do would help them in the first task. But if they stayed alert and concentrated on the sentries, they might very well be able to save Frank's and Kevin's lives.

If it came to gunfire, of course, the plan went up in smoke. But plans could be made anew. A dead friend couldn't be summoned back to life.

It was a tense few minutes, that became a tense half hour—and then stayed tense for another quarter of an hour. Kevin and Frank weren't rushing anything. Rod was sure that Nickerson would be letting the Cherokee set the pace. And where even a modern soldier with Frank's training would have moved much more quickly, Griffin had the patience taught him by a lifetime. Rod knew what he was doing. Move a few feet; stop; wait a few minutes.

Then do it again. Never moving long enough to allow the target to spot you. Just enough that, even if they heard something, they'd never see you. And then there'd be no further sound for minutes.

Rod spent a fair portion of that forty-five minutes thanking the stars that he hadn't been born and raised in the eighteenth- and early nineteenth-century frontier. He finally understood just how hairy that must have gotten. Imagine going to bed every night *knowing* that somebody like Kevin Griffin might be creeping up on your cabin.

When the assault finally happened, it went so fast Rod barely understood what he was seeing through the scope.

Griffin appeared, right in front of one sentry. His hand flashed to the convict's throat. Rod never saw the knife, but an instant later the con was going down, clutching his throat and silent.

Nickerson, with his size and strength, didn't bother with a knife. He just seized the convict and slammed his head against the brick wall of the armory. Since the man wasn't wearing any sort of head covering, that produced a thud so faint Rod couldn't hear it at all. He was sure the four sentries standing guard at the main entrance hadn't noticed a thing, since they were farther away than he was.

That head smash might very well have killed the convict. But, an instant later, Nickerson had him by the hair and shoulder, holding his throat open for Griffin.

It was over. Rod shifted the scope to study the four guards at the main entrance.

Nothing. They were still chatting away, where alert guards wouldn't have been talking at all. But Luff hadn't exactly been able to take his pick from the few and the proud.

"Okay," he whispered to Marie. "Let's all move up. We can circle around now, and get out of sight."

Five minutes later, they were all gathered just to the side of the armory, out of sight of the sentries at the main entrance. Moving briskly but not as if he were up to something—one of the sentries might still look over—Rod found the key to the armory and unlocked the door.

Silently cursing himself for being an idiot. Luckily, either Griffin or Nickerson had figured out that the two of them needed to remain standing in front of the armory. Just in case one of the other sentries looked over, saw no one apparently on guard, and decided to wander over to see what had happened to them.

Rod hadn't even thought of that. If he had, he might not have used Nickerson at all. True, one of the convicts they'd slain had also been black. But he was nowhere nearly as big as Frank. Fortunately, Frank had been quick-witted enough to figure that out also. So, he'd spent the whole five minutes slouched against the wall, figuring that one slouching man looked about the same as another seen from a distance. And staying in the darkest part of the area, since his uniform wasn't remotely the same color as the con's coverall.

Fortunately, as dark as it was, the distinction between blue and orange wasn't readily noticeable that far away. Griffin hadn't taken any chances, though. He'd quickly dragged the other convict out of sight, stripped the corpse of its coverall and put it on over his own clothes. That man was just enough larger than Kevin was to make that possible. He'd be sweating under that double layer, in this heat, but Kevin Griffin could make any of those ancient Stoic philosophers look like crybabies.

The door opened, Rod positioned himself so he could keep an eye on the guards at the main entrance, and waved everybody in. One at a time, spaced five seconds apart, as they'd been told.

Rod was the last one in. Just before entering, he reached down, seized the collar of the convict Nickerson had taken down, and dragged him into the armory. Once inside, he summoned one of the men in the K-9 team.

"Strip him of the coverall, put it on, and take Nickerson's place outside. You're about the right size and color."

Kelly Evans chuckled. "I got a much higher moral fiber, though. I swear I do."

That done, Rod went to see what they'd found.

A minute later, like all the guards in the armory, he was trying not to laugh out loud.

Almost everything was there! Very little had been taken from the shelves and hauled inside the walls.

Luff was either paranoid or he had good reason to be. Most likely both, of course.

"What do we do?" asked Marie. "We can't possibly carry all this stuff out of here."

"Not the weapons, no, except for some of the rifles. But we can take out most of the ammunition for the rifles. Without ammo, they're just clubs. Not very good clubs, at that."

"The pistol ammo?"

"Leave the pistols and their ammo. For the kind of war we'll be fighting, they won't be that much use. It's the rifles that matter." He paused. "Well . . . let Kidd take one of the pistols and plenty of ammo for it. That'll make him happy, and I figure a happy hit man is worth a little extra work."

Geoffrey smiled serenely.

Softly, Rod clapped his hands. "Okay, people, let's get at it. You know the plan."

They were running slightly behind schedule, so Rod didn't dare spend more than four hours at the work of emptying the armory. They still had another important assignment tonight.

It was slow work, too. Gathering the stuff up and depositing it by the door went quickly. But the rest was time-consuming. First—and only one at a time, since a group of people might be noticed moving, even in the dark—they had to leave the armory carrying as much as they could. Walking slowly and as silently as possible, until they reached the cover of the woods. Dropping the burden in the first small clearing and coming back. Timing it so there was never more than one person moving visibly at the same time.

Rod exempted Marie from that task. She was still too worn out from her exertions, and they needed someone good with a rifle shot anyway, keeping the men at the main entrance in sight and ready to shoot if need be.

At least the work wasn't too tiring. The ammunition they carried was heavy, but they had to move so carefully that everyone had plenty of time to rest in between stints. And after an hour, they were able to shed some of their precautions. Those cretins at the main gate "standing guard" had started a campfire! A few minutes' worth of staring into the flames would make them effectively night-blind. All they had to worry about thereafter was making any loud noise.

Forty-five minutes before the time he'd allotted ran out, to Rod's surprise, they'd emptied the armory of every single round of rifle ammunition in it. It had been so long since he'd done simple manual labor that he'd forgotten how much a few people could do, just using their own muscles, if they kept at it steadily.

"Okay. We'll take as many rifles as we can. But forty-five minutes, that's it."

That work was physically much easier. Rod wouldn't let anyone carry more than two rifles, one in each hand, even though they could have easily handled more weight. He wasn't taking any chances that somebody might stumble out there in the darkness and wind up dropping several rifles in a clatter.

Even with that limitation, they managed to empty the armory of most of its rifles. All that was left in the way of usable weapons were pistols. Henceforth, Luff and his men would be able to use whatever rifles they had just as long as their magazines still had rounds. Well . . . Luff had probably stashed some rifles and ammo in his own quarters, too. Still, the one great nightmare that had haunted Andy and Rod had been the overwhelming firepower the convicts possessed. Which they had now lost.

When the four hours were up, he spent a couple of minutes chewing on the unexpected problem their success had created. The rest of their mission was important, sure, but *nothing* was as important as getting the rifles and ammo now stacked in the clearing back to the cave. Or, at the very least, hidden somewhere the convicts couldn't find them.

That would require a change of plans. The intention had been that they'd use everyone in the mission for the next stage. But Rod decided that he could make do with just himself, Marie, and . . .

Cook and Kidd, he decided. Cook, because for whatever reason, Hulbert had come to have a lot of confidence in him. Kidd, because if things went sour, it might come to a gunfight at close quarters. In that sort of gunplay, he was pretty sure Kidd was the deadliest man alive. Literally, in this new world.

Besides, it would be safer with just four of them. They couldn't do as much, but they could probably do enough—and there was much less risk of being spotted.

Marie led the way to the supply room, with Hulbert bringing up the rear. The room was located between the administration building and the gates that led to the prison cells. The men who'd designed the installation almost a hundred years back had arranged things so anything a prisoner might want or need was beyond a prisoner's reach in the event of a prison riot. They wanted to be able to starve the prisoners into submission if they had to.

That worked in their favor. Obviously, Luff had decided the original design suited his purposes as well. The areas were deserted at night.

They made their way to the first floor cafeteria, then crossed the large room and entered the back area using Marie's keys to get in. Marie stood outside the door, watching, while the others got busy. They each had a list of what Carter Leffen had called a "Recipe for Destruction." Using everyday cleaning products, they were to mix up explosives and divide them between each set of double entry gates. They wouldn't be able to time exactly when they'd explode, but when they did, Leffen thought they'd destroy the gates. Enough of them, he said, might even take down part of the wall. Even if just the gates went, nothing Luff and his people could jury-rig in their place would be nearly as strong.

They had two hours to make up the explosives, he figured. Then, with whatever they had, they'd set them and be gone. By then, Nickerson and Griffin and the others would have been able to haul the rifles and ammunition at least a half mile into the woods and have found a safe place to hide them. Kevin had said he could manage that well enough that only an expert Cherokee or Choctaw or Chickasaw woodsman—"maybe a few white men too, I guess"—could eventually find it. But none of the convicts at Alexander had a cold chance in hell.

As he was carefully finishing with his fourth bomb, Marie appeared at his side. Her face looked very pale, but that might have been a trick of the dim lighting. They were working by the light of a small electric lantern.

"Rod, you have to see this," she whispered. "You just *have* to."

Puzzled, he followed her into the cafeteria. Marie headed straight for the big walk-in freezers. The door to one of them was open. That, alone, told him how agitated Marie was. The light inside was spilling into the interior of the building. Hopefully, given the few windows, nobody would spot it. But he'd still have to chide her about the carelessness.

When he got to the open door, though, he forgot all about reproving her. His jaw dropped.

"Holy Christ," he whispered.

He was sure his own face was pale. Most of the shelves were stacked with naked human bodies. Headless naked bodies. The heads that had once belonged to them were stacked on a different shelf.

"Get Cook and Kidd," he said. After Marie left, remembering, he closed the door to the freezer. Not all the way, just enough to eliminate almost all of the light coming out.

When Cook and Kidd arrived, he opened the door little. "Look inside."

They did so, for about ten seconds. After an initial little intake of breath, Kidd pursed his lips. There was no expression at all on Cook's face. In fact, after a few seconds he said, as calmly as could be: "They must have gotten the generators back up."

"What the fuck is going on here?" hissed Rod. "I want a straight answer."

Cook and Kidd withdrew their heads and he closed the freezer. Then he went to check the next one.

It was also full of corpses and severed heads.

The third one was almost full. After Cook saw that, he shook his head and said—in that same maddeningly calm voice—"I wonder what the maniac will figure out next. Once this claptrap solution runs out of steam."

The man's calm was almost infuriating. "What the *fuck* is going on? You didn't tell us about this!"

He barely caught himself before shouting the last sentence.

Cook shook his head. "We didn't tell you about it because it hadn't happened before we left. Remember—I did tell you that Luff was using us Boomers as his body-disposal unit. After we were gone"—he shrugged and hooked a thumb at the lockers—"I guess this was his next solution. And if it finally dawns on you that Luff is jumping from a frying pan into the fire, I told you that also. You know that phrase, 'penny-wise, pound-foolish.' Probably dates back to one of Luff's ancestors."

"Jesus." Being fair, Cook *had* told them that Luff's madness took the form of solving one problem at the expense of creating a bigger one. But neither Rod nor Andy had imagined anything this . . . this . . .

"Jesus," he repeated. "It's like a photo I saw once. Some place in Cambodia, during the Pol Pot regime."

"Tuol Sleng," Kidd provided. "I was thinking the same thing."

Rod stared at him. Kidd smiled.

"And if you're wondering how I'd know that, there are three possible explanations. I'm a man of many parts. I have a keen interest in the photography of the grotesque. I was looking to see if I might spot some professional tips. I'll let you decide which explanation is the right one."

"I vote for 'you're a man of many parts,'" Marie said immediately.

"Smart lady. I think I'll vote the same way myself."

Rod sighed. "God help them. How many bodies are in there, do you think?"

"Dozens," said Cook. "For a professional estimate, you'd have to let me look inside again."

Rod shook his head. "No, let's get back to work."

They set as many bombs as they had, just in time to make Rod's new deadline. Now, they had to leave. The first light of dawn would be appearing in less than half an hour.

Once they got into the woods, they looked back.

"How soon, do you think?" Cook asked.

"Don't ask me. I told Leffen I wanted detonators that, whatever else, wouldn't go off too quickly. But how that weird chemical setup he designed works, I have no idea. There wasn't even a fuse."

"Burning fuse would've been spotted by the first man who saw them," said Kidd. "Way it is, even if somebody does see the bombs before they go off, they'll just think some lazy con left a bunch of jars full of piss lying around. And"—here came his shark's grin—"being lazy cons themselves, won't even think to haul them out."

Rod understood why Cook had asked the question. He was tempted to wait himself, to see what would happen when the bombs went off.

But that might take hours, for all he knew. They'd been up all night and they were all tired, especially Marie. They needed to get at least a mile into the woods—two would be better—before looking for a place to sleep.

"Let's go," he said. "We'll know soon enough. Once Andy hears about those lockers, he's gonna go ballistic."

"Andy Blacklock doesn't ever go ballistic," said Marie.

Rod chuckled. "Fooled by appearances. I don't mean

ballistic as in blowing his stack. I mean 'ballistic' as in figuring out the same thing I did. Luff's regime is self-destructing. Best to help it along as fast as possible. Watch and see if I'm not right. This isn't going to be a slow war of siege and attrition."

After a while, he added: "And there's something else. I don't really understand it, because it's not my nature. But Andy Blacklock *cares* about his prisoners. The word 'guard' means a lot of things to him, besides a paycheck and keeping the streets safe for politicians to go campaigning in."

CHAPTER
⟨ᴍᴍᴏ 50 ᴏᴍᴍ⟩

Adrian Luff leaned back in the chair in his office and gave the punk standing in front of the desk a long, cold stare.

The punk shrank inside his paper coverall, the only thing Luff allowed men to wear any longer, unless they were one of his own. It was harder to conceal a weapon in the paper folds. And if anyone was planning to run, they'd think twice if even their clothes would be gone after one or two days out there with the dinosaurs.

"Do you think I'll pull out the ankle shackles and put you on a chain gang clearing the side of the road?" Luff tried to remember the punk's name, but it wouldn't come. "Forget that. I won't lock your ass down, toss you into the hole for a month, or any of the nice things you would have gotten from Blacklock. You will die. Slowly, but not all that slowly."

"Listen, boss. I ain't dissin' you. I don't know nothin'."

"You were on the wall when the gate blew. If you didn't see something, you should have."

577

The punk shook his head. "I don't be lookin at nothin' 'cept the cock in front of me. I just tryin' to stay alive."

"You're just some poor bitch having to turn tricks to get by. Right?"

The punk looked at the floor and nodded.

"Well, you either remember something worth remembering, and give me a name—or you will spend the next six hours in a dentist chair. Ever had a healthy tooth pulled with no anesthetic?" Luff didn't wait for an answer. "It makes for a substandard day. On the bright side, having no teeth might be a professional help to you. Logan, take this dickwad to the infirmary. Pull every tooth in his head. When you're done, bring him back to me. I think he'll be more willing to chat then."

"No!" The punk trembled, his face graying. "Wait! I'll tell ya, I did see somethin'. A man!"

"Too late. You can't miss a dental appointment. We'll talk afterward. Or rather, I'll talk and you'll mumble."

The punk didn't know anything, Luff was sure of that. But someone did. And when word got around about the dentist chair, those who did know would stand in line to tell him what was what.

It has to be Bostic. And Cook, probably. And they must have had inside help.

Bostic had been gone almost a week. He'd disappeared the day of the riot, after hooking up with Boomer's boys. Cook had probably gone with him too, although no one had seen him.

That was fine. Let the bastards leave. He hoped one of those things with the big teeth and big claws got them.

But why would Bostic blow the gate, too? It made no sense. The man had wanted to tuck tail and run south, not run the prison.

The armory had been stripped, which did make sense. Luff and his men still had pistols, but it wouldn't be long before the ammunition for the rifles ran out. If another big riot broke out, they'd be in a real jam. After that, they'd be down to pistols, and cons weren't that afraid of sidearms. Not afraid enough, anyway. Sooner or later, some of them would work themselves up to rush Luff's reliables. When that happened, they'd get their hands on at least a few of the pistols and there'd be all hell to pay.

There was only one solution. It was time to tighten the screws again. This time, hard and fast. Break everybody's spirit all the way down, including that of his own people. He couldn't take the chance that another Collins might emerge. That was the reason he'd had the four guards watching the main entrance immediately executed. The armory had been plundered right under their noses!

No second chance, no mercy. Do as you're told, do it now, and do it right. Or you go into the freezers. Or wherever else Luff figured to put them, once the freezers finally filled up. Which would be by tomorrow morning, he reminded himself.

At first, he'd thought maybe Blacklock and the guards had done it. But that didn't make any sense, on at least two counts. First, the whole operation had been too ruthless. Everybody knew Blacklock and Schuler were softheaded. And maybe they'd died and now Hulbert was running the show out there, but Hulbert wasn't bright enough to have figured out something like this.

For Christ's sake, the man was one of those survivalist goofballs. Spent his weekends voluntarily doing what no one in his right mind would do for money. A guy like that was hardheaded, sure, but he had a brain the size of a walnut.

Besides, Luff knew from Collins what Blacklock and his people had taken out of the prison when they left. They'd had no explosives. Whatever had been used to blow the gates had been something jury-rigged. Probably from the kitchen locker room supplies, from the looks of things. What upstanding officer of the law would know how to do that?

Answer: None. Even Collins had been a dummy, that way. But Bostic might very well know. And if he didn't, one of Boomer's boys would. Carter Leffen had been one of the men spotted leaving the prison in that faked "plague" caravan. Everybody knew he was a wizard at making things go boom.

Adrian enjoyed solving puzzles. It was the only pleasure he had left.

CHAPTER
51

"No," Andy said firmly. "We go as fast as possible. We wait just long enough for that one catapult to be finished. That'll be enough to send over the smoke bombs that Leffen's making up. To hell with anything fancier."

Rod scratched his jaw. He'd known Andy would want to move quickly, but he hadn't foreseen anything *this* quick. They hadn't gotten back and given their report but three hours ago. "A smoke bomb won't hurt anybody."

"I know that," Andy said patiently. "But it will confuse them—and by now I'm sure that regime of Luff's is held together by nothing more than chewing gum and baling wire. I mean, Jesus. Three freezers stuffed with corpses and severed heads? And we already knew from James here that Luff started his killing spree almost immediately. By now . . ."

His normally ruddy face looked ashen. Rod knew that the news that hundreds of the inmates had been slaughtered was affecting him. The problem was that he thought it was affecting his military judgment too.

But, to his surprise, Chief Watkins spoke up in support of Andy's plan.

"I agree with the captain," he said. "Most forts get captured because the defenders are caught unprepared. That's how the Red Sticks took Fort Mims." He chuckled. "That backfired on them, of course, once Andy Jackson got into the act afterward. But that fucking asshole's nowhere around to save this Luff fellow's bacon." A bit grudgingly, he added: "Not that he probably would have anyway."

Cook weighed in, then. "Yeah, let's just do it. But I don't agree with one thing in your plan, Captain Blacklock. Just rushing the main gate seems . . . well, silly, to be honest. We should go for the armory again, too."

"The *armory*? No matter how crazy Luff is, he's bound to have that well-guarded by now. And that door wasn't . . ." Blacklock trailed to silence, his eyes widening.

"Sure, we didn't blow it up. So what? We got the key, still. And I can guarantee you that whatever else Luff has, he doesn't have a locksmith with his tools to have changed the lock."

"He might have it barred or chained from the inside, though."

"So? Worst that happens, we create a diversion. But I'm willing to bet he doesn't. In fact, I'm willing to bet my life—I *will* be betting my life, since I'll volunteer to lead the attack—that Luff still isn't worrying much about what sort of threat might come from the outside. He'll have analyzed our raid on the armory and come up with exactly the wrong conclusion. There must have been somebody on the inside involved. And he doesn't know who it is. That's what he'll be fretting over."

Blacklock studied him, for a moment. "Is he that crazy?"

Cook shrugged. "It's just the way the man's mind works. He's a *manipulator*, Captain. He doesn't lead a gang, he engineers one. He's smart, but I remember what the Boom said about him. Luff will always ignore a straight-forward answer if he can find a complicated one. Look at that attack on me he told Butch Wesson to do. What was the purpose of it? I spent some time trying to figure that out, and finally had the sense to ask Boomer. He said Luff was trying to get me to be cooperative with him, since I had access to the infirmary. But instead of just asking, or figuring out some way to bribe me, he went about it ass-backwards."

Blacklock thought about it. "All right, I can see your point. But he'll still have at least a dozen men guarding the armory. Some outside, but most probably inside."

Cook smiled. "You still don't get it, Captain. Luff won't have *anybody* inside the armory. He won't trust anybody in there. He'll have it locked inside and out—with him having the only keys. The guards won't be in the armory. Some of them will be on the outside, and some might be guarding the inside door—but not inside the armory itself."

He glanced over at the Boomers sitting a distance away from the leadership conference. "We can handle the guards on the outside easily enough. Kidd alone could probably do that. What happens next, I don't know. If the guards on the inside are steady enough, we'll pretty much be stymied. Opening that second door and just rushing out would be dicey as hell. But by then you'll have started

the main attack and I don't think they'll stick around.
They'll be too rattled. Those guys aren't what you'd call
Delta Force, you know."

Rod had been thinking about it, while the two talked,
and the more he did, the more he liked Cook's plan. If
nothing else, even if Cook and his men couldn't get out of
the armory, they'd have taken it. Luff wouldn't have access
to it either. And he was pretty sure Cook's assessment was
right. Whatever guards were assigned to watch the inside
door probably would abandon the assignment, once the
crap hit the fan.

Andy, apparently, had come to the same conclusion.
"All right. I take it your proposal is to turn the whole job
over to you Boomers?"

"Seems sensible. Look, let's face it. Some day we may all
be good buddies and make jokes about Botany Bay. But
right now, your guards and us Boomers are about as
comfortable together as cats and dogs sharing a lifeboat.
With the dogs getting hungry and the cats in a foul mood.
Trying to mix us together on the spot into a single combat
team is just pie in the sky. You know it, and I know it. So
you take one assignment—you and the Cherokees—and
concentrate on getting through the main gate.
Meanwhile, we'll see what we can do at the armory."

"I think he's right, Andy," Rod said. "To be honest, if
you were to add the Boomers to my platoon, I'd just
scratch my head and tell them to keep out my way. I
wouldn't know what else to do."

"Yeah, I can see that. All right, Cook. No, I guess I'd
better start calling you James, huh?" That came with a
little smile. "But what do you propose to do assuming you

succeed and get out of the armory? We need to be careful we don't wind up shooting at each other."

Cook chewed on his lower lip for a few seconds. "We'll go for the watch towers. You'll have enough on your plate as it is."

"All right. I'll make sure all my people know. But keep in mind that we're almost certainly going to be taking fire from those towers before you can take them. If you can even try at all. So if you do get into any of the towers, we need some sort of signal that lets us know they're now in friendly hands."

"Those Spanish blankets are distinctive—and it's one thing we know Luff and his people can't possibly have. We'll cut some strips and take them with us. If you see one hanging from a tower, pretty please stop shooting at it."

"Okay." Andy looked around the small circle gathered at the campfire. Him, Hulbert, Watkins, Kershner, and Cook. "Sergeant, how are you and your men doing with the new rifles?"

"Very well—except I think Susan Fisher's niece will be getting jealous. Pitzel is talking about marrying his new rifle." In his heavy Swabian accent, he added, "I am struggling against the temptation myself. Fortunately, unlike Pitzel, I have read the Bible and know that such a joining is forbidden by the Lord."

Between the accent and the young man's solemn face, it was hard to know if he was joking or being serious. "Uh . . . where does it say that in the Bible?" Rod asked.

"Leviticus. Somewhere in there, almost everything is forbidden."

It'd been a long time since Hulbert read the Bible;

even then, he'd only read parts of it. He was pretty sure he'd skipped over Leviticus because—well, yeah, it had seemed like page after page of you can't do this and you can't do that or you must do this and do it exactly this and that a way. Still, he thought it unlikely that God had said anything specifically about .223 caliber semiautomatic rifles.

"I guess," was all he said, though. Arguing Biblical interpretation with a nineteenth-century German-American was probably as pointless as arguing it with Brian Carmichael.

"Let's get going then," said Blacklock. "Edelman tells me the catapult will be finished today, and Leffen will have enough bombs put together. I want us moving out at dawn. Two days from now, we take Alexander back."

CHAPTER
52

Margo stared up at the ceiling, her hands clasped behind her head. Given that her body was only covered by the sheets from the waist down, Nick found the sight distracting. Which was odd, perhaps, given that he could hardly claim to be sexually frustrated. In fact, he was feeling a little exhausted. Margo made love with the same enthusiastic verve she drove her SUV.

"Do you ever wonder what's happening to those poor people, Nick?"

"Yes, I do. At least three times a day. But I start by reminding myself that they aren't 'poor people' to begin with. They're my kind of people, actually. I grew up in an Ohio town not that much different from the towns that produced the guards and nurses at Alexander."

He reached for a cigarette, and shook one loose from Margo's pack when she extended her hand. Both he and Margo smoked, which was bad for their health and getting less and less socially acceptable as time went by—but was very handy, from a romantic standpoint. No matter how different they were in other ways, they shared the smoker's sense of withstanding a bitter and relentless siege shoulder to shoulder.

After he lit hers, and lit his, he lay down next to her—shoulder to shoulder—and looked up at the ceiling also. "As for the Cherokees, I think they'd resent being called 'those poor people.' I know some Cherokees. Even today, after all that's happened to them, they're a proud people. At least, the ones I know are."

"Well, yeah. But . . . most of them are convicts. Maximum security type convicts at that." She exhaled cigarette smoke and chuckled. "Of course, I guess that just reinforces your point. Not even knee-jerk bleeding heart liberals like me really think felons are hapless waifs."

They smoked in silence, for a while. Then Nick sat up, stubbed out his cigarette, and offered her the ashtray to do the same. Like most things in Margo's quarters in the facility, the ashtray was simple and utilitarian. Aside from her politics and her knuckle-tightening disregard for each and every principle of defensive driving, the only extravagance the woman seemed to have was a devotion to ice cream that bordered on idolatry. She'd had some sort of enormous mostly ice cream dessert after dinner, and had then insisted on stopping at a Dairy Queen on the way back to the mine. How she managed that and kept her slim figure was a mystery. Just one of those people with a furnace for a metabolism, he guessed, rather enviously. Nick gained weight easily, if he didn't watch his diet and slipped on his exercise program. That had been a problem for him even as a young man, much less at the age he was now.

"We just don't know, is the only answer," he said. "And we never will know what happened to them—or is happening to them. Malcolm says it's theoretically possible, with enough data—which we might even have, with this event—that we could someday send a probe of some kind that might find them. But theoretically possible and technologically feasible are two completely different things."

"As any physicist can tell you, especially particle physicists like me. The experiments we could do—*if* we could generate the energy." She gave him a look he couldn't quite interpret. "Do you pray for them?" she asked abruptly.

"Yes. Every night."

She nodded. "I'm not religious, as I think you know. But if you want to say prayers now, please feel free. Or any time you're with me. I won't join you, but I won't mind, either."

"Thank you. I will, then."

After he finished, she stroked his arm. "This is going pretty well, I think."

"Yeah. So do I."

"But I'm not budging on the driving. Forget that crap about the man taking the wheel."

Nick chuckled. "I can live with that. Or not. But I noticed that Alex included a very nice life insurance policy in that package. So I guess I can't plead mercy for my poor kids left orphaned."

"Poor kids! One of your sons is a lawyer, one of them's a computer technician with his own consulting business, and the third is studying to be doctor. And both your daughters look to be doing well for themselves too."

"Well. True. I did pretty good by them, for a trash-hauler whose father was a steelworker." He lay back down next to her, cupping an arm around her shoulder, and stared at the ceiling again. "It's too bad we'll never know. Because if we could, I'd bet you dollars for donuts those 'poor people' will do just about the same, give 'em three generations. Including a fair number of the inmates."

CHAPTER
53

James Cook moved quickly through the basement of the administration building. The smell down here was even worse than he remembered. Spending the last few days in the cleanest air he'd ever known—whatever other problems the Cretaceous had, manmade pollution was not one of them—had had its effect on him. Using the beam of a flashlight, he took the stairs two at a time, shoved open the door to the main level and breathed in air that now carried a different stench. This was the smell of too many humans living without bathing or plumbing. Sweat, urine, and feces.

The rest of the Boomers followed close behind. All of them except Kidd and Leffen. Kidd was lying back at the armory, with Leffen—who'd really be pretty useless in a fight—left there to watch over him and, hopefully, keep Geoffrey from bleeding to death.

Getting into the armory had been a simple matter of

gunning down five not-wary-enough sentries and unlocking a door. Getting *out* of it and into the rest of the installation had been a different story altogether.

What James simply hadn't foreseen was that, once inside the armory and at the door leading out, they'd have no way of knowing if there were any guards waiting beyond. In the end, after he dilly-dallied for a couple of minutes, Kidd had told him to just open the fricking door and he'd handle the rest.

Which he had. There'd been four of Luff's men on the other side of the door, it turned out, all of them with pistols. Kidd had gone through rolling, come up, and taken out all of them. The whole incredible gunfight hadn't lasted more than three or four seconds.

But he'd taken two bullets himself. One a minor flesh wound in the arm, but the other . . .

Kidd would make it or he wouldn't. In the meantime, James didn't have any time to spare.

Blacklock had given them a five-minute lead. Then, they'd start the main attack on the gate—which, from the sound of things, had already erupted. The Boomers needed to reach West Tower while everything was still chaotic and confused for the prison's defenders.

The Boomers moved through the door, crossed the floor, dropped down a flight of steps, and then took off through the perimeter tunnel at a near run. They arrived at the base of West Tower short of breath, then leaned or squatted against the wall waiting for their breathing to even out. The next stage of the operation was going to take stealth, not speed.

"Sounds like a war out there," Morelli said.

Boyne snorted. "There damn well better be a war going on out there, Dino, or we're dead meat."

"Yeah, I know. I was just sort of, you know, reassuring myself."

When James was sure all the men were capable of breathing slowly and silently, he took off his shoes, tied the laces together and draped them across the back of his neck and over his shoulders. The others did the same. It was time to climb the one-hundred-plus steps to the observation deck.

He wanted to rush, but didn't. Instead, his pistol in his hand, he climbed a few steps and then waited a few seconds. Unlike Hulbert, who'd kept his eyes to the scope, James had watched the way Griffin and Nickerson had stalked the guards outside the armory. He'd been impressed by the Cherokee's cold-blooded patience and it hadn't taken him long to understand the key.

One or two sounds were hard to interpret. A succession of sounds is what brought sense and meaning.

He took another few steps. Then waited a few seconds. Then another few steps; another. And so on, all the way up the stairs.

Time ticked away. James had to force himself to stay patient. He might be overdoing it, sure. Morelli had been right—that *did* sound like a war going on out there. The convicts in the tower above were probably not paying attention to anything else. Still, he forced himself to maintain the stalk.

None of the Boomers objected, even though they must all have been feeling the same impatience. By now, James knew his authority over them was unchallenged. In fact, it was probably even stronger than Boomer's had been. James wasn't erratic, the way the Boom could be.

The stairs ended six inches above his head and the floor began. He motioned for everyone to be still and then took the next step so he could get a peek inside. The small room was full of cigarette smoke. A body was curled against the far wall. The man's head was down, his chin on his chest, as if he were asleep. James couldn't see the face. But the blood that soaked his entire coverall made it obvious he was dead. Some guard out there—probably Hulbert or Nickerson or Marie Keehn—had hit the sniper's triangle.

The cigarette smoke was coming from two other convicts, still standing at the firing windows with rifles in their hands. Next to the windows, rather, keeping under cover. The sniper's bullet that had taken out the con against the wall had obviously made them cautious. As James watched, one of the men spit out his cigarette, raised his rifle, took a quick step to the side, fired three shots, and scuttled back under cover. He couldn't have possibly been able to really aim at anything. But, in a way, that didn't matter. James knew that all the firing outside was just covering fire from Blacklock and his men. Unless the Boomers could take out the tower, any attempt to rush the gate would produce bad casualties.

James dropped his left hand so Boyne and the others could see. Two fingers. Two cons. He pointed toward Boyne and then to the right. Boyne nodded.

James took a deep breath and lunged into the room. The con who'd spit out the cigarette saw him coming, but before he could bring the rifle around, James had started shooting.

James wasn't a gunfighter and he wasn't a hit man. He'd never fired a pistol at anything but a target in his life, and hadn't done that all that many times. But he had steady nerves—very steady—and he knew how to use a gun, and he wasn't worried about ammunition. They had plenty of pistol ammunition.

And it was very close range.

Later, he figured out he'd fired eight rounds. All but one of them hit the convict, somewhere in his body. Three of them had been fatal wounds.

He looked to his right. Boyne had done the same, obviously. The rounds he'd fired combined with James' own had left James feeling a little dizzy. The noise had been pretty incredible, in that enclosed space.

He saw John's lips move.

"What?" he asked. Then, pointed to his ear.

Boyne came closer and almost shouted. "I'd forgotten how much noise a pistol makes in a room." He grinned. "That's what got me the hard sentence, you know. If I'd just shot the bastard humping my wife once or twice, they mighta gone easy on me. But I emptied the whole clip. Wadn't much left of the dirty rotten fuck, by the time I was done."

Jealousy wasn't an emotion James approved of, probably because he suffered from it fairly badly himself. Any time he spotted Elaine in what looked like a friendly conversation with another man, he got a little twinge. But he was bound and determined, this time around, to keep it under control—and he wasn't really worried about her anyway. For one thing, she was at least as possessive as he was. The squint in her eyes was a sight to behold, whenever she spotted *him* talking in a friendly way to another woman.

Still, even in his worst days—even drunk—James couldn't imagine himself actually murdering somebody out of jealousy. But . . . who knew? He'd never caught a girlfriend in fragrant deliction, either, or whatever it was called. On the other hand, why had Boyne been carrying a gun in the first place? The adultery couldn't have caught him *that* much by surprise. Unless he packed a piece everywhere he went, which wasn't likely. Boyne had been a machinist, not a gangster.

And why was his mind wandering? They were, in fact, in the middle of a war.

"Get a blanket up here!" he yelled down the stairs.

A moment later, the strip of blanket was passed up, hand to hand.

Crouching to stay out of the line of fire, James moved to the open window and tossed most of the blanket strip through. Then, squatting by the wall and holding the other end in his hand, he wondered what he could use to anchor it. That was another thing he hadn't given any thought to, earlier.

So much for his budding career as Julius Caesar or Alexander the Great. For a brief instant, James felt a powerful spike of longing for his familiar job as an emergency medical technician. That had sometimes gotten stressful, but it was a stress he was *familiar* with.

Boyne squatted next to him. He'd apparently analyzed the same quandary.

"We gotta leave two guys here anyway, boss. That was the plan. But I figure we may as well leave three. Hell, leave four. Now that we done it once, the truth is that having a lot of Boomers along is pretty pointless. Two, three, four guys can take a tower, or it can't be done at all." He pointed to the strip-end in James' hand. "One of 'em can take a break by sitting here and holding the blanket. Two guys watch at the window with rifles. One guy watches the stairs with a pistol."

As plans went, it was better than the one James had drawn up. He let Boyne pick out the men to stay at West Tower, while he steadied himself for the next task.

He thought they'd still have the advantage of surprise, at least. This tower had been the critical one, since it was the tower that covered the main entrance. He could already hear the sounds of Blacklock's men pouring through the entrance. The Cherokees were out there too. Their war whoop was distinctive. Scary as hell, too. James didn't think any of the cons in the other towers would be paying much attention to anything else.

He could be wrong, of course. But they'd find out soon enough.

The battle inside the prison was now in full swing.

The moment Andy Blacklock saw that strip of Spanish blanket coming out of the tower window, he ordered the charge on the entrance. By then, the catapult Edelman had designed and the Cherokees had built—Jeff called it a "trebuchet," with his usual fussiness about terminology— had fired more than a dozen of Leffen's smoke bombs. The entrance area was almost completely obscured. Anyone firing at them as they charged would be firing blindly. It had been the danger from the tower that had really kept everyone pinned. At least one of the cons up there was a marksman. Two of Andy's people had been killed by him, already.

Not in a while, though. Hulbert had taken out one of them, and that might very well have been the sniper. The men remaining up there, after that, had just satisfied themselves with little quick bursts of rifle fire.

It was all a moot point now, though. Cook and the Boomers had done their job.

Four more guards went down charging the entrance. As closely spaced as they were—had to be, given the dimensions involved—even someone firing blind was bound to hit somebody, at least a few times. Unfortunately, while the bombs Hulbert's raid had planted had destroyed the gates, they hadn't been powerful enough to really damage the walls.

Then, finally, they were in the smoke, searching for the defenders. Leffen had told them the smoke wouldn't be too hard on the eyes—but if this was his idea of "not too bad on the eyes," Andy didn't want to think what the little convict could produce if he was deliberately trying to blind someone.

Still, squinting or not, a little teary-eyed or not, they could see well enough. There were five convicts still left in the area when they came through the gate. All five went down, along with one of the Cherokees. Two of the convicts were shot while trying to run away.

They'd lost seven people so far, that Andy knew of, at least four of them killed outright. But they had the entrance to the prison. That was the critical thing. There was no longer any way that Luff and his men could get it back.

CHAPTER 54

Frank Nickerson led eight guards into the armory. Blacklock had ordered him to make sure it was secured, and then—if the situation permitted—position himself and his people as snipers on the roofs.

The armory itself was empty. Just beyond, they found Geoffrey Kidd on the floor, with his back propped against a wall. He looked to be bleeding pretty badly. Carter Leffen was kneeling next to him, fussing and fidgeting and obviously doing the man no good at all.

Frank looked around. The bodies of four convicts were scattered around the area. All of them had been shot in the neck or upper chest.

Kidd's work, obviously. Frank didn't care what the general attitude of the guards was. He was starting to get very fond of Geoffrey Kidd.

"Leffen, leave him alone. You're probably doing more harm than good."

Frank looked over the people he had. Bird Matthews,

he thought, had the most medical training of any of them.

"Matthews, you stay here and do what you can for Kidd. Jenkins, you stand guard. The rest of you, come with me."

"What do I do?" asked Leffen plaintively.

"I have no idea. Just stay out of the way. And don't burn anything down, fiddling around."

"Why would I do that?" Leffen said, more plaintively still. "Ain't no insurance companies left."

In the machine shop area that he used for his war room, Adrian Luff moved three tool bits across the diagram of the prison. "Haggerty, get out there and tell Hancock, Olszanski, and Thaxton to get their squads up to cover the entrance. Those guys there will need reinforcements."

Haggerty left. Luff moved another couple of tool bits, while crooking a finger at Walker. "Jimmy, you go round up Metcalf and Michaels. We need to take back the armory."

Walker left. Whatever reservations or doubts he or any of Luff's top lieutenants might have had about the situation, they were buried deep in their brains and out of sight. By now, Luff's authority was absolute. And there was something very reassuring about the way he kept calm and collected under any circumstances.

Walker even thought they were going to win this battle.

Haggerty could have warned him otherwise, by the time Walker reached the area where Metcalf and Michaels were supposed to be. But Haggerty was dead by then.

Haggerty had passed through D-block on his way to find the squads Luff had sent him to find. The building was mostly empty, by then, with not more than a fourth of the cells still occupied. He was caught completely off guard by seven convicts rushing out of one of the cells. All these cells were supposed to be locked! There weren't any reliables in D-block.

He only got off two shots with his rifle, and neither of them hit anything but the walls of an adjoining cell. The first con who grabbed him had gone for the rifle and had wrestled it aside.

Haggerty would have died eventually from the beating that ensued. But a sharpened pork bone driven through his eye and into his brain made sure of it. Not even Luff's maniacal regime, it turned out, had been able to keep inmate ingenuity suppressed.

When they were done with Haggerty, the convicts went back into the cell and hauled out one of Luff's men. One of his "reliables," as he called them. His name was Jack Mayes. The man had remained cowering in a corner, after agreeing to unlock the cell for them.

Seeing the convict yanking the pork bone out of Haggerty's eye and coming toward him, Mayes squawked. "Hey! We had a deal!"

By then, two other cons had him by the arms. A third con, standing behind, kicked his legs out from under him. A fourth con seized him by the hair and jerked his head into position.

"We lied," were the words that came with the pork bone.

Dino Morelli led the attack on the next tower. James had planned to do it himself again, but the Boomers simply wouldn't let him.

They wouldn't allow Boyne to take part, either. At some indefinable point between towers, those men had started accepting that they might actually have a future.

"You ain't got nothing to prove, boss," was Morelli's comment. "Neither does John."

Morelli did a better job anyway. He wasn't as purely murderous as Kidd would have been. But a man doesn't commit that many armed robberies without leaning how to use a pistol, even if a smart armed robber like Morelli never actually fired a shot in the course of his crimes. The reason for his long sentence—the judge had thrown the book at him—wasn't because he'd hurt anyone in the course of the robberies. But he'd terrified lots of people and he'd done so damn *many* of them.

Six shots were all he fired, and he took down two men with them. The Boomer with him, on the other hand— that was Quentin Jackson—emptied his whole clip at his target.

That was mostly just personal, though. Jackson was quite good with a pistol and knew perfectly well his first three shots had taken care of his man. But since the man involved was Tom Davidson and they had plenty of ammunition, Jackson saw no reason not to satisfy an old grudge.

"How does it feel being shot to doll rags, you fuck?" He started unzipping his coverall.

"Jackson, cut it out," said Morelli. "We ain't got time for you to piss on him."

"Sure we do. You and me supposed to stay here and guard the tower. We got plenty of time."

"Fine. I don't want to *smell* it, how's that?"

In the end, Jackson satisfied the last of his grudge by muscling Davidson's body out of the window and letting it plunge to the concrete far below. Between that and all the bullets he'd put in him, the man would spend his afterlife a mangled mess. Jackson was a Rastafarian, of sorts—a one-man sect in the creed—and believed firmly that you went into the afterlife looking the way you did when you died.

"Think there's any weed in the here and now?" he asked Morelli, a half hour later.

Morelli had been wondering the same thing. From what he could see and hear, they'd be having a celebration tomorrow. And Morelli didn't approve of liquor. The stuff was bad for you.

Frank took down the first two convicts advancing on the armory with four shots, two for each. The fusillade that followed from the guards with him took down three more. The rest ran.

"Anybody hurt?" he asked.

Thankfully, nobody was.

Behind them, Bird Matthews finished with her first aid.

"Amazingly enough—assuming nothing gets infected— I think you're going to make it."

"Hope so." Geoffrey hissed a little at the pain. "I'm worried about my kids."

Matthews shifted to a squat and looked at him. "Wouldn't think you would be. That much."

"Meaning no offense, ma'am, but what you know about the heart and soul of a big city hit man could be written on the head of a pin. Where were you born and raised? From the accent, I'd say Podunkville, Middle-of-the-Sticks. Population, five hundred."

Matthews smiled. "Okay. Fair enough. Why'd you do it, then?"

He started to shrug, but the pain that gesture caused drew another hiss. "Hard to explain, exactly. Looking back on it, I think I'd've done better to take up hamburger-flipping. In the long run, anyway. At the time, though . . ."

His eyes studied nothing in particular on one of the walls. "When you're a kid growing up in Chicago's Englewood neighborhood, with a whore for a mother and a string of men coming through instead of a father, your options look pretty limited. And you got the moral code of an alley cat. By the time I was fifteen, though, I knew two things for sure. And two things only. First, I was queer. Second, I was tougher'n anybody I knew. Way, way tougher than anybody my own age. So . . . one thing led to another. It doesn't take too long before you realize you've burned every bridge that might have existed behind you. After that . . ."

He was silent, for a while. "The funny thing is, the only thing I really regretted was that I figured I'd never have kids. And now I do. So, here I am. For the first time in my life since I was a kid myself, worrying about something."

"Well, I know that feeling. It's the one thing—the only thing, and I stress that—I miss about not being straight."

Kidd peered at her. "You're the dyke, right? The one they say has a motorcycle jacket?"

Matthew chuckled. "Yep, that's me. Of course, I never wore it on duty. But if I can get my locker back, I'll show it to you."

He managed an actual grin, despite the pain. "I'd surely like to see that jacket. The prospect's enough to keep me living, I figure. Between that and the kids."

They were at the administration building, now. Andy Blacklock and Jeff Edelman worked their way across the building's large entryway. A half dozen guards bolted up the stairs, checking the upper floor offices. Another dozen went through the main level payroll offices looking under desks and inside file cabinets. And another half dozen went downstairs, to the basement area, checking behind boilers and inside tool rooms.

A few slow minutes passed and the *all clear* call came from everywhere.

The gates to the prison's interior were closed and locked, but they had a key. It slowed them down, but didn't stop them. None of the prisoners had stayed behind to protect the area.

They went through the first set of gates. The second set, the ones dividing the guardhouse from the prisoner holding area, was open. So was the third set leading from the building to the main street inside the walls.

"Where *are* they?" Andy muttered. He was starting to get a little rattled, almost. Except for one brief firefight with a small group of convicts shortly after they took the entrance, they hadn't run into any opposition. And that firefight hadn't lasted more than a few seconds. One guard went down, with a leg wound, and two convicts were killed. The rest ran.

In fact, the prison seemed eerily deserted.

At Andy's command, four COs left the main body of guards and veered left. They went through a door and up the stairs to the holding area reserved for men who needed close watching. The stairway was narrow, just thirty inches across. And instead of the normal eight inch run and eight inch rise with a tread of eight or nine inches, the stone stairs had a six inch tread. And their rise and run varied from step to step. Eight inches, six inches, nine inches, four inches. The stairs, built without a handrail, had been designed to slow prisoners down. They were difficult to climb and treacherous to descend at any pace above a snail's.

The guards, four members of the prison's extraction team, went up the stairs sideways, at a pace most people wouldn't have thought possible. Once at the top, they fanned out. It didn't take long to check the cells, bathrooms, and guard's station. The wing was clear. No prisoners.

Inside one of the cells was a small wooden sculpture of a woman. Her perky nose, full hair, and large eyes almost matched a photograph lying on the bottom bunk. Scrawled on the wall opposite the bunk was a message written in bright green paint:

I am murdered

Beneath that message was another:

No honor among thieves

The men looked at the graffiti. After a few seconds,

Lowell Van Wagenen sighed. "It's not like Mark to leave his wife's picture on the bunk."

The others nodded. Mark Huston carried Peggy Huston's photo everywhere he went. The man showed it to anyone who would look at it. He had once said it was his life ring, the thing that kept him sane. No one ever pointed out that sanity was not the man's strong suit. Or that Peggy's photo looked just like Reba McEntire when she was young. Or that, according to his prison records, Mark had never married. Instead, they were grateful.

From the time the picture showed up until the day of the Quiver they hadn't had to rush him to the infirmary because he had eaten glass or razor blades. They hadn't had to put him on suicide watch or in the hole for fighting with other prisoners. And not once did a CO get gunned down with a bucket of piss and shit.

Mark loved his Peggy and their two children, a boy and girl who looked like kids out of a Sears catalogue. He was always full of stories about their antics in school and how they helped their mother. He made no phone calls and received no letters. But he could always tell you what they did over the weekend. A three-time loser who would never see the outside, he talked about the things he would do with his family once he got home. The fishing trips they would take, and the vacations to Yellow Ray and Disney World. He even took classes at the prison school so he could earn a living once he was on the outside. He planned to go straight. He was going to do it for the kids. He wanted them to grow up right. He wanted his son to be a doctor and his girl to marry well. There would be no jailbird for her.

Gently, Lowell put the photograph in his shirt pocket and said, "Let's go."

A few minutes later they rejoined Andy and the other guards, who had just finished with cellblock A. It was as empty as the one the extraction team had checked and no one was happy about it.

The prison felt like a trap waiting to be sprung. The empty buildings and empty walkways echoed with their footsteps and whispers. The mix of guards, Cherokees, and U.S. soldiers no longer fanned out quite as quickly when they entered a new area. They wanted to stay clustered together; their faces mirrored their emotions.

They crossed the prison checking each cell house, garbage dumpster, and abandoned vehicle they passed. Methodically, they worked their way to the exercise yard.

They could hear an occasional gunshot from somewhere in the prison, and a fair amount of shouting or screaming. But not enough. Not two thousand prisoners enough.

Rod Hulbert was on the roof of the administration building watching Captain Blacklock and Chief Watkins. Marie Keehn and two dozen of the guards were waiting at the east gate. Their plan had been pretty straightforward. They would attack the prison from the front and the west, herding the prisoners through the safe-looking east opening. Once through the wall, Marie and her people would start dropping them until and unless they surrendered.

Rod was nervous. So far, he had counted only thirty-three prisoners moving around. Most of them were dead, thanks either to him or Blacklock's people. And Cook's Boomers had taken out three of the towers, which accounted for another half dozen to a dozen.

That was *way* too low. Things were about to get deadly. They had to. There were only four buildings left to go through: C-block, D-block, the infirmary, and the machine shop. And for two thousand men to be in those buildings, it would be elbow to elbow.

He watched, ready to take down anyone he could spot. Andy and a dozen guards, backed up by Kershner and his men, were about to storm the infirmary. Most of those who would remain outside surrounded the building, their weapons trained on every window and door. A dozen others stood with their backs to the buildings. If any prisoners had been missed, and tried to come at them from behind, they would be ready.

"Goddamit, where's Haggerty?" Luff demanded of the two lieutenants he still had with him in the war room. "And Jimmy should be back by now, too."

But Jimmy Walker was in pieces, by then. Preoccupied and worried because he hadn't been able to find Michaels and Metcalf, he'd made the mistake of passing too closely by one of the locked cells in C-block packed with unreliable inmates. Hands—many hands—had seized him and yanked him against the bars. The hands tried to take his rifle, too, but the rifle had come loose and fallen on the floor too far away to be reached.

Still, the hands had Walker. And while the men who owned those hands couldn't get out of the cell, they could go to work on him. And when they tired, pass him to the hands in the next cell.

He spent the rest of his life seeing nothing but hands. Black hands, white hands, brown hands. Some of them were very strong. All of them were very eager.

He didn't see anything, after a while. His eyes were gone. Soon after, he stopped screaming. His throat was gone too.

"What do we do, boss?" asked Boyne. "We didn't expect this."

James didn't have an answer. He'd thought they'd be occupied the whole time taking the towers. But after the second tower, that Morelli had taken, the towers were empty.

Somebody had been in those towers. Cigarette butts were strewn all over. But they were gone now.

In a clearing in the woods just out of sight of the prison, Jenny Radford and Barbara Ray did another check of their supplies. There was no point to that, really. They'd gotten their improvised battlefield medical center set up long since. The handful of guards Andy had left to protect them—against predators, more than the possibility of convicts coming out—at least had that duty to keep them busy. Jenny and Barbara had nothing. Another useless check of the supplies at least kept them from having fits.

CHAPTER
55

Andy approached the door to the infirmary, praying his vest would take whatever came out the window at him. Nothing came. He halfheartedly pulled on the doorknob, expecting it to be locked. It wasn't. Hurriedly, he stepped into the entryway. The second set of doors was also unlocked. His nerves were stretched tight. His heart was in his throat. None of this made any sense.

He jumped through the door opening and turned around, checking the mirrors over his head. All the halls were empty.

There was a strange, pungent odor in the air. He couldn't quite place it.

The other guards and Kershner and his men were now just two steps behind him. They moved slowly across the floor. He waved at the examining room and one of the guards disappeared into its interior and returned in a short while, shaking his head. Another guard had moved on, checking the break room and then the records room.

Again, a headshake. Andy looked at the stairwell leading up to the second floor and couldn't help but wince. The moment they were inside the stairwell they would become sitting ducks.

He opened the door and stepped through it, motioning for the others to follow. As quickly and quietly as possible, they climbed the stairs and reached the top.

Again, the door wasn't locked. He opened it, gave a soft shove, and it swung wide. The strange odor was there, stronger now, but no prisoners. They moved quickly, fanning out.

"Blacklock. Over here."

Kershner and Pitzel were staring into a row of three cells. Andy hurried over.

Bodies were stacked inside all of the cells, reaching from the floor to within a foot of the ceiling. All of them were headless. All of them were naked.

"Over here," Watkins called.

They turned and went over. It was another cell. This one was lined with heads.

"Jesus," one of the guards whispered. "We knew about the meat lockers, but . . ."

Andy's stomach churned and he could feel the room spin. He took a deep breath and regretted it immediately. He recognized the peculiar scent, now. But it wasn't the scent that nauseated him—that was just the smell of powerful disinfectant cleaning fluids, mixed with . . . ammonia, maybe. Or bleach. What sickened him was the realization of what had happened. Having filled the freezers, and still not knowing what to do with more bodies, Luff must have decided this was the best temporary solution.

Drenching the corpses with this homemade let's-hope-it-works hideous brew must have been what he decided would keep the bodies from decaying before he could figure out a final solution.

There was always a method to the man's madness, as mad as it might be.

"Okay," he said. "I need an estimate. How many dead?"

Jeff Edelman walked toward them, his face pale. "There are a hundred and forty-two names on this list. Every one of them except the last nineteen has a line drawn through it." He handed Andy the clipboard he'd found on the desk.

They found the guillotine in C-block. Along with—thank God—hundreds of convicts still alive, packed in their cells. And, outside the cells, what was left of a convict that Andy thought might be—might have been—Jimmy Walker.

Andy walked down the line of cells, staring at the still-living inmates. For their part, they stared back at him silently. Some of them were crying.

Eventually, one of the inmates cleared his throat and said: "Nice to see you again, Captain Blacklock. Where you been?"

"Nice to see you, Franklin. I've been detained by other business, I'm afraid. But I'm back now."

Franklin cleared his throat. "Good. We wound up missing you. A lot."

"Where's Luff?" whispered the inmate next to Franklin.

Andy shook his head. "We don't know yet. But we'll find him."

"When you do, kill him. Kill all of them. Please."

Andy didn't reply to that. He'd already come to the conclusion himself that that was probably the only rational solution. But being back inside the place he'd worked for many years—the place that, strange as it might be, had shaped his sense of duty, even his sense of self—he didn't feel able to give that order. What he could order with regard to foreign conquistadores, he simply couldn't do with regard to inmates who were under his authority.

Rod would think he was nuts, of course. Rod was probably even right. But Andy wasn't Hulbert.

"Don't worry about Luff," was all he finally said. "Whatever else, he's done."

There came the sound of a fusillade, from far away. A big one, and it was ongoing.

Andy keyed his radio. Before he could even ask, Marie's voice came over it, providing the answer.

"A lot of inmates are trying to make a break through the east gate. We're gunning them down. But they keep pouring out. Must be fifty of them already, and there's more coming."

"Are they armed? Can you handle it?"

"Yes, they're armed. Rifles, mostly. But they're completely panicked, Andy. They're not even shooting back. Just trying to get to the woods."

They had to be Luff's own people, then. Between what they'd learned from the armory raid and what they'd seen since storming the prison, Luff had disarmed every convict except his own inner circle—and most of that inner circle was now trying to get out.

"Shoot as many as you can, but don't take any risks. If some of them make it to the woods, we can live with it.

Their ammunition won't last long, no matter what. After that, it's them barehanded against the dinosaurs."

"Right. My money's on the dinosaurs."

It sounded as if Marie and her people could handle it, and Andy needed to concentrate on taking the machine shop. This was almost over, and he wanted to finish it. Now, before the horror just overwhelmed him. He knew that, to the day he died, he'd never be able to get those images out of his mind. And would always blame himself for the slaughter, in the end, no matter what reassurances people gave him.

The horror had happened on his watch. For someone like him, with his sense of duty, that was all that mattered. The only thing he could do now was end it.

Watkins came up to him. "Don't worry about the ones who make it into the woods. Kevin and a few others can take care of that problem, over the next few days. Might take a week. Probably not."

Andy stared at him. Watkins smiled. "For Kevin, it'll be like hunting deer. Except deer are more dangerous."

All things considered . . .

"Okay, fine. We'll leave it to him."

Hearing a little commotion, he turned. James Cook and about half of the Boomers had come into C-block.

"The towers are secure," Cook said without preamble. "And one of your guards—I don't know his name—told me to tell you that they've cleared D-block. They found a couple of hundred prisoners in there still alive. All of them locked up except seven, and those went back into a cell without putting up a fuss. So what's the plan now?"

Hearing that two hundred people had survived in D-block was something of a relief. But not much. That block had held over three times that many inmates, just a few weeks earlier.

But Andy pushed that aside, for the time being. First things first. "Machine shop. All that's left."

Cook nodded, then gave the cells packed with still-living inmates a long, considering look.

"You want, we Boomers can pick out some worthy men for you. Have them take the lead in the charge." He gave the prisoners that distinctive smile of his. The one Andy thought would probably terrify Las Vegas casino owners if they saw it coming. It was obviously terrifying some of the inmates.

"Least the fuckwads can do," Cook added.

The offer was tempting. But Andy wasn't about to go there.

"No, we'll handle it. Our job, not theirs."

"Get ready," said Luff. "We'll butcher 'em as they come in, and it'll all be over."

The twenty men he had left didn't say anything. A couple of them nodded.

Luff decided things had probably worked out for the best. Reliability was the key. With steady men, you could accomplish wonders, and the last hour or so had been a ruthless selection process. Any of Luff's reliables who weren't quite reliable were trying to get out through the east gate. Or trying to hide somewhere.

The ones left were really reliable. All he needed.

"Come out with your hands in the air! You will not be asked again. You have exactly ten seconds to respond."

From inside the building came a reply. "Fuck you!"

Andy looked at his watch and waited. "Five seconds!"

There was no response.

"One second!"

Crack!

That shot almost hit him. He could hear the bullet whizzing by.

Before he could even give the order, three guards lobbed gas canisters through the building's broken windows.

Hulbert could see movement through the open windows, even with the smoke. He said to the guard lying next to him on the roof: "I'm right—you're left."

That was Bradley Scott, one of the guard force's sharpshooters. Scott fired a moment later. By then, Rod had a man in his scope and took him down. For the next few seconds, firing from the vantage point of the roof and working from each side, they shot every man inside the machine shop who made himself visible. Six, all told, and maybe two others. Not all of them would be dead, though. Three of the shots Rod had taken had been at exposed limbs, and he was sure the same was true of Scott.

Nickerson and the other shooters on the other buildings were doing the same. Two minutes went by. After the first ten seconds or so, no shots had been fired from the machine shop. There'd been no counterfire at all.

During that time, other guards kept lobbing gas canisters into the building. By now, Rod knew, the inmates inside would be in bad shape.

Suddenly, waving a white strip of some kind of cloth, five men burst out of the building. Two men came behind them, but those last two were shot in the back by someone still inside before they could get out of the door.

The five men who'd made it out were coughing, their eyes running. Two of them vomited the second they were through the door and took their first breath of fresh air. Vomiting or not, though, they scrambled to the side, out of the line of fire of anyone in the machine shop. The other three men had already done so.

None of the guards moved.

Andy went over, crouching low, and caught one of the prisoners by the shirt. "Who's still in there, Sternwood? Answer me, damn you."

"Luff. Him and Krouse and Ray." He coughed. "Everybody else is dead in there, 'cept us. Maybe one or two more are alive, but they's hurt bad."

One last charge, then. If that much gas hadn't forced Luff and the other two out, adding more wouldn't help.

Andy would lead the charge himself. It was his responsibility.

He dragged the prisoner over to the next building, letting the other four make their own way on hands and knees.

Once that was done, he started giving orders into the radio. But James Cook interrupted him before he got very far. Somehow or other, he'd gotten his hands on a radio. He must have been standing next to a guard holding one, and had told him to hand it over. The guard would have obeyed, probably without even thinking about it. Cook was one of those people—Andy was another, himself—to whom authority came easily.

"Andy, that's nuts. Fuck the machine shop. I've been talking to Boyne and he tells me most of the equipment in there will survive anyway. It's steel and cast iron."

"Survive what?"

"I'll blow the damn thing. Give me ten minutes to go find Leffen. Then give him half an hour—hell, give him an hour—to figure something out. Fuck going over the trenches. Luff ain't worth it. Just snuff him like a rat in a hole."

"He's right, Andy," came Rod's voice. "We can take the time. We've got the whole building surrounded and this one doesn't have any connecting underground corridors. Let's do it Cook's way."

Andy hesitated, then realized they were right. His fierce urge to lead a charge into the building was just a half-suicidal way of trying to atone for his lapse in duty. But, whatever else, he had no right to risk the lives of other people in the doing.

"Okay, we'll try it. James, go ahead. Take as much time as you need."

By Andy's watch, it took exactly one hour, six minutes, and fourteen seconds. Without any preamble except a brief alert over the radio—that was for the benefit of the sharpshooters—Cook appeared in the courtyard, pushing a supply cart ahead of him. He was moving fast, almost but not quite running. The cart was loaded with bottles. Big ones, most of them, all connected by some sort of fuse arrangement. God only knew what was in them. God and Carter Leffen, whose peculiar genius was now completely unrestrained by the need to avoid casualties.

As soon as Cook appeared, Hulbert and the other sharpshooters starting firing into the building through the windows. As covering fire went, it was absolute and complete. If Luff or either of his two men tried to shoot at the oncoming cart—if they even raised their heads enough to see it in the first place—they'd be dead.

When Cook got to the open door, he planted his foot on the rear axle of the cart and put his weight on the handles. That was enough to hoist the front wheels into the building. Then—damn the maniac—he took the time and risk to enter the building pushing it in front of him.

He'd have no covering fire, now. Not from Hulbert and Scott, anyway. He was right in their line of fire.

The sharpshooters on the other buildings kept firing, though, and that was evidently enough to keep Luff and his men down.

A few seconds later, Cook came out of the building. Running as fast as he could.

"Get down!" Andy half-shouted into the radio. "Everybody. Down!"

The charge blew. Andy hissed in a breath. Leffen, the arsonist, had designed a bomb that was mostly an incendiary. The building didn't come down. It shook a little, but that was all. If they could put the fire out, they'd still have a machine shop. If they could put it out soon enough, they might even still have all of the machine tools and equipment intact.

But Luff was dead. He and Krouse and Ray were probably unrecognizable at all, any longer. That incredible first bloom of fire had been hot enough to be felt reflected off the walls. Inside, it must have been like having a miniature atom bomb going off.

He stood up and spoke into the radio. "Get the fire-fighting gear. Quickly, people." He shifted channels. "Marie, what's happening out there?"

"Nothing. Haven't seen anybody in a while. I figure maybe thirty of them made it into the woods. Tops. Probably not more than a couple of dozen."

"All right. We'll deal with that problem later. Once you're sure there's no danger, check to see if there are any survivors among the ones you shot."

After a brief hesitation, she said: *"Yeah. Will do."*

Up on the roof, Rod smiled. His girl, sure enough. And it was time for him to make good on the boast.

He gave Scott a sidelong look. "Brad, you know what Andy's like. I figure he'll be having enough nightmares as it is, without adding another one." He used his rifle to indicate the five men in Luff's inner circle. "You with me, or do I handle it myself?"

With a puzzled frown, Scott looked down at the five men below who'd made it out of the machine shop alive. They were sitting against a wall, under the watchful eyes of a guard. They'd stopped coughing by now, but they still looked teary-eyed, even from a distance.

After a few seconds, the frown disappeared. "Oh. Yeah, sure."

"Come on, then."

Hulbert appeared, with Bradley Scott alongside. Andy only noticed him coming with part of his mind. He was preoccupied with getting the firefighting organized. The machine shop wasn't particularly flammable, as a building, nor was the equipment in it. But he was worried about the oils in there. They'd just be cutting oils and cooling solvents, not gasoline or anything like that. But, given enough heat, almost any kind of oil could ignite.

Hulbert nodded toward the five men against the wall. "Since you're tied up, I figured I'd take care of this. We should get them into a cell. Keep the other prisoners from killing them, if nothing else."

Andy gave the men in question a quick glance, then looked back at the burning machine shop. "Yes, you're right. Use any cell you can find that'll suit the purpose. We'll deal with them later."

Hulbert went over to the prisoners. "On your feet. Now. You boys are getting locked up again."

That seemed to relieve them more than anything else. Still bleary-eyed, they got up and starting walking in the direction Hulbert pointed to with his rifle. Rod and Scott followed, a few steps behind.

Andy went back to worrying about the fire.

Not more than five seconds after Hulbert and his charges disappeared around a corner, he heard a short fusillade of shots. His rifle at the ready, and with two other guards following him with their own weapons, he raced to see what had happened.

He found Hulbert and Scott, standing over five corpses. When he got closer, he saw that all of them had been shot in the back.

"What happened?"

"Stupid bastards tried to make a run for it."

Bradley Scott nodded solemnly. "Shot while trying to escape."

Andy stared down at the bodies. They were still lined up in a row, the same way they'd been walking. He stared up at Hulbert.

"Let it go, Andy," Rod said softly. "Just let it go. This part of our new world, you leave to me and Kevin Griffin, will you? I promise I won't meddle with the rest."

The sound of distant rifle shots came. Not a fusillade. Just one shot. Then, a few seconds, another. Then, a few second later, another.

Hulbert smiled. "And Marie, sounds like."

Andy sighed, and wiped his face. "No more, Rod. I'll look the other way, with Luff's men." His tone became very hard. "But not one inch more. If that's not understood, I will make it understood. Believe me, I will."

"You got it, boss. Not one inch more."

They got the fire under control, before the oils in the lockers got ignited. Any of the small open cans of cutting oil lying around had gone, of course. But those had probably been ignited during the explosion itself, and they hadn't contained enough to do any real added damage.

Once the fire was out and the building had cooled down enough, Boyne accompanied Andy into the building. While Andy looked for the bodies, John inspected the damage to the machine tools and the other equipment.

"We still got a machine shop," he pronounced, after a while. "A couple of the drill presses are scrap, but that's no big deal. The drill bits are okay, which is all that really matters. And we'll have some work to do, repairing the

Bridgeport and the small lathe. But the other two lathes and the Cincinnati are fine."

He looked down at the three objects Andy was studying. "Which one's Luff?"

"I have no idea."

Fortunately for the mythology of their new world, they were able to figure it out soon enough. They found Luff's dental records in the infirmary. There wouldn't be stories floating around for years about how Luff might have made it to Argentina on a submarine—or even into the woods. The monster was dead.

So were one thousand, four hundred and six of the inmates who'd still been alive when Andy left the prison to look for the Cherokees. And at least another forty weren't going to be alive much longer, from the effects of Luff's rule.

CHAPTER 56

"Andy, you have to let this go," Jenny told him quietly, a week later. "The truth is, most of those men would have been dead anyway, within a year or two. Luff targeted all of the sickly, all of the old, anyone with an infectious disease, anyone with a heart condition, anyone with cancer, anyone with emphysema, anyone with a really serious blood pressure problem, anyone who was diabetic, anyone who was psychotic—anyone he thought was weak at all. You saw it. He had his office piled high with the medical records. He even had everyone on Death Row murdered, probably figuring they'd be more trouble than they were worth."

"I know that. We also found his notebook where he made the calculations. So many dead, so much food saved—and then, so help me, he filled four pages calculating whether keeping a sick man alive instead of a healthy one would be cost-effective in terms of food, figuring that a healthy man needs to eat more. And came up with the conclusion that he'd always be ahead if he thinned the herd—that's the expression he used in his notes—by working from the bottom up.

"I also know that, in his sick and twisted way and certainly not because he gave a damn about them, Luff probably saved as many lives of Indians out there as he took inside the prison. Probably a lot more. Whatever else happens, we won't be spreading AIDS and hepatitis and half a dozen other diseases in this new world. Not now."

He fell silent. In the hopes it might lighten his spirits, Jenny said: "And we won't be spreading smallpox, either. If I remember right, that was the big killer after the New World was discovered by Columbus. Not because of Luff, but because we'd pretty much eradicated it anyway. There hadn't been a case of smallpox anywhere in the world in years."

Andy shook his head. "I know all that, Jenny. And it doesn't make any difference. Not to me. My job was to be a guard commander. I might have taken a man to be executed, but I didn't pass the sentence and I didn't carry it out. And until the sentence was carried out, by lawfully appointed persons, my job was to protect society from that man and protect him as well."

He wiped his face with a big hand. He'd been doing that a lot, these past few days. "And there was one of those men on Death Row that most of us thought was probably going to be exonerated and released soon. Once the lab report on the DNA evidence came in. Leland Jefferson: Quiet, soft-spoken, spent fifteen years on Death Row waiting for one appeal after another. Never budged from his claim to be innocent—and, privately, I eventually decided he was. The truth is, we all liked him, after a while."

They'd never found Leland Jefferson's head. When Andy finally thought to inquire, the Boomers told him Jefferson was one of the men whose bodies they'd incinerated in those early days. He was just ashes, now, slowly spreading across the world of the Cretaceous.

"Andy, let it *go*."

A few minutes went by, as they sat together on a log just outside the prison. By now, the area around Alexander was quite safe. In the course of scouring the area for escaped convicts, Griffin and his Cherokees also reported any dangerous-looking animals they spotted. Kershner and his men would respond immediately. They carried modern rifles as backup, but they always fired the first volley with the muskets.

Hulbert was right about that. It remained to be seen how the muskets would do against something the size of a tyrannosaur or an allosaur. But those were few and far between, and none had been spotted within two miles of the prison. Against the smaller predators they did encounter, one volley of .69 caliber bullets was enough. Certainly enough to take them down. The rifles were only used to finish the kill, if needed.

Eventually, Jenny sighed. "All right. I know you well enough to know you probably won't let it go. Not ever, at least somewhere in your mind, till the day you die. But would it help any if you held me, in the meantime?"

"Sure would."

"Then do it. Start right now, and never stop so long as we're both alive."

CHAPTER

57

"Hernando!"

De Soto turned his head; something was coming from beyond the rise.

"Run! Run!"

His men were scattering, moving faster than they had moved in days.

Then he saw the demon.

"Cowards!" he shouted.

He drew and fired his wheel-lock pistol. Then drew the other from its saddle holster and fired again.

There'd be no time to reload. He drew his sword and spurred his mount.

The horse threw him. Then fled.

De Soto staggered to his feet. The demon might have gone after the horse, except that de Soto's fury was too great. On foot, he charged, staggering and reeling. He was still half-stunned from the impact of being thrown. Calling for the blessing of the virgin and the saints.

No man is a villain, in his own eyes. And whatever virtues were absent in the man named Hernando de Soto, courage was not among them.

All who observed his end, and survived to tell the tale, agreed that de Soto never stopped fighting. Not even after the demon's jaws had closed upon his middle and lifted him high, and his blood and intestines spilled everywhere. Still, he struck at the reptile head with his sword; and struck again, and again.

Some swore he struck a last blow as he disappeared into the maw. And believe he fights still, in Lucifer's very bowels.

CHAPTER
58

The seven-year-old girl's eyes looked as wide as saucers. "You promise you won't hurt him?"

Esther Hu stooped and took Linda May Tucker's little hands in her own, which weren't all that much bigger. She didn't have to stoop much, either. The paleontologist was a very small woman.

"Linda May, believe me, the very very very last thing we're going to do is hurt the little fellow. He's more precious than gold."

The girl stared at her, for a bit. "Well, okay, then. I guess."

"And you can come visit him any time you want to, just to make sure he's all right." Esther glanced up at the girl's parents. "We'll be glad to pay the cost of the trip, folks."

The mother nodded. The father just looked relieved.

Watching, Margo had to keep from laughing. Quite obviously, the father had heard the same stories about what happens to baby alligators kept as pets that she'd heard.

Linda May Tucker, now satisfied enough, started examining the room curiously. Her eyes fell on a very big, thick book lying on a table nearby, kept under glass. "What's that?"

"That?" Esther straightened up and studied the book for a moment. "We call it Exhibit A. What it is, though, is a very old Bible. Really old."

"Can I touch it?"

Margo stepped forward. "Better not, honey. It might get damaged. It's really, really old."

She was fudging, actually. True, looked at from one angle, the Bible was slightly over four hundred years old. But, measured from the likely date of printing, it was no older than some of the books in Margo's own library. And it was very sturdy.

Still, they weren't taking any chances. Not with a German-language Bible, printed in Fraktur typeface, from the last decade of the sixteenth century. There was no date printed anywhere in it, but the expert Nick had brought in said he could place it and date it quite precisely—to the satisfaction of any antique or rare book dealer in the world.

More to the point, he could place it and date it so precisely that not all of the king's men nor all of the king's lawyers nor all of the king's national security experts could deny the fact.

Nick had been right. In less than eight months, they'd turned up seventeen people in the area around Grantville who'd discovered something, before the federal agencies clamped down. The Bible had been among the things they'd found. And then, encountering the blank indifference or even outright hostility of the authorities, had decided to keep those items quietly as a private possession and say nothing further.

Margo still wasn't sure she agreed with Nick's plan, to wait until there was a change of administration before holding the press conference. Somewhere in the darker recesses of her mind, she had a faint lingering suspicion that Nick was trying to avoid embarrassing the current holder of the White House. He admitted himself that he'd voted for the bum, even if she was pretty sure he'd come to regret the fact as time went by.

Still, she understood Nick's insistence that politics be kept out of The Project's policies. And his reasoning was hard to argue with. The election was only a short time away, after all. And a new administration, regardless of which party's candidate won, wouldn't feel compelled to hold the bunker of folly at all costs. Not even the party which now controlled the White House, with a new President.

Not after The Project held the press conference. With—so far—four Nobel Prize winners having quietly agreed to attend and give their support. With—so far— dozens of eyewitnesses who could report things that were completely at variance with the official government line. With—so far—well over two hundred objects of one kind or another that did the same.

All of it backed up by the massive data The Project had collected over the years here in Minnesota. Data, further- more, that had been duplicated at least in part by more than a dozen research facilities elsewhere in the world.

And they had Exhibit A. Which was now, of course, demoted to Exhibit B.

Margo beamed down at the new Exhibit A, which had just arrived from a farm located three miles from the spot where Alexander Correctional Center had once stood.

The baby velociraptor peered back up at her.

"His name's Chucky," the girl explained.

Esther and the paleontologists *swore* the critter wouldn't get any bigger than a large turkey. Margo hoped they were right. Even as tiny as it was, those teeth looked sharp—and the big claws on the feet looked even scarier.

There wasn't much question it would grow up, either. The girl who'd found it, just coming out of the egg, had lavished tender loving care on her new pet. It was obviously quite healthy.

"He likes Chicken McNuggets. And french fries. But you gotta break them up into little pieces first. So he doesn't choke or anything."

Linda May leaned over, reached a finger into the cage, and stroked the creature's neck. Margo would swear the little monster arched its neck in response. And it made some sort of noise that sounded almost like a purr.

Couldn't be, of course.

EPILOGUE

⚭ ⚭

"One year to the day," Edelman pronounced. "Well. Formally, I guess."

Jenny smiled at him. "What's the formality involved, Jeff? We *have* kept track of the days. This is the three hundred and sixty-fifth. Don't tell me you're trying to screw us up with a leap year."

Edelman grimaced. "The folly of common sense. Jenny, what—exactly—is a 'year'? It was three hundred and sixty-five days where we *came* from, sure." He waved his hand airily. "I will graciously ignore the additional fraction of a day that required a leap year on occasion. But you're presuming a constant day—and we know the Earth's rotation slows down, as time goes by."

He tapped his watch. "That's why we have to keep adjusting these things, each and every damn morning. The day's shorter. You see my point? Sure, it's been three hundred and sixty-five days. Three hundred and sixty-five *shorter* days. Who knows how many days it takes to make a year, in the Cretacean Here and Now?"

His expression got a little smug. "Ask me in a couple of years, though—however many days that takes—and I'll be able to tell you."

Andy leaned over the side of the former watch tower, which had been turned into a favorite picnic area for most of the time and was reserved for the colony's cabinet in session when they wanted it, and looked at the pile of stones some distance away. "Is *that* why you've got those poor kids building Stonehenge for you?"

"Poor kids, my ass. They love it."

They probably did, at that. Except for Brian Carmichael's church, nothing captivated the immigrants who kept trickling into Schulerville more than Jeff's various science projects. Of course, Andy was all but certain that most of Edelman's students had their own religious interpretation of what he was doing. He knew for a fact from Kevin Griffin—who'd become almost fluent in the main immigrant dialect—that the term usually applied to Edelman was the same term applied to Carmichael and Elaine Cook. "Shaman" was the closest translation.

Hulbert cleared his throat. "Uh, folks. If the esteemed parties present would tear themselves away from idle speculation, can we please return to the subject which Mr. President plopped before the cabinet." He looked at his watch. "I'd like to settle this before the wedding, if we could."

"Fair enough," said James Cook. "I propose we accept my advice as a formal proposal. Or if you want to get fussy about it, I recommend somebody else makes it a formal proposal."

Technically, Cook didn't have any formal cabinet post,

just as Geoffrey Watkins didn't. They sat on the cabinet ex officio, as the respective heads of the two other political entities who made up the confederation: in his case, Boom Town, and in Geoffrey's, the Cherokee town of Saluka.

But, especially in Cook's case, that was a technicality. With Watkins, there was more substance to the distinction. As friendly as they were, and as closely connected as they'd become, the Cherokees still maintained a certain distance. Residual wariness, if nothing else.

Andy couldn't blame them, given the history involved. Even though he knew, and so did Watkins, that there was no chance at all of that history being repeated in this world. In the North America they'd come from, the Cherokees—the other Indian tribes, perhaps even more so—had simply been overwhelmed by the sheer numbers of Europeans who kept arriving, and their offspring. Eventually, although it had never really vanished, their culture had gotten pressed flat under the weight. That couldn't possibly happen here. If anything, Andy thought the cultural adaptation was tending at least as much in the other direction.

Besides, as far as sheer demographics went, the residents of Schulerville and Boom Toom and Saluka were *all* minorities. Small minorities, at that. As time passed, they'd discovered more and more villages of pre-Mounds Indians—and, just four months ago, had finally stumbled across the Mounds culture. Thirty-five miles away, it turned out, the Quiver had deposited Cahokia itself. The Mounds people didn't call it that, of course. They called it something Andy still couldn't pronounce, no matter how hard he tried, and neither could anyone else in the cabinet except Watkins. So they kept using the term Cahokia as a practical convenience.

By their current estimate, between thirty and forty thousand people had wound up in the Cretaceous, of whom more than ninety percent were Indians from somewhere in the centuries before the arrival of Columbus.

True, disease was hitting them pretty badly already. But Jenny didn't think they'd be hit nearly as badly as had happened in the world they came from. If nothing else, there was no smallpox. And most of the villages within fifteen or twenty miles of Schulerville had accepted Jenny, Susan Fisher, and the other nurses—James Cook too, in a pinch—as shamans. They'd readily follow their advice, at least on medical matters. That helped a lot too.

"I'll make it a formal proposal," said Jenny. "And I agree with it."

Hulbert scratched his jaw. "I dunno. I'd trust Bostic as far as I could throw him."

James rolled his eyes. "Rod, who said anything about 'trust'? Bostic sure as hell didn't. I spent five full days in his town, dickering with him and getting the lay of the land, and I can assure you the word never crossed his lips once. His point, though, is that we have no objective reason to quarrel with him; and he doesn't, with us. So why not make it a formal treaty?"

Hulbert kept scratching his jaw. Cook tightened his. "And if that doesn't move you, maybe this will. I was *there,* Rod, you weren't. If we pick a fight with him—don't have any doubt about this—we'll be starting a war with all of his people. You keep thinking of Danny Bostic as a criminal and a gangster, but for those people he's their hero. He's fucking Beowulf, I kid you not. The valiant warrior from distant parts who showed up with a handful of stalwart companions and took care of the monster who'd been ravaging their villages."

Cook's irritated look was replaced by a mischievous one. "He did it the same way you did, by the way. Dug a big pit and served himself up as tyrannosaur bait."

That piqued Hulbert's interest, naturally. "No kidding?"

"Allosaur bait," Edelman said wearily. But that was a battle he'd lost months ago. Whatever the huge theropods might "really" be, everyone except him had long ago decided that "tyrannosaur" just plain sounded better.

"Yup, no kidding." Cook's expression got more mischievous still. "He even made the same silly mistake you did. Took the time and effort to line the bottom of the pit with sharpened stakes."

Rod chuckled, a bit ruefully. He and his hunters had spent days getting those stakes ready. And had then discovered—which he admitted he should have realized from the beginning—that the stakes were pointless. A complete waste of time and effort.

No land animal who ever lived, be they never so fierce and ferocious, could survive a plunge into a fifteen-foot deep pit. Not when they weighed better than six tons. Most of the stakes had just splintered, without ever piercing the monster's thick hide. It mattered not at all. Half of its bones had been broken, including its spine, its hip, one leg, both arms, and its lower jaw. All they'd had to do was wait by the side of the pit until it finally died.

"But that was about the only mistake he made. A dumb gangster would have tried to take over by force. Bostic just did his heroic deed, made modest hero-like noises, and bided his time. The only problem he ran into was that all three of the chief's eligible nieces started quarreling over him. That took a while to sort out. But, eventually, it did."

Nieces, not daughters. Like all of the Indians they'd encountered, including the Cherokees and the Cahokians, the village societies were matrilineal. Descent ran from mother to daughter, not father to son. And while males always occupied the position of chiefs and—in the case of the Cahokians—the top priests, their own lineage was reckoned through the children of their sisters, not their own. Which meant that when the current chief died, Danny Bostic was in line to succeed him. So were several other men, of course, but the tribe would decide among them—and what tribe in its right mind was going to pick anyone else for chief, when they had Beowulf sitting right there?

Andy thought it wouldn't take more than a generation— two, at the most—before matrilineality became established custom in Boom Town also. The population of that town was still overwhelmingly ex-convict. The final deal Andy and Cook had worked out concerning the surviving prisoners had been that the Boomers would nominate people for a pardon, and a committee of guards appointed by Andy would make the final decision—but they could only decide from the list presented by the Boomers. Balance of powers, so to speak. Then, there'd be a sort of parole that would last for somewhere between six months and six years, depending on the inmate involved, although it could be shortened if the Boomer panel and the guard panel jointly agreed.

During that stretch of time, the parolees were under one and only one restriction: they were forbidden in Schulerville and Saluka. They had to go live in the new town the Boomers created—or anywhere else, for that matter, but almost all of them wound up in Boom Town.

In essence, the Boomers had wound up being the confederation's parole officers. And they were parole officers whom it was *really* tough for an inmate to fool. They knew every trick in the book. After a few months, the guards had gotten confident enough about the situation that the pace of releasing prisoners speeded up a lot. There were only a hundred and forty-six inmates still locked up in the cells, and the truth was, except for a handful, those men would probably stay there the rest of their lives. Not even the Boomers wanted any part of them.

Feeding those remaining inmates had been something of a strain for the colony, since they didn't contribute much in the way of useful labor, until the legend spread through the surrounding villages—Andy suspected Cook was behind that, although he denied it—that the remaining inmates were demons who needed to be placated until they finally went away. Thereafter, quite regularly, small parties of villagers would show up with food offerings for them.

The villagers always got a guided tour of the former prison when they brought the offerings, which was an added attraction. For people whose culture was barely beyond the Stone Age, the installation that had once been Alexander Correctional Center was deeply impressive. Sort of a cross between seeing the Pyramids and visiting Disneyland—except Disneyland never had real live demons you could look at, locked behind bars. And, after a while, some of the inmates decided the situation was amusing and started putting on a show in their cells.

The one big problem that remained, of course, was that Boom Town's original population was entirely male, except for the former Elaine Brown. And James Cook wasn't about to tolerate his people getting wives by violence. The three men who tried had been executed. Not summarily, either. There'd been no need to use the services of Geoffrey Kidd—although he was always there in the background, just as a reminder to everyone.

No, the Boomers had held real trials. They'd even asked Andy to provide the judges. Found guilty by juries, the men had been hung on a knoll just outside the town.

Which, of course, promptly got the name Boot Hill.

That meant any man who tired of the absence of female company had to go out there, some way or another, and sweet talk the villagers. That turned out to be reasonably easy to do, if a man had any sense and was willing to work. At least, for inmates who hadn't spent a lifetime behind bars and lost any useful skill—but Luff had murdered most of those anyway.

Still, while they were willing enough to accept Boom Town swains—even eager, sometimes, with ex-inmates with certain skills—the villagers retained their own customs. They were usually matrilocal as well as matrilineal, although they didn't insist on the former. Still, any children born to the union belonged to the mother's family, not the father's. And while the former guards in Schulerville might have put up a struggle over that issue, the ex-inmates didn't much care. Most of them had come from dysfunctional families to begin with, and didn't see anything particularly unusual about having a mother instead of a father at the head of the family.

Andy stopped ruminating. By now, he thought Rod had had enough time to digest Cook's proposal concerning Bostic. They needed to settle this. Andy had decided from the beginning that James' attitude was the right one to take. Bostic wasn't a threat—and the much larger Cahokian culture might very well turn out to be one.

There was a society Andy didn't like at all. A harsh theocracy, essentially, much larger and better organized than any of the village cultures, and with some truly repellent features. They did, in fact, practice ritual human sacrifice. Nothing on the scale of the ancient Aztecs, granted. But it was woven into their customs nonetheless.

What made the situation all the more explosive was that, six months earlier, the damn Spaniards had tried to seize Cahokia by brute force and impose themselves on the Cahokians as a new aristocracy.

With less than two hundred men, almost no ammunition left—and de Soto killed by a tyrannosaur long before, according to the stories they'd heard. Whoever had wound up in charge of the survivors must have had delusions of grandeur that he was another Cortez.

John Boyne, it turned out, knew a lot about the history of Mexico. He'd explained to Andy, once, that the two main reasons Cortez had been able to conquer the Aztecs weren't the much-ballyhooed advantages of having guns and horses—much less the Quetzalcoatl myth—but the facts that disease had already ravaged the Aztecs and that most of the soldiers he had were allied Indians who had their own good reasons to hate the Aztecs.

Even then, the first time the Spaniards seized their capital, the Aztecs had counterattacked and driven them out.

The same thing had happened again. Only, as someone once quipped, history had repeated itself as a farce. These Spaniards had only one horse left. Ran out of ammunition before they got into the capital complex. Had no allies; in fact, they were hated by every Indian village that knew them. And a leadership whose only resemblance to Cortez was ruthlessness.

In the end, according to what they'd been able to piece together, probably not more than forty or fifty Spaniards had survived. And those men had disappeared somewhere. For all intents and purposes, de Soto's expedition was simply no longer an important factor in the political equation. Eventually, one way or another, those men who'd survived would just get absorbed into the villages.

But, not surprisingly, the attempted conquest had made the Cahokians belligerent and suspicious—and they had a culture for which suspicion and belligerence came easily to begin with.

Some day, Andy figured, they might even wind up having to fight another war. If so, why go out of their way for no good reason to make enemies elsewhere? The day might come when they'd be approaching Bostic for an alliance, not simply a peace treaty.

"I think James is right, Rod," Andy said. "We should draw up a formal treaty and present it to Bostic. And if he agrees, sign it and be done."

Andy looked at his own watch, now. "We don't have much time left, people. Any discussion?"

That really meant, did Rod still want to hold onto his mulish recalcitrance. Andy knew, from private conversations, that everybody else in the cabinet had already come to the same conclusion he and James had.

Hulbert shrugged. "Yeah, sure. Beside, it's your decision, Andy. A cabinet vote's not binding on you, anyway."

"Officially, no. Have you ever seen me override a majority of the cabinet, though? Answer: no. That's because I'm not stupid. Any proposal or policy that can't win a majority of the cabinet is not something I figure the people out there will swallow either, if I try to shove it down their throats. This little confederacy of ours is about as far removed from Prussian autocracy as I can imagine."

Rod smiled. "True. Okay, I'll vote in favor also. Holding my nose, but I will."

Andy rose. "That's it, then. Let's get down to the church."

The moment he finished that sentence, the church bell started to ring.

"I love that sound," said Jenny. "Even if it is tinny."

James had just gotten to his own feet. "Give John a break. As he'll tell anyone who asks, he's a machinist, not—toss in at least four expletives here—a metal caster. That bell's the best he could come up with. So far, anyway."

It *was* a tinny-sounding church bell. But Andy agreed with Jenny. And, in his case, not simply out of sentiment. He was coming to believe, more and more as time went by, that in the long run that tinny-sounding church bell was more likely to bring down any enemies they might have than all the rifles in the armory.

As they left the tower and headed for the big wooden structure just outside the walls of Schulerville, he found himself pondering the matter.

Andy had mixed feelings about the church that Brian Carmichael had founded—and which Elaine Cook had then boosted enormously.

The colony had two really good singers. Elaine and Marie Keehn. Personally, for his tastes, Andy thought Marie was a little better. But it hardly mattered either way. Better or not, neither Marie's style of singing nor her own religious beliefs would have allowed her to throw herself wholeheartedly into building Brian's new church the way Elaine had.

True, Elaine and Brian got into some ferocious theological disputes, from time to time. She'd belonged to a church that, while fundamentalist in many respects, didn't share some of the extreme views of Brian's church. But since Brian was naturally easygoing and was never willing to force an issue, as long as everyone was willing to respect what he considered "the basics," Elaine usually got her way. The end result was a church that, whatever quirks it might have from Andy's viewpoint, didn't dwell too much on theological fine points. And it was vibrant, lively—and, most of all, cheerful. Brian's sermons focused on the love of God and Jesus, and came with the man's natural ebullience and goodwill. It was hard to imagine anything more remote from the spirit that had filled the stern churches of the old Puritan colonists. You'd never hear Brian Carmichael describing the streets of hell paved with the skulls of unbaptized children, the way Cotton Mather had. Carmichael barely talked about hell at all. The devil simply didn't interest him.

The man was odd, that way. As was about to be demonstrated again today.

The same Brian Carmichael who would insist that the Quiver was God's way of demonstrating the falseness of the doctrine of evolution—the logic there was enough to make a pretzel shriek in agony—and could recite, literally, chapter and verse from the Bible, simply didn't seem to care about the way people filled his teachings, exactly. As long as they did it in what he considered a Christian spirit—which, for him, ran heavily toward love of fellow man and spent little time at all scolding that same fellow man for his failings—and were willing to follow a few "basic rules," he was satisfied.

Even the transparently idolatrous aspects of the way most villagers interpreted his teachings was something he was willing to ignore. It turned out the effigies and carvings the villagers paraded around with on holy days and religious festivals weren't *really* icons—much less papist saints—they were actually "symbols of upright folk." So spake Brian Carmichael, anyway. And since he was the prophet, in the Cretaceous, who was going to argue the point?

The sermon done, Elaine would trot out and start the singing, and within two minutes the entire congregation was joining in. On their feet, clapping and dancing—and using musical instruments upon which were often carved representations of the same "upright folk."

Andy had come to the conclusion that he could live with the quirks. Like Rod, holding his nose sometimes.

Because he was pretty sure, now, that every sermon that went by, every raucous and happy congregation, was another little trickle slowly undermining the cultures around them, where they needed to be undermined, and cementing them where they needed that instead.

Carmichael's church was growing rapidly, much more rapidly than any other denomination, and by now most of its adherents came from the many Indian villages in the Quiver Zone. And some of those converts, starting about three months ago, were coming from Cahokia. Or, at least, from the villages around it and under Cahokia's rule. Andy realized that, in a century or two, his descendants might have to deal with another theocracy. But at least that one wouldn't practice human sacrifice—and, in the meantime, Andy was pretty sure that within a few years Carmichael's missionaries would make a war with the Cahokians something of a moot point. Those damn priests of theirs, with their sacrificial rites, were more likely to be overthrown from within.

"I *still* can't figure out why they're doing it," Rod said, after they left the walls of Schulerville—which, in its own peculiar way, had become another factor undermining the priestly caste that dominated Cahokia. Sure, their mounds were impressive. But the walls and towers of a town that had once, in another universe, been a maximum security prison, were a hell of a lot more impressive. Even if the architects who'd designed it so long ago would be astonished to hear the news.

The new murals helped a lot, of course. They'd turned the once bleak and grim walls of Alexander into something extremely colorful and vivid. And if the origins of those intricate and fascinating designs were gang symbols, who cared? Certainly not the villagers who came to stare in wonder.

The prison gangs still existed, in a way. But given that Luff had slaughtered all the gang leaders, and everything else that had happened—not to mention that Cook's rule in Boom Town could get very iron-fisted if anyone really provoked something—their competition had wound up taking a predominantly artistic form. The gangs were really more in the way of competing art schools, now. Each one got part of the walls assigned to it, which they kept painting over to match some new challenge. They pretty much had to do that anyway, of course. Schulerville's paint stocks were too limited to turn over to them, so they had to make do with what Susan Fisher and some of the villagers came up with. The colors were usually bright, albeit the range was limited—but the paints didn't last too long, either.

And if the competition got pretty rough, sometimes, well . . . so had the streets of Oxford and Cambridge and the area around the Sorbonne in Paris, in centuries gone by.

"And *I* don't understand why you can't figure it out, Rod," said Jenny. "What's so complicated? They're bound and determined to get their orphanage up and running, and to do that they need to get Brian's approval. Every orphan around is from a village. The Cherokees take care of their own, and we don't have any because—so far— we've only got a total of one kid. Kathleen Hanrahan's boy, who'll grow up Cherokee anyway. Now that Kathleen moved in with Geoffrey."

The Cherokee chief looked a bit smug. "We get along quite well, too. It's nice having a woman again. I think we may even get married, after a while."

Cherokee marital customs were a lot looser than anything Carmichael liked. But it didn't matter, since only one Cherokee had ever joined his church and it was unlikely there'd be any more coming. That Cherokee had been considered more or less the town idiot. The Cherokees remained patient with Brian and his missionaries, but that style of Christianity just wasn't what suited them.

Jenny looked back at Rod. "Don't you understand? The orphans will have to be village kids—and who gets them first? Brian, that's who. They just wander in on their own, or people who find them drop them in front of the church, not knowing what else to do. Give Brian a month, and they're budding little church members who accept his authority."

"Fine. But—"

"But *what*? They're just being practical about it. Brian insists that any orphanage has to be run by a married couple, or it isn't respectable enough for him to be willing to turn any kids over to their care. And a marriage is something that can only happen between a man and a woman. One of the basic rules. Period. You know Brian. As long as people follow the rules, and he likes what they're doing for other people, he's not going to question their own purposes and private intent. As he puts it maybe eight times a day, judgment is the Lord's, not his."

"I still think it's nuts."

So did Andy, in a way. But he couldn't deny that there was a certain charm to the whole thing, too.

"We are gathered here, dearly beloved—"

You had to hand it to Brian Carmichael. He didn't so much as blink. Not once, all the way through the ceremony.

Sinners they might be, but they'd followed the rules. Judgment belonged to the Lord, not him.

Geoffrey Kidd, at least, wore a jacket that covered most of his tattoos. He'd even worn gloves, to cover the tattoos on his knuckles. In fact, he almost looked like a respectable groom.

Bird Matthews, on the other hand, while she'd finally been willing to bend to the letter of Carmichael's rules, wasn't about to let him get away with the spirit. So, sure enough, she wore the jacket to her wedding.

Dykes on Bikes.

At the reception afterward, Andy couldn't resist trying to tease Kidd a bit.

"So. Tell me. Are you looking forward to the wedding night with any trepidation or anxieties? Most newlyweds do."

"'Course not. The orphanage has separate bedrooms for husband and wife. The kind of modest and proper living arrangements you ain't seen in a century, almost."

Kidd glanced to the side. "You won't see Bird and me watching each other like hawks, the way those two do. Even though neither one of them has the slightest reason for it. There's never even been a trace of gossip."

Andy looked over. James and Elaine Cook were chatting with Marie Keehn, each with an arm around the other. You might have been able to get a crowbar between the two of them, if you were willing to spend some time at it and sweat a lot.

"Nope," Kidd went on. "You watch and see. This will be the most troublesome-free marriage in the Zone. Who knows? We may even set a trend."

"Dinosaur stakes," Andy muttered.

"What was that?"

"Nothing. I was just reflecting on wasted effort."

Kidd grinned, as only he could. "You mean like trying to needle a reformed serial killer? In the *Cretaceous*?"

"Like I said. Wasted effort."

The Following is an excerpt from:

The Sorceress of Karres

Eric Flint
Dave Freer

Available from Baen Books
January 2010
hardcover

Chapter 1

Threbus looked more than a little alarmed at the sudden appearance of the slitty little silver-eyed vatches all around them. "I suppose . . . these are the kind that can't be handled by your mother?" he asked of Goth, his middle daughter. The tone was faintly hopeful. The expression was not.

His daughter shook her head. "I reckon not. Captain, how about you? You're a real wizard with vatches."

Pausert considered the problem. It seemed clear enough that the little fragments of otherwhere, pieces of impossible whirling blackness called vatches, had appeared because of Pausert. Pausert was a vatch-handler, a vatch negotiator, he who had done the impossible, and made friends with the creatures who were normally puppeteers playing with humans for a sort of dreamlike amusement. It would seem that there was such a thing as too much success.

Eventually, he shook his head. "If I tried and failed—even

on one, it'd be pretty fatal. I think we're going to have to learn to co-operate with them, Threbus."

"How?"

"Rather like one deals with the Leewit," said Pausert.

Threbus groaned. "One does not deal with my youngest daughter, Pausert. One merely tries to limit the damage and then distract her."

Captain Pausert, who had had plenty of experience of the Leewit, grinned at his great-uncle. "Yes. That's it, I think."

Threbus took a deep breath. "Pausert, you have repaid us for what we did to you."

Because of the Karres witches, Captain Pausert had been though more near-death experiences than he cared to think about at any one sitting. He patted his great-uncle—and future father-in-law, if Goth had her way—on the shoulder. "I hope so. It was a bit rough at first. But I wouldn't have missed it for all the worlds in the Empire."

"More to the point the Empire wouldn't have survived, without you getting through it," said Threbus.

Pausert nodded. "I understand that . . . now. And I wonder if the vatches are not doing the same thing for Karres."

Threbus looked thoughtful. "You can hardly have spoken to the precog teams, Pausert. It's because of what they're seeing that we're glad you came back here so quickly. They've been giving us worrying and confused views of the future. Not all good, either. I wonder if this is another klatha talent starting to manifest in you?"

"Nope," said Pausert. He'd been through enough of the otherworldly klatha development phases to recognize that feeling. "Just common sense. Karres has faced two terrible dangers. Been all that stood between man and Manaret, and between the Empire and the nanite plague."

"Could be," said Goth slowly, "that Karres, just by existing, draws trouble."

Captain Pausert felt an eerie prickle at the back of his skull. Some kind of klatha force was at work here.

It was plain that Threbus felt it too. "We can't exactly stop existing. We've always operated, if not in secret, at least not obtrusively. We could hide back in time or something . . ."

Goth shook her head, her high forehead wrinkled in concentration. "It wouldn't make any difference. Whatever causes this is like Big Windy the vatch. I reckon it's not limited to space or time as we know them. Not even this dimension. Manaret and Moander were pulled from somewhere else. Another dimension, thousands of complicated dimensions away . . . they *thought* it was by accident. But what if it wasn't?"

"I'd say we're in trouble. Again," said Captain Pausert, shrugging. "We're getting quite good at that."

"Clumping right," said the Leewit, arriving suddenly in their midst. "What are all these stinkin' little vatches doing here? Where is Little-bit? She's okay. I didn't invite all these other ones."

"Perhaps she's here, somewhere. It's a bit confusing," said Pausert.

"Well, go away, you lot," said the Leewit to the vatch-swarm. "Or I'll whistle at you. I don't know if it'll bust you up. You want to find out, huh? Anyway, Pa, I came to tell you Maleen is here at the palace."

Threbus brightened perceptibly. He was a fair man, Pausert knew. He never played favorites among his daughters. But he plainly had a soft spot for Maleen, his oldest child. "If they won't go away," he said, looking at the vatches, "I suppose that we could."

The Leewit looked warily at her father. "Not the Egger route . . ."

There was a boom as air rushed in to fill the space. The vatches flickered and rippled around where the four Karres witches had been moments before. They'd find them again of course. They had their flavor.

Chapter 2

"I didn't know that it was possible to teleport that sort of mass," said Captain Pausert, impressed.

Goth squeezed her father's hand. "Oh, yes. So long as you've got a hot witch doing it, it works pretty well."

Threbus wiped his brow. "If the range is not particularly great, I can manage large amounts of mass. But I'm pretty well limited to a few hundred yards. A group of us can manage a few miles."

"Still a pretty hot witch," said Goth. "I can only do a couple of pounds."

Threbus smiled. "You've got the range on me though. And you're young yet. When I was your age I had just started to discover a few klatha powers but they were so slight that I didn't actually believe they were real."

"That must have been just as well on Nikkeldepain," said Captain Pausert, thinking of his home planet. It was a very conservative and traditional place. Quite stuffy in a lot of ways. Karres witch tricks would not be happily received there.

The thought made him chuckle a little. Most of the people of Nikkeldepain would be horrified by the company he was now keeping. It had not been the easiest place to grow up in, in some ways. Not if one was just a little bit out of the ordinary. Captain Pausert could see now that might easily have been the start of his own klatha manifestations. But it had given him enough trouble at school, and later in the Nikkeldepain space navy.

That, and the infamy of his great-uncle Threbus, the very man who had just teleported them. It had been difficult growing up in the shadow of the stories about great-uncle Threbus. Harder because he'd never known quite where to stand on it all. His mother had always stood up for her strange uncle, in spite of what people said. Pausert had had a few bitter fights about it at school. He'd always held out that the stories had to be exaggerated. Now he had to wonder whether it had not been Nikkeldepain that had been the victim, not his eccentric great-uncle.

They were joined by Maleen, who was with a young man Pausert didn't know. Pausert hadn't seen much of Maleen since the day that he had left the three witches of Karres back on their home planet after rescuing them from slavery on the Empire world of Porlumma. He'd always been a little suspicious about that. The witches were certainly capable of rescuing themselves from most situations. Maleen was a precognitive Karres witch— which gave him enough ground for extreme suspicion.

Precog was not an exact science. But it was good enough for her to have prepared a tray of drinks for them. Tall green Lepti liquor for Captain Pausert and her father, and a pale frothy brew for her two sisters. When Pausert had last seen her, Maleen had been a pretty blonde teenage girl. It made him sharply aware of the passage of years to see that she was now definitely a young woman.

"Captain," she said proudly, taking the young man's hand possessively, "this is Neldo. My husband."

Pausert extended his hand. "Pleased to meet you." Well, she had said that she would be of marriageable age in two years, Karres time. Pausert was still not too sure just how long a Karres month was. But he, together with Goth and her little sister, the Leewit, had been on quite a number of adventures since then. Come to think of it, he wasn't entirely sure how many months it had all taken.

Neldo shook his hand warmly. "I've heard a lot about you." Then he turned to his father-in-law. "Maleen has got some great news."

"We're going to have a baby!" said Maleen excitedly.

Threbus beamed and hugged both of them. "Would it be too much to expect for a precog to have some idea what sex it's going to be?"

Maleen blushed. "You know we're not supposed to do that kind of thing."

"So you got Kerris, or one of the others, to do it for you," said Goth, grinning.

Maleen and Neldo smiled at each other. "You might be right. We might even know what we've decided to call her."

The Leewit stood in front of them, her arms folded. "There is only one 'the Leewit.'"

Maleen laughed. "We know that. And it still didn't put us off having children. Her name will be Vala."

"Why?" asked Goth.

"We don't know," answered Maleen. "It's not a name that either of us had ever heard before."

Captain Pausert was a little taken aback by the name. It brought back a flood of memories which he had thought were gone for ever. "I knew a Vala once, back on Nikkeldepain."

Goth looked suspiciously at him. "You said that . . . sort of funny. Who was this Vala?"

"Just a girl I knew when I was growing up." Pausert had a bad feeling his ears were starting to grow slightly red.

"I bet she was your sweetheart, Captain," Maleen sniggered. "Hope she was better than that insipid girl, what was her name, Illyla."

"She wasn't a bit like Illyla," said Captain Pausert reminiscently. "Actually, if anything she was more like Goth. Except that she had red hair and was a bit older. She got me into a fair amount of trouble, but I don't remember that I minded too much. Like the lattice ship that came to Nikkeldepain at about that time. She was one of those people that you never really forget. Oh well, it was long ago. It's a beautiful name. I'm glad you chose it."

"Huh!" said Goth, looking at Pausert from under her dark brows. "Anyway, I've never had much time for babies, not until they grow up a bit."

Toll came in. "And then they turn into something like

the Leewit," she said, looking at her youngest daughter and smiling.

The Leewit shrugged. "Babies are no fun anyway. I have decided that I'm going to stay with the captain for the next while. Things happen around him. And he takes pretty good care of us. Makes us wash behind our ears even."

That last was plainly something that she felt was a little unnatural. Pausert had to smile to himself. The Leewit was a handful to deal with, but at least he felt that he was dealing with a child, even if he knew very little about how to do so. With Goth he was less certain. She was growing up. Fast.

According to the Karres precogs this was going to be a very important year for Goth. The year had started with their departure from the Governor's palace on Green Galaine, on a life or death mission to escort the Nartheby Sprite Hantis and her Grik-dog Pul to the Imperial Palace. Of course no one had seen fit to tell him that the trip was going to be quite as risky as it had turned out to be. It had been a period during which the captain's own klatha skills had grown immeasurably. But although Goth had matured, he could honestly not say that it had been that much of an important year for her development. Except . . . they still had a couple of months to go. Pausert could not help but be a bit nervous as to what they might bring her.

A little later, when Goth had gone off with her sisters, Pausert broached the subject of his next mission with Toll and Threbus. His relationship with the Witches of Karres was an interesting one. At least in theory, Captain Pausert was just an independent trader, with a fast armed merchant ship. But in practice he was part of the community of Karres. That was more about a willingness to do what was needed, than merely a reference to your citizenship or place of birth. And if Karres needed him, he was willing.

"The Chaladoor," said Threbus, referring to a dangerous and mysterious region of space, the lair of pirates, the Megair Cannibals . . . at one time of Manaret and the Nuri globes lurking within the Tark Nembi cluster of dead suns and interstellar dust and debris.

"Oh?" said Captain Pausert warily. He'd survived one crossing of Chaladoor. Admittedly, he'd been in more danger from those inside his ship—spies and the notorious Agandar—than from forces outside it.

"There is something going on in that area of space. Since Manaret was destroyed, quite a few ships have risked the crossing. And none of them have made it. The Daal of Uldune has also thought to expand his power in that direction . . . And he has been repulsed."

Pausert raised his eyebrows. He knew the hexaperson that was the cloned and telepathic ruler of the one-time pirate world rather well. Sedmon the Sixth was not a trivial foe. The Empire still trod warily around him, and the forces at his command. Whatever the danger was that lurked in the Chaladoor, it was something serious. "You . . . want me to do what, exactly?"

"You will be a kind of bait, to be honest, Pausert," said Threbus. "All we want you to do is encounter the problem, and then run away as fast as you and the Sheewash drive can manage. The Chaladoor is a large, complex region.

Karres could hunt for some years without encountering whatever the problem is. Problems tend to avoid whole worlds which are also spacecraft."

He looked at his grand nephew with a twinkle. "And we do really mean 'run', Pausert. You've proved yourself far more than just capable with problems. And you've taken good care of my daughters in the process. But not with something that was big enough to deal with eight of the Daal's cruisers and a battle wagon. They barely had time to say they were under attack on sub-radio, before being destroyed. Whatever it is, it is no easy foe to deal with."

Threbus cleared his throat and continued. "You have a ship which is very nearly the equal of a single cruiser anyway, as far as speed and detection equipment is concerned. We'll have it refitted with some more of the very latest equipment, at our expense. Your armaments are not quite to the same standard, but they are certainly up to holding off an enemy until you can engage the Sheewash drive. Now that you have also mastered the drive, and with Goth and the Leewit to help you in emergencies, we think you should be able to deal with running away. Leave us to the clean up!"

"You wouldn't take unnecessary risks with the girls anyway," said Toll, smiling. "My daughter has already made her plans for you. And you wouldn't be foolish enough to try and spoil them now, would you?"

Goth's plans were to marry the captain as soon as she was of marriageable age. At first the captain had not taken her terribly seriously—just as Threbus had apparently not taken Toll's similar plan too seriously. And see where it had got Threbus! As time had gone on and Pausert and Goth had shared adventure and danger together, Pausert had come to realize that he was very fond of her too. But he was a normal man, and she wasn't yet properly grown up.

Yet . . . the witches did have some other avenues open to them. He knew that Threbus must be at least eighty years old by now. Yet he looked to be no more than in his mid-thirties. He also knew from what they had learned on Uldune that Toll too could change her age at will. As they turned to leave, Pausert cleared his throat and braced himself to ask, "Er. Toll. About age shifts . . ."

Toll turned back and raised one eyebrow at him, with a quizzical half-amused, half-dangerous expression on her face. "What?" she said, in a way that would have made most men say "oh nothing. Nothing at all." But Pausert was quite brave. Or quite stupid. He was not too sure which of he two he was being right now.

"I was wondering," he said, "about, well, the age shift thing."

Toll smiled. "Oddly enough, Goth's been raising the same subject lately. The answer is 'no,' Captain Pausert. Compared to Nikkeldepain our way of raising children may seem a little strange to you. Karres children are very independent. They have to be. But, captain, they are still children, and need to go through stages of development, just like any other child. There are a number of important formative experiences Goth still has to go through. We did not let our children go with you lightly, Captain Pausert. We have ways of knowing that you are absolutely trustworthy. And anyway, because of the parent-pattern in their heads, we're around in a way, even when we're not."

Captain Pausert had encountered the Toll pattern in Goth. He'd wished that he too could have a resident instructor and mentor, sometimes. But Karres had decided that he was best left to learn on his own. "I've always done my best for them all," he said. "And if you think that is best for Goth, then we will just have to let it all happen at its own speed."

Toll patted his shoulder. "And it will. Take a step back from it, if you can. Age shift is one of the things we don't teach the young witches. Every single child among them wants to be grown up instantly. What child doesn't? Well, we found that although they can cope very easily with the physical changes in their bodies, it's not the same with their minds. Only time seems to achieve that properly." She cocked her head slightly and smiled. "See, it wouldn't just be an older Goth . . . my middle daughter is quite an old soul in a young body sometimes. But can you imagine what it would be like if the Leewit could suddenly choose to be grown up, or at least have a grown-up body?"

That was quite a thought! "Could make applying a piece of tinklewood fishing rod adapted to be a switch very interesting," said the captain. "I think I see your point. I don't think the galaxy is quite ready for that yet."

"Goth, you're being a dope," said the Leewit. "Isn't she, Maleen?"

"Shut up," said Goth. "It's more complicated than you understand, you little bollem."

Maleen, looking down on her younger sisters with the

vast tolerance of an older, and now married woman, smiled. "Don't you like the captain any more, the Leewit?"

The Leewit looked affronted. "He's not a bad old dope. Okay. He's not even so old. And he's not really a dope. I like him quite a lot, actually. He's good to have around especially when things go wrong. But I don't see what Goth's all upset about." She sniffed. "And don't tell me that she's not, because she is."

Goth gave her a look that would have sent sensible wildlife running. "It's your baby's fault," she said to Maleen.

"I didn't tell you everything Kerris and the other precogs said about her."

"Don't know if I want to hear," said Goth crossly.

Maleen put a hand on Goth's shoulder and pushed her down into a chair. "Well, you should. Because it is important. I need to talk to Toll and Threbus about it too, but I couldn't with Captain Pausert there."

"Why? What did they say?"

"Pausert's going on a mission to Chaladoor."

"I know that. We leave . . ."

"Except that you're not going to be with him," said Maleen.

Goth shook her head. "He needs me around. He doesn't have a pattern in his mind to guide him through the klatha stuff. And he . . . experiments. Look what happened with the Egger route. We ended up back in time. He'll get hurt or killed, for sure, if I am not there."

Goth knew full well that Captain Pausert had actually done all right a couple of times without her. But a girl had keep an eye on her man. And she was double uncertain right now. That episode was well back in his past, but she was not ignorant and naive enough not to know that the captain had given his heart to this Vala. Also, his tone said that she'd meant something very different to him than his former fiancÈe Illyla.

Illyla, Goth could deal with, just like she'd dealt with Sunnat. This Vala . . .

Goth hadn't liked his reverent tone. And she didn't like the fact that, in a way, the girl couldn't have been much older than Goth was now, when she got her claws into the captain. Well. He wouldn't have been a captain then. But still.

"You know what precog is like, Goth. No one ever sees the whole picture, but they do see what they see, right? And this is what Kerris said. You—Goth, nobody else—have got to do this or else he's not just going to get killed. It'd be like he never was. It's got something to do with what is going on in the Chaladoor."

Goth took a deep breath. "You tell me all that you know right now, Maleen." This was much more serious than some old girlfriend he'd never got over.

"Well, you know precogs measure might-be's. They predicted Vala's name. We both heard it and loved it . . . and they said that it was really important that she be called that. And they said that some power from the Chaladoor was going to murder Captain Pausert."

"What!" Goth leapt to her feet. "We could dismind him, like Olimy. Or he could put himself in a cocoon like he put the Leewit and me in . . ."

"And it happened when he was fifteen," said Maleen.

"There is a ninety eight point probability that he died before he ever left Nikkeldepain. Maybe some enemy figured out then it was a good idea to get rid of him before he developed any klatha powers. Before he had Goth and Karres to protect him."

Goth said several words that even shocked the Leewit.

"The captain will wash your mouth out with soap!" said the youngest witch, primly, as if she herself did not delight in using terms that would make a docker blush. Although she was usually careful to do so in a language that Captain Pausert could not understand. Her klatha gifts ran to the ability to translate and speak any language.

"Not unless you tell him, he won't. And I'll make you swim back to Karres on the Egger route if you do," said Goth. "You're going to have to look after him in the Chaladoor, little sister. I'm going to have to go and deal with this."

The Leewit nodded, wide eyed, looking at her sister. It was going to be quite a task. But that was pure Karres. If something needed doing, you did it. Karres people weren't much good at waiting for someone else to take the responsibility. "How are you going to get there?" she asked.

Goth gritted her teeth. "The Egger route. And there's not going to be anyone else to help me at the other end either."

That could be nasty. Really nasty. But by the look on Goth's face that wasn't going to stop her for an instant.

"I think you'd better talk it over with Toll and Threbus first," said Maleen. "And this may not be the perfect time."

Goth took a deep breath. "I am not going to be able to sleep unless . . . isn't this a paradox? Like, he must have survived or we wouldn't have met him?"

Maleen bit her lip. "You'd think so. But all precog could give us was that somehow they avoided the time paradox."

"Time is too complicated to play around with lightly," said the voice of Goth's Toll pattern, issuing from her lips. "Dimensionality comes into it."

They went to find Threbus and Toll. And, not surprisingly found them in consultation with several of the senior precogs. "You know the prediction that it was important that you spent the next year with my grand nephew Pausert?" said her father. "We've got a little more clarity on that."

"We're trying to establish the precise dates right now," said Toll. "But you will be leaving on the *Venture* with him, and then we think you're going to have to jump to the past, via the Egger route."

"I worked that out," said Goth, gruffly. "Been talking to Maleen. But why can't I just go now?"

"Because the flight schedules have been published and we are still trying to establish exactly when you have to go to, Goth. We have established you do . . . or did go back to Nikkeldepain. We have only one other insight, Goth. A lattice ship."

The Leewit bounced. "Yay! I want to go too! I want go too! I love the circus!"

"Well, you can't," said Goth firmly. "I need you to keep an eye on the captain. Anyway, you're the only one beside him that seems to be able to do anything with those little vatches."

Threbus grunted. "We need them to clean out nannite-infected people. But the follow-up on that has been a bit chaotic. It seems that they only do things because they like Pausert. We don't really have any way of motivating them."

"Little-bit likes me too," said the Leewit cheerfully. "I got used to her."

As if the vatch had known she was being spoken about, the tiny fleck of blackness with the hint of silver eyes appeared, flickering around the room. **Hello big ones. I have taken the others to watch a play. They like them nearly as much as I do.**

Goth chuckled. "I guess you've got your motivation."

Threbus nodded thoughtfully. "There are going to be a lot of traveling players visiting the outlying provinces of the Empire in the next while."

"On an imperial cultural uplift programme," said Toll smiling. "I'll have some words with Dame Ethy and Sir Richard."

"Should be pretty interesting with that sort of audience! They'd better not let the shows get stale or the little things will liven 'em up," said Goth. "But it could work."

Threbus nodded. "I like it. It gives us something the vatches want. The other issue with the nannites is that we've had the imperial scientists working non-stop on the material—dead material so far. They haven't given us anything to use to combat the plague, other than a possible repellant. But they have said that they're absolutely sure that the plague is an artificial creation.

The nannites were engineered. Made. They were programmed to do what they did."

There was a moment of silence. "That's a pretty powerful enemy."

Threbus nodded. "And one that has been around for a very long time. Working on records from the Sprites of Nartheby, the plague came from somewhere toward the galactic center. We, of course, probably weren't the targets. But it could be that something in there knows that their plague has been defeated."

"So they might be getting the next attack ready."

Threbus rubbed his jaw. "It's also, in a way, why humanity were able to expand off old Yarthe with such ease. We found so many habitable planets with traces of old alien civilizations on them, but no other existent aliens, except for the Sprites on Nartheby. But we have to face the possibility that the nannite plague might just have been the alien equivalent of a pest-exterminator, cleaning up before the new occupants got there. And the nannite problem won't just go away. It's with us for the foreseeable future. Even if we track down and destroy every nannite in the Empire, they could still be hidden away somewhere—inside or outside the Empire, in the smallest colony, and could burst out again. We're going to have to be vigilant. And get people used to having Grik-dogs to smell out the nannite exudates being something they must have."

"Well, at least I like Grik-dogs," said Goth. "And I guess keeping an eye out for nannites will also mean that we're ready for other problems."

Threbus nodded. "We're going to be stretched pretty

thin though, for the next few years. We'll have to keep Karres people undercover, scattered around. And Karres itself will probably keep a low profile. We will have to find ourselves a new sun to orbit, because the planet will be top of their target list."

"I reckon," said Goth. "And we like the old place."

Chapter 3

Pausert was not prepared for Goth to sniff loudly and retreat, when he made a joke about his lousy take-off, instead of teasing him. The captain was almost sure she was in tears. But he couldn't leave the navigation controls just then to follow her and find out what was wrong. When she came back, her face looking recently washed, he started to ask. But she waved the question away.

She remained taciturn for the rest of the day—and all of the next, and the next. By then, Pausert was really starting to worry.

He tried to pry the Leewit, to see if she knew anything. But the little witch seemed to be in one of her non-cooperative moods.

By then, they were approaching the Chaladoor, and Pausert had something else to worry about.

❈   ❈   ❈

Neldo stopped vibrating after a while, and started breathing. "Touch-talk," he gasped, just as soon he had enough breath. "The things I do for love. Maleen couldn't come because of the baby. And I've had a team of witches damping the klatha output. We hope that Pausert is unaware of this, but I need to be quick."

Goth put her hands against him, and made contact with Maleen. "What have you got for me?" she demanded.

"Quite a lot. We tracked back the date a lattice ship last landed on Nikkeldepain. And discovered that a girl called Vala, the daughter of Sutherb and Lotl, was a student at the Nikkeldepain Academy for the Sons and Daughters of Gentlemen and Officers, for six months in the same year. Got a picture of her from a yearbook. It's you, all right. But your hair is curled and red. I've sent curling tongs and the dye that mother thought best match, with Neldo. You'll have to light-shift it a bit longer at first, but long term it's easier not to have to do light shift all the time. Oh, and here's a safe set of co-ordinates for you to go to—an impression of a place on Nikkeldepain. Father supplied that."

The image flooded into her mind. "Suberth and . . .?"

"Mother and father, you dope," said the Leewit. Complex codes were obvious to her. Mere anagrams were a joke.

"Oh. Yeah."

"The Leewit. You need to know seeing as Goth isn't going to be here. Someone is spending huge amounts of money on finding the *Venture* 7333. Offering a small fortune for her flight times and schedules. Whatever is happening in Chaladoor has fingers in crime in the rest of the Empire. We're digging for whoever has put up the money. But, even by Karres standards, they've been spending it like water. And the odd thing is they have a description of someone who looks a lot like mother, that they're also looking for."

"What's so odd about that?"

"The person has wavy red hair, and her name is Vala."

Goth put on as many layers as she could. The Egger route was tough on the body. The captain thought that he had some way to stop the vibration, but she couldn't ask him about it now. Anyway, his klatha skills were very powerful . . . and a bit scary and off the wall.

The Leewit was oddly silent during the whole process. A little wide-eyed and apprehensive. The Leewit *really* did not like the Egger route. Actually, Goth didn't like it much herself.

"Well," she said, taking a deep breath and fixing the touch-talk mental co-ordinates in her mind, "Here goes. Look after the captain for me, Leewit. And don't forget to wash behind your ears."

"I won't," said the Leewit, not arguing for once in her life, her voice a little small.

THE FANTASY OF ERIC FLINT

THE PHILOSOPHICAL STRANGLER

When the world's best assassin gets too philosophical, the only thing to do is take up an even deadlier trade—heroing!

hc • 0-671-31986-8 • $24.00
pb • 0-7434-3541-9 • $7.99

FORWARD THE MAGE with Richard Roach

It's a dangerous, even foolhardy, thing to be in love with the sister of the world's greatest assassin.

hc • 0-7434-3524-9 • $24.00
pb • 0-7434-7146-6 • $7.99

PYRAMID SCHEME with Dave Freer

A huge alien pyramid has plopped itself in the middle of Chicago and is throwing people back into worlds of myth, impervious to all the U.S. Army has to throw at it. Unfortunately, the pyramid has captured mild-mannered professor Jerry Lukacs—the one man who just might have the will and know-how to be able to stop its schemes.

hc • 0-671-31839-X • $21.00
pb • 0-7434-3592-3 • $6.99

And don't miss **THE SHADOW OF THE LION** series of alternate fantasies, written with Mercedes Lackey & Dave Freer.

MORE ...
ERIC FLINT